DISK OF DRAGONS

P M F JOHNSON

Dedicated to Sandra Rector Johnson, my eternal fire.

Chapter One

"Any who would wield the Disk of Dragons must prove worthy under fire, sky and stone, or fail and die in pain, alone."
"Prophecy of the Disk," from The Chronicles of Sinnesemota.
24th of Goblenmoon, Year 1007A.

A strange haze hung over ancient Shendasan.

Rev Caern and Dan Zee hustled through the crowded marketplace that morning, hunting a discarded leaf of cabbage, a scrap of meat, anything to eat. Outcasts and shunned, the two boys kept an eye out for disapproving stares that might lead to kicks or blows.

Being a year or so older, Rev felt responsible. He had impulsively promised Dan they would find food today. But even rotting castoffs were hard to come by, since all trade to the east had ceased.

No work was available for anyone from the slums.

Despite being an orcen, a tall race of powerful reptiles with sweeping tails, Dan looked to his human friend with a naïve hope. Rev was constantly thinking up schemes to find food. Though barely teenagers, they were on their own, since Dan's grandma was frail, Rev's Ma was sick, and Pa wasn't worth much these days.

The haze slowly thickened. Smoky, purple-grey tendrils, nearly hidden by the mist, drifted through the crowd, touching one person after another.

Magic.

Tallying a count? Hunting someone? Rev shivered, uneasy. A tendril drifted towards them. He quickly pulled Dan aside.

"What's that?" Dan asked.

Rev's answer was drowned out by screams from the far end of the marketplace. People flooded into the plaza. The crowd jostled the vendor tables, and food toppled off everywhere.

All was chaos.

The unwritten rule was that anything dumped in the dirt scavengers could grab. But a fresh *neve* steak?

Rev snatched up the steak, and Dan grabbed a handful of fallen pears. They ran off at full speed into an alley.

Someone shouted for the city guard.

After scampering through a dozen cramped streets, Rev and Dan stopped in a garbage-strewn alley deep in the slums. A desultory rain started. Their hearts were thumping.

"Did you plan that?" Dan asked, his eyes wide.

"No," Rev said, then, "Well, something like that."

He never had such a twisty, excited feeling.

"Stealing is wrong." Dan sounded regretful. "Even stuff lying on the ground. It's not right to take good stuff."

"We can't return it now," Rev said. "They'd catch us."

Rev felt guilty. He did not want to end up like his father, sponging off friends, complaining about old injuries, drinking away his life. But what else did the slums offer? Life as a thief, a lookout for some dust dealer, or a beggar. A good job, like joining the city guard, was possible only for those with connections.

Pa was a good enough man, he taught Rev to hunt. They went up into the mountains, where Rev grew skilled. After all, a miss with the bow meant a hungry night, and arrows were hard to get. In turn, Rev taught his friend Dan.

But a month ago the guard had closed the city gates to residents, cutting off all trade, along with any chance to hunt in the mountains. And city rats were harder to hunt than mountain squirrels. People competed for them.

Rev dreamed of being a great spell caster, like in the old stories of Sinnesemota, or a monk who could walk on air and overpower enemies with his thoughts alone. He wanted the respect that mages earned. That successful thieves had.

"So much food. I can't believe it," Dan said, eyeing their haul. "You put us right there at the perfect time."

He waggled his tail happily. "Rev Caern, you are one canny human."

"We did it together, hunt-brother. You're the best friend anyone could have."

Pleased, Dan flushed a dark grey.

2

Disk of Dragons

Dan Zee had the broad snout, hairless skin and reptilian face of an orcen, quite a contrast to his shorter, curly-haired human companion. Orcen were practical, so Dan might accept his lot, but Rev Caern had been beaten and starved too much, and bore that human stubborn streak. He wanted out of this town.

Lately, he felt as though spying eyes watched everywhere. Nothing you could pin down, but it was creepy. Yet Rev couldn't leave Shendasan. His mother was sick, he had to care for her.

"Dan," Rev said, moved by their success to be serious. "Someday, I'm gonna be as big as anyone in this kingdom. I'll make a place we can all live, where no one has to steal, no one has to go hungry. We'll have healers, we'll take care of each other. A place where if people work, they'll be paid decent."

"No place like that exists, Rev. Not in the whole world. You think any kings or nobles would let you do that?"

"We're going to make it exist, Dan. You and me. Someday. Watch and see."

Dan laughed. "You've always had a million crazy schemes, Rev. That's no wilder than any other. Fine. I'll help you. But be careful. Someone might be listening who could hold us to that."

Rev laughed, but he looked around anyway. No one was close.

The boys split a fresh pear, then Rev cut the *neve* steak into three pieces with his belt knife. One piece for Rev's family, one for Dan and his grandma, and one for Minthala, an old orcen neighbor who lived alone in her shanty.

Pa would beat Rev if he found him giving away food, but the old orcen lady had so little, and she was always nice to them. Rev hoped she wouldn't realize the steak was stolen.

Folks said Minthala was crazy, praying every day for justice and mercy, but Rev liked her. She was Ruskiya orcen, like Dan Zee, a proud people, honorable and tough. Rev loved her tales about Sinnesemota, the ancient empire that ruled after the defeat of the vampyren, and how Sinnesemota would return someday with its heroes, human, orcen, dragon and dwarven, its justice, peace and magic. She said Rev's family had been important back then. So Dan was wrong, kind of. A place like that had existed, once. An empire of peace and justice. Sinnesemota.

3

Rev never felt the spying eyes around Minthala. She wore a little token as proof against bad magic, and hung another in her hut. Maybe that was why.

The rain tapered off. A rain spout gargled merrily, its mouth carved in the shape of a surprised leopard.

"People running everywhere," Dan said, collapsing backwards and spreading his arms wide in amazement. "Stuff to grab all over the ground. You're a *lord* slick."

His words drowned out more distant screams.

"What do you mean?" Rev asked.

His orcen friend sat up. "Knowing something was about to happen, figuring where to take advantage, you're always calculating like that."

His pointy ears drooped. "Me, I'll be lucky to find work swamping out a tavern, but Rev, you're too smart for this place."

Rev shifted, uncomfortably. He wasn't used to praise.

Then, faint but clear, came another scream.

"Wait a moment." Dan's eyes narrowed in suspicion. "You didn't know anyone was going to scream just now, did you?"

"No." Rev felt embarrassed.

"So you didn't know about those earlier screams, either?"

Rev's answer was interrupted by a shout.

"Here they are." At the mouth of the alley, a sergeant of the city guard was pointing at them.

Half-a-dozen orcen city guards stood behind him, blocking any escape.

Rev and Dan scrambled to their feet. At the opposite end of the alley other guards appeared, sunlight gleaming off their spear blades.

A wave of misty purple tendrils was counting the guards.

"Give up, thieves," roared the sergeant in triumph.

"We didn't steal anything," Rev said. "The food was lying on the ground. Free to anybody. That's the rule."

"Prove it. Show us that the meat is spoiled."

Rev hesitated. He hadn't thought of that.

The sergeant flashed his fangs. "I know you, Rev. Useless thief. You're doomed for dead."

The sergeant was named Eg Bror. He said poor folk were to blame for their own misery, and beat people who didn't pay him off.

4

Now he and his followers raised their weapons.

Rev and Dan drew their knives and stood back to back.

"I'm starting to think," Rev said, "we shouldn't have grabbed anything."

"Rev Caern," Dan declared, "if I survive, I will never take anything not mine again, on the ground or not."

Orcen never went back on their word.

"Drop your weapons and we'll kill you quick," offered the sergeant.

"Rev, you could come up with another fancy idea about now." Dan sounded strained.

A tremendous cry arose. A wall of smoke whipped into the alley. Behind it a wave of chest-high brown, cockroach-like creatures poured into the alley, marching in orderly ranks. They each had four legs and two arms. Half wore black pants, the rest black skirts. All had bronze breastplates and carried short black spears.

Foreign invaders.

The guards spun around, raising their weapons as the cockroach people attacked. Spears clattered against spears. Someone screeched in pain.

Keeping his wits, Rev hustled Dan over to a pile of boxes. They clambered on, then shimmied up a downspout to get away, as the city guard fought for their lives.

From the rooftop, Rev and Dan looked out over the city. To their astonishment, fires billowed everywhere and smoke rose in columns. The scorched smell was horrendous. On the streets, people screamed, fled, or fought the invading cockroach people.

Rev had always thought of Shendasan as an eternally drowsing cat, unchangeable. Now he saw how rapidly change could come. It scared him.

Only the vast Shendao monastery behind its sprawling walls remained unaffected. A ray of sunlight lit its highest tower as a bell rang for morning prayers, an eerily beautiful sight amid the haze and confusion.

"Grandma," Dan said, his voice thick with worry.

He found stairs on the far side of the building and raced down them, then away. Gone.

Rev followed more slowly, wondering about his own family. Shame blossomed. Pa would be out somewhere, drunk for sure. He hadn't come home last night.

But Ma was sick. So Rev headed for his parent's shanty.

5

On the street, he passed a few dust dreamers in the shadows, pipes clutched in hand, skeletal people indistinguishable from grime-streaked statues. Screams of fear and defiance pierced the murk.

Rev's purloined groceries remained back in the alley. In a funny way he was relieved, not having benefited from the theft.

Then he noticed a bundle of clothes in the street.

Even for the poorest of us there is a childhood time of innocence, when the familiar seems eternal, when the baby next door does not seem to change, but remains forever a baby. So children think, memories and fantasies merging, dividing, dancing around each other. No danger is real, only the casual pain from bumps of exploration. Then the illusion shatters, leaving us in a world of the impermanent, the tawdry, the cruel.

Minthala, the old lady Dan and he befriended, lay dead before him, an alien-looking short spear stabbed through her gut.

Grief struck him. Who would hurt a harmless old woman? Had they murdered her because of her little talismans?

Sad and scared, he ran until he reached a trash-strewn lane. Halfway down it stood a shack of salvaged brick and sticks, with a half-painted board roof. Home.

He ducked a misty purple tendril at the door. "Ma?"

Against the far wall inside lay a bundle of familiar rags. The rags stirred. Ma was drunk, but alive.

He released his pent-up breath, relieved. Now, what tavern would his father be in?

Half-a-dozen cockroach soldiers rushed into the lane outside, accompanied by purple tendrils. Their mouths bore mandibles, and their hands sported two front claws and two back fingers, along with a thumb.

Rev's heart sank.

"What do you want?" He stood his ground at the door, trying for a no-nonsense tone, but his voice quavered.

"Bow to the Order."

Two soldiers aimed spears at his belly, two others flung him to the earth, two others peered into the shack.

Their mandibles clicked as they talked in Hazhean, the common tongue.

"Ttt. She's lying down in the midst of the day."

"T. Human rot."

Rev rose to protest, but a soldier struck him with a spear butt. He collapsed in pain.

Rev's father arrived, roaring in outrage. "What do you mean by this? Roaches and vermin. This is my—"

The blow to his head sounded liked wood smacking meat.

The leader of the soldiers spoke in a high, hissing voice. "T, t. You are now servants of the Chisen Empire, observing the duties each day, bowing to the Unity on his throne. T, t, t. Doing as you are told, conducting yourselves as productive contributors to the Order. Tomorrow at dawn reporting to the East Gate for duty. You understand?"

Without waiting for an answer, the cockroach warriors departed.

Rev shakily rose to his knees. Beside him, his father lay unmoving.

Chapter Two

"After their defeat, the Chisen withdrew from the world's stage. Little congress passed between their country and others, and our historical analysts declared the Chisen would remain forever so. Your pardon, High Fer Gleni. In this analysis, I explain why the recent bloody expansion of the Chisen Empire could have been anticipated."
<u>*Introduction to Low Fer Sicari's Thesis on the Chisen War*</u>*, presented in Remula, Ilmari, Year 1036 After the Fall of Sinnesemota (Initial Thesis Rejected by the Council of Historians, Later Accepted as Emended).*

Midnight sat heavily on Shendasan. The Chisen goblen had imposed a curfew after they conquered the city, so even after four years few went out past sunset. Anyone caught without a pass was liable to be executed for being non-orderly. The waist-high, cockroach-like Chisen clung to orderly behavior as burrs clung to wool.

Which meant Rev Caern had this particular alley to himself. With a certain aplomb, he sat upright in the shadows, surrounded by garbage, a rolled-up rug beside him hiding a sword within its folds.

Beyond the alley lay the Great Plaza where half-a-dozen Chisen guards, a full pod as they reckoned things, lolled by the fountain under oil lamps that illuminated the only statue in the Plaza, a marble woman who symbolized justice.

Pigeon dung streaked the statue.

The Chisen guards looked like so many arrogant insects, sure of their world. Rev didn't know why they had invaded, but he survived their brutal rule, resenting every cruel moment.

Now he wanted some of his own back.

His latest scheme would not be easy to pull off. Chisen magic lurked everywhere. Purple tendrils tracked through any crowd, imps and other magical servants nosed down every alley, while more of the weak or careless were arrested each day.

Disk of Dragons

Only the Shendao monastery remained unconquered, maybe because the monks were great fighters, or maybe because they had so little worth taking. Either way, the Chisen never attacked the monastery, and over the years commerce grew up between the two sides. With permission, people could come and go through the monastery gates.

Admiring the monks, Rev had taken refuge in the monastery, where he now worked as a guard. But he was outside the monastery walls tonight. And the Chisen were dangerous.

Over the last few years, whenever he went abroad in the city, he had to avoid frequent patrols, and the purple tendrils seemed to concentrate in the areas he once lived. They crowded around his old shack, around the taverns his father once preferred, even around Minthala's old hut.

They hung around Dan Zee for a while, but Rev's friend lived in a boring fashion. Dan humbly accepted the back-breaking workload the goblen imposed, and although poor, lived a tolerable life in the slums. His days were confoundedly repetitious, and the tendrils finally gave up on him.

Rev had grown broad-shouldered and tall as an orcen. With his curly dark hair he might have been handsome, but his ribs showed — from sharing his meager rations with his mother. He was all she had. Rev's brother Var vanished during the Chisen conquest, and the goblen later killed his father, along with many others.

Yesterday, Rev's mother finally died of her wasting illness. Last night, with tears on his cheeks, he buried her as deeply as he dared in a nameless plot in a cemetery outside the city walls. He did so without permission — the poor never received permission. It bothered him that he could do no more for her, but a headstone would merely guide the Chisen to her body, which they would dig up and cast on the city midden.

Time to get out of this town. After his one piece of unfinished business.

On the far side of the Great Plaza, on the gaudy façade high above the double doors of the City Hall, hung a sword that had been in Rev's family since the days of Sinnesemota, a famous sword that Rev's ancestors loaned to the city as a symbol of their faith in justice.

Every Midsummer's Festival his father had carried the sword in the Honors Parade, a glitter in his rheumy eyes.

But when Rev's father climbed up to retrieve his sword the first Midsummer's Day after the conquest, the Chisen arrested him, and the governor, Norwe Hesketh, ordered Rev's father executed for theft. Another reason to hate the Chisen and Norwe Hesketh.

It wasn't fair. Rev's father wasn't the thief. Not that time. That sword belonged to him, not the city, and especially not the Chisen.

Rev was determined to take back that sword, gambling on his own skills versus the whole Chisen empire. Maybe his optimism was getting a touch out of hand. He grinned with little humor, as he nocked an arrow to his bow.

The cloud cover broke to reveal the golden disk of the moon. A moonbeam highlighted the sword. For some reason, the contrast of light and darkness raised the hackles on Rev's neck, as though the light were somehow contesting a shadowy magic. Was the moon's strength used by some power opposing the Chisen?

The goblen guards in the Plaza stamped their feet, unused to the chilly mountain air. He had to get around them. If the Chisen noticed the sword's disappearance they would suspect him. And kill him.

But Rev, being Rev, had a plan.

From inside the rug at his side, he unwrapped a battered practice sword, purchased from a drunk for eleven coppers. Swapped for his father's blade, the practice sword high up on the wall should fool the Chisen. For a while.

He would have been glad for some amazing magic that allowed him to fly up to his sword, like the Disk of Dragons, which supposedly gave the powers of a dragon. But the Disk had been lost for a thousand years, so Rev must resort to this more mundane approach. Legend said the Disk would reappear at the beginning of the Dark Battle, when the evil Goddess Thana would try to enter this world, while opposed by the gentle Goddess Luwana.

A shout rang out. The guards had noticed an orcen youth scurrying across the far end of the plaza – Rev's friend Dan Zee. The plan was begun.

\#

"T, t, reptile, you are going where?" asked the corporal, moving to intercept Dan Zee.

"I'm on an errand." Dan's tail nervously tattooed the pavement.

The goblen soldiers stood only waist-high, but all six carried spears.

"I have a pass," he went on.

Would Rev's forgery stand up? How had Dan let a human talk him into such horrible behavior? A forgery was a lie, Dan argued, but Rev answered the Chisen wouldn't even look at it, since they knew orcen never lied, so it wouldn't be a lie. If it functioned as a pass, it was by definition a pass. Right?

Rev's logic made Dan's head hurt, but Rev had saved his life that time. Well, all those times. So Dan owed him. To whom a Ruskiya orcen owed his life, he owed loyalty, and Rev was using that fact, burn him.

To Dan's dismay, the Chisen corporal did study his pass. Dan stuttered, and almost blurted out the truth. Only the fact that Rev swore Dan to silence kept his tongue quiet.

Life should be straightforward, that was the orcen way, not this mealy-mouthed manipulating. Thankfully, the forgery passed muster, and the corporal gave the pass back. Or maybe the delicious smells from the basket distracted her.

"Ttt. What do you carry?" She grabbed the basket, opened it. "Muffins!"

"They're from the bakery, for the morning breakfast." Dan was trying to stick to the truth, but imply more. His not-quite-lying made his voice squeaky. Burn Rev.

"And your master will punish you if you don't deliver them? Too bad for you." The corporal turned to the others. "Enough for each for us."

"I have a receipt." Dan frantically waved a second scrap of paper. It was a real receipt.

The corporal gave Dan a kick. "T, tt. Get out of here."

Gratefully he fled, his task accomplished, determined to insist he would never even semi-lie again. It hurt his heart.

#

As the eastern sky lightened, Rev climbed City Hall, finding handholds on the ornate stone façade. Below, the guards snored, half-eaten muffins scattered around them.

Rev exulted as he swapped the practice sword for his father's blade. He did it!

But as he descended, footfalls rang out across the plaza. Arriving too soon. Surprised, he swung into a niche behind a buttress. A pod of Chisen troops marched into the plaza. The changing of the guard was not due for another hour's glass, but there they were, ahead of schedule. Chisen were never off-schedule. What was going on?

The arriving sergeant kicked a prone guard. "Ttt. Sleepers, awake."

Rev listened, having learned their language. He had an ear for such.

"Get up, you slugs. Falling asleep while on duty, bad as the soft skins. We are receiving new orders. Doubling the guard. The conjurors' imps are being restless. Probably just some wandering drunk."

One soldier sniffed at a muffin. "Sergeant, they were drugged."

"Ttt." The sergeant rattled his contempt. "If they were drugged they'd be having their throats slit by the soft skins."

He kicked the sluggish corporal. "Sleepers on-duty have no need to sleep off-duty. Be reporting at the end of your watch to the kitchens for more work."

"T. I am bowing to the Unity, sergeant," the corporal said, her voice thick with sleep and mortification.

She swayed, trying to sit upright.

The sergeant looked around and Rev cowered back.

Once again, Rev had the sense of energies contending far above him, the golden disk of the moon opposed by... an absence. The shadows themselves, maybe. Nothing you could actually see.

While Rev was suddenly sitting in a beam of moonlight, as though holiness surrounded him.

But why would any magical being support him?

The goblen did not look upwards. Instead, the squad marched off as the groggy Plaza guards lumbered to their feet. None spotted the human who swung down the building and slunk away down the alley.

Nearly a whole day passed before a sharp-eyed Chisen guard noticed the counterfeit sword.

Chapter Three

"The goblen, learning of priestly magic from the orcen, used this knowledge in their own way. Instead of humbly petitioning for power, they demanded it, opening gates to the Other Side and forcing magical beings captured there to do their bidding. In this way they discovered conjuration magic."
<u>*The Histories of Teren: The Age of Magic.*</u>

That evening, hiding in a whitebeam tree in a remote garden of Shendao Monastery, Rev considered the irony of his situation. He had returned to the monastery before dawn to grab his things and get out. But just after he slipped inside, relying on his financial arrangement with the guards to allow passage, all the monastery gates were unexpectedly ordered to be locked. Trapping him.

Hoping to learn why, he fell in for morning assembly, when all monks and initiates gathered to learn the news and participate in meditation. Sure enough, the wailing monks, who cried out the news in their huge voices, had an announcement: tomorrow the monastery would swear in every initiate as a full monk, in a new, special ceremony. No exceptions.

An uneasy buzz broke out in the ranks. This broke with timeless tradition: endless youths had passed through the monastery as initiates, without ultimately taking the onerous vows of a monk. By this arrangement, the monastery reaped cheap labor and potential recruits, while the youths learned a trade. Why the change?

The High Master himself had to call for attention to silence the crowd. But he did not explain, only demanded order and obedience.

The announcement reinforced Rev's intent to get out. Living in the monastery exasperated him. He was a free spirit, used to his own ideas, while the monks demanded unyielding discipline.

Rev almost wished he had taken Dan Zee's way, accepting the daily tasks the goblen assigned and living in the slums. As it was, even if Rev did escape the monastery, how could he survive in Shendasan without a daily pass and a place to live?

Anyway, he did not dare remain where the very shadows seemed to be hunting for him. He must leave town.

Beyond the city, the Hiyin Mountains loomed in a wilderness so huge it beggared the imagination. He would have to make it through that wilderness as well.

Rev carried a small pack and the family sword, having stashed his hunting bow in a cubbyhole outside the monastery. In tales about heroes imprisoned during the Shadow Years, a forgotten gate always existed through which the hero fled. Rev loved such stories, but all gates of Shendao Monastery were locked and guarded. He had spent the day checking.

Footsteps rang on the flagstones. Rev shrank closer to the bole of the tree as two short figures wearing saffron robes approached. Cowls covered their heads. They paused near his tree. Monks had almost an extra sense due to their skill at shi, a way of manipulating life energy, so they might sense him.

Rev tried not to move, nor think. He was merely part of the tree, taking in the last light.

The broader monk spoke first. "The conjurors say the outlawed one is inside the monastery. Their imps sniffed out his trail to here. He has the sword."

"T. So my pod best find him," said the thin monk, "or we're the ones who will be answering? Why not send in the imps?"

Rev started to sweat when he heard the click of mandibles. These were goblen standing on their back legs. To conceal their race? He knew of no goblen monks. These must be spies inside the monastery. And who was the outlawed one? Him?

"Tttt. We can't use the imps in here yet. The monastery has... protections to be removed. But the disorder of this place is ending. Even monks admit reality when it's chewing on them."

"T, t? There's been a change?"

"T. Their High Master is under Governor Norwe's heel. They found something on him, I am supposing, to change his mind. Forcing these ungrowns to swear in as monks and submit to the knife. Brilliant. These

14

humans will never be rebelling. T, t. The Chisen Empire free to expand westward, you will be seeing it."

Rev did not care for their talk about forcing the initiates to "submit to the knife." What part of him did they plan to cut? His sweaty hands slipped.

At the slight noise, the thinner monk looked straight at Rev.

"Tt. The outlaw's in the tree. Rev Caern is right there."

Rev swung down from his branch and launched himself out of the tree. The goblen lunged for him. Claws brushed Rev's back, but he avoided their grasp and fled.

Goblen ran more quickly than humans, but these two were hampered by their robes, so Rev gained on them as he sped through the garden.

He skidded around an elegant shed, scattered a row of hoes to slow his pursuers, then raced across a bridge over a koi pond. Out of sight, he dove into the underbrush.

The two spies thundered around the shed. Not seeing him, they halted, clicking and cursing. Numerous paths wended away in different directions.

Using a ravine as cover, Rev slipped away, up a hill. Meanwhile, the goblen started off in the wrong direction.

Rev ran the entire way to the cell of a monk he knew, the Elder Fu Vehma. The elder's cell sat off by itself deep in the gardens. Somehow Rev had forged a friendship with the roly-poly monk, bringing bowls of rice, helping clean his meditation cell, and conversing with him. The Elder Fu was quiet where Rev liked to talk, still when Rev proved restless, and wiser than Rev ever could hope to be. The old monk also made an amazing cup of tea.

To Rev's delight, the Elder Fu had begun to teach him shi: using one's will to sense the flows of energy in the world, and manipulate them. Rev, being Rev, immediately starting using the knowledge to avoid the purple tendrils of the goblen conjurors as he prowled the city. He had not admitted this to the Elder.

Night had fallen, but a welcoming candlelight flickered within the hive-shaped cell. Rev hesitated outside the door. "Elder Fu?"

The Elder Fu sat inside, cross-legged, palms up to receive the descending beneficence of the universe. The monk was ancient and bald, with amazingly bushy eyebrows, a wizened ball of a man. Happiness poured out of him every day, which made him one of Rev's favorite people. The elder might have been part orcen, his faintly iridescent skin gleamed with a golden sheen, and in certain lights seemed scaly. But with no tail, he must be mostly human.

"Elder, I got a worry," Rev said, catching his breath.

"You have too many, young one. Release a few." The Elder Fu smiled. "Come sit."

Wriggling nervously on the guest mat, Rev told what he had heard.

"You are in danger, then," the Elder Fu concluded.

"They know I overheard them. They'll mark me at any moment."

The monk tilted his head, as though listening. "No, young Rev, they have gone for help."

He raised one bushy eyebrow. "Why were you in the gardens? Do you intend to flee after the announcement?"

"Yes, Elder," he admitted. "I didn't enter the monastery to be a monk, I came here with my mother after the Chisen invasion."

His voice failed. He remembered his mother's last days and the fever that took her.

"I am truly sorry for your loss, Rev."

Rev bowed his head. "Thank you. I miss her terribly. Her and my father."

He sprang to his feet. "But I can't stay here, they'll blame you. How can I get away?"

The Elder Fu pursed his lips. "You reviewed the walls and gates?"

"I didn't find any slither hole out. Is there one, Elder Fu?"

The monk spoke softly, almost to himself. "In you, young one, I sense possibility. You may be one we seek." He looked up. "But you have drawn attention, so we must cloak you."

"Cloak me from what?"

"From the evil that takes an interest in you." He shrugged, enigmatically. "As for how, your success in following a certain path should suffice. Since one side has shown interest in you, perhaps we can entice another side into the game. If you successfully traverse this path, that will draw some beneficent attention."

"How many sides are there?" Rev asked.

16

"Three, by one measure. First, the vampyren seek to sow corruption and divisiveness, from which they gain power. They want a return to the Shadow Years, when the vampyren ruled the world. They are opposed by a second, evil people, the followers of Thana, the Goddess of... well, some say Submission, others say Death. Either way, those who follow Thana mostly form insurgencies against corruption, then reveal their own cruelties later. Corruption and insurgency go together like honey and bread."

"I don't like either, myself."

"Those peoples are led by the Hand of Thana, an ancient human. She is almost incorporeal, having lived so long her body has crumbled to dust, all but one Hand. She cannot move about, but only continues as a sort of living death. She guides the worshippers of Thana."

Rev shuddered. "Someone I never want to meet. But you said there were three sides."

"Yes. The third side is made up of people who want a world of justice and peace. However, despite the growing threats, most people only want to be left alone. Only a few consciously choose any real third side."

"Us, you mean," Rev said, his eyes shining. "Those who want to bring back the Empire of Peace. Like the old stories say."

"Us? Well, as for that, we must first make it us. Young one, I must have some security from you for lending aid."

At Rev's expression, he laughed.

"Don't look so chagrined, payment is required for any service in life. Remember, without justice, there can be no peace. But I warn you, if you take this path you will be marked, not have a quiet life." The Elder Fu sighed. "I would say do not undervalue a quiet life, but you are young. Well, let be what will be. What I require is simply an honest answer: will you work for the return of the Peaceful Empire of Sinnesemota and the betterment of our world?"

The way the elder spoke resonated inside Rev. The question was an old one, right out of the Chronicles of Sinnesemota, one asked of Aspirants in the Quest to re-establish Sinnesemota, the Empire of Peace, after its betrayal and fall. Joining the Elder Fu in a struggle for peace appealed to some deep part of him. Anyway, his cynical side felt sure that he could fulfill such a requirement on his own terms.

"Yes, Master." He used the rote words. "Though it may take all my life."

He felt something in the universe go click. It was a spooky moment.

We spend so much of our lives pretending our actions have no consequences and our words can always be reversed. When a moment of consequence does occur it raises the hackles on our neck and reminds us there are deeper connections we flout at our peril.

Uneasily, Rev wondered if it would be possible to slick out of this promise. Only far down inside did he understand the commitment was made and the reverberations begun.

The Elder Fu bowed his head. "Rev, you have the chance for a grand future, but no one has happiness who holds such painful secrets. You must release them. Yet here is a secret that isn't shameful, so you may keep it without pain: many people band together for good, in ways not visible to the casual view. There is reason for hope."

"A shadow empire?"

"Not shadow. Say rather, a band who work for peace. They govern only themselves. These people use the sign of the dragon in greeting." His left hand curled as though holding a ball, but with the thumb widespread and a gap between the middle fingers, mimicking three talons.

"I'd like to join them," Rev said impulsively, making the sign himself.

"You have. They live over the whole world." The old monk smiled. "Young Rev, I shall hear how you are doing. That is, if you safely traverse the path."

This old man had always guided Rev with kindness, although he never went to holy services and the other monks actually seemed unaware of him. In fact, despite his watching over the initiates like a hen over chicks, even they rarely noticed him. Rev might be the Elder Fu's only friend.

The weight of trust lowered Rev's head, and his shame welled. "Elder, I ain't always been good."

"As though any of us has." The monk chuckled. "I have watched you help the hatchlings, the children, and protect them. You treated your mother honorably. You are a good man. Young, I grant you... foolish, I grant you... flawed, I grant you... but good. Anyway, without weakness there can be no growth of wisdom. Now, we go." He rose. "If you solve the puzzle of the path, you can leave the monastery unchallenged."

18

"A puzzle? What's the trick to solving it?"

"The riddle is different for each of us. That's the way of any decent puzzle, don't you agree?"

They started towards a complex of stone buildings, and after a few steps entered a maze of turns between walls. Soon Rev was lost. Maybe his curiosity was distracting him.

"Elder Fu, why did the Chisen invade Shendasan? We weren't hurting anybody."

"The world loses its balance. We see the loss of justice even in our remote nation."

"Isn't that just what happens? Tyrants see an opportunity and attack?" Rev felt his cynicism rising.

"It is more than that, this time." The Elder Fu paused, before choosing the passage to their left, a dim way between tall walls. "The Alliance of Free Nations recently collapsed. The vampyren are reappearing after a thousand years, to hunt the Artifacts. They are patient, and do not readily expose themselves to danger, so something momentous must motivate them. They push to advance, attack, conquer. As though little time remained."

"And that affects the Chisen?"

"Yes, and perhaps it is why the followers of Thana are also on the move. I fear good people will be crushed between these evil forces."

"What can we do?" Rev asked, worried.

"Work to restore justice. Take control of the Artifacts, as the Prophesies point us to do."

"All Nine Artifacts?"

"Used together, the Artifacts ruled Sinnesemota. Together, they can restore justice and peace. Divided, in the wrong hands they must bring oppression. Until they are brought forth, the Disk of Dragons must not open the Hall of the Empire."

"Why do we care about opening the Hall of the Empire?"

It all seemed troublesome and confusing.

"The Hall contains the Heart of Light, the Jewel that can contact Lord Vos, patron God of Sinnesemota. Justice flows from Vos, as mercy flows from the Goddess Luwana."

"So the Heart of Light is the real key?"

"Once the Artifacts are working together, yes."

"Where are the other Artifacts?" Rev asked. He was delighted the old monk was telling him so many secrets.

"Most are hidden. We know the Rose of Understanding grows in Gy Pe, and the Labyrinth lies in the heart of the vampyren empire. A great evil in the Labyrinth must be cleared away before it can join the other Artifacts. That was never done in the days of Sinnesemota, so the Empire ultimately collapsed."

"The task of bringing together the Artifacts sounds monumental." The thought sobered him.

"Someone must do it."

"Isn't someone assigned by the Prophesies?"

"Whoever takes up the Disk of Dragons. The Disk comes first."

"The Disk of Dragons. I know its stories," Rev said, proud to show off. "You can fly with it, you can breathe fire. It's like you're a dragon. Anyone with it can succeed easily."

"I suspect you underestimate the difficulties. And overestimate the power of the Disk."

They reached an open gate where the golden disk of the moon revealed a garden of night flowers, filled with the cries of nighthawks. A path wended away.

"From here you must find your own way, young one," the old monk said.

Rev hesitated, caught by surprise. "What about my show-a-card on how to escape? My clue?"

"Simply follow the path you prefer."

Astonished, and with some trepidation, Rev stepped into the garden. He had the peculiar sensation that he was looking at two separate places at once: first, the garden of the monastery under the moon, but second, and at the same time, a clearing in a wild forest under some diffuse light. The second view was disturbing, in the way the bright red berries of deadly nightshade are alluring.

The path at his feet glowed golden, a rivulet of dissonance.

"Follow the strangeness," came the elder's words, as though from a distance.

Rev turned, but the Elder Fu was gone. Unsettled, but excited by the gamble ahead, Rev reminded himself he could always turn back, and started down the glowing path.

#

The orcen Eg Bror bowed, his bobbed tail trembling as he faced the creature in the dark room, in this dark city. He survived by yielding to the conquerors, doing as they demanded, and found he liked their harsh ways. He had not considered he might be under observation himself.

His mind, paralyzed with fright, refused to consider what sort of creature this must be.

The shadowy creature spoke in a low, threatening voice, like the grinding of rocks. "The boy Rev Caern. The one who took the sword. If you wish to live, orcen, you must find him for us." There was a pause. "Find the sword and him. And perhaps, bring back his ears for a bonus."

#

As Rev stepped forward along the glowing path, it was as though two paintings were being carried past on both sides, the closer one semi-transparent so the other world showed through the first. Was this a way out of Shendasan? He hoped so.

The dual scenes made him dizzy. The second world, darker and more distant, fascinated him. Small movements and sounds arose, maybe made by magical beings. Did those creatures know all his failures and weaknesses? How he had stolen to eat? His shoulders rose rebelliously. He just had to do better in the future.

The glowing path split into two branches, a brighter branch leading back to the mundane world of the monastery, and a second one heading into the strange forest, which path dimmed as it progressed.

The dimmer path disturbed him. A pile of white objects like bones gleamed on one side, beside which rested a large, glowing stone, with depths that flickered and shifted. With dread he stepped forward to peer in. Then he stopped.

Whatever awaited there, he was not prepared to see.

But with a sudden boldness, he chose the second path into the forest, hoping its golden color promised good.

Who has not had a surge of hope, a sense that we are bound for better things if we take a chance? Borne by such a feeling, it may be impossible

21

*not to rush forward. And perhaps, when reflecting back, we see our choice
turned out for the best. Perhaps. But we have an almost limitless capacity
for fooling ourselves, and Rev was still very young.*

With those first steps on the new path, he endured a terrible dizziness.
Then an unearthly resonance tolled at a pitch almost too low to hear.

"You've gone and dealt it now," he muttered.

The monastery and its buildings vanished. He walked in a fragrant
night forest, a place of wondrous beauty. The temperature was warmer,
and distant peaks glittered beneath a pale light, the same and yet not the
same mountains he knew. The moon had vanished but stars blazed down.
Every leaf's edge gleamed, every color shone, every scent wafted to him
with an unearthly richness. The light arose from nowhere and everywhere.
His very fingers were translucent in that weird light. He could be at peace.
In this place no one knew his secrets.

Implications unfolded as he stood overwhelmed in thought. His sense
of self faded.

Time passed. He lost memory after memory, unaware they were
vanishing as he remained motionless, without regard to hunger or thirst,
his breathing slowing...

A disk of golden light appeared in the air. Across it twisted the image
of a Dragon, coiling around images: a thorny Rose growing from a coffin,
a blazing Staff, a smoking volcano. This Disk was a well of power, the
very heart of danger and intent.

Disturbed... delighted... trapped... he had the confused impression the
Disk of Dragons was sentient. Words whispered in his mind. He must
understand. He could just about...

That old man. The monk. What had he said about secrets?

His curiosity contested the eerie lethargy. The Disk of Dragons sucked
at his will.

He fought it, forcing himself to remember his name, Rev Caern.

He struggled against the alluring majesty of the Disk, seeming to offer
a place at the heart of things. Of course, he wanted to believe it. Wasn't the
Disk supposed to be good? It was filled with light, after all. Wasn't the
Light always good?

But he was a boy of much experience, and therefore many suspicions.

What drew Rev back was his simple core of self, which did not believe he was the center of the universe. If life taught him anything, it was that he was just a man. So, as if struggling through thick mud, he took a physical step away, then another.

The Disk bathed him in a brilliant, golden glow. Then it vanished. With it went the lassitude.

Surely that meant he had won free of its influence. His relief lasted only until he realized the path was gone. Where was he?

He heard something lumbering closer, through the brush. Cautious, he slipped into a thicket.

A great bear, its shoulders as high as his head, shuffled past, a deadly, monstrous looking being with narrow, cruel eyes and long, wicked claws, a terrifying sight. The bear, striped golden and brown, sniffed the air.

Rev had the impression it noticed him.

He nearly fled, but the bear moved on. Hunting the Disk of Dragons? Or obeying it? Whatever was happening, Rev was just a tiny piece on a very big board. And none of the bigger pieces were showing much care and concern. They would use him and discard him. He best remember that.

Once the bear departed, Rev hurried off in the opposite direction.

But he began to wonder, did any path lead out of this dim forest, this other world? Was there no way out? Panic flooded him. He fled, blindly tripping over unseen roots, bumping into tree trunks, until something caught at his ankle and he fell.

On his hands and knees, he tried to collect himself. Flight availed nothing. He must think his way out. Shaky, he climbed to his feet. He had reached here by seeing two worlds at once. Could this world be overlaying his own? If so, could he find that path between the two again?

He set out, adopting the inner silence required to draw on the power of shi. Silence. The peace of belonging. He concentrated on that.

He smelled an ethereal incense, along with an eerie sense of separation. His inner calmness grew. A breeze rustled the leaves. Starlight poured down. Complexities. Subtleties. The mundane world reappeared behind the view of this world.

He yipped for joy, but instantly the mundane world wavered. So he calmed himself, and in so doing, found the faint glow of the golden path.

The path branched ahead, the brighter branch leading home.

In a few paces he walked into a barren, windswept terrain, back in Shendasan, onto the empty slope of a hill. The city wall loomed to his right, the monastery to his left. The lights of the city shone below. He had escaped the other world.

The sense of eyes constantly watching was not there. The Disk had maybe protected him from that, as the Elder Fu said, which was good.

But the Chisen were still looking for him, and they could use mundane spies as well.

Chapter Four

"The Goddess Luwana wandered this world, and through Her Love, life sprang up and the hills grew green, but Thana, Goddess of Silence, grew angered by the songs of birds fashioned from the wind. As Luwana rested, Thana crept up and stabbed Her Sister. Luwana's Blood flowed, filling the world with life's magic, but Thana, Goddess of Death, fled in shame. That no God of Chaos might benefit from Luwana's Blood, Vos the Maker created a Veil between the Outside and this world across which even the Gods cannot cross. But where Luwana fell a Rift opened, home to many evil things."
The Histories of Teren: The Age of Legend.

Six months later, Rev Caern and Dan Zee approached a mountain town near noon on a spring day. Flowers nodded and birds chattered. Though Rev did not realize it, this was Vosday, twenty-fourth day of the month of Dwarvenmoon and his nineteenth birthday.

After such a long flight westward, he had nearly forgotten his worry of someone chasing them for the sword. After all, the Chisen would not know its story, nor its purported powers. Others did, but nobody talked to the Chisen. And it was his sword by right. That sense of shadows chasing him must be just a boy's foolishness, him pretending he was more important than he really was.

Rev continued the argument he had been having with Dan Zee. "We got no money. So we need to make a play here."

Dan's tail whipped uneasily. "There must be a better way, Rev. We're not in the slums anymore. We're doing fine in the wilderness. We lived off the land right through the winter."

Rev was now nearly the size of his friend, tall even for an orcen, but they were both underfed. With Dan that showed in his tail, narrower than it should be.

"But do you *like* it out in the bracken?" Rev said.

25

"I like the peacefulness. And these hunting bows I made are better than those old ones."

"Oh, admit it, you hate duckweed worse'n me by twice. Foul-tasting stuff. Now, who's stood by you?"

"You have." Dan sighed. "You always help me, it's true."

"And when I asked if you wanted to come along?"

"I agreed. But Rev, it was the middle of the night, I was mostly asleep."

"Well, I couldn't stay in Shendasan with conjurors hunting me, could I?"

"No," Dan said, his tail drooping. "The Chisen were searching hard for you. The whole town had that old-sweat stink from conjuror magic. You stirred them up, sure enough. Vintage Rev Caern."

"But we got away, right? Haven't seen any purple tendrils since. Using shi to avoid them worked, I tell you. My next plan will work as well."

Dan shook his head. "I gave my word not to steal. And I won't lie for you anymore, or carry forgeries or anything like that. You got too many tricks, Rev."

"Did I say I planned to slick anything? And we got nothing to lie about." Rev gave his friend an encouraging smile.

Living on roots and seeds had not changed his view, though he now knew that if he must, he could survive out in the wilderness. But he didn't *want* to live off whittle shrubs and ground gophers.

One suspicion he didn't share with Dan was that they had been led here somehow. Such an alien satisfaction rushed through him at the sight of this town gate that he felt alarmed. Hadn't he broken free of the Disk of Dragons' influence? Was he still playing some unfortunate part in that conflict of larger powers?

He put that fear aside as they entered the town's tumbled-down gate. They had to earn a living somehow, and they could not be too proud. He intended to buy Dan a decent apprenticeship, but the few coins he had saved so far were not nearly enough.

Dan had no idea Rev was building a stake for him.

Inside the gate, the town looked patched-up and raw, with limestone buildings lining the curving, dusty street, but the folks who bustled along and the wagons of goods in the street indicated a growing, cheerful place.

"Jaunt's End Restaurant," said a sign, with a rather wicked likeness of a fat orcen bending over a food-laden table, seen from behind with his tail high (a fellow named Jaunt, no doubt) painted in the primary colors orcen preferred.

Rev ignored his annoying conscience, which pointed out all sorts of ways to earn a living without stealing. He felt excited. A wagon outside the general store appeared unwatched, loaded with sacks and barrels, a piebald gelding placid in the traces. He peered inside the wagon. A sack of nails, another of dried lingonberries. Very interes—

"Can I be of aid, stranger?" A woman emerged from the store.

Rev hopped back from the wagon. The woman stood tall and slender, with honey-blonde hair that caught the glory of the morning sun. She carried an ornate walking stick, and was human like himself, though these were Afen orcen lands. Her nose crooked a bit, and her dress was a practical grey, but what a wonderful world that contained such a beautiful woman. Unfortunately, her hazel eyes narrowed in suspicion, and she studied him as if examining a worm that might require squashing. "What are you doing?"

"I, that is, I was wondering if you needed a driver for your rig."

"You were reaching for something in the wagon bed."

Rev flushed. "Thought I saw a mouse."

Dan sadly shook his head.

"I just put those sacks in that wagon." Her tone turned sharp. "There was no mouse."

Thankfully, a thunder of hooves interrupted them. An orcen stumbled in through the town gate. He was dusty, with streaks of blood on his shirt. A crowd of orcen men on horseback followed, laughing as they struck at the man with whips.

The woman shouted at the newcomers. "That's enough, you thugs."

Rev was glad her attention shifted away. He started to ease on down the street, but Dan kept watching the confrontation between the riders and the woman.

One of the riders mocked her. "Well, if it ain't the nurse of Zhopahr."

"Shame on you, have you no sense of justice?"

He laughed. "Say, nursie, want to learn to ride?"

That sounded like trouble that would get Dan involved. No Ruskiya tolerated disrespect for a woman. Sure enough, his friend's tail started to whip angrily.

Rev sighed and put down his pack. He would have to intervene to keep this peaceful. Forty-to-one odds would not deter Dan. The Ruskiya believed one's doom must be followed, though death be inevitable. Orcen could be annoying that way.

The rider addressing the woman was a huge orcen with a grease-stained vest, a wide, reptilian face and a bare head painted in a threatening red and black. He carried a long spear, and leered at the woman.

As for her, instead of acting scared, she stood before the thugs as though she confronted a few unruly schoolchildren.

Spurred by her courage, Rev stepped forward.

Dan spoke. "Quit bullying people."

The man noticed Dan and Rev. "You drifters lost something over this way?"

Rev made a placating gesture. "We're just asking you to leave her be."

"You're interfering? Then die." The man aimed his spear at Rev and spurred his horse. He kept the blade aimed at Rev's gut, coming closer and closer.

At the last instant, Rev spun aside and slapped down the shaft of the spear. Its point bit into the earth. The butt drove into the orcen's stomach, levering him out of his saddle. The man cartwheeled through the air and slammed onto the street.

He lay gasping for breath.

The other thugs looked up to find Rev nocking an arrow to his bow.

"Drop your weapons," Rev ordered. Dan Zee also had an arrow ready. The thugs were caught unawares by this, no weapons in their hands. They had not expected resistance.

One thug grabbed for his sword. Rev's arrow hit him in the shoulder, knocked him out of the saddle. In one smooth motion Rev drew and nocked another arrow. Dan and he hunted with bows every day; they had gotten quite good. The thugs growled, but at last dropped their weapons.

"You brought trouble on yourself, human," said one orcen, his tail whipping. "Know who that is, yonder?"

He pointed at the first orcen in the dust. "That's Khat Trun."

Rev felt a stir of deviltry. "It's good of you to come right out and admit who you play with, alley cat, but I didn't hear the right tone in your voice."

"Tone?"

"I'd be thinking you'd have shame in your voice, admitting such a thing." Rev shook his head. "You ain't been dealt the cards today. Best gather up your friends and leave."

Using his bow, Rev indicated the two orcen in the dust, and they slung the wounded men onto their horses.

"Your appurtenances will be at the general store tomorrow," Rev told them.

The belligerent orcen glared. "We'll be back for you, sure as my name's Lum Tar."

"If you feel lucky, come ahead," Rev said pleasantly.

The man swore at him and the thugs rode off.

A loud cheer arose, and people rushed out to shake Rev's hand. The greeting astonished him. These Afen were a strange sort of orcen, to hide when ruffians attacked a lone man in their midst. Ruskiya orcen like Dan would charge to a man's defense, Shendasani orcen would ignore such proceedings, figuring it was the victim's doom, and of course humans mostly went along with the crowd, but Rev never imagined any orcen acting afraid. Didn't the Afen believe fate was unavoidable, as other orcen did?

The woman calmly climbed onto her wagon, not acting unduly impressed.

"Are you unhurt, ma'am?" Rev asked.

She sniffed, as though he should be embarrassed, then clucked at her horse, starting off. He felt ridiculous. Her learning he was a thief kindled his desire to keep moving. He did not belong here, or anywhere, really. Not if he kept stealing.

But as Rev slung on his pack, an older orcen in an elegant riding coat and carrying a gem-studded cane limped up.

"Sir? May we talk?" The fellow spoke as though to a favored underling. Two orcen men in fine clothing stood behind him. These Afen had narrower snouts than Dan, and brighter clothes.

Rev cautiously bowed.

"First, let me say that was amazing," their leader said.

The crowd cheered, and the woman stopped her rig to listen.

Rev waited, uneasy. News of his skill at unarmed fighting could give away his connection to the Shendao monastery. The monks were famous for bare-handed combat. As a monastery guard he had trained in the techniques. He wanted no pursuers discovering where he was. They might be after the sword, still.

"I'm Lot Sun." The man leaned both hands on his cane. "I run the largest ranch in Zhopahr valley. Our town has a position open for Boundskeeper, and we're wondering if you're the man to keep the peace."

Rev felt slugged unawares. Him? Keep the laws? He was a thief.

But a rush of longing to belong somewhere swept him.

The man went on. "Our Town Council is prepared to pay six silvers a month, along with room and a horse to keep after two months. Interested?"

Whenever Afen orcen mentioned money, they were dickering. Actually, any time they opened their mouths, they were dickering. The Afen loved to bargain.

"Six silvers is far too low, sir," Rev responded automatically, "but the offer is intriguing."

The human woman spoke up. "Watch yourselves, friends. This man just—"

"Murder," cried an orcen at the town gate, interrupting. "There's been a murder!"

The orcen wore the smock of a potter's apprentice, and had prominent, but slightly mismatched ears. He clasped his hands in appeal. "Follow me. Please, we need help."

Rev and Dan charged after the man up the road to a trail into the woods east of town. The trail led to a clearing where a trio of young orcen waited. A woman sobbed in the arms of another, while a man stood vigilant. Sunbeams revealed blood sprayed everywhere. A body sprawled on the ground, limbs and torso shrunken, as a scalded scent of burnt roses faded away.

"Bhat," shouted Lot Sun. "By the Gods, no."

The rancher threw himself down beside the body, unmindful of his elegant clothes.

"We were coming for a picnic when we found him," said the man guarding the women. "It's Bhat Sun. His brother." He indicated Lot Sun. A throng of townsfolk had followed, so maybe the Afen weren't fearful of danger, exactly. Then why hadn't they helped defend that man?

A man carrying a smith's hammer spoke. "He's not been here long. The critters haven't found him. I saw Bhat this morning, leaving town. He nodded to me."

"Whoever did this is probably still around," said a plump orcen, his tail whipping.

Lot Sun got up from his knees. "Whoever catches the killer of my brother..." His voice faltered, then resumed. "That person wins my brother's ranch and five hundred *neve*."

A murmur buzzed through the crowd. Five hundred *neve* was a lot of cattle. And an offer without any mention of bargaining? Lot Sun must be crazed with grief.

Such wealth would bring more respect than Rev ever imagined. And this remote valley was months from Shendasan. Surely the Chisen wouldn't find him here. If he couldn't make a life for himself here, where would ever be any better?

"Lot Sun," Rev said, "pay me 18 silvers a month along with the horse and a place to stay, with Dan Zee here as my assistant, and I'll accept your offer to be Boundskeeper."

The rancher nodded. "The position is yours."

Dan Zee's tail flicked in astonishment. His narrowing eyes hinted he would have plenty to say, later. Rev shrugged, feeling some dismay himself. He had asked for too little or there would have been more dickering, but 18 silvers seemed exorbitant already.

Rev squared his shoulders as people milled about. Importantly, he asked them to clear away so an investigation could start, but no one complied. Rev was a stranger and no one owed him anything.

Finally, another man urged folks to return to town for safety reasons. This man radiated such confidence that people readily listened; he was easily the largest person around, but sported long, golden hair and had no tail, so he was no orcen, though he wore the regional garb, homespun hemp pants and a leather fringed vest, a green kerchief around his neck, and a long knife in a sheath. His friendly argument carried weight, and the townsfolk dispersed.

He introduced himself to Rev and Dan. "I'm Yarrow. Like the herb."

A lunching table sat in the clearing. This must be a popular picnic spot. Steam rose from the foliage, lending an unearthly atmosphere, and the tree trunks were pale, like huge ghosts crowding around the clearing. An enchanting little river chuckled through the trees, and the first blue starflowers bloomed.

As flies buzzed, Rev, Dan and Yarrow searched for evidence. Pools of blood had kept people away from the body, so Rev found two interesting tracks. First was a large paw print in the blood made by some large cat. The snow leopards he tracked with his father were too fastidious to step in blood. Was the cat sick?

The second track was a partial impression of a man's boot, not made by the dead man, nor by Lot Sun, so possibly the killer had made it. A notch was missing from the heel print. Neither the dead man's clothing nor his skin bore bloodstains, though blood pooled everywhere.

Lot Sun knelt beside his dead brother. "He never wanted to ranch. Always wandering. Told him he'd find trouble in those foreign towns, but he laughed. Now he's been killed right here in Zhopahr. We were orphaned. I was older, always made sure he ate. He was a good man. Why did someone do this? Everyone liked him."

"We'll help you carry him home, sir." Rev patted the man's shoulder.

Lot Sun stood, unsteadily. "Thank you. Bhat was a bachelor, so we'll bring him to my place. We'll hold the funeral tonight."

Yarrow, Dan and Rev made a stretcher out of saplings. Rev tried not to look at the man's face, twisted into a rictus of pain, as they loaded him on the stretcher for his last walk home.

Chapter Five

"Afen orcen. Traders, mostly, some farming and wool textiles. Backbone of their society is debts, favors and bargaining. People keep careful track of debts. Honesty very important. Explain this to Fin Su — don't let our apprentices be caught lying. Afen don't laugh as much as other orcen, but not as quarrelsome, either. Main city is Khav, in the valley of the Ganjense river. Don't offer our best silk first."

Secret Notes of a Caravan Lord. Probably Vien goblen from internal evidence, about the year 830A. Such caravans plied the Great Spice Road in great numbers. Collection of the Museum of Thehar.

Ghund Rejeen entered the town through the front gates. He was a nondescript human, no one to look at twice. He considered that a blessing in his business.

This seemed like any other mountain village, no reason to believe the human he hunted would be here, but his master would know if Ghund skimped in his searching. Ghund was not good at deception, so he relied on being strictly obedient.

His master even fed him meat on occasion, when he had a particular success. He never asked what animal supplied that meat, but he had suspicions. Another reason to stay loyal.

It was a good life for a simple human from Shendasan.

Despite the lateness of the day, Ghund headed for the general store to ask questions.

#

Lot Sun's ranch was a large, well-tended spread commanding a hill that rose a couple thousand paces southwest of town. The stone barn and outbuildings looked original to the ancient town, but the ranch house was a new two-story log building with a porch, cedar shakes, and gardens of vegetables and flowers.

33

They laid Bhat Sun's body in an outbuilding smelling of dust and leather riding tack. Rev and Dan helped prepare the body for burial, in the process confirming Rev's initial impression that no wounds marred the corpse. So how had the blood drained out? It would take powerful magic to wreak such an effect, and a nasty mage to think of such a spell. Rev felt chilled.

#

Too many funerals can be the death of a man, some wag once said, anyone attending enough might be inclined to agree. The room is invariably hot, with some unwashed relative indulging in too much juniper liquor, who crowds you and talks too loudly. And when someone dies untimely, pain makes any conversation difficult.

Rev hoped not knowing the departed would make this experience less miserable, but that wasn't true so far.

Forty-two candles burned in the room where Bhat Sun's body lay shrouded, one for each year of his life. Lot Sun opened the door, and the entire town of Zhopahr turned out to pay respects.

Everyone brought something to remember Bhat by: some gambled with him and brought rolling bones, some brought buckets of ale, since Bhat had been something of a carouser, and the memorial table quickly filled, as a quitara softly played and people sang the old orcen drinking songs the dead man loved best. The mourners passed a shiny blackstone from hand to hand. Such wish stones mirrored the face of each person who looked into them. Legend said a bit of each mourner stayed in the stone, which went into the grave as a wish for the soul's peace.

Lot Sun stiffly clasped the arms of each arriving mourner, but seemed barely able to respond to the condolences. He had ashes of mourning on his face and his fine clothes were torn, like a small boy in a costume he did not wish to wear. He leaned heavily on his cane.

Rev and Dan wished on the stone in turn. Rev felt his own resonant grief from the recent loss of his mother, and more distant loss of his father.

"The whole town must have loved the man," Dan said, his voice low out of respect.

Rev felt a bit overwhelmed. Most people here were Afen orcen, though a few goblen of indeterminate nationality attended. He was only a slicker from the slums, how was he going to catch the killer? But his optimism quickly returned. This was an opportunity to learn the town, and start a list of suspects. He put aside his own grief and the memory that he had never cried for his father. It made him wonder if something were wrong with him, that he did not have the feelings normal people did. He shook his head. Enough of that.

He circulated through the crowd, greeting the business owners, the miners from the hills, the farmers from the plateau to the south. Everyone greeted him as "sir," the laboring types even treating him deferentially, as though surprised he would talk to them. Rev joined a group of orcen men in homespun red shirts and pants dyed blue; all wore heavy miner boots, their knuckles oft-broken, their faces knotted with lumps and scars.

"This seems like a nice town," Rev said. "You folks lived here long?"

"Only about a year, sir," said the tallest, with a respectful bow. His grey skin had paled, indicating he was older.

"A murder seems out of character. Are there many rowdies?"

A fellow with one squinting eye answered. "People enjoy to have fun here, sir, but not more than other towns."

"You think someone just got drunk and killed him? Are there a lot of killings in town?"

"Killings?" The tall orcen looked at him coldly. "Maybe there's a cutting or two happens over to Madame Coo's, but that ain't murder, that's a fight got out of hand. Whole different thing. People got a right to let off steam, and if it's rough on some, well, they died like they lived. But Bhat Sun, he was respectable. He enjoyed the tavern with us common folk, as though there was no difference between us. Staked me with a sack of beans once, and me a commoner. But this town has gotten mean, people at each other's throats. You'll see, Bounder. We didn't deserve anyone so good as Bhat."

The man walked off.

"I think the thugs hereabouts might have robbed him," said the squint-eyed miner. "He had more money than the rest of us, with that big ranch and all."

"He never made a copper off that ranch," disputed the third miner, a wide-shouldered man. "You and me, we get paid regular, he had to trade a cow every time he wanted groceries."

"Had he just sold a cow?" Rev asked.

"Might of, sir," the wide-shouldered man answered, "but he ran an account most places, paying off his debt with a calf, then charging more. Never generally got down to having coins. His brother Lot Sun, he's the rich one with those fancy clothes and high-tone ways. If you were going to lay for someone, why not him?"

"Thieves are dumb," the squint-eyed miner said. "Who'd be a thief, always looking over your shoulder for fear of hanging, and nobody willing to talk to you?"

Rev felt his face heat, but he kept smiling. No one knew him here.

"Way I figure," the squint-eyed miner went on, "it was the thugs."

"You mean the group on horseback today, whipping that man?"

"The very ones. There's a motley pile of them living in the foothills east of here."

"Why do people let them stay?"

"Who's to stop them?" the squint-eyed miner said. "You humans, you'll attack a king with a song and a sling, but we Afen are more cautious. Doom comes to us all, but no need to hasten matters, especially not over somebody else's foolishness. Anyway, it would take a full-out battle to roust those thugs."

Rev interviewed more folks with little result. But as he returned to Dan, a trio of middle-aged orcen approached, wearing plain brown shirts and pants cinched at the waist by white sashes, modest clothes but clean, and barefoot, not uncommon among orcen. Dan also never wore shoes. The orcen smiled stiffly and held out their hands to shake while still several paces away.

"Bounder," said the lead orcen, oldest by his white temples. Bounder was a shortened title for Boundskeeper. He shook Rev's hand with vigor. "Can't tell you how glad we are the town's returning to lawfulness, with your hire. I'm Kek Nin. Arms wright. This is my brother Nan, makes the best cabinets sold locally. You'll find us friendly people."

His brother spoke. "What do you think of what's happened, Bounder?"

"A sad day. Any idea who might have wanted to kill him?"

None voiced an opinion, but their expressions soured.

"It's a shame the town is coming to this," Nan said vehemently. "Something's got to change." His voice carried, and a few mourners looked over, their glances cold.

36

The third man smiled fixedly but never said a word. Nobody introduced him. Kek Nin shook Rev's hand once more and the three moved on.

"Creepy people," Rev murmured.

"I wonder if their white sashes got some sort of meaning," Dan replied.

Over in a corner, two men confronted each other, their gazes locked and their muscles swelling, before their women steered them apart. Rev and Dan watched, surprised.

"That felt kind of ugly," Dan said. "Dangerous."

Rev shook his head. "It's a funeral, people will be on their best behavior." But maybe the Afen were even more impulsive than most orcen. He wondered if the killer was in the room.

Three women arrived, all dressed in grey cloaks. The room's buzz hesitated. The first woman had honey-blonde hair – she was the woman Rev clashed with this morning. He felt a jolt of nervous interest. He had never been good at talking to girls. She stood as tall as her orcen companion, but not nearly as tall as the third of their trio, a huge, insect-like woman.

The human gave her condolences to the family, then proceeded around the room to offer greetings, moving with a lanky confidence, as though she had trained for a courtly world, but rarely inhabited it much.

Her two companions circulated separately, finally introducing themselves to Dan and Rev as healers. Ma'tha Mahn was a slender, older orcen with sparkly green eyes who wore her grey skirt cut at her knees, a racy length for an Afen. She swayed prettily as she talked and kept glancing sideways at Dan, who began to grin in an embarrassed fashion. Dan had never had a girlfriend, either.

The second lady, Laia, was a trollen. Rev had heard stories of this race of strange mortals. She was pale cream in color, fading to silver on her triangular face, preying-mantis-like in appearance and nearly twice the height of a human woman. Her voice was deep, her manner dignified, her grey dress of a modest length. Laia gave no family name, but people treated her with as much deference as Lot Sun himself.

At last, the human woman approached. "You're still in town, traveler?"

"My name is Rev Caern." He bowed. "This is my friend and assistant, Dan Zee. I've taken the job of Boundskeeper for Zhopahr."

She laughed, then covered her mouth as though embarrassed to make a merry sound at such an inopportune time. She took a moment to compose herself.

Ma'tha smoothly made the courtesies, covering her companion's social gaffe. "Rev Caern, may I introduce Gabryal Lansdon, who assists our healing work."

The honey-blonde nodded, amusement in her eye. "We've met."

"I have a question," Rev said, "since something tells me you'll be openhanded. Why was this job available? It pays well."

"Pays three times what you would receive in any other town, you mean," she answered briskly. "Excuse me if I can't believe you'll be honest in return, but why are you here?"

"You hurt me, Gabryal," he said, affecting an injured air. "Truly you do."

She laughed despite herself.

"We're looking for a place to settle," he explained, returning her smile.

"Keep that job and settle here you will, Rev Caern, in a nice plot in the graveyard with your own little wishstone. No Boundskeeper has held the job for over a month in the last year."

"Why's that?"

"You've faced the reason why." Gabryal made a sour face. "Forty thugs headed by that vile Khat Trun. People live in terror of them."

He admired her plain speaking, despite the sparks she and he rubbed off each other. "So my situation is somewhat dangerous?"

"Oh, somewhat. The last three Boundskeepers died violently. You be careful, Rev, the thugs will be hunting your hide."

"Thank you for your concern. I hope to disappoint them. Any idea who the killer might be?"

Gabryal shook her head. "I can't believe the killer is from here. It's a quiet town, aside from the miners and the thugs. And the ranch hands on payday. Look for a drifter, I'd recommend." She considered him. "I suppose the shoes are why Lot Sun decided you're of the professional class, deserving of a job like Boundskeeper. No common laborer could hold such a job, but being a foreigner, the Afen don't know exactly how to rank you. Have you noticed how respectful everyone has been?"

"I wondered about that," Rev said. "What do you mean, professional class?"

"People fall into social castes. Your friend Dan here is a common laborer, his bare feet put him there. But you, shod, are more puzzling. They'll call you sir until they figure you out. Interestingly," she smiled thinly, "thieves are ranked in the lowest level, as outcasts. Afen only speak to such if absolutely required, and then only in the third person. Drunks are outcasts, as are rag-pickers."

"Rag-pickers don't hurt anyone," Rev objected.

"Of course, but it is the Afen way, disputed at your own risk. Best to wear shoes, Rev."

The ladies made their goodbyes. Rev watched them go, stirred and upset. Gabryal showed a reckless streak and an intriguing unconcern with petty conventions, which struck a resonant chord in him. And she was beautiful. "I'm glad we're staying in Zhopahr."

"For Gabryal?" Dan snorted. "Think she'll have anything to do with you after today?"

Rev shrugged carelessly. "Maybe. Anyway, you looked interested in Ma'tha."

Orcen turned a darker grey when they blushed. Dan became almost rosy-black, and his tail thwacked the floor. "I don't know nothing about her," he mumbled.

Rev clapped him on the shoulder. "Not yet, but looks like we're staying a while, hunt-brother. You got time to learn."

His mind went back to the murder. The dead man's skin had a terrible, sunken quality, and the lack of wounds on the corpse bothered Rev, as had the faint scent of burnt roses that lingered in the area of the murder. Roses didn't grow in the deep woods.

At Lot Sun's urging, Rev and Dan slept in an out-of-the way shed that night. Rev awoke as the sun came up. He enjoyed mornings, they made him want to roll his shoulders and set to work, get things done.

The morning was foggy. Dan slumbered on, but Rev had never been one for lying abed until noon; that would make him too much like his father. He grinned wryly.

Hoisting his pack, he walked the wide path of crushed rock back to town. The town gate was off its hinges, a security concern. The full weight of the responsibility hit him. Little children lived here, under his protection now.

He headed out to where the body was found. Catching a murderer would prove his worth, and becoming a ranch owner and a wealthy man would give him respect. Respecting a person by class was weird. Either you had money or you didn't, what else mattered? That was how people rated each other in Shendasan. Sensible. He daydreamed about buying things, about people nodding to him on the street. He felt his soul expanding.

Sunlight slanted through the forest, creating a misty effect. Someone stood in the shadows by the murmuring river. He hesitated, but she was already turning, a staff in her hands. It was Gabryal, surprised to see him. A sunbeam highlighted her blonde hair.

"This is a lonely place to be, Healer," he said, overwhelmingly aware of her beauty.

"I spend much time alone, Rev." His presence seemed to disturb her as well. She put her hand to her hair. Then her jaw set decisively. "You should see something."

She led him to a grassy spot where a small rock, glowing orange, lay half concealed in the turf.

He reached down, but it burned his fingers. "Aiyy. It's hot." He dropped it, then laughed involuntarily. In the instant he held it, a welter of emotions had assailed him: arrogance, hunger, lust, greed, yearning, despair. "What kind of rock is that?"

"I don't know." Her tone was defensive, her words too quick. Was she lying?

He felt awkward, as though questioning her were accusing her somehow, but he was determined to do what he must. "Why are you alone where someone was murdered? Ain't you afraid?"

She flushed. Her eyes glittered. Anger? Grief? "I knew him."

Rev nodded. Had she been romantically involved with Bhat Sun? He felt an instant jealousy. But he was honest enough to admit that humans and orcen were similar enough that it happened, sometimes. People were people, they would love who they loved. Usually causing no end of uproar in both families, though.

"I'm sorry for your loss," he said, clumsily.

She nodded. "If you would excuse me?"

She hurried off towards town. An intriguing woman, and one strange encounter.

Oddly, just by using the meager protection of a handkerchief to lift the glowing rock, Rev prevented it from burning him, and from releasing the burst of emotions. The rock pulsed a deep orange as he put it in his belt pouch.

He would show it around and see if anyone could tell him what sort of magic it was, and why it might have been dropped at the spot of the murder.

Of course, that might also alert the killer that Rev was on the trail.

Chapter Six

"Orcen have skin of a grey hue; that of the Afen has a bluish cast and is less pebbled than the Ruskiya or Murkung. The Afen also wear bright clothing. The Ruskiya and Murkung wear furs ornamented with bone, tooth or claw, and the Ruskiya often display tattoos."

"Ethnographies of the Eastern Continent of Hazhe," author unknown, collected in <u>The Histories of Remula</u>, 930A.

Rev was now Boundskeeper, and therefore the number one target in town. Under the afternoon sun, he thought about how he could protect himself as he made his way to a small tower near the west gate. Lot Sun mentioned the Bounder's keep last night, telling him the tower was his home as long as he held the job, a well-built, easily defensible place. There were a lot of empty buildings in town, so it wasn't that surprising a perk, but he liked it.

Inside, a great circular room comprised the first floor, dragon shapes decorating the flagstones, as dragons formed decorations all over town. He lived here now? Emotion unexpectedly choked him up, and he realized how much he had hungered for a place of his own. He took in every discolored stone, every gap in the mortar to be lovingly repaired in the days ahead, as he dropped off his pack in the second floor bedroom. Home.

He paused, then hefted his father's sword. While he never handled a sword beyond some basic training at the monastery, he was glad to have one now. He felt surprised, not for the first time, at its plainness. For a weapon proud enough to hang on the town hall, it bore no ostentation, no ruby in the pommel to ruin its balance, no breakable gold wire wrapped around the grip.

But it had hung open to the weather for years, and needed no sharpening nor care. That did imply magic. So maybe there was reason for the Chisen to hunt it down.

Proud or plain, the blade carried his family's history. He felt the sharp edge of grief, thinking of his father. He fantasized about facing Norwe Hesketh, the governor of the Chisen, sword-to-sword. Rage swept him, and the sword in his hand seemed to intensify his emotion. Should he put it down? Reject his rage?

Rebelliously, he belted on the sword. He must stay ready with a killer around, must improve his swordplay.

#

To get a sense of his new responsibilities, he explored the town, even heading out the north gate into the ruins that circled the city. Low walls from the collapsed remains from taller buildings formed passageways through the brush. Here and there he found strange holes gaping in the soil. He examined one, found the recent marks of a spade.

A thousand paces or so into the forest, he reached the ruins of a wall even larger than the current town wall. The original city wall? If so, what now served as the town wall must have been just the bounds of some palace or temple complex, implying the old city had been huge.

The strange holes were abundant along the old wall. He imagined dozens of people creeping around, digging like crazy at midnight. He wanted to laugh, but actually it seemed creepy. A breeze hissed through the eerie ruins.

He had a disquieting feeling again, as though he were *supposed* to be here.

On the heels of that feeling, he heard footsteps crunching through the ruins, on a course as though someone had been following him. On impulse, he crouched behind a low wall – not really believing anyone would be following him, but not ready to meet anybody from town out here alone in the ruins, either.

He caught a glimpse of the man, passing along. He looked like a plain and ordinary human, nobody special, not as greasy as the thugs. Rev did not recognize him from the funeral, but surely quite a few people lived here he had not met as yet.

The man moved with purpose, carrying a spear like those the city guard carried in Shendasan. His skin was mottled, and he was skinny and frail, as though he had not been eating well recently. When he had passed on, Rev chose to go another way.

Passing around the corner of a head-high wall, he suddenly found a building so perfectly preserved he thought he had stepped back in time. An ancient crabapple tree in its courtyard shaded the entry, which had a marble façade and a lintel carved with the likenesses of a stag, doe and two fawns, the stag protective before the others. An orcen in full armor stood at either side of the door, each holding a long spears and wearing a white sash. Somehow, the scene struck him as disturbing. As though some unpleasant magic were being conducted here.

Rev found his voice. "What place is this?"

"The Temple of the Goddess, served by the Priestess Uulong," answered the guard on the right. The guards drew aside their spears.

Rev's impulse was to flee as from a trap, but he stepped inside. An acolyte knelt there with an offering basket. Embarrassed by his thin money pouch, Rev dropped in a copper, while the acolyte stared straight ahead. She also wore a white sash. The dark, cool temple smelled of sandalwood and a wooden altar filled the center of a room lit by candles. Fresh scratches marred the hardwood floor near the altar. Brocaded tapestries blanketed the walls and a stairway led down out of sight.

Rev had seen a different temple in town. Did two temples indicate a rift between competing theologies? He never attended any temple, though his parents taught him about the Goddess Luwana's Mercy and made him memorize the major (short) prayers from The Book of Vos. Disturbed by the temple, he departed, heading westward through the ruins until he found a private spot in a once-magnificent dooryard, where the pale walls were mostly intact. Two tangled bushes released a sweet scent from their scraggly red and golden blossoms. Rev sat on an old stone bench.

It was a perfect place to practice shi, so he started to meditate, clearing his mind.

To sense shi is simple, the Elder Fu had said. *Bring one finger from each hand together until they nearly touch. Slowly. You can feel the energy of shi between them. All things generate flows of shi. A sheath of energy surrounds all living things. This energy flows slowly where blocked, as in a swamp, and quickly where it moves freely, as with a young stream tumbling down the mountain.*

Rev concentrated on feeling the flows of energy.

Shi is subtle, difficult to control. Sense what the energy around you is doing, young Rev, and why.

Working with shi calmed him, though sometimes a sense of separation, from manipulating the energy, overwhelmed his calmness. Then he would quit, frightened that the separation might prove deadly. He knew so little. That did not happen today.

Done with his shi exercises, he worked with his sword on the martial forms he learned as a monastery guard. He was going to need both shi and sword.

#

When Rev returned to the keep that evening, Dan Zee was there, preparing a savory goat stew in the cauldron, newly baked pine nut biscuits on the counter, and baby lettuce garnished with violets plated on the plank table.

"Smells good." Rev plopped in a chair at the table. "Did I ever mention you're the best cook I ever met? Too bad you ain't a woman."

Ladle in hand, Dan stared at Rev. "Long day?"

He overrode Rev's answer. "What with signing me up to be your assistant and all."

"Didn't you want the job?" Rev asked, astonished. "I thought you wanted honorable employment more than anything."

"You never dickered for my pay. So I'm working for nothing."

Rev returned Dan's hangdog look. "And why should this job be different than any other you've had?"

They both laughed, and Dan sat.

"Anyway," Rev took a biscuit, "I'm thinking you do half the work, you get half the pay."

Dan slapped down his tail. "I won't take that much. You got the title, you'll be dodging the big arrows. Pay me three silvers a month and that's fair."

"Six," Rev said, "and you cook." He spooned up some stew.

"Five and you clean."

"Deal."

Dan furrowed his brow. "Was this bargaining a little backwards?"

Rev gave him an innocent look. "Sounded right to me. This stew is amazingly good."

"Rev, why are you willing to be Boundskeeper? The last thing you ever wanted was some work-a-day job."

"That's being nice. What you mean to say is, *Rev, you're no peace keeper, you're a thief.*"

Dan darkened with embarrassment. "I didn't say that."

"I don't know why I took it. Maybe to see if I *could* hold a job. A man should have a purpose. Being the Bounder will be a challenge, but we'll pull it off together." He felt more nervous than he admitted.

Dan hoisted a biscuit in salute. "That's Rev, looking at the bright side. Anyway, you'll outthink any ruffian. Who knows more about breaking the law than you?" He leaned forward. "How come you took the good room on the second floor?"

"I got here first. Besides, you'll like the third-story room fine. Everyone knows orcen don't mind a few dead flies."

"I don't remember reading that in the Orcen Explanatory Manual."

"It was in the appendix." Rev nodded his head solemnly. "You got to read those kind of books all the way through."

"Absolutely I will. Soon as someone actually writes such a book."

Finished eating, Rev used jug water to rinse out the cauldron. "I need your help to hunt this killer. I think if we find anyone with a reason for vengeance against Bhat Sun, they'd likely be who killed him."

"We ain't found anyone like that."

"But there had to be a reason he was killed." Rev flung the waste water into the bushes outside the front door.

A fellow was standing out there, some distance away. Rev had the impression he was just idling around, but then the man headed off as soon as Rev stepped outside. Rev did not get a good look at him; the same human he saw in the ruins?

Rev went back inside, closing and latching the heavy door. "If we keep asking who folks were at the time of the killing, either folks will verify each other's story or we catch someone in a lie."

Dan nodded. "That means figuring out exactly when the killing happened."

"Only a few flies were buzzing around, no ants, so he couldn't have been dead very long." Rev had seen dead bodies in the slums. "So, the same morning we arrived in town. It'll narrow down who could have done it."

"Assuming it wasn't a robbery by some drifting stranger," Dan said.

#

Next morning, Dan and Rev ran into Yarrow on the street, who bowed with a flourish and invited them to one of the tea houses. Yarrow had sparkling, tawny eyes, and his skin possessed the same slightly golden, iridescent sheen as the Elder Fu's. Rev again marveled at the size of the man. With his curly yellow hair he was no orcen, though he might be half orcen.

Over a porridge of *neve* milk, Yarrow agreed to talk about the town.

"Who do you think killed Bhat, sir?" Rev asked, carefully lifting his tea cup. He wasn't used to delicate plate-ware; a mug was more his style.

"Might have been a magic user or someone supplied by a magic user. A bloodless corpse sure hints at death by spell."

"Who are the mages in the valley?" Dan fed pastry crumbs to a sparrow bold enough to sneak in the door. Dan had an affinity for small animals and birds.

"Hard to say. Some hide their spell casting. But that healer Gabryal carries a staff openly. Elemental mages use staves, so anyone carrying a staff might be one. War mages, folks call them."

Rev glanced at his own quarterstaff in the corner.

Yarrow laughed. "That is, assuming it's not just a cut-down sapling."

"Hey, that's a finely worked implement of defense, I'll have you know."

"If you say so. Conjurors, clerics, healers and so on don't use staves. But as for a killer, I'd think about those thugs in the hills east of town."

Yarrow did not follow the general cultural rules of the Afen, there were no 'sirs' from him. He spoke to them as to comfortable equals. He did wear a pair of hand-tooled leather boots, slightly scuffed from use. "There are about forty ruffians causing trouble in the countryside, stealing, bothering women, drinking and gambling. They carouse most evenings at the Bolstered Fowl tavern. Gang up on a Bounder, if you give 'em the chance."

Rev shrugged. "Players got to know the rules at the beginning of the deal. And a confrontation might reveal any magic user among them and we're further along."

"Or dead," Dan said, who had the sparrow taking crumbs from his hand now.

"True. We have to be careful. Who are other magic users?"

Yarrow pursed his lips. "Ma'tha and Laia also belong to the Grey Women, the same healing order Gabryal is in. The two priests. Qur Sil, he's been in the valley five years or more, and Uulong probably use priestly magic. She's been in the valley about three months. You got that goblen conjuror living out east, Xul Bil Be, and another in a cabin north of town. Skarii is her name. Be surprising if Khat Trun's thugs didn't have a magic user to attack caravans and such."

"A big list," Dan said morosely. The sparrow on his shoulder flew off.

#

In the Bolstered Fowl late that afternoon, the orcen thug Lum Tar wiped off beer foam, and glowered at the little, nondescript human before him. "You're a liar."

Lum Tar swatted at the man, a stranger in town.

The man dodged. "You'll see, sir."

Humans were fast and tricky. Lum Tar hated them. He was second in command of the rebels, as they styled themselves, with notions about making his leadership permanent, if he could get rid of Khat Trun. Therefore he could not appear a fool. If this human lied and Lum Tar believed it, he would look bad. If the human was telling the truth... Lum Tar's head hurt.

"Ha. I'll kill you," he decided. He would seem strong even if the human were telling the truth about a new sign.

But the human dove out the open window, devious as all his race. The other rebels roared with laughter. Lum Tar lumbered to the window. No sign of the man. Coward. Lum Tar went to the front door, then paused, not wanting to get too far from his source of ale.

Paper fluttered on the community notice board, across the plaza. Annoyed, Lum Tar realized this was the sign the human meant, so he trudged out to the sign, the other rebels following. The paper looked like a chicken had walked along it.

"What's it say?" he asked no one in particular.

"Those are the new town laws, Lum Tar." A human leaned against the willow by the town well. "Rules I've been hired to enforce."

It was that new Bounder, Rev. Had that skinny human known Rev was here, set Lum Tar up for some reason? Not that Lum Tar would have avoided Rev. He feared no human. So he sniggered. "But I can't read, can I? So I don't have to obey."

The other thugs laughed.

The human showed his teeth like a wolf. "It says: *'No spitting or cursing before women. No drawing of weapons or breaking the peace. No damage to the property of others. No harassing citizens or visitors. No robbery, murder, or other thuggery. No dastardly activities.'"*

Lum Tar felt uneasy. "I won't listen to no such thing." But he almost said *sir*. Astounded at himself for such weakness, he tore down the notice.

Rev approached. "Tearing down that notice constitutes breaking the peace. You'll have to come with me."

"Make me," said Lum Tar happily, and swung a huge fist.

#

Rev ducked, and the blow went over his head. Rev drove a hard left into the orcen's face, splitting the skin over the man's right eye. A crowd gathered, hungry to watch, and Rev knew he was in trouble.

A fury comes out in a crowd surrounding a battle that its individual members would never admit feeling otherwise; an electricity of hate, for battle fury is a living thing that does not care who satisfies its thirst.

If Rev lost he would die. His opponent had no mercy, the crowd hungered for blood, and he was a stranger, a human in an orcen town.

Lum Tar swung his huge fist at Rev's head. Rev twisted so the blow glanced off, but its force knocked him down anyway. His vision went black. The gang of thugs screamed approval. Desperately, Rev rolled away, blind. Lum Tar stomped down, but missed him. The thug cursed, whipping his tail in frustration. Rev scrambled to his feet, his head clearing. His foe advanced with a snarl. Lum Tar meant to crush Rev.

Rev considered grabbing his quarterstaff, leaning against the willow, but he hesitated, thinking he must beat this man in a fair fight to win respect. A mistake.

Hands seized him from behind. Lum Tar roared in satisfaction as Rev struggled to free himself from the thugs who held him.

The crowd called out. "Human's doom. Human's doom. Kill him."

A rumbling voice interrupted. "One at a time, fellows."

Yarrow was there, twirling his broadsword like a matchstick. No one wanted any part of an armed man who stood a head taller than the largest orcen. Dan stepped up next to Yarrow and nocked an arrow to his bow. The thugs reluctantly released Rev and backed away. One of them was that nondescript human Rev had seen around town.

"Thanks, you two," Rev said to his friends. Yarrow and Dan waved for him continue, making no further move to help – Rev was starting to dislike this orcen penchant for letting people suffer their own doom. Lum Tar swung a roundhouse right, but Rev stepped inside it and smashed the heel of his hand against the orcen's face, further splitting the skin over his brow. The man roared furiously and rushed. Rev caught Lum Tar's left arm with his own left hand and threw the orcen over his outstretched leg.

Lum Tar hit the ground heavily, but sprang to his feet cat-quick. He looked surprised. Maybe no human ever took a blow from him and remained standing, but Rev had fought in the slums all his life, and as a monastery guard learned some of the science of fighting. Rev felt the excitement and fear that always marked a fight.

"Come here, human, and I'll destroy you." Lum Tar had a mad gleam in his eye.

He charged again, but Rev coolly stepped aside, caught his wrist, and threw him down once more. The orcen hit the ground, this time rising more slowly. His eyes squinted, assessing Rev with a new respect.

Rev was not as tall, but his shoulders were as wide and he had spent months hustling food in the wilderness, hard work that strengthened his muscles, while the thug lived the soft life whenever possible. Rev felt good, breathing easily, his limbs loose.

The onlookers screamed, the ones with white sashes caterwauling the loudest. Lum Tar came at Rev warily, his eyes bright with hate. Cautiously, Rev circled to his left.

As Lum Tar turned he crossed one leg before the other, out of position. Rev lunged, swinging a fist against the orcen's temple, staggering him. Then they traded blows, Rev shifting and ducking to avoid the full force of any attack except on his arms and shoulders. Still, it was like taking blows from a man with a hammer. The effort became a mindless thing, as Rev struggled to beat down his opponent, to succeed, to live.

At last Lum Tar lurched, leaving a momentary opening. Rev managed a clean shot to his chin. Lum Tar swayed, and Rev drove his left into his foe's face, remorselessly widening the split over his eye. Blood poured out. As the orcen brought up his hands to protect his face, Rev swung a right and left into his wind, doubling the man over.

Panting, near the end of his energy, Rev yanked the orcen's head down as he brought up his knee, pulping the thug's face. Lum Tar screamed. Rev smashed his right against the orcen's open jaw, breaking it with an audible snap. Lum Tar fell sideways into the dust, moaning.

Rev backed away, breathing hard. It was over.

Dust rose into the sky. Around him stood people who had been shouting for his death, thugs and townsfolk. His eyes coolly moved from face to face and they dropped their gazes, embarrassed to face the slum kid hired to protect them, whom they betrayed at the first chance.

What did I ever do to you, he wanted to snarl, but it was just that he was human. An expendable stranger, nothing personal, same as back in the slums.

"You." He pointed at the largest thug standing. "Nail that sign back up."

Cowed, the thug obeyed, using a splinter as a nail and a rock for a hammer.

Rev looked, but didn't see the red-and-black head of Khat Trun among the gathered ruffians. Too bad.

Rev raised his hand. "Those who follow these rules are welcome in Zhopahr. Rule breakers will be taken for justice. Repeat violators will be required to leave the valley."

Rev reached down, grabbed Lum Tar's shirt, and dragged the orcen away.

To restrain Lum Tar until the town council could meet in the morning, Rev dumped the man in the third floor room of their keep, on a canvas tarp. They would not give him one of their beds, he surely bore vermin.

"It ain't like he's gonna be ambitious about sneaking out," Dan commented, as they returned to the first floor great room, where Dan laid down his bedroll for the night.

Rev felt roiled inside, unhappy at having to fight, despite winning. He prowled the great room, restless and lonesome, pocketing small items.

Dan watched without comment. Someone rapped at the door. Rev opened it to discover Gabryal and Ma'tha.

Rev felt a nervous pleasure at the sight of the tall, hazel-eyed Gabryal.

"I'm glad you're here, Healers." Rev bowed them in, despite not knowing if a Bounder should bow to healers here. "We got an injured man needing attention."

"The Town Council sent us, Bounder," said Ma'tha in a low, melodious voice, with a brief curtsey. Healers were of the professional class. Her grey skin was so smooth it glowed, but pale at the temples, indicating she was not so young. Her bright orange dress complemented her green eyes and her grey bag matched her cape.

Gabryal's leather vest and leggings showed off her athletic figure while allowing her freedom of movement. Her hair was back in a braid. Her staff was thick and knotty, the wood black. Rev's heart thudded, being near to her.

Ma'tha greeted Dan with such pleasure the young orcen turned dark with embarrassment, then Rev led them up the curving stairs.

On seeing the patient, Ma'tha clucked. "You must be strong to do such damage, sir."

She opened her grey bag, drew forth scissors, a linen roll for bandages, and pouches with moss, herbs and other materials, then set to work, as Gabryal made poultices for the man's contusions. The room filled with the comforting scent of green growing things, and Rev abruptly felt hopeful, an effect of their healing magic, evidently.

Rev found the interplay between the two women strange. Ma'tha did the bulk of the work, but remained subtly deferential, though she set the man's broken jaw swiftly and professionally.

Rev sensed the movement of energy as she healed – not the familiar water-like flow of shi, more like fabric being stretched and realigned on a frame, an alien sensation, but pleasant. Could she have used her magic to kill Bhat? Something was off-putting about Ma'tha.

When she finished, Lum Tar slept soundly.

"He'll spend the night like that, Bounder." Her voice was clipped, as though working the magic alienated her from the world. Magic did that.

"Thank you, ma'am," Rev said, hoping ma'am was the right form of address.

"He's the one who should be thanking me, sir."

Ma'tha murmured a healing spell for Rev. It evoked a strange sense of release, a giving up of control like falling backwards in a dream, then the shivery feeling that invisible beings plunged unseen fingers inside him, manipulating tendons and joints. He didn't care for the sensation, but did feel less stiff afterwards.

An aura of detachment surrounded her. With an effort, she seemed to cast it off before she headed for the door, pausing near Dan.

"I enjoy tea in the evening at Playa's Local Tea House, but doing so alone is so tiresome, don't you agree, my handsome hawk?"

She left Dan gurgling at the familiarity. Gabryal gave Rev one last unfathomable glance, which left a happy twist in his heart.

Neither Rev nor Dan much felt like sleep after that, so they sat up watching over Lum Tar. Stars gleamed through the window, as the injured man snored deeply. Rev threw an old blanket over the man.

Rev mentioned his suspicions about Ma'tha, but Dan shook his head.

"She was healing folks all that morning, I already checked."

"Checking up on her already, my handsome hawk?" Rev asked innocently.

Dan growled. "And where was your lady love, Gabryal?"

"She's not my lady love and I don't know."

"Yet," Dan said, slapping his tail on the floor.

"Yet," Rev agreed, enjoying the ambiguity of the word. For a moment, his uncertainty overcame him. "Honestly, Dan, I ain't much comfortable in this job."

"There's a surprise, since you've spent your whole life as a thief. Give it time, Rev."

"I keep wondering who I'm hoping to trick with this notion of being a Boundskeeper. Am I making a fool of myself?"

"I'd say so," Dan said, "but that's a role you *should* be comfortable in." He avoided Rev's mock punch. "I'll take the first watch. Wake me when you get tired and I'll take the rest of the night. You're gonna need sleep after that."

#

The next morning, Sennaday, a bright day under a blue sky, Rev led his still-groggy prisoner to the town plaza for the council's judgment. Rev wore his sword.

Where the street widened out into the plaza, the local cooper, Jho Iun, intercepted them, trotting with tail out and head down as though to butt anything in his way. An orcen woman followed, her sour expression adding years to her age. The cooper's wife, Rev suspected. She wore a white sash, Jho Iun did not. He looked as short and wide as the barrels he made.

"So, Bounder," he squeaked, planting himself in Rev's way and bowing without looking Rev in the eye. "Don't wish to distress you, never that, but have you heard?"

"Good day, Cooper," Rev answered.

Something about Jho Iun seemed greasy. The cooper rubbed his hands together ceaselessly and wore a perpetual smirk. "That fellow Khat Trun, he's vowed vengeance on you. Says he wants you *dead*. That fight'll be interesting, won't it?"

"Not how I'd have described it," Rev said, feeling a surge of dislike for the cooper. "Where were you the morning of Bhat Sun's killing?"

"With my wife at her tea house, sir."

His wife nodded, to Rev's disappointment. Not that Rev thought the cooper capable of such a bold feat.

"Did you come here hunting the Disk of Dragons?" the cooper asked. "It'll be trouble for whoever finds it, but you wouldn't mind, you're tough. You're actually out there hunting Bhat's killer. Imagine taking on a doom like that, but that's humans. The killer will hunt you down, you know. Let the human die, everyone thinks, especially if Khat Trun is the killer. He's scary. They won't help you. How does that make you feel?" Jho Iun was practically salivating.

"My job is to uphold justice. That I will do. Goodbye, Cooper." Rev stared at Jho Iun until the man flinched and shuffled away.

In short order thereafter, the Town Council, seated in five chairs beneath the willow in the plaza, decided on a punishment of ten lashes. Rev bound Lum Tar to the tree with a rope while Jho Iun ran to find a lash. As Boundskeeper, Rev carried out the punishment, feeling sickened.

The thug screamed like a child while the townsfolk laughed at his weakness, Jho Iun laughing the loudest of all.

Afterwards, Ma'tha put salve on the thug's back.

Once she finished, Lum Tar faced Rev.

"You ain't seen the last of me, Bounder," he mumbled, his jaw still swollen. He stumbled off, out of town.

Chapter Seven

"Inland from Pangodia live all manner of strange beings. Reliable sources report a city of the dragon folk high in the Hiyin mountains, whose lairs hold gold unmeasured. The Nine Lost Artifacts are held by these greedy, cruel creatures. Of the mortal folk, the Afen are the greatest marvel, for their heads grow directly out of their chests, and they hop around on one foot all day, food dropping from the trees into their waiting mouths. This writer has seen these people, and can attest to the absolute truth of these tales."

Romance of Pangodia and Interior Lands, by Canne Truatha, published under the auspices of the Council of Historians in the city of Remula, the nation of Ilmari, Year 327A.

After Rev and Dan finished lunch, Rev started a fire to heat water.

"These people don't seem to care if we live or die," Dan said, "as long as we don't bother them. Bhat Sun they cared for, but he was one of their own. Should we just keep moving down the trail?"

"We *are* strangers," Rev answered, "and do folks in Zhopahr treat each other much differently than in Shendasan? Not that I've noticed. And we need the money." A rough feeling arose. "Anyway, I want to shove it to them, after cheering against me like that."

"And what about that Gabryal woman?" Dan teased him.

Rev grinned. "She's intriguing. It ain't so much that I'm falling for her, as I just want to get to know her better."

"So you tell yourself alone at night, anyway. You think she's the killer?"

"We saw her right before the body was discovered, so I doubt it. I don't suspect your Ma'tha, either. Why would they have?"

"A year ago you wouldn't have taken on such responsibility," Dan turned the subject away from Ma'tha. "You've changed."

"I had enough of living in the wilderness. Now I know what ground squirrel tastes like." Rev made a face.

"Hey, I did a good job cooking those squirrels."

"Then why didn't even the robber jays want them?"

"Aw, what do birds know? So, what *do* you want, here?"

Rev hesitated. "We've both lost family unjustly."

Sorrow crossed Dan's face. His grandmother had been killed by the Chisen.

"We can help other people from going through that. Maybe get justice for Bhat's murder. I keep thinking about the shock on Lot Sun's face. The killer is out there, Dan, and may kill again. Also, despite a few hotheads, I want to establish us here. My folks never valued community, but I do, and we got a chance to belong in Zhopahr."

Rev noticed a family on the street yesterday, and something about the tender way the man looked at his children touched a lonesome spot inside Rev. The children were neatly dressed, the wife smiling. That man would matter to someone all his life.

#

As Rev patrolled the streets, the cloud cover broke and the bright sun appeared. One or two persons nodded hello, but others turned away. He had no idea why folks might be avoiding him. He noticed that non-descript stranger who had been hanging around town. The man was across the street, and back a ways, as though he had been following Rev. He carried a long wooden tube.

Rev headed straight for him. "Stranger, I want a word with you."

The man's eyes widened. He fled down an alley. Surprised, Rev took off after him, but the alley curved between tall buildings, and when he came out the other side, he was on an empty street. A short way down each direction, other streets intersected with this one. No one was on the street, and there was no evidence which way the man had gone. The dirt held too many tracks to pick out one set in particular.

He gave up, but decided to keep an eye out. Something was suspicious about that fellow. He remembered the man had been in the crowd supporting the orcen thugs, during Rev's fight with Lum Tar. What was the tube for?

Near the north gate a building displayed a sign having a cup with steam rising. Inside, three orcen men, their temples grey, sat on brightly colored cushions, their tea service on a low table. Rev recognized the wagon wright, though not the other two. They nodded to him as to an equal, so at least they seemed to accept him.

"I don't understand." The smaller orcen spoke. "How come you don't use iron axles, Os Gar? They'd last better. We're seeing more ironmongery all the time."

The wagon wright drank some tea. "Ain't that I can't make 'em, Nip. Using iron for all those tools in my shop, ain't I, and chains on the harnesses? But what do you do with an iron axle what's bent? Can't repair it out on the road. White oak's plenty strong and easier to replace. Anyway, it's lighter. Only issue is, wood for a wagon you got to season two years. The greatest danger to any freight wagon is in its wheels – your wheel shrinks if it ain't seasoned proper, and the tire works loose until the whole contraption suddenly falls apart. Busts all the spokes right where they enter the hub, and *then* you got some repair work."

In the pause, Rev asked: "Sirs, I've noticed a bunch of holes outside of town. Anyone know where they come from?"

The wagon wright Os Gar laughed. "Bunch of fools wasting effort, Bounder."

The smaller orcen nodded. "People have some crazy notion there's a massive magical Artifact hidden hereabouts, sir."

Rev remembered his name from the wake. Nip Rew.

"It's not massive, Nip, it's powerful," the wagon wright corrected. "The Disk of Dragons is actually not big. But how folks think digging at random will find something hidden a thousand years, I have no idea."

"The Disk of Dragons? The Artifact from Sinnesemota?" Rev asked. "That gives you the power of a dragon?"

"It does more than that," Os Gar answered. "The Disk is the key to opening the Hall of the Empire. Whoever finds it can reestablish the Empire of Sinnesemota."

"So the finder gets to rule the world," Rev said, intrigued.

"Well, the stories never said that," said Os Gar. "I suppose if you try to rule the world, folks are going to oppose you. Be a long fight."

"And the Empire is supposed to be the essence of peace and justice," said Nip Rew. "So there's a paradox right there, establishing a world of peace by starting a war."

"The Hall of the Empire is the prize," said Os Gar. "It contains the Heart of Light. Heart of the Goddess Luwana. A huge jewel, they say. The vampyren could use that Heart to conjure up more vampyren. Not many vampyren left, no matter what you hear. Takes big magic to create even one vampyren. So their ruler, the Cabalmaster, could start a whole new army of vampyren with it. While anyone else could use it to reestablish Sinnesemota. A world-wide empire. Finding the Disk of Dragons is the first step to opening the Hall, and getting all that power. So people want it. The Cabalmaster sends its Watcher all over the world, snooping for it. Scary thought."

Rev remembered his vow to the Elder Fu to try to reestablish Sinnesemota. Should he be looking for the Disk of Dragons? The thought of confronting that Disk again made him go cold. Was it controlling him even now? He didn't *feel* controlled.

"I'm aiming for a smaller payoff at the moment." Rev raised his voice so the proprietress in the kitchen might hear, but he tried not to be too loud. Politeness was important to the orcen. "I'm looking for some help about town."

"If you're looking for men and willing to pay, I might be interested, friend. What are the duties?" Yarrow entered the tea room, his golden hair agleam.

"I'm looking for someone to help Dan and me keep the peace, Yarrow."

Yarrow dropped onto a cushion beside Rev, raised his hand to the proprietress for a cup of tea. "Keep the rest of the thugs off your back whilst you fight 'em one by one? Already proved myself there." He had a devilish glint in his eye. "What're you paying?"

"Be careful, sir," said an orcen at a nearby table. "Make Yarrow pay his own board. I hired him to build a wall on my stable, and paid in food. He near ate me right out of my home."

Rev grinned. "I'll take that to mind, sir. How's the wall?"

"A mule kicked it just this morning. Never wiggled. He built it strong."

Rev turned to Yarrow. "You take orders from me, or if I'm not around, Dan Zee. I'm paying three silvers a month, paid whenever I am paid."

"Fair enough."

Yarrow did not dicker, Rev realized in surprise. He was not Afen, obviously. A small boy wandered away from the table where his mother was conversing to her friends, snuggled right up against Yarrow's ankle and fell asleep; the mother glanced over, then went back to her conversation. That was Yarrow, such confidence flowed from him that people relaxed. With Yarrow and Dan Zee behind him, bringing peace to the town did not seem so impossible. Yarrow and Rev drank black tea to seal the bargain, Afen fashion, and ate some fresh baked raisin muffins. In their discussion, Rev found Yarrow knew the location of the camp of the thugs.

"That could be useful knowledge," Rev said. "They seem to be the first suspects for any crime committed."

"You going after them right quick? Maybe I should've asked to get paid in advance."

"Absolutely not. That's my guarantee you'll slick me out of trouble when needed."

"You surely lay a worth on three silvers a month, my friend," Yarrow said wryly.

Yarrow talked slowly, running his hand through his hair when thinking. He was cheerful, but though he never exactly said anything bad about anyone, Rev absorbed a clear sense of many of the town's inhabitants.

"I'm wondering about possible reasons for the murder," Rev said. "How about jealousy?"

Yarrow shrugged. "Maybe. Bhat had a woman he was courting, Dores was her name. Folks thought they might get married. Brought her out from Khav, last time he went down there. His brother was happy Bhat found someone, him being not so young, but Lot Sun did have his reservations, since she wasn't a professional, nor merchant class. Afen lay a real worth on such things. Bhat was kind of foolish about her, growing her flowers and buying her ribbons. Sweet, really. They both liked to drink, maybe that was an attraction. But she's a woman who looks where the money's hid, and Bhat had none. She made the mistake of thinking rancher is the same as rich. She left him last fall. He took it hard, hid in the cabin all winter, not much help with the cattle. Wasn't until a month or two ago he started getting out, taking an interest again."

60

"Where's the jealousy motive come in?"

"She moved straight to the rotgut side of town and started an establishment, and not with Bhat's money. She didn't have any cash when she got to town, so who gave her some, and why?"

"They didn't get along after she left him?"

"They had a huge fight the night before he died, at the front door of her establishment. Half the town heard it."

Rev tapped his finger on his cheek. "I'll have to ask this Dores some questions. Bhat didn't carry money, someone said."

"Not much. Local merchants would be poor suspects if the motive was robbery, they all lost money on his death. Or would have, except Lot Sun went around and made his brother's debts good. Even the thugs knew Bhat carried no money."

Rev shook his head. "I don't know enough. For instance, there are an awful lot of thugs for such a small area. So many can't be surviving by robbing townsfolk who have no coin, so what makes it worth their while to stay?"

"Maybe the traffic on the roads," Yarrow said. "See, Zhopahr sits at a trail crossing of the Great Spice Road, which caravans take to Khav and beyond, and the Smuggler's Road, which goes north and south, avoiding Khav altogether. My, that muffin is good." He took another. "A fair amount of business passes through Zhopahr, then."

"There's call for luxuries that folks never used to want, East loves West and West loves East and all that. The thugs hit the caravans and occasionally get away with it."

"Don't the caravans have guards?"

"The big rigs hire those Shendao monks. Nobody wants to fight them," Yarrow said. "The little wagon trains got mages, or guards. But sometimes not enough."

Rev felt nervous, learning that monks would be passing through town. He changed the subject. "How have you been making your way, Yarrow?"

"I was punching cows for Bhat before the murder. Made my living off cattle longer than I care to remember."

That made Rev wonder how old Yarrow was. The man looked young, but something in the tilt of his head or crinkling of his eyes suggested great age.

"What do you know about these folks in the white sashes around town?"

Yarrow shook his head. "Touchy subject. White-Sashers are folks who have taken to attending services with the new priestess Uulong, and abandoned the older congregation of Qur Sil. Those two priests haven't said so much as howdy to each other in the three months Uulong's been here."

"A situation to watch?"

"Nobody's started a fight yet, but you know religious people." Yarrow grinned. "Always killing folks who disagree with them. Following the will of a loving God, I guess."

As they stood to leave, Yarrow quietly handed the sleepy children and puppies circled around him back to their mothers. Rev was glad to have hired Yarrow. Outside, Yarrow agreed to patrol the town while Rev learned more about the ruins, then meet for dinner at the keep.

"One last thing," Rev said. "Folks seem to be shunning me. Any notion why?"

"Sure. They don't want your doom rubbing on them. They figure you for a dead man."

"Doesn't that disturb you?"

"Nah." Yarrow shook his head. "Seen too many fellows die to fret about one more."

Rev rocked his head back, amused. "Well, there's a comfort to me, I can't tell you."

#

Later that afternoon, Rev traveled through the forest edge north of town, examining the ruins for defensible positions. Abruptly, he had the feeling of being watched. Was that human around?

Sword in hand, he put his back to a wall. The forest seemed too quiet. He looked up. On a branch overhead, he saw a white leopard. A demon cat.

His breath caught. Legend said the vampyren could turn into white cats to hunt. Could this be a vampyren? He remembered the paw prints around Bhat's body. Had a vampyren drunk the dead man's blood? Rev shuddered. Vampyren were the enemy of the mortal races. Only a few hundred vampyren ever existed, but they were cruel, strong, and steeped in evil, murderers and shape-changers, delighting in the pain of others. The cat gazed into his eyes, and he felt hypnotized. Breathe, he told himself. Breathe. His first lesson in shi, the calming exercise. With breath came the ability to move. He raised his weapon.

The leopard snarled and leaped away onto the forest floor. There it hesitated, turning as if inviting him to follow. Involuntarily, he shook his head no. The cat seemed to understand, or perhaps was disgusted with him for ruining its hunting spot. It vanished into the underbrush.

Rev fled, and was halfway back to town before he slowed enough to notice strange tracks in the dirt. He felt familiar with most spoor, but not these; they resembled hand prints, like the tracks of the monkeys living in the monastery gardens. The depth of the print indicated a weight greater than most men. A larger ape. The beast traveled alone. He decided to discuss the tracks with Yarrow – but in the end, forgot to do so.

#

Rev and Dan emerged from their keep on Vosday morning to discover Lot Sun dismounting from his horse. The rancher wore an outfit of brushed white leather, with a matching wide-brimmed hat. "Rev, we didn't agree about the when of your pay, so I'll use the schedule I pay my hands, once a week. 18 silvers a month, split by four weeks, would be four silvers a week. Every week on Vosday. There's two more days in a month than that, and you get two more silvers a month, so first of each month I'll pay you the other two silvers. Today's the first of Goblenmoon, so you get those two coins for this month now. Reasonable?"

Lot Sun held out a handful of coins.

"Thank you, sir. More than reasonable." Rev tried to keep his voice calm, but his awe rose at the coins in his hand. Six silvers!

"You've been doing a fine job, Bounder. See that you keep working diligent."

Lot Sun remounted and rode away.

Dan's eyes widened. He whispered. "Flames of the pits. Rev, we're rich."

They raced back into the keep and Rev poured the coins onto the table. They jumped around the room in glee, hollering and laughing.

Dan abruptly halted. "Silver. They really are silver. Rev, how can I be worthy of this?" His jaw trembled.

Rev was solemn, too; the first legitimate pay in their life. Now they were like normal people who worked; respectable people. He whooped again. "From now on, we're going to get paid this much. Here." He split the six coins into two piles. "Half for you."

"No," Dan said, "we already been through that. Give me two now, then one per week." He took two coins. "You need the rest for expenses, anyway. Paying Yarrow and all."

"You're right about one thing," Rev said. "I'll keep working hard. I'm going to be rich and important."

Dan hesitated. "I'm afraid for you, when you get that money you're always hungering for."

"That's the strangest thing I've ever heard, hunt-brother."

"Rev, what will you do when you get all that money and it doesn't make any difference?"

Rev scoffed. "No wonder you're poor with an attitude like that."

"I'm not poor. We're both of us earning more than we've ever seen in our lives."

"It's not the money, Dan. I just want to be respected. I want to walk down the street and have people know my name."

"Does that mean you're going to stop stealing from them?"

Rev looked at his friend in astonishment. How had Dan known Rev had been pilfering? "It's only little stuff, nothing anyone cares about. Flowers. A bowl, once."

"We're not in the slums anymore. You had to steal there, but this is a nice town, and you got a good job. Why ruin it?"

"I'm not going to ruin it. Leave me alone." Rev looked at the ground, humiliated." Anyway, this is my job just until I catch that killer. That's my real chance, catch that killer and I'm a ranch owner. Hundreds of *neve*. I really *will* be somebody."

Could Rev become so famous his brother Var might learn where he was? He wondered if his brother was still alive. Someday he would go looking for Var.

"Why aren't you happy just to be someone to yourself?" Dan kept at it.

Rev felt defensive. "Sometimes you don't understand. And I don't know how to explain. Anyway, let's stop this pity talk, and go celebrate."

#

Disk of Dragons

The first of Goblenmoon was Greening Day, celebrating the return of spring. Bundled daffodils and hyacinths hung from doorways, everyone wore their brightest clothes, and a rousing dance took over the marketplace. Musicians stood on a wagon serving as a makeshift stage. To one side, miners competed in a log-tossing contest to assorted cheers and jeers. Children hurried from person to person, offering crocus nosegays.

But Dan only ate one tiny bag of sweets before mumbling an excuse and hurrying off. Where was his friend going? They had not even eaten.

Disappointed, alone, Rev wandered from booth to booth until he found a tooled leather scabbard for his father's sword. Half a silver in cost. He wished his parents could have seen it. He did not know what to do with all this money, the number of coppers returned in change for the silver to buy the sweets was ridiculously high.

To his nervous delight, when he entered a tea house, he discovered Gabryal about to sit at a table.

"May I join you, Gabryal?" he asked, pleased at his nerve. He could even afford to court a woman, a wonderful, expansive feeling.

"That would be nice, Bounder." She shook out her honey-blonde hair.

He ordered a pot of tea and a large plate of tiny sandwiches, then found himself having to make conversation.

"I..." he started. His brain froze up.

He felt like an imposter, a slum kid trying to live in a fancy world high above himself. The whole Afen world seemed so alien, the tiny sandwiches, formal teas, all of it. Finally, the dutiful part of his mind took over. "I believe the murder happened the morning I arrived in town. I'm hoping to locate where everyone was."

"I was in the general store shopping much of the morning. Tay Hich and his wife Kesa were there, the owners. Their kids were playing with Pura Rew's daughter."

"Thank you, Gabryal, I appreciate your help."

She smiled more warmly. Their gazes met.

He felt excited. "We haven't gotten along smoothly, but I'm hoping we can start over. I like you, Gabryal. You have such a sparkle, you're direct, and no fool, either. That's my impression, anyway."

"You're kind, Rev. I don't trust you, but despite myself, I actually like you, too. There's something refreshing about your slick ways."

He bowed. "Thank you, I guess. Really, what I'm wondering is, who are you? Are we as alike as I suspect?"

"Me?" She made a self-deprecating gesture. "I'm the kind of woman who takes whatever comes, I don't expect too much anymore. You do have the direct part right. It's embarrassing, women are supposed to be sweet and demure, but take a typical woman and find her opposite, that's me. A good woman is indirect? I'm too frank. Kind? I think of myself that way, but demure? Please." She grinned. "And not much humility."

"I've never been much for bowing my head and scraping my feet either."

She leaned backward for an instant, making him aware of the smooth fabric of her blouse.

"I flatter myself to think I have courage," she said, "but maybe it's a lack of common sense. When I was a girl, a dog protecting the neighbor's house would bark when anyone passed, flinging himself at the fence. I said to the other kids one day, 'He's just lonely.' They thought I was crazy, they *knew* he was serious. They bet I wouldn't go in there, but I wasn't going to be a scaredy-snake, so I shimmied over the gate. You never saw such a surprised animal, he didn't know whether to bite me or run. I stuck out my hand, he gave me a lick and we were best buddies the rest of his life. Great dog. Fierce. I wouldn't do that now... all right, I would, but there'd have to be more in it these days. Still, I am who I am. I've needed to be tough."

"So, we're nothing alike," he said, and they both laughed.

At last, she said she must return to her patients.

"I'd like to do this again," Rev said. "This was fun."

"Thank you, I enjoyed myself as well." She smiled at him before she walked away, then turned to wave, which twisted his heart in a crazy way.

#

Ghund Rejeen stood at the rise to the Eastern Road, watching the strange little messenger he had called to him depart afterwards, slithering eastward through the brush.

In a way, this marked a failure. Ghund had tried setting an ambush, but Rev was always checking his back trail, paying attention to his environment. He was harder to sneak up on than any human Ghund ever stalked.

Ghund had no intention of drawing the attention of Rev's friends. That huge, blonde fellow looked dangerous as a cobra.

So Ghund was sending for reinforcements. He would bring the full attention of his masters to bear on Rev. Sadly, Ghund had not killed Rev, nor seized the sword; the Bounder always kept it on his person. But even finding Rev should be enough to win a reward. Maybe he could hit Rev with a poisoned dart from a safe distance. One way or the other, Ghund stood to benefit.

Chapter Eight

"Where a dragonet you spy,
There's a dragon right nearby."
Children's rhyme, from the streets of Pacesacre.

Evening painted the trees that surrounded the clearing gold, and birds fussed in the forest, voicing their last songs before dark. In a shaded area of the clearing, a vampyren prepared a spell, one that must be cast far from any intervening presence. The vampyren was unconcerned. It could sense any mortal presence out to a hundred paces, and none was close. The vampyren were birthed out of shadow, and the Shadow Folk became more powerful in darkness.

This spell would search for the Disk of Dragons, which could open the Hall of the Empire, where lay the Heart of Light. The infinite power of the Goddess Luwana radiated from that jewel.

On a black silk cloth, the vampyren laid out a scrap from the ancient vestments of a High Priest of the Dragon, a marble candlestick with a candle made from the grease of a human skull, and a brace of bound and quivering rabbits. The vampyren lit the candle. At the first few words of the spell, the rabbits slumped, dead. Scarlet light flared over their bodies.

Other reddish lights flared in the underbrush, one after another: death calling death. Wherever something died recently such lights appeared, a side effect of ritual magic. Power coursed through the clearing and the vampyren felt the familiar hunger ritual magic stirred. A stench of mortal decay permeated the area.

With an effort of will, the vampyren stopped the casting.

The seductive call of power was nearly overwhelming, and the red lights whipped wildly, blown by a rising wind, but the spell must not be completed yet. Ritual magic, also called ceremonial magic, was only used by vampyren. Anyone who traced a ceremonial spell back through the ether would know a vampyren cast it.

Ritual magic occurred in two parts: the locus where the spell actually fired, discoverable by magical reverberations, and the triggering, which could not be located. Due to this drawback to ceremonial magic, vampyren mostly used conjurations or elemental spells. But ceremonial magic was the most powerful, and needful at times.

The vampyren's fangs showed. *I will eliminate those Grey Women.*

But only from ambush, when each was alone. Grey Women had killed many Shadow Folk over the years. Typical of vampyren, this one lived in an obsessive fear of death. And it had reason to fear. Clues hinted a dragon lurked nearby. Shi was being used, which was dragon magic, and a heavy magic presence weighed in this valley, consistent with one of the Jeweled Folk. And dragons hunted vampyren.

However, one did what one must. Especially since the vampyren recently felt an unsettling sense of watchfulness. It was being watched. Such feelings happened on occasion, it had always assumed they came from the attention of the Cabalmaster, keeping track of its minions, but the Cabalmaster did not explain itself to the rank-and-file. Fortunately, the attention was fleeting this time. But the vampyren felt a little more trapped, a little more pressure to perform its duties, no matter what the cost.

Putting aside its fear, the vampyren conjured an imp to remain in the clearing here, and report back the results of the spell. Then the vampyren departed.

Later that evening, in its lair, the vampyren spoke the word that would trigger the spell, send the scrap of parchment flying to the location of the Disk of Dragons.

Impatiently, it waited. Far too quickly, the imp appeared.

Results? the vampyren demanded, in thought.

The parchment burned to nothing without moving answered the imp.

Foiled, the vampyren flew into a rage, flinging items about the room. Its gaze fell on a rat in a hanging cage. Slowly, the vampyren crossed to the cage and opened its door.

The rat inside squealed in terror.

#

The healers sat on willow branch stools before their tent. They occupied a vacant lot not far from Zhopahr's south gate. The ruins of nearby buildings sheltered them. A log reflector helped their fire warm the area. As the conversation took a confidential turn, Laia watched for passersby, her antennae turning this way and that.

"I'm worried a vampyren is nearby, Ma'tha," said Gabryal. "We should warn people."

"To do what, panic? What can normal people do against a vampyren?"

Gabryal felt foolish.

"Anyway," Ma'tha went on briskly, "you reviewed the area where that man was killed and found no evidence of a vampyren."

"I was interrupted before I could finish," Gabryal said.

Embarrassed, she remembered that day at the picnic spot, being caught there by Rev, her half-lie to put him off.

She knew he liked her, which was flattering, it had been a long time since any man had noticed her in that way, but she could not tell him the truth: the Order of the Grey Women did not just heal, they also hunted vampyren. It was dangerous work, secrecy was imperative.

The man was no better than a thief, and dangerous. Look how he handled that orcen thug. Why did some voice inside keep insisting she tell him all about herself? No, that was vanity. Rev might even be the vampyren; he obviously had secrets. Few people knew much about vampyren. The Shadow Folk were said to be fearful of garlic and mirrors, to be ten feet tall, to be invincible. They were used as tales to frighten children.

But a vampyren had killed her beloved husband, and she wanted revenge, so when she learned the hidden purpose of the Grey Women, she joined the militant branch of their Order.

Pitch flared in the fire, throwing the shadows into stark relief. Nearby, Gabryal's staff was planted in the ground, taking in elemental power, recharging. Elemental magic required such a storage device, regularly replenished from the magic pooled in the earth.

"What disturbs me," Gabryal said, "is that Bhat Sun had no blood left in him. More than one old tale say the vampyren suck blood."

"Untrue stories though," Ma'tha said. "Vampyren use magic to draw out the life's energy, not the blood, of their victims." She slapped down her tail for dramatic effect.

Gabryal was the youngest and least experienced of the three of them, so by the traditions of the Order she must defer to her elders, but she wondered if Ma'tha knew the whole truth. Vampyren were ancient and horrible, feeding on all mortal races. Maybe the Shadow Folk also used a spell that sucked out blood. Sometimes Ma'tha took the threat of the vampyren with less than complete seriousness, being distracted by men. She was always trying to find a stable life.

"The young one may be sensing something," Laia spoke. "I also feel disturbed. Go to check your detection spell, Gabryal."

If Laia felt disturbed, Gabryal must be cautious. Trollen women had uncanny abilities. They followed one another into the tent. On the table where Gabryal had her divining spells, ripples stirred in a bowl. The water glowed red: a vampyren's spell had been cast, not far away. An ozone stench hung in the air. Despite the rush of confidence that came as a side effect from casting elemental magical, Gabryal felt an ominous chill. A vampyren WAS nearby.

#

As the sun topped the Hiyin mountains on Arsday, the second of Goblenmoon, Rev stood on a hill in the cool air, peering down the Eastern Road to where it climbed into the foothills. Far off, a great number of people approached; army or nation, his responsibility either way.

The townsfolk already looked to Rev, their Bounder, for leadership. Rev enjoyed this newfound respect, but wished he were confident about handling the approaching strangers.

Having reconnoitered the threat, he re-entered Zhopahr, as people in the street discussed the strangers in grim tones, and miners clustered by the general store, clutching pickaxes.

A burly miner in a wide-brimmed hat bowed to him. "I've heard about these people coming, Bounder. Refugees. Hundreds, but if we band together, we can keep 'em out."

"Refugees from what, Miner?" Propriety among the Afen required that when first conversing with a person, one must refer to the nobility as Lord or Lady, to merchants and professionals by their name or as sir or ma'am, and laborers by their name or as man or woman. Fortunately, you could always use a person's profession as an honorific, no matter what their social status.

The orcen snapped his tail, the equivalent of a shrug. His reptilian snout was broad, and he had light grey skin, mottled and scarred from fighting. He wore an impeccable maroon velvet jacket that matched his hat, and an elaborately filigreed sword in a tooled leather scabbard. He spoke slowly. "Some war or other. I've seen the like, back in the lands of the Pers. They come down from up north whenever the karken go raiding."

"To be openhanded, I don't know your name, Miner."

"Ash Wal. Own the big silver mine up in the hills east. Got three dozen miners working for me. We're at your disposal, Bounder." He treated Rev with the deference a laborer gave a professional. Rev didn't think he'd ever get used to that, coming from an obviously wealthy man.

"Thank you. First, I think we should learn what they plan to do."

"They aim to settle in right here. I talked to 'em yesterday, I had trading business eastwards. They're Ruskiya orcen, a warrior tribe."

Forewarned, Rev took charge. He felt awkward, but folks seemed glad for his directions. The town walls served as a defensive barrier, though the gates remained broken. He had not started to repair the town's defenses. He felt guilty, but too late now.

He set defenders to lay wagons sideways across the gaps of the gates. The town had maybe 150 fighters, men and women, the miners carrying picks, the shopkeepers having spears and a few swords. The people wearing white sashes talked belligerently and flourished their weapons, and Rev worried they might provoke a conflict.

He directed most defenders to protect the eastern gate, those with bows atop the walls, and had the weaponless gather old clothes for bandages and pails of water to wet down the roofs against fire. Next he sent a runner to inform Lot Sun and other nearby ranchers.

He would direct the town's defenses from atop the wall, since he possessed a bow. Enough defenders carried spears to form a sortie, and these he placed at the gate under the command of Yarrow.

At noon the refugees appeared at the crest of the eastern road. An impressive and disquieting sight, so many armed people. Their column halted a few hundred paces from town, and a tall Ruskiya orcen raised his

72

hand. Two wings of archers swung out and marched up within bow range. Rev's mind raced through possibilities.

The advice of the Elder Fu came back:

Consider the facts, make the best decision you can, don't second guess. Take deep, slow breaths, and make no decision based on fear.

The deep, slow breaths were not so easy to manage.

A contingent of the newcomers approached, led by an old woman with a grey cloak that sported a long tassel, like a tail. Woven into the tassel were finger bones, and the cloak's clasp was two large claws. She wore a studded leather hauberk and a metal cap, and looked tough as a raven. The other orcen wore dark furs, with claw, antler and tooth necklaces. Their skin was mottled in regular patterns. Tattoos?

The parleying party halted twenty paces from the wall. The woman spoke in a gravelly voice. "I am Dunortha, Rus of the Red Bear Clan of the Ruskiya orcen. These are my people. Close you this road against us?"

Ash Wal called out. "Woman, what makes you believe you can move in on us?" He addressed her as one would a common laborer, despite her position at the head of her clan.

An angry murmur ran through the men behind Dunortha, and their hands tightened on their spears. Perhaps two hundred refugees stood before the gates, with sixty or so fighters who looked well acquainted with their weapons.

Rev felt the bite of panic. This must not spiral out of control. Orcen were impetuous, this could explode into a fight. He leaned forward to speak. As he did, a small something hissed past his ear, just missing him. What had that been? He jerked aside, puzzled.

Fortunately, Rev was not the only one working to control the situation. Dunortha made a small, lordly gesture and her people fell still.

"You are speak for your people, orcen?" she asked the mine owner. "Your name?"

"My name's my own," Ash Wal said in his slow, belligerent voice. "If you try to stay here, we'll drive you out."

"No one is fighting anyone yet," Rev interrupted. "Lady, I'm Rev Caern, Boundskeeper of Zhopahr." Unlike Ash Wal, he spoke to her as though to a noble.

"The Boundskeeper speaks for the town," declared Lot Sun, just arriving and out of breath. His ranch hands fanned along the top of the wall. "Though we make important decisions in Town Council, Lady." Townsfolk nodded. As a Council member, a landholder, and the wealthiest man in the valley, Lot Sun's opinion carried weight. He gave her a noble title as well.

"Why did you come here?" Rev asked Dunortha, relieved for the rancher's support.

"We are refugees who seek a place to rest, Boundskeeper. We are travel with children, not as a war band." Dunortha maintained her calm, holding her warriors in check. Rev had never seen anyone in such control of people without doing anything.

"Rev Caern, we have sick people among us and injuries. The Murkung and their karken apes drive us from our homes. They worship the Goddess Thana. We serve not the Lady of Doom, but we weary. We ask you allow us to rest, until we are strong to go on."

Women and children waited well behind the Ruskiya warriors, looking ragged, some wearing no cloaks despite the chilly day.

"You have armed folk," Ash Wal said, his hand on his ornate sword as his nostrils flared. "You could lull us, then kill us all."

"We build our fort at a distance. We are raise our own crops, and leave you alone. We seek no charity." Her voice rose proudly. "Grant you leave for us to remain in your valley?"

"You've fought since you left your home?" Rev asked.

Dan Zee worked his way through the crowd, headed for something behind and below Rev. Rev had no time to consider why.

Dunortha answer. "Sa. Many battles, but we are Ruskiya and we survive."

"Are you followed, Lady?"

"It is probable, sir." She had the direct manner of all Ruskiya.

"Who follows you? The Murkung?"

Her eyes glinted in appreciation at the thoughtfulness of his question. "Nay. We fight, three weeks before today, an army of the Chisen goblen. Why the Chisen expand their territory we do not know, but they have no love of orcen nor human, Rev Caern. If they are here, you are glad of our arms in your defense."

"Don't trust these refugees," Ash Wal objected. "They got enemies."

The woman Dunortha stared at Ash Wal. "Sa, an army follows, a thousand soldiers who burn and pillage. Also, savage karken roam and slaughter many. I warn you this. You stay in your village and believe yourselves safe, but I sharpen my weapons and build my walls and not make new enemies, am I you. Fell things arise again from evil times before Sinnesemota."

A baby started crying among the refugees.

"Our town hasn't got enough food for so many people," Ash Wal said. His widened eyes gave him a fanatical appearance.

Several men in white sashes loudly agreed. "They're poor. They'll bring crime. We have to take care of ourselves. Let others be responsible for themselves for once."

"We have goats and seed. We grow crops," Dunortha said.

"There's a more serious issue," Ash Wal said, pointing at the refugees with his stubby forefinger. "These people admit bringing an army down upon us. They endanger us."

"Fah. The army goes where it does." Dunortha's voice remained smooth. Great leaders rarely revealed when they were upset, she certainly did not. "We are no influence, we are not rich in the spoils an army seeks. You are yourselves more targets."

Rev tried appealing to the Afen love of dickering. "Lot Sun, maybe we can find a deal. Would you consider allowing the refugees to stay on Bhat's ranch in return for protecting his cattle?"

The townsfolk held their breath. This new possibility might defuse the situation.

But Lot Sun was an Afen orcen, not about to rush into any agreement. "Who might pledge for the honor of these refugees, sir?" Lot Sun pointed his ornate cane at the Ruskiya. "How can I trust them not to steal and eat the cattle?"

The Ruskiya orcen stirred angrily, and one man stepped forward. "We are a people of honor. Do you question us?"

"I'll pledge their honor, sir," Rev said. The old lady in Shendasan, whom Dan and he used to find food for, was Ruskiya. Maybe this way he could pay back Minthala's kindness to two young slickers. "No tougher people exist than the Ruskiya orcen and none more honest. A Ruskiya would die rather than go back on her word. If they promise to stay in peace, protect your cattle and defend our town in common against any enemies, I'll pledge my word against any damage they might do."

"But who will pledge for you, Rev?" Gabryal stood at the gate, holding her staff. She spoke in an amused tone, but with a hard edge. Despite that pleasant, even flirty meal together, she obviously remembered how suspiciously he acted at their first meeting.

Rev flushed. "It's on my honor to serve the town, Gabryal. I'll stand for these people, and it's up to Lot Sun whether he accepts my pledge of their good will."

The Ruskiya seemed mollified by Rev's trust, but Ash Wal addressed Lot Sun. "Sir, it ain't loss of face to refuse aid to strangers. These people got no face with us."

Agreement murmured through the miners.

"You were new to the valley yourself once, Ash Wal." Lot Sun's dark eyes shone coldly. "And you were staked to a few meals, as I recall. Seems a mite churlish to deny others what was freely given you."

Caught unawares by this argument, Ash Wal lowered his head like a lizard hunting a way out, then bowed stiffly. "You're right. I've lost face after all. I'll make it up to my ancestors, but we ain't done with these refugees, mark my words."

Lot Sun had made himself an enemy, not that he seemed to care. The gaunt orcen rancher was as stiff-necked stubborn as anyone Rev ever met.

"Sir, if an army is coming," Rev said, "we'll need people for our defenses. Why not allow the Ruskiya to stay through winter, provided they abide by the posted laws and agree to leave Zhopahr valley next spring unless the Council votes to allow them to stay."

"A generous offer, Bounder," said Dunortha.

Lot Sun looked unconvinced. "There may be no army, Bounder. Then what would be the advantage to us?"

"We pay to stay here, rancher." Dunortha recognized the start of a dickering session.

"Pay?" the rancher asked, leaning on his cane, suddenly more interested.

"We pay a silver a day and watch over the cattle," said Dunortha. "Any cow that dies we pay three silvers kine-guild."

"Ten."

"We are already watch the cows. Five."

"Eight."

"Seven."

"Done," said Lot Sun, his head rising proudly, "if your clan pledges to peace and honor."

These Afen would dicker over their own deaths, Rev thought in amazement. "What of it, Ruskiya?" he asked. "Do you pledge?"

Dunortha stood straight, the sun illuminating her. "Hear ye, townsfolk of Zhopahr, I, Dunortha Layanava, Rus of the Red Bear Clan, agree to these terms, and so bind my people, that we attack no people of this valley except in self-defense, we submit to punishment for any law we break, and we care for the kine. So we pledge to this man, Rev Caern."

"To Rev?" Lot Sun began to object. The tip of his forked tongue flicked out, as though tasting a change in the air. The orcen rancher obviously expected the refugees to pledge to him. But he nodded. "I accept these conditions. These refugees can stay on my brother's ranch."

Dunortha bowed. "We thank ye, people of Zhopahr. May all your hunts be worthy."

Rev bowed in return, wondering what he had let himself in for, but exhilarated at having negotiated a peaceful settlement. People slapped his shoulder, as much to share in his success as to show their support. It felt good.

Ash Wal waved to his miners. "We got a mine to work, men." The miners followed him out, passing the refugees without a glance. No miner wore a white sash, Rev noted.

The folks who did wear white sashes were grumbling, and one orcen with a narrow snout and pebbled grey skin came up to Rev. "Do you stand against our priestess?"

"We're all working for peace," Lot Sun said. "Give our Bounder a chance, man."

The man glared at Rev. "We watch you." He walked away.

"Thanks for supporting me, Lord," Rev said to Lot Sun. He was finally getting the hang of how to address people, ironically by listening to the White-Sashers do it wrong. The rancher nodded acknowledgment.

Ma'tha approached. She wore her grey cloak over a red dress. "A brave and uncommon act, Bounder, your offer to help these people. I commend you."

Behind her, Gabryal nodded shortly. "It's good to have a glib tongue on occasion, Rev." She leaned in close. "You did well, I'm proud of you." Her gaze sucked his breath away.

He managed a bow. "Thank you, Healers." His voice squeaked a little.

Dan approached, but never looked over at Ma'tha as the healers hurried away.

"Dan," Rev said in a low voice, "here's your chance. Go talk to Ma'tha. Don't be shy."

"Oh, that's over already."

"You've never had a honey girl before in your life," Rev was flabbergasted. "How could it be over so quickly? I didn't even know it was started."

Dan darkened in embarrassment. "You're a little slow, Rev. Anyway, shouldn't you be guiding the Ruskiya to their new home?" Dan kept his head down, not meeting Rev's eyes.

Puzzled at what he missed, Rev patted his friend's shoulder. "You're a good friend, Dan, and a gentleman. I'm thankful you're with me."

"One other thing, Rev. While you were talking, someone... I think they shot something at you. I tried to see who it was, but he got away. A human."

An assassin? That was unnerving.

Rev nodded. "Thank you, Dan."

He would have to be careful, from now on.

#

The next morning, as Rev approached the bordello run by Madame Coo to interview Bhat Sun's former honey girl, he noticed the cooper Jho Iun hanging back in the shadows of the entryway next door. Was that the cooper's home, or did he have business in this section of town?

Inside, the bordello had a large open room with a scattering of tables and chairs. A greasy deck of cards decorated one table. The woman behind the bar, the only person visible, spoke. "Bounder. How glad I am to have you patronize us. I am Madame Coo."

Disk of Dragons

Madame Coo was tough-looking even by orcen standards, with a large black mole on one cheek, badly covered by grey face paint that didn't match the color of her skin. She wore a black hair wig, a disturbing sight on any otherwise hairless orcen, and her dress was also black, with red straps. The falsies in its cups were far larger than any orcen breasts in history, and hung too high on her chest. She tossed back a drink and came around from behind the bar, grabbing the bottle and a pair of glasses.

"I'm looking for Dores, ma'am," Rev said quickly.

Madame Coo stopped in plain astonishment. "What'd I...?"

Her voice lost its slickness, giving Rev an insight.

"That's you," he blurted. Yarrow said she had opened an establishment.

She sat heavily at a table, poured drinks into both glasses, shoved one his way, and drank off the other. "That's me, Bounder. Dores Coo."

"I'm here to talk to you about your boyfriend, Bhat Sun."

"Boyfriend?" she responded with a shrill hilarity. "If you call any of the five men I meet each night a boyfriend, I suppose he was one, too. You know what I do for a living?"

"Yarrow says you weren't in this business until last fall," Rev answered coolly, "which makes me curious how you got set up with this establishment so quick."

"I found some money, and knew some girls."

"Why did you leave Bhat?"

"No money." Her voice turned casual. Rev wouldn't believe anything said in that tone.

"Five hundred *neve* is no wealth? You have high standards."

"Ah, he was always out with his cows," she said in a derisive tone. "He never spent any money on me. You can laugh, but a girl wants to have fun."

"Why not return to Khav? Not much fun around here."

"No way to get back alone. Didn't know it was so remote out here."

"You had a huge fight with him the night before he died. What did you fight about?"

"He wanted me to give up my business, but a woman needs a business to protect her. Men aren't reliable, Bounder."

Rev studied her. "Your answers all sound practiced. Why is that?"

"I don't know." She grabbed his drink and downed it, too.

"Who do you think murdered Bhat?"

She stood. "I told you, I don't know. If you'll excuse me—"

"No, you didn't tell me. Afraid they might hurt you, too?"

"In my business, you better be afraid of that every day." She walked away.

He followed. "Who staked you to this business?"

She turned on him, and gave a faint, triumphant smile. "Why, Khat Trun did. Now I'm sorry to leave you, Bounder, but work calls."

She departed out the back door, leaving him astonished and alone.

Chapter Nine

"Where the Goddess Luwana fell, a fierce volcano grew, which cast forth both the undying dragons, who glittered like gems, and the Heart of Light, a great jewel, the Heart of Luwana Herself made present in this world."
<u>*The Histories of Teren: The Age of Legend.*</u>

On a rainy Lunsday morning, Rev interviewed Jho Iun in the front room of the cooper's home. Jho Iun called the cramped, dingy box of a room his guest parlor. The cooper did live next door to Madame Coo's environment.

"Madame Coo killed Bhat, Bounder." The cooper simpered. "I'm sure of it." He leaned over his cup of tea. "Or had him killed. She's been involved with the deaths of several men. I hear her talking, you know, all sorts of things go on next door." The cooper wore a furtive, excited expression. Jho Iun living next to a noisy whorehouse was more than coincidence. Disgusting thought.

"You've heard her order people's deaths?"

"Near enough. She's always flirting with that Khat Trun, and he's a killer. They're lovers. *That* I know for a fact."

A woman shouted something next door, proving the shared wall between the cooper's shack and the bordello really was too thin.

"They don't like you, Bounder," Jho Iun wiped his mouth on his arm, slurped more tea.

Rev was too repulsed to try his tea. "But you never heard her actually plan the murder."

"That night, afterwards, they were practically cheering in there. Well, she was. Maybe her girls were just being polite with the boss. Some of the thugs snuck in, and they sounded pretty happy, too. Oh, she either did it or knew about it."

#

At noon, Rev made his way to the Grey Women's campsite. As always these days, he kept an eye out for the nondescript human, believing that must be the assassin, but did not spot the man. Maybe he'd moved on.

Rev found the three healers eating lunch. The rain had stopped. Rev hoped to make Gabryal an ally in hunting the murderer. He respected her standing up for herself, and anyway, he liked her no-pretense dealings with everyone, from ranch owners to the rag pickers living in the ravine.

"Rev," she greeted him. "That new scabbard looks quite handsome."

He bowed in thanks. "And the embroidery on your dress is beautiful, Gabryal."

"Ma'tha's work." Gabryal indicated the healer, who wagged her tail in acknowledgment. "Would you share some lunch with us?"

"I'd be honored." He happily accepted a bowl of potato soup. "How long have you healers been in the valley?" He had been so glad to be with Gabryal that day in the tea house he forgot to ask questions, so he was determined to ask now.

"A couple of months." Her voice suddenly sounded strained. Was something strange about the question?

"Why did the three of you stop here?" He felt clumsy at interviewing.

Gabryal seemed to take offense. "We're healers," she said stiffly. "This valley was underserved. We belong to the Order of the Grey Women, after all."

"The whole Order of Grey Women is healers?"

"We are."

"Healing is a noble profession." The rising humidity made him grateful for the breeze. "There's so much I don't know. For instance, the murder looked done by magic. But I have no idea what school of magic could do such a thing."

"Are you asking if healing magic could do such a thing?" Gabryal challenged him. "I was with you when the body was found."

"I remember." He had dreams of impressing this woman, but this interview was not going well. He tried to pacify her. "I doubt any of you would be the killer."

"Then why accuse us?" She put down her food and stomped off.

Unhappy, he watched her go. If searching for the killer cost him a chance at romance, well, you didn't win every pot. He had given his word to uphold justice in Zhopahr. She had to take him as he was, as he must accept her as she was. That was fair.

"I don't know all schools of magic that might accomplish such a deed, Bounder," the trollen Laia calmly answered. "Healing magic could, but neither Ma'tha nor Gabryal have the necessary skill."

"Do you, Lady?" He had heard others give her the noble title.

Her antennae quivered with amusement. "I have never tried."

"Ah." He wondered how to proceed. "Can you confirm my guess as to how long Bhat had been lying there when we found him?"

Ma'tha answered. "Well, he was stiff with rigor mortis, Rev, so more than a couple turns of the hour glass. But people saw him alive early that day, so sometime that morning."

"Thank you. That's about what I was thinking."

Gabryal returned. "I am sorry for flying off like that," she said, uncomfortably.

"I'm sorry for being insensitive. I'm not good at asking people questions, I know."

The awkwardness dissipated as Rev helped Gabryal clean up. "I'm amazed at how small a space you use. Where do you keep your supplies?"

"Would you like me to show you?" Gabryal asked in a tone of making amends.

"I'd love that." He held his hands firmly behind his back to keep his stealing problem under control as he followed her to a shed standing against a stone wall. The shed was packed with paraphernalia.

"The top shelf is bandages. Ma'tha and Laia put this together. The middle shelf is potions. Here are the splints, beakers and dishes—"

"You need a better place than this." The words left his mouth before he thought.

"Better than the open air?" Gabryal said, her voice growing a little tight again.

"Absolutely. We can do better as a town. I'll lead the effort to build you a new hospital."

"We can't ask you to do that," Gabryal protested, following him back to the fire.

"It's only right." His enthusiasm grew. "Your presence benefits the community. We could have a building bee."

He could maybe prove his worth, and besides, he liked to plan things. True, recently it had been heists and whatnot, but he could turn his talent to good. Couldn't he?

"Friends?" Laia returned from the street. "Look."

She carried the body of a rabbit tied into an elaborate, bloody knot. A stench of decay rolled before her.

Ma'tha collapsed onto a stool.

"What does it mean?" Rev asked.

"Only a misunderstanding, Bounder," Gabryal said, too quickly. "It's nothing. We're taken by surprise, that's all."

Ma'tha cut in. "Bounder, we do need to prepare for this afternoon's appointments."

"Please, just go." Gabryal's voice was tense.

Surprised and hurt, Rev took his leave as the women stared in dismay at the throttled animal. He was sure it was a threat being delivered. But who would threaten them, and why?

#

Since Rev could do nothing about the healers' troubles if they would not confide in him, he headed off to Lot Sun's ranch in a light rain, finding the orcen rancher preparing to ride out with his men. When the rancher spotted Rev, he waved the others on ahead and invited Rev inside, to a room that overlooked the slope westward. The window had real glass.

How had they packed in glass to such a remote place? The window showed off a landscape of pine and deciduous trees to the north, giving way to meadows and grasslands to the south. Three fruit trees graced the yard. A fire in a grate combated the damp air.

"What can I do you for, Bounder?" Lot Sun asked, after they completed the ritual of compliments, gifts offered and refused, and other formalities Afen inflicted on visitors, and sat down with cups of tea. Despite his elegant black riding outfit, Lot Sun looked unwell. His grey skin had paled and dark circles showed under his eyes. His cane rested by his chair.

"Sir, I want to learn more about your brother," Rev said. "Get a read on how he played his hands, who might have known him. Maybe I can find out who killed him."

"Everyone knows everyone hereabouts," Lot Sun said. "That'll be no help."

84

"Maybe not. But it might help to know who he was talking to and where he went."

A mountain oriole landed in one of the yard trees, and commenced an insistent song, loud enough to be heard inside over the crackling fire.

"All right." Lot Sun pursed his lips. "Bhat used to travel. Went to the lowlands a few times, to Khav." His breath caught. "Now he'll never be coming back, waving some book and shouting about his wonderful find."

"Was he a member of either congregation in town?"

"We attended services ever since Qur Sil came to the valley. That was a few years ago, now. It makes the wife happy, and Bhat enjoyed talking to folks."

"You never went to the services of the other temple?"

"We went once or twice." Lot Sun added a log to the fire. The log began to steam.

"So there wasn't any falling out with the White-Sashers?"

"I've never had any problem with any of my neighbors."

"I meant with Bhat."

"Him? He'd get along with a polecat. Everybody liked my brother, easy going as they come." Lot Sun's voice trailed off.

The oriole's whistle gave way to an abrupt series of chirps. A hawk swooped by the window, pursued by two smaller birds chasing it away from their nest.

"Sir, we will find your brother's killer, but it may take a little time. Anything you can tell me about him, what liked to do, who he liked to see, would be of help."

Rain pattered. Mists rose in streamers over the hills, giving the world a lonesome aspect.

"Bhat was always one for digging up things," Lot Sun offered.

Rev felt a prickle of curiosity. "Digging up things? Hunting the Disk of Dragons?"

Lot Sun made a dismissive gesture. "No such foolishness. Old pitchers, bowls, domestic things. He had an interest, especially if they had a nice design."

"What did he do with them? Sell them?"

"I don't think he did much of anything with them, he just liked them. You saw how his ranch house was jammed when you helped us search it the other day."

The oriole landed on a tree outside, carrying something in its mouth, maybe straw for a nest or food for chicks already hatched.

"Was anyone else interested in the same sort of thing?"

"Believe that goblen Xul Bil Be hunted old things, yes." Lot Sun shifted uncomfortably. "I'm afraid I'm a bit of a stickler for the particulars of social interaction, sir. Mostly, I frown on gossip."

Rev nodded. Few Afen were much for telling jokes or making fun, but Lot Sun seemed so upright it hurt. He was the most humorless man Rev ever met. Not a bad man, just stiff-tailed. "One thing I do wonder. Everyone knows Khat Trun heads the thugs, so why hasn't the town just hanged him and been done with it?"

"He maybe killed my brother." Lot Sun's eyes went dark and flat. "But as for hanging him, well, you're not Afen. Honor says there's got to be proof. If we hung the wrong man, how could we make that up to his ghost? An angry spirit hovering around your home ain't good, it messes up your doom. Best to be sure." The orcen paused, his tongue flicking. "But I do want answers from that Khat Trun."

A hand-sized carved dragon sat on a stand in one dark corner. How long before anyone would miss it?

The thought horrified Rev. How could he overcome this evil yearning? A little temptation inside him pointed out that just thinking about stealing would do no harm. He was not doing anything wrong, he was a fine upstanding member of the community. No one would suspect him. With an effort, Rev put his thoughts back on Lot Sun.

"Weren't many folks in the valley until about five years ago, when Ash Wal found silver. Just us and our ranch hands. Others drifted in for the mining and farming, or to cater to the caravans. Skarii, the goblen witch, she arrived last year, and the new priestess Uulong about three months ago. Both my children have taken to wearin' her white sashes." Lot Sun shook his head. "First saw Khat Trun a year ago. Evil man."

"What brought in all these recent people?"

"Well, the latest batch of bandits appeared after the mine opened, that might be it. Another thing, last year Bhat sold off those gold coins he found. Folks started showing up in heaps after that. Might've started it, treasure hunters hunting more coins. No one's found any more, though."

"Gold coins?" Rev asked, astonished. "Bhat found gold coins?"

"Only a few. He gave me one, actually."

"So someone could have murdered him to get his gold coins."

"He didn't have any left," Lot Sun protested. "They went to pay debts and buy cows."

Rev shook his head. "Folks see gold once, they'll be convinced there's an endless supply. Did he tell you where he found the coins?"

"Out in the ruins someplace."

"That's maybe what all those holes are about. Why would anyone think the Disk was nearby, when the capitol of Sinnesemota wasn't anywhere around here? Hunting gold makes more sense to me. What do these coins look like?"

"I'll show you one." Lot Sun grabbed his cane and limped out of the room.

Alone, Rev crossed to the carving; jade, an exquisite dragon, with wings uncoiled. Rev palmed it and slid it up his sleeve, where the jade felt cool against his skin. He stood eyes closed, as fear, hot excitement and shame came over him.

No. He made himself put the carving back down. He walked to the far end of the room and looked out at the gardens.

Lot Sun re-entered the room. "Ah. You found my little carving."

Rev jerked involuntarily, astounded the rancher had noticed. Rev had placed it back exactly where he found it. "I was looking at it, yes. How would such a carving get here?"

Lot Sun smacked down his tail. "See, that's maybe why people think the Disk of Dragons was here. Bhat thought folks must have come here from Sinnesemota's capital, after the Collapse. Maybe brought the Disk with them." He handed over a gold coin, which had a dragon etched on one side, a detailed picture of a disk on the other. The edges felt sharp, as though newly minted, despite the coin's obvious age.

Rev's hackles went up: the Disk on the coin was an exact replica of the vision he fought that day leaving the monastery, the same volcano, staff, and dragon. How could that be? Trying to stay calm, Rev moved to return the coin, but Lot Sun waved him off.

"Hold onto it for evidence."

"One more thing. I understand Bhat had a falling out with the woman he was courting, could you tell me more about that?"

All emotion vanished from Lot Sun's face. "No, sir. There's too little I know. He brought her back from Khav last time he was there."

"The time he brought the gold to sell?"

Lot Sun's tail stirred. "A canny observation. Yes, she seems like a woman interested in gold lying around loose. Bhat didn't have any. I'm thinking when she learnt that, she left him and went back to her element." The rancher stood. "Bounder, you never came to pick up that horse we promised."

"Not yet, sir." Rev also rose.

"Too much ground to cover by foot if you're to protect the valley, so a horse was part of the deal. A man's got to live up to his side of a deal. I got a horse in mind. You ride much?"

Rev felt a rush of alarm. "Not much."

"Well, she's a gentle mare. Go all day if you take care of her." He picked up his cane. "We'll get you set up with an outfit."

The drizzle had ended, although the sky remained overcast. As they walked to the stable, carrying their tea cups, Rev asked, "Was your brother the one who found the silver lode?"

"No, that was Ash Wal. Wasn't no more than a prospector, but he found color and staked his claim. Got the biggest mine on the hill now, scores of men workin' for him, and loyal, too. Don't go crossing Ash Wal without thinkin' hard."

The stable was as neat and well kept as the rest of the ranch, with the tack hung on wooden pegs, the stalls square, the floor swept. It smelled of oiled leather, hay and horses.

"Ash Wal and your brother must have run into each other."

"Could be. Bhat never spoke much about the man. Ash Wal ain't much for raisin' an ale, all he ever does is work. Bhat spent more time with fellows who enjoyed themselves."

At the corral, three horses stood under a copse of trees. Lot Sun whistled, and the horses walked over, two bay geldings and a grey mare. Lot Sun had Rev give a carrot to the mare. She nuzzled him.

"Were Xul Bil Be and your brother acquainted?"

Lot stared at Rev hard. "You hauled out an awful pile of questions, didn't you?"

"Part of my job."

Lot Sun grunted. "Suppose it is. Well, ever'body knew ever'body, like I told you."

"Your brother and the conjuror shared an interest in antiquities, though, I'd think they would have talked over what they were finding."

Lot Sun looked doubtful. "That Xul Bil Be, he pretty much stays to himself."

Lot Sun showed Rev the tack, and Rev saddled the grey mare while Lot Sun saddled a gelding. Rev knew barely enough about horses to curry and saddle them.

"You can keep her in town at Dril Plu's livery," Lot Sun said. "I'll go the cost of stablin' for two months, that'll settle the debt up to now. Agreed?"

"Sounds like a smooth deal to me."

Lot Sun nodded, business-like. "Bounder, I got to get back to work. Leave your cup, the help'll get it."

"Thank you, sir. She's a wonderful horse. What's her name?"

"Grace." Lot Sun switched his tail in an embarrassed way. "Didn't name her myself. The wife, you know," he said apologetically.

As Lot Sun rode off, Rev felt frustrated, but he was not exactly sure why. Lot Sun had answered his questions, but still it felt as though the rancher had been evasive.

Rev decided to make one more stop before evening, so he headed northeast past town, riding Grace, but he knew little about riding a horse, and they could not come to any agreement on a direction of travel. Finally, in frustration, he dismounted and led her. He was tired, but felt driven to find that killer – he wanted his new home safe, wanted people secure.

This was a way to win respect he had never considered. It felt better than stealing, but the thought that he could fail at being a Bounder was scary. Rev did not know which magic could kill Bhat Sun in such a gruesome manner, except that Laia said healing magic could do so.

Did trollen ever murder people?

He tried to catch any sense of the Disk of Dragons influencing him. But the attempt seemed foolish, making himself over-important. Wouldn't Dan find amusing the idea Rev had a secret connection to one of the nine Great Artifacts?

And why is that, Rev? Where did this connection come from?

Why, it just appeared one day, Dan. No, honest.

He felt embarrassed. Those encounters must have been all in his head, despite the vision of the Disk. But how explain the exact details being on the coin? The dragon, the staff, the volcano. That was spooky.

The goblen conjuror Xul Bil Be lived in a tower atop a bluff overlooking the town. As Rev led Grace up the path, he thought about the big cat that had tracked through a puddle of blood at the murder site. Rev recalled his father saying snow leopards always acted fastidious. Why did this one not avoid the blood? Was it a pet of the killer? One legend said vampyren could turn into leopards, an unpleasant thought.

Rev tied his horse to a nearby bush. At the oaken door, a huge, red-veined eye appeared out of thin air. Rev jumped, then held still as it examined him. A faint stench of sweat exuded from it, and a cold cruelty iced through him – markers of conjuror's magic.

He worked a shi exercise to throw off the sense of cruelty.

Above the eye, a disembodied, sneering mouth appeared. "Yes?"

"I've come to speak with Xul Bil Be. My name is Rev."

"About what?"

"Is this Xul Bil Be?" Rev asked.

"Do I look like him?" the disembodied mouth asked.

Rev stifled the temptation to say it didn't look like anything at all. Again he used shi to calm himself. "I'm the new Boundskeeper in the valley, I wish to speak to the man."

The eyeball and the mouth disappeared. Rev felt taken aback. Had it gone to report? Heaps of slag sat in spots around the tower, the vegetation looked scraggly, and a skim of ooze covered a nearby pond. The tower itself was made of catstone, a stone whose gold and green stripes shimmered in the sun that broke through. The forest covered a ridge eastward, where a few birds sang and flowers bloomed in crannies, as though battling the local oppressiveness.

"What do you seek from me?"

At the door stood a goblen, chest-high on Rev, slender, with dark, intense eyes, wearing a dark robe that covered his golden, cockroach-like body down to his four ankles. An underlying rage radiated from him.

"I was hoping to speak with you, sir."

Xul Bil Be's mandibles clicked. "Tt, why are you in this country? You're new."

"I am. I've taken the position of the local Boundskeep—"

"You haven't said why you came to this country."

"Looking for work."

"Ttt, no one comes here looking for work. Too remote. What are you concealing?"

Rev felt embarrassed. He could not say it was none of his business, or the man would respond in the same way. "I wasn't coming *here* exactly, I was passing through."

"From where?" The questions were staccato, relentless. If conjurations made a person cruel, this man had evidently been conjuring a long time.

"Shendasan."

"A human from goblen territory. Ttt, a refugee?" Derision colored his tone. "Or a partisan run out of the country, perhaps a common criminal, ttt, no family, no ties."

"I have the task," Rev mustered his dignity, "of learning the circumstances of Bhat Sun's death. I'm here to ask questions of one who knew him."

The mage clicked in surprise, and hissed cautiously. "Why do you think I knew him?"

Rev's own suspicion flickered. "How long have you lived in this town?"

"I have been here a year."

"Are you Chisen?"

"I am not from the Chisen nation."

Rev was not surprised. With his golden color and jerky movements, Xul Bil Be seemed little like the Chisen. "What's your business here?"

Deep within the mage's eyes a light glowed dangerously. "T, t, t, I seek ancient things."

"An antiquarian? Did you know about the gold coins found hereabouts?"

91

The goblen hissed in annoyance. "I am not interested in gold coins."

"Did you know that Bhat was interested in antiquities?"

"I do not speak of the dead." The answer came out flat.

Rev waited for more explanation.

Xul Bil Be grabbed Rev by the shirt so quickly Rev had no chance to defend himself. "I yield no more answers. T, t, t, leave here, or suffer consequences."

Rev remembered the eyeball hanging in the air. What sort of curse could this man cast? But Rev was stubborn. "I'll not ask of the dead, but I do have one more question. At the site of the murder I found a rock that glowed unnaturally, an orange color. Do you know about such things?"

The man glared without reply. The interview was over. Rev wondered whether the goblen mage was the member of a full pod, but now did not seem the time to ask.

"Thank you for your time, sir." Rev mounted Grace.

Xul Bil Be stood staring, until Rev rode out of sight behind some trees.

Chapter Ten

"Now, your neve cow is a boisterous beast. She'll forage in the high woods where you ain't going to run any other type cattle. Horns close enough to her head that she can slip through the thickets, but long enough that even snow leopards rarely try for a full-grown neve. Bulls have thicker horns than the female of the species. Any stranger they stalk like a cat. Don't want to come on them in the woods when you're afoot."

Musings of an Afen Puncher in the Foothills East of Khav, as recorded by the roving ethnographers of Ilmari in the years before they formally organized into the Historians of Remula. Exact year unknown, but certainly prior to 623A.

Two mornings later the sun was rising and a warm breeze tickled the treetops. Anything at all could be accomplished on such a glorious day. Gabryal looked up from her breakfast to see Rev, Dan and Yarrow leading a line of horses and riders, cattle, squalling children, women carrying baskets and men marshalling cartloads of lumber hauled by oxen, with everyone singing. Her jaw dropped.

"It's Vosday," Rev called merrily, "and since Vos is the God of making things, we've come to build your hospital."

"Oh, Sweet Gods of Order," she said. "Ma'tha, Laia. Come look."

As the two healers rousted out from their tent, Gabryal said to Rev, "Every time I meet you I'm amazed. How did you get everyone to help?"

"Told them we'd have a party later and you'd dance with the men who helped. Yarrow agreed to dance with the ladies, turns out he's danced in the courts of kings."

"I'm to dance with everyone?"

"Well, and me twice for putting the building bee together."

"No fair, no fair," cried Dan. "You're getting greedy."

She raised a hand and smiled. "I'll think about it."

#

Ma'tha took over directing the building project, renovating the building next to the healer's vacant lot. Inside would be rooms for examinations, operations and recovery. Ma'tha seemed to know how to do everything, and put everyone to useful work.

Rev found himself moving logs with the wagon wright, Os Gar, hauling each from a cart to the far side of the building.

"Os Gar, I'm wondering why anyone would want to kill Bhat Sun." Rev struck up a conversation as they went for a log.

"A hard question to answer, Bounder, the man didn't have any enemies."

"He found some gold coins."

"He spent those long ago, paying debts. He wanted to give me one. I couldn't change it, he didn't owe near that amount. He finally went to Khav to sell the coins. Caused quite a stir down there, I heard, but he got smaller coins and paid me off."

They grabbed another log from the stack, and Ma'tha pointed where she wanted it.

"The coins caused a stir?"

"So he said. Don't know what he meant, they looked like any other coins. Foreign, of course." Os Gar put down his end of the latest beam first. Rev followed.

"Were he and Madame Coo on good terms after their... after..."

Os Gar went coldly formal. "Bounder, I know nothing of the woman, nor of any interactions between her and Bhat. I liked Bhat Sun. He was a man of honor."

"I, yes," Rev said in confusion. Bordellos were evidently not to be spoken of in Zhopahr. "Maybe someone from Khav killed him."

"Maybe. You know, Bounder, I don't seem to be of much help."

Ma'tha was calling for a volunteer to wield an adze and Os Gar raised his hand.

"Actually, you have helped, wagon wright," Rev answered. "Thank you."

Rev returned to haul more logs. No one believed Bhat had anything worth stealing, and the search of Bhat's home had yielded only broken pots and arrowheads. Rev knew of no motive for murder other than jealousy over Madame Coo, though that would be reason enough for Khat Trun. Had Bhat Sun maybe found the Disk of Dragons?

Laia joined Rev in hauling lumber. They worked quickly. Laia lifted beams with an astonishing ease: her arms had an extra set of joints, giving her great strength, and she towered over him like a huge preying mantis. She wore the same practical one-piece grey dress. He did not know the fabric, a durable-looking weave, and asked about it.

"It's spider silk blend, Rev. Traditional among my people."

She was quiet but courteous, with a low, musical brogue, using an occasional word from the trollen language.

"Lady, trollen use oracular magic, true?" Rev asked, as they rested between loads.

Her antennae bowed acknowledgment.

"Can you divine who killed Bhat Sun?"

"I am sorry, Rev, I have not that skill."

#

The biggest surprise of the day was Dan Zee. Having an honorable job made him bloom, laughing and even joking with strangers. Rev was glad, but it sort of made him lonesome. Once, he found himself alone near a bucket of tools. The hunger to steal seized him, then a flood of shame. Stealing would ruin everything for Dan, and himself too. Anyway, this was too public a place. Now if he were by himself...

Enough. As he made himself walk away, he noticed Xul Bil Be, the goblen mage, talking with Ash Wal, the burly mine owner. Xul Bil Be glanced at Rev and moved on, as though he had just paused to exchange a pleasantry. Hard to imagine that goblen saying anything nice, but Rev was glad the community seemed to be knitting together during his building bee.

#

Observing people had been part of Gabryal's duties as a girl attending grand diplomatic functions with her father, where generally she had been overlooked by the dignitaries; she would report each night to her father. Today, one man acting differently than she expected was Yarrow, gentle and courtly, even to the small boys who gathered up courage to ask a question, the result being the huge man had a line of children following him, mimicking as best they could his nonchalant grace. Ma'tha was of

95

course enamored, but he answered her flirtations with such diffused politeness the healer was stymied. In fact, he did not show any of the ladies special attention, which roused speculation. Did he have a girl?

Yarrow seemed to notice everything himself. At one point a man, a stranger in town, was hanging around the edges of the worksite, when Yarrow turned toward him. To her surprise, the man fled, running away at full speed, dropping a tube as he went. Yarrow deliberately stepped on the wooden tube, snapping it. She wondered what that was about.

Then Ma'tha and Pura Rew tried to draft Gabryal into asking Yarrow about himself, but she begged off with some distress. She felt every inch of her own awkwardness with the handsome Yarrow. Give her Rev, who was not put off by her bluntness. She thought too much about Rev, she told herself sternly. Her eyes glanced to where he helped frame the roof, in camaraderie with the other men. When he smiled at her she smiled back, but looked away. How could she think of someone else when her own true love lay cold in the ground?

#

By the end of the day both the hospital and the healer's home next door were walled and roofed. As the sun went down, Lot Sun and his men slaughtered a trio of *neve* to turn on spits over the fire, and the celebration began.

Os Gar knew the flute, his wife kept time on a drum and her sister possessed a vast repertory of songs. The refugees took their leave, everyone else stayed. Gabryal did dance with all the men, but to Rev's delight she reserved several for him. In his arms she felt light and soft, and her eyes sparkled. He felt good with her, not needing to fill every pause with words, and since he did not feel forced to talk, words came easily. They gazed into each other's eyes as they danced, the heat stirring.

Ma'tha proved endlessly knowledgeable about party games – fashioning small presents and toys for the children and sending everyone off for treasure hunts, hide-and-seek, pull-away and assorted other games. Deeper in the evening she gravitated to the rough men gambling by the well, and soon was laughing, drinking a mug of wine and leaning on the shoulder of a farmer to offer teasing pointers as he cast the bones.

Rev snuck glances at the ground, seeking any track with a notch missing in the heel, like the track at the site of the murder, but saw none.

As folks were making their good nights, a thunder of hooves at the east gate sent Rev and the other men scrambling for weapons. Into the firelight trotted a score of scruffy horsemen, Khat Trun at their front. His head, painted red and black, gleamed in the light of the flames.

"Who's ready for a party?" Khat Trun shouted, holding up a skin full of drink.

"The party is over, Khat Trun." Rev stepped forward.

Khat Trun was drunk in the saddle, and it took him a moment to focus on Rev. "It's the little man in the street, he's still talking." He turned to his companions and guffawed. "Why's he still talking?" He turned back. "Little man, shut up."

"The party was for folks who lent a hand, but they are tired now and going home."

"Tha's all right," Khat Trun said belligerently, "we'll just stay and work on you."

Rev kept his temper. He did not want a fight to break out with families everywhere.

A voice called from the shadows. "Khat Trun, you murderer." Lot Sun stepped forward, followed by a dozen men. The rancher's eyes glittered. "Did you kill my brother?"

"Didn' have a thing to do with it," Khat Trun sputtered. He swayed and grabbed his saddle to keep himself upright.

"Why don't you take on someone who *can* fight?" Lot Sun drew his sword.

Khat Trun laughed, a crazy sound, as he fumbled for the hilt of his sword. Children cried and grabbed their mothers' skirts.

Rev stepped between the two men, his own sword sheathed. "No one will fight anyone tonight. Lot Sun, there are women and children here."

"The Bounder's right, Khat Trun." Ash Wal came up the street, backed by a score of miners. "We'll all be going home."

Khat Trun made a sour face. "Jus' wanted to join the fun."

"Fun's over," rumbled Yarrow.

Khat Trun stared coldly at Rev. "Whole town's rallying around you, Bounder. Gettin' to be a problem, you are."

Khat Trun jerked his horse around and spurred away, his men following. Lot Sun stood sword in hand, gazing after the thugs.

The remaining mothers swept up their children and hurried off.

"Something has to be done about him," said Dan in a shaky voice. "I think he's the killer."

"Maybe," Rev said, "but does the style of the murder fit Khat Trun's approach? He's more a bludgeon and axe type."

"Khat Trun's willing enough to kill," Yarrow pointed out.

"Eager, even," Rev agreed, "but why kill Bhat?"

"Someone did."

Yendre Pindo, the goblen White-Sasher, marched up. "Rev, these thugs grow bold, and you do not deal with them. Ttt. I will report this."

"Report to who, Yendre?" asked Dan. The goblen did not deign to answer.

"You will suffer consequences, if others are hurt," Yendre went on.

"I'm surprised you White-Sashers would have anything to do with a party like this," Dan said. "You seem to disapprove of anyone having fun."

Yendre glared at him and stalked off.

"The White-Sashers are getting nastier," Dan concluded.

"They haven't caused any trouble," Rev said, stifling a grin at his friend's bold words. "People like their organization, and they take care of each other. I saw some down in the ravine fixing up houses, and that priestess Uulong parcels out food to whoever. Half the spare cloaks we collected for the Ruskiya came from them, no dickering, just gave them over. They ain't all bad."

Dan slapped his tail down. "I still say they're going to cause trouble."

"Rev," Yarrow said. "Noticed you've been practicing your sword. I'd be glad to spar, if you're looking for a partner."

"I'd appreciate that. And anything you can teach me of swordplay, as well."

Yarrow glanced at him with amusement. "I know a few techniques."

#

That night, the last the healers would spend in their tent, Gabryal could not sleep. She found herself entirely too comfortable around Rev, and yet uncomfortable as well, in a delicious way. Not even her beloved ever made her feel as relaxed as Rev did, with his small jokes and willingness to be silent rather than jabbering half the night. Thinking of Zhac, her husband for that briefest moment, squeezed at her heart, and she felt as if spending time with Rev somehow betrayed her lost love. She did not want to have such feelings if they meant forgetting the man she loved.

Her eyes stared into the blackness. Remembering Zhac stirred her determination. She had followed the faintest trail of the vampyren who killed her husband: a casual comment in a tavern east of Khav; an inexplicable death further east a week later. The trail led here. She trembled with rage that her husband was dead, while the evil one who killed him lived on.

Since she was wide awake, she decided to hunt the vampyren. She put on a robe and slipped outside, to avoid disturbing Laia.

If the vampyren were disguised, it could have been here today. She set sticks on the fire, then started a spell. Confidence bloomed in her. That was the positive emotional side effect of casting elemental magic, but she must be careful, every type of magic generated both a positive or negative emotion, and the negative emotion for elemental magic was arrogance. Elemental magic also called up the ozone scent of lightning.

Ma'tha was nowhere to be found. That cute farmer had brightened at her attention, and Ma'tha never let such a catch escape. Gabryal felt a stab of annoyance, more than half jealousy, at how Ma'tha could always get a man. Gabryal put Rev's strong face and easy laugh out of her mind; she had work to do.

Now, if only the vampyren had been foolish enough to kill that rabbit with ceremonial magic. Holding the carcass, Gabryal widened her spell to encompass the area where people had worked today, the fire magic showing as ghostly flames. The flames coalesced over one spot, then another, before fading. Her heart thudded in excitement. The glowing areas were places the vampyren had lingered in disguise. First, near the lumber. A man? Second, where the food was cooked. A woman? Who had moved between the men and the women all day?

Nervous, she looked over her shoulder, but the street was empty.

She had a terrible thought: Ma'tha's farmer spent a great deal of his day in those spots. Well, she could not drag Ma'tha home on no more than a suspicion. Anyway, the person who came to mind was Rev. He was hiding something, and why did he pay her such attention? She was too tall, her nose was crooked, and she certainly had not been leading him on. A vampyren might court her to throw her off guard. Was that what Rev was doing?

She must be too tired. Little suggested Rev was a vampyren. Still, she would keep her eye on him.

#

Rev moved through the town in the night, studying each street before he started down it, testing the shifting eddies of shi for traces of any presence, human, orcen or other. The starlight overhead helped some, though shadows grew deep in many of the alleys.

He was learning the ways of the inhabitants – Os Gar walked each night around his block, keeping an eye on things, sometimes visiting his brother Rhon, the blacksmith. Dril Plu had trouble sleeping, and spent much of each night at the door to his stable, staring at the stars, smoking his pipe. Trouble mostly started down at Madame Coo's, though the thugs generally avoided the town these days.

He carried his bow, a quiver full of arrows over his shoulder, his sword at his hip. It reminded him of Shendasan, passing along like this with as little trace as possible. He encountered no sense of the creepy shadows that haunted Shendasan though, and none of the old sweat smell of evil conjurations.

He wondered how the Ruskiya were settling into their new home. He would have to go over and dicker for some of the soft leather shoes they made, good for someone who wanted to move without notice. They were good people, unless you were on the wrong side of a fight with them.

When he reached in the loneliest part of the town, he paused to listen. The occasional creak of a building settling, the faint hiss of the breeze beneath eaves, the moan of a cat a few streets away, courting his love. Shi energy moved through the area smoothly, without any binding. All seemed well here. He passed on, stepping as quietly as possible. Better to see any trouble before it saw him, that notion had kept him alive.

Scattered clouds crossed the sky, blotting out the stars here and there. The breeze was fitful, making it hard to sift out the normal sounds of the night from anything unusual. He reached the top of another street, one he rarely walked down. He paused there to watch at the top of a hill. The clouds had thickened, and it was very dark, impossible to see to the far end of the street. Dan was resting, ready to take the early shift. Yarrow was

100

probably at home, asleep, though Rev had no idea where he spent each night, come to think of it.

Gloomily, he stared up the street. Something was moving on the hill. A dog, maybe, or one of the half-feral pigs that roamed the area. He kept himself still, down in the pool of darkness. This was a good town, a lot of hardworking people here, trying to better themselves, help their families. Many sent money back to their homes in Khav, or even further places, entrusting the coins to caravan masters. It was a tolerable arrangement, the caravan masters taking a cut for the service.

He hadn't seen any more movement. The breeze was moving down the hill, so any dog would not know he was here. Might not matter to it.

Why had he stopped here? What did he care about these people? None were kin. He had no idea they existed until that morning he faced down Khat Trun. He liked the respect folks gave him, well, many folks did. He liked wearing the pin of a Bounder on his chest.

Someone was easing down the hill, by the shape a human. He could hear nothing. Shi revealed nothing either, though he was not as good at shi as a full monk. But few mortals could pass so unnoticeably.

Rev's clothes were similar in color to the buildings around him, and he stood in the shadows near a wall. Clouds covered the stars overhead, so seeing anything more than a few paces away was extremely difficult.

His fingers brushed the hilt of his sword, and he wished he had trained with Yarrow already. Was this the vampyren Gabryal mentioned? Or that strange, nondescript man who'd been hanging around?

Innocent person, or assassin?

"They know where you are, now." The voice came out of the darkness, a stranger's voice. "I sent message you are here."

"Who are you?"

"I saw you once in Shendasan," The stranger's voice was a bit closer. "Burying your father. I thought, someday I shall bury you. It was my idea to arrest him for taking the sword."

He paused, as though considering. "Or I should say, the shadows put that thought in my head. The shadows watch us, all of us. It's the Watcher."

Rev crouched, his sword out, bow in his left hand, remembering stories of the vampyren, how they grew stronger in the night, how a lone mortal rarely had a chance against them.

"Now I shall win the credit, before Eg Bror arrives."

The stranger must have expected a flinch at the name from Rev's past. He chose that moment to close the distance.

Just the faintest brush of shoes against the earth. The glitter of a blade.

Rev flung himself aside, feeling his enemy's weapon shave the hairs from his arm as it passed. He swung his sword with all his strength. It struck another weapon with a clang. The shock staggered him sideways.

He got his feet under him and drove out and upward with his blade. He felt it hit, but something struck his bow heavily, knocking him off his feet. He landed on his back, kicked out at his opponent's legs. He knocked his foe back, and scrambled back to his feet.

He drove his blade forward, slashed left, missed. He dodged left, following the momentum of his swing. His shi awareness picked up his foe coming in from the right. He slashed with his sword, missed, slashed, missed again.

Where in flames *was* the man?

Behind him.

He jumped forward, and the blow aimed for his head nicked the back of his neck.

Rev spun, knocked his opponent's blade aside with his own, and swung his fist. It smacked into the man's head. His enemy staggered. Rev lunged forward with his blade, skewered the man's shoulder.

The man jerked back, and his sword fell, clattered on a stone.

A glimpse of the man's face in the moonlight showed a rictus of fear. "I'll call an army down on you."

He fled.

Rev ran after him, but the man was quicker. He reached the city wall, went up the steps on the inside of the wall like a cat. He reached the top and leaped over the parapets, dropping out of sight.

Rev reached the parapets, looked out. Nothing moved in the gloom in the fields below. It was a drastic fall, but no form lay crumpled at the base of the wall. No rope, no cushion, no explanation how he could survive such a fall.

Rev waited, ready for the next attack, but suspecting, from that look of fear, that the man was gone for good.

The last of the clouds cleared overhead, and the moonlight, seeming twice as bright, shone down. The man – it must have been that nondescript human – was gone.

Rev was breathing hard. He had lost his bow in the fight, so he stooped, reached around and found it, then rose slowly.

So the shadows watching in Shendasan had not been his imagination, and the danger was real: whatever intelligence was behind them had sent a killer. He survived this time, but which stranger might be next with a knife?

Chapter Eleven

"The human Rhys appeared before the Emperor, and with his crooked, humble smile, requested the Colobites form the Emperor's personal guard, putting aside the Rainbow Clan. Counselors warned that the Colobites served the vampyren, but the Emperor was headstrong and granted the petition. The Emperor was assassinated that same night. So began the Troubles, which lasted until the Empire collapsed."

"The Last Hundred Years," from <u>*The Chronicles of Sinnesemota.*</u>

As Rev was settling down to sleep in the early morning, someone banged on the keep door. Rev jumped, his nerves on edge. He found an orcen woman standing outside.

"Bounder, someone's been stealing from me."

"Tell me about it, ma'am." Rev had a sinking feeling as he waved her in, but forced his face to stay genial. Dan came into the room.

"Someone's taking chickens from my coop. Thasday nights. Figures it'd be the day dedicated to the Goddess of Death. One bird at a time. I sat out with my bow. I'd have done for him," she patted her bow. "but he must've spotted me."

"How many chickens?"

She looked confused. "Well, it's happened three times, an' I thought he got a chicken, but when I just counted, only the one chicken is gone. I'm thinking I scare't him off once or twice maybe, and miscounted. I'm asking you keep a watch on the coop next Thasday."

"We'll certainly do that," Rev assured her.

After she departed, Dan stared at Rev. "I gave my word to uphold the rule of law. That includes catching thieves. Any thief. Do you understand me?"

Something steady and honorable rang in Dan's tone.

"Absolutely." Rev knew how false-hearted his own voice sounded. "We'll make sure no one ever steals from her again."

Rev could not meet Dan's gaze, and hurried out the door. He knew how hard Dan found it to say those words. How could Rev put his own friend in such a dilemma?

I returned all the chickens but the one. How did that one get away on me? What if I bought a replacement, and snuck it back?

Even as that thought arose, Rev raged at himself – he *had* to stop stealing. He didn't want to play this stupid game any more, taking things, then seeing if he could return them. That woman could not afford to lose any chickens, and he was troubling her into the bargain, making her worried about thieves. What was wrong with him? How could he make it up to her?

Trying to put his shame behind him, he went to help with the finishing touches on the hospital. Well, to court Gabryal.

It was Arsday, so from every door came the scent of soap, billows of dust beaten from rugs, and the sounds of folks singing traditional cleaning songs, generally mournful laments of lost loves that fled when they learned how much work housekeeping truly was.

At the hospital, the patients were admiring the building. Several praised Rev for bringing the town together, despite his protests that his part had been small compared to Ma'tha, Yarrow and others. Gabryal was busy with a patient, but smiled and said she would have time later.

Disappointed, he offered to help Laia whitewash walls and hang curtains. The trollen was amused at his interest in Gabryal, but answered questions about her friend so vaguely he gave up asking and simply enjoyed the work. Once they finished indoors, they went out to dig a well. Laia chose the spot, and they reached water in short order, then erected a temporary wooden cover over it.

Laia nodded, pleased. "I'll start on a stone sleeve for the well tomorrow, Bounder. This afternoon I'll put a wooden roof over the well to keep out leaves and detritus."

They took a break in the shade of a wall.

"You get a lot done in a hurry, Lady," Rev said ruefully. His muscles ached.

"I take pleasure in working, it keeps me from having to think too much." Something cool in her manner kept him from pursuing that line of conversation.

"What were you healers doing during the morning of the murder?"

"Gabryal was shopping, as you already confirmed, while Ma'tha and I saw patients. You'll confirm that with the tavern keeper Pura Rew. She was here. The clothier Papas Sekulto was here as well." She smiled. "You'll forget to ask him to confirm our story."

An earthy scent increased; the scent of oracular magic. He shuddered. It was creepy that trollen could see the future, but still, she was nice.

For lunch, Gabryal and Rev found a spot on the town wall to enjoy the breeze, where they had bowls of rabbit stew and anise candy Rev brought. Below, a caravan of twenty wagons and perhaps fourscore Vien goblen traders approached, dust rising from the wheels as the wagon masters cracked their whips and shouted weird, ululating cries. They made camp with militarily precision, circling the wagons, unhitching the mules and leading them to corrals built against the town wall. The mules brayed, heading for water troughs. A town delegation appeared and faint, glad greetings arose. This caravan must be a regular visitor.

The time passed pleasantly. A certain heat smoldered, but the two picnickers were content to let it build slowly, a delightful way to picnic. Rev learned Gabryal was from the Angin, an island nation of humans far to the west. The Angin were traders, and her father had been an esteemed merchant until summoned to court.

"The king asked that my father take on a duty for the nation. Naturally he agreed," Gabryal said proudly. "He always believed community is most important. Without people upholding their duty to help each other, how could any have peace or prosperity?"

"Hard to argue with that." Rev offered her a piece of candy.

Their eyes lingered on each other as she slowly devoured the sweet. She smiled, then continued. "He became a diplomat to the court of the Pers, in the city of Thehar, which meant taking us halfway across the world."

"What was your mother like?" Having never been so close to a girl, he felt drunk on being so close to her, alone and intimate.

"I miss her." She laughed lightly. "Mama, she was wild, a wild woman. He married her, I don't know why. My parents were crazy for each other but never thought a thing alike. Father wanted me to be a good merchant's wife, oversee the home and the servants, but Mama told me a woman has to have strength, and taught me elemental magic. War magic. Father never found out. He would have been scandalized." Her glance at him was positively wicked.

He wanted her to be scandalous with him. His heart was beating powerfully. Being unpracticed with girls, he did not know how to move to the next level of intimacy. The next question popped out of him. "Why did you leave Thehar?"

She shook her head. Her expression cooled. He wondered what he had done wrong, then realized he had asked one too many questions. But she answered anyway.

"I found a man exactly the ideal my father preached to me, a wonderful man, a tribute to his people and a Defender of the Throne. I loved him, and strangely, he loved me. His name was Zhac Krin'sohn. He asked me to marry him, and I agreed." She smiled, remembering.

Rev disliked the man already, but as she went on, his compassion for her overcame his petty thoughts.

"He was Pers, a foreigner, tall and handsome. My father was furious. Since Zhac was an orcen, Father said I betrayed our people, and the morning of my marriage, he threw me out." The pain of memory etched her face. "What did it matter? I was to live with my husband. But there was a call for the Defenders. Zhac paused only long enough to pledge our vows and give me my marriage kiss, then rushed off to duty. I was so proud of him. I was so ignorant."

She picked up her bowl, fussed with it. "They found a vampyren. Cornered it. But the vampyren killed them all. Including my husband."

The wind ruffled her hair. Sadness for her overwhelmed him, and he took her hand.

The men below shouted as they worked, small sounds in the distance.

"My new relatives called me bad luck and cast me out, so on the night of my wedding I was on the street alone." She made a small sound. "I walked until reaching what turned out to be a haven for the sick set up by the Grey Women. The next morning I took my turn ladling soup, and from then on had a home with the Grey Women."

"Do you ever see your family?"

She shook her head, gently drew away her hand. "I still receive letters from Mama. Father has bent now that his daughter is a widow, but I wrote Mama he must see who I do marry before he gets hasty in forgiving me."

The sun warmed their faces. Gabryal brought up a new subject. "I heard that Khat Trun's men were seen in the ruins near town. Be careful, Rev."

Their heat had cooled, but a new intimacy remained.

"It has to be done," he said, pleased at her concern. "Lot Sun said his brother was an antiquities lover, and found coins in the ruins. Have you seen the like?"

He handed over the gold coin.

Gabryal stared at it in dismay. "Bhat Sun found this here? This is a coin minted by the Priests of the Dragon."

"Who?"

"The orcen priests who protected the Disk of Dragons after the fall of the Empire of Sinnesemota. During the Troubles, their whereabouts were lost to history."

"The wagon wright told me the Disk of Dragons is the key to the Hall of the Empire, that you can't enter the Hall without the power of the Disk. But why is the Hall important?"

"The Hall contains the Heart of Light, a jewel that serves as a Gate a God could use. As Vos did to send messages to this world. That's what made the Empire of Sinnesemota so magnificent. With the power of a God, who could stand against you? I'm sure many folks in town are after the Disk. Including dark powers." Her voice dropped. "I fear a vampyren lurks nearby."

"This would draw a vampyren?" He shook his head. "The vampyren have been in hiding for a thousand years, is the Disk of Dragons that important?"

"The old books hint a God could use the Heart of Light to enter this world. Any God."

"A God?" Rev said, disbelieving. "You think a God might come here?"

"To this world. Using the Heart of Light as a Gate."

It was too much to take in. "Who would the vampyren be struggling against?"

"We're not far from the traditional home of the Murkung tribes. The vampyren seek the Heart to make alliance with Ars, the God of War. Ars might help them make more vampyren, replenish their ranks. While the Murkung seek it for Thana, the Goddess of Death. Both powers are evil, but they struggle against each other. Innocent people get caught in the middle."

"Maybe someone wanted to learn where Bhat found those coins," Rev said uneasily. "Judging from the expression on his face, he died in pain. Tortured, maybe."

She suddenly seemed impatient. "I must return to the hospital."

"I got things to do, too," he said, torn between gathering the remains of their picnic and trying to kiss her. To flames with the dishes, he decided, but she was already stepping away.

Then she hesitated. "Rev, I had such a wonderful time." But the expression on her face was sad, and he knew she was thinking about her husband.

"Give me a moment to gather these things, and I'll walk you back."

He must be patient.

#

That evening, Rev found a note propped against the door of his keep.

Quit snooping if you want to live.

He looked around. Who would threaten him? He did not recognize the handwriting.

When Dan came in, Rev was at the table, poring over a map he had commenced. "I'm looking for some pattern, but I ain't seeing it. The local goblen tend to live outside town. Same with the magic users. Not that we can guarantee the killer lives out of town."

He sighed, pushed away the map, then showed Dan the note. "Think I'll start looking at samples of handwriting."

"You show that note everywhere, you might make its sender upset, hunt-brother, and those thugs can be sudden, I've noticed."

"I might also make the sender nervous, and get him or her to act too quickly, make a mistake. But there's more to it." Rev related what Gabryal said about the vampyren and Murkung possibly hunting the Disk.

Dan wriggled his tail uneasily. "I lost a cousin to a Murkung raid up north. They're brutal. Folks say they're getting restless, and so are the karken, maybe this is why." Dan studied the map. "But it's our duty."

109

Rev shook his head. "Who'd of thought you'd be willing to fight a vampyren? This job is making you a rock of the community, Dan. Next you'll be chatting up strangers and running for mayor."

"Like you ain't changing? What about you giving up slicking?"

Rev mumbled something.

"Oh Gods. You stole something again today, didn't you?" Dan thumped his tail. "Even after that lady this morning. I'll have you up before the Town Council, don't you understand? Can't you stop for me, at least?"

"I returned it already. I was only seeing if I could, well, never mind."

"Who can believe if that's true? I'm thinking you'd lie even to me."

Rev lowered his eyes, ashamed.

#

In the evening half light, out in the ruins, a circle of ape-like creatures, grey-furred, with frighteningly intelligent eyes stared at the man in their midst. These were the karken, voracious and evil. Many tales told of their depredations, stealing in through windows, unlocking doors, slaughtering the innocent. It was said they were bred in the Shadow Years by priests who wished an army to fight the vampyren.

Despite the man's allegiances, he felt uneasy, which made him angry. "Gods, it's hard to deal with you creatures. Never know if you understand a word or you're just scratching your fur and wonderin' how to eat me."

One of the older apes shifted.

He stared at it belligerently. "Go after me and you answer to the Goddess. Anyway, you got to stay concealed, that means not killing anyone."

Several of the apes shrieked. Would the Goddess Thana really care if they killed one of Her servants? He kept up a bold front. "Quiet, you. Want me bringing tales back? You'll get your chance at man flesh, but your job now is to hunt that vampyren. Find it, and tell me. Now go."

That they understood. In a moment the clearing was empty. He wondered if they would hold back, denying their murderous hungers. Probably not. Actually, the thought pleased him.

#

Early the next morning, Rev went riding on his horse, Grace, out the north gate. He dismounted to drag aside the thorn bushes he set up each night to keep out wild animals. They needed better gates.

Rev had a few goals today: he wanted to know if any thugs hid in the ruins. He also planned to study who had easy access to the murder site, and finally, he aimed to get practice at riding. People hid smiles, watching him flop around in the saddle. Lots of other folks could ride, how hard could it be?

So he hung onto the saddle horn as he rode, and tried to reach some accord with his mount. He felt vulnerable, in case another assassin came around, but he had to continue to live his life. He'd told Dan and Yarrow about the man he'd fought, that there might be more such assassins appearing.

"Following you from Shendasan?" Yarrow asked, and Rev nodded.

"I'm thinking that it's separate from Bhat Sun's murder, but I guess I can't be sure of that."

He mentioned what the man said about the creature in the shadows of Shendasan, watching and directing. "Was that one of the vampyren, maybe?"

Yarrow did not discount that offhand. "There are old stories, very old, of the Cabalmaster, leader of the vampyren, controlling such a creature. If the Watcher is abroad again, that would be evil news indeed. It guides the Cabalmaster in conducting war."

The day was sunny and warm. Grace showed patience with the rider jostling on her back like a loose sack of grain, but she seemed frustrated about his skills at communication. As they wended through the ruins, she stopped suddenly, though he had no idea why, turned left for no reason that he could see, and came around in a full circle despite his patting her on the neck, trying to make friends. But when he jostled the reins, she moved forward again at a walk.

He found no evidence the thugs were hiding close to town, so he headed deeper into the woods. His mount showed considerable concern for him, avoiding hanging branches and holes, taking the easiest route.

At the murder scene, only some trampled vegetation remained from the struggle. The site was a thousand paces from town, behind a small rise. The goblen conjurors Xul Bil Be and Skarii both lived outside of town, as did that priestess Uulong. As did Khat Trun and his thugs. So any one of them could have come here unwitnessed, murdered Bhat, and left with no one the wiser. Nor could he count out Madame Coo. None had given an alibi.

Rev headed north, not so much guiding Grace as being carried by her, while sunbeams and shade dappled the forest and birds flitted through the underbrush.

Dan had learned most of the miners had alibis, except, interestingly, Ash Wal. The mine owner said he had been in town, but no one had seen him. A lie?

Rev had not found the boot that made the print at the murder site, and had no idea if the scent of burnt roses after the killing mattered. Was that some form of magical scent? He had met the snow leopard that left the print by the body. The pet of a magic user? Or was it the vampyren in a shape-changed form?

Rev rode into a clearing, only to encounter a trio of *neve*. Grace broke into a brisk canter as Rev grabbed for the saddle horn, remembering she was a cow horse.

The *neve* took off, two cows and a calf, and Grace smartly herded them, discovering at last what her rider must have intended. Rev was amazed at her skill. She rounded up the cattle in a trice, and stopped them by a mound of rocks in the clearing.

A bright red shawl was spread across the rocks. To his surprise, an orcen woman sat among the stones, her eyes narrowed in the stoic expression of someone in pain. She clutched at her knee. He recognized Dunortha, the old woman who spoke for the Ruskiya orcen refugees.

The *neve* eyed her skittishly. *Neve* had sharp horns – if they charged, the old woman could be killed.

"Need some help, Lady?"

"You take care of those animals and I am on my way, Bounder," she growled.

Rev dismounted and squatted next to Dunortha. "You ain't going anywhere with that knee."

"You know not our ways, Bounder. I am Rus, leader of my clan. You touch me, even to help, and the men of my clan must kill you."

Rev leaned back. "Seems unneighborly."

"You are not allow to touch me. You insult me and dishonor my clan." She seemed a shade less confident. "How are you to help me?"

"I can't leave you here among the cattle." He mounted Grace, and with some work backed off the *neve* a few dozen steps. Hitching Grace to a shrub, he gathered boughs and vines to weave a rough travois. "I'll haul you. Be a mite rough, with no binding on your knee."

"I bind my own knee."

"I'll get you the materials."

By noontime, she was on the travois, her leg bound tightly so as not to jostle. The best splint he could find was his new scabbard, so he insisted she use that, over her protests. With the travois hitched to his saddle, he led Grace off, carrying his bare sword as his horse dragged the travois. The day had grown humid and hot, so they rested once an hour glass, as best he could judge. At one stop, he mentioned that she was quite a ways from her camp.

"I am Lothut. A finder. This is one reason they choose me as Rus. I find the proper camp place. It is talent, more than just locate a few quail for to hunt." She paused. "It is good to do. When I die or my mind fades, they choose another. We are a tough people, the Ruskiya. From us the first Emperor of Sinnesemota is once chosen."

"That's right, the Emperor Layal was Ruskiya."

"Sa. You remember." She sounded pleased. "Few do who are not Ruskiya."

"My Pa used to tell old stories sometimes, and I liked hearing them." Rev had a pang of sadness, realizing how much his father had taught him. How to bait a hook, set a snare, tricks to staying alive in the wilderness.

Dunortha went on. "Proud, we are, but these days are difficult. The karken." She spit. "Apes. From the north. Agents of evil. I tell you this. Dangerous. They are expand their home, move south."

"They're following you?"

"Fah," she said. "We are not important enough. We are see their tribes, many of them join the Murkung, and battle is our future. We prepare." She was a woman who might face death itself, admitting its strength but marching forward anyway. He understood why her people loved her.

"Your people come from the north?"

"Sa. Four months we walk. Our men hunt, the women gather, the children help. Three times the karken attack, once the army of the Chisen goblen. We are still here." Her gaze was fierce.

113

"What were you searching for, out in the woods?"

That question she refused to answer.

They continued slowly, aiming to jar her as little as possible. She kept her eyes closed against the pain. As evening lengthened, they reached the refugees' camp, and a rough voice from the darkness challenged them in a language Rev did not know.

Rev answered in the common tongue. "I'm bringing in one of your women. Hurt." The man made an expression of astonishment, then let out a piercing whistle. Within moments Rev was surrounded by men armed with spears and bows. Angry murmurs arose, until the old woman spoke in her own language. The men seemed grudgingly mollified. Rev felt grateful she remained alert.

A burly, dark-faced orcen with a broken nose challenged Rev. "This true, what she say? You find her and carry back? Not dishonor her?"

"I found her fallen amid some rocks, yonder. I never touched her, Guard."

The orcen glared, then nodded. "Thank you for help her and for respect her."

The men unlashed the travois and lifted it onto their shoulders. The old woman leaned over the side. "Please come into camp and we thank you properly."

"I'd be obliged."

Several men ran ahead. When they arrived in a clearing between the tents, preparations were underway for a small feast. Rev was given a chair beside the fire near Dunortha, who lay on a litter with her leg elevated, while the rest of the clan sat on low stools. She chewed a scrap of willow bark to help with the pain, and a female clan healer tended her leg.

Rev was amazed at her ability to shrug off such an injury, but she assured him she would seek the trollen healer Laia the next morning.

The fire crackled and sparks lifted up into the gloaming. The Ruskiya made a fuss over him, bringing dishes of spicy food and mugs of bitter ale, laughing and joking in their strange, rich language. They wore feathers in their hair, of owls, hawks and eagles, along with bone jewelry and claw necklaces. They carried their weapons close to hand. Rev would not worry about any assassin when surrounded by these people.

Their clothes were of fur and leather, beautifully stitched and embroidered with blue, red and yellow beads, and they all bore the Red Bear clan tattoo on their left cheek. The warriors had tattoos of leopards and wolves, mothers had moons for each child, and elders had designs of the sun and stars. The higher their status, the more tattoos graced their skin.

They had begun a palisade around their camp. Wise. Rev found himself enjoying these quiet, tough people. He hungered to learn about different people, so he spoke with those who understood his tongue, and they shared observations about the northlands, and their customs.

Dunortha turned to Rev. "You help us, so we ask what we do not understand. Why are your people not attack us?"

Rev stared in astonishment. "Why should anyone attack you?"

She made a dismissive gesture. "We are close by, and some among you oppose us."

"You ain't on their land, so they got nothing to say about it."

"You are a strange people, Rev Caern."

"Different customs."

"Sa. I know this duty of yours, Boundskeeper. It is an honor thing, protect people. We are a people of honor. Twice you protect us and we owe you debt. You send us cloaks for our little ones. I declare, Rev Caern, you are welcome of the camp, a guest of honor."

The Ruskiya buzzed in agreement.

"Listen, my people. This man helps us. When the Chisen goblen are come, we join him for strength in the fight, we come to the need of his town. Do ye agree?"

"Sa," the people shouted agreement.

One warrior approached with a pot of dark ink and a needle. Rev kept his face impassive as the warrior applied the needle to his left shoulder. He felt as though each stick of the tattoo needle tied him to these people, a growing sense of being located at the center of the clan, as though through the tattoo, he could find any of the members of the tribe, and they could find him. A wonderful sense of belonging flooded him, and the theft-hunger vanished. The belongings of the tribe had become his, and his theirs. The discovery left him with a surprising sense of relief. Done, the tattoo was an intricate blue star. He heard whispers of approval that he did not flinch as the star was detailed.

Afterwards, the men slapped him on the back and offered drink from a skin. He took a pull, but nearly choked on the heat of it. Everyone laughed and the skin was passed around. The men began a strange, stooped-over dance. Rev could not understand how they kept their balance, but soon was out learning the dance. Stringed instruments and whistles started up, then all were dancing and singing.

At a break, Rev learned the High Priestess Uulong had tried to win converts.

"We chase her away." Dunortha readjusted her knee to a more comfortable position. "Such foolish things she believes. But she is dangerous, Rev."

The refugees considered the karken their natural enemies, and the monsters had been increasing in recent years. They told spellbinding tales of narrow escapes, and long journeys. Rev learned where the old Ruskiya lady in Shendasan learned to tell stories.

"These are bad days, same as the Troubles after the Collapse of Sinnesemota," Dunortha said. "Evil is come. The karken have the love of Thana. The Murkung call Thana the Goddess of Submission and follow Her. We call Her the Goddess of Death, since She orders death to who does not submit to Her." Dunortha examined her bracelet, worked silver and turquoise. "The Murkung grow hungry, but I am an old woman, sa? I have no care for things that matter when I am young, that other peoples fear us. All I care is they leave us alone. Once I conquer, now I teach." Her eyes sparkled. "We sit too long in talk, when this is time to celebrate. Rev, dance us another dance, and let this old woman watch and enjoy."

As Rev spent the night among the clan members, he experienced the large feeling of being accepted just for himself. The Ruskiya were a confident, hard working people, with no illusions, enjoying simple pleasures, and acknowledging him as one among them. In some way he could not explain, he felt these were his people. The people of his heart.

As dawn lightened the sky, Rev returned to show his respects to Dunortha.

"Rev Caern, today, you are become Star Friend to the clan of the Red Bear, under the Goddess of the Wilderlands, Lacrima Ferae. We do not forget. You need help, we come. Soon, you need help."

"If you need help, I also will come," he said. "I thank you for your welcome. To be a people alone and yet be generous is an admirable thing. So I see you." He paused. "I asked Lot Sun the extent of this ranch. It runs from the northern trail on the east to the two stone buttes on the west, and from the long hill north to the river south, beyond which is Lot Sun's land."

"Sa, a good place for *neve*. We watch over them until we leave." Dunortha nodded solemnly. "Rev, we thank you. Good travel to you, friend."

"And to you." He had already learned the traditional Ruskiya farewell. "May your hunts be worthy."

As he saddled his horse, he felt pleased at their offer to join him if a fight came. Now he had a knife in the hole if needed, and something told him Dunortha was right.

He was going to need their help soon.

Chapter Twelve

"Oh, my dears, do let us consider the Great Spice Road! What romance! What intrigue! Who has not marveled at the noble deeds of Restelte, leaving his home among the Fuen'te to seek his lost love? He wanders from Ilmari on the Oceans of Storms, to Hazhe and east until he comes to the mysterious city of Xan Hes, and finds her the queen of those foreign people. Who has not delighted in the teas, silks, and spices that traversed that mighty road, through sand storms and bandits to bless our own humble tables. It makes my heart quiver, quiver to think of the men who tramp that road, dark, dangerous strangers with a sword in their hand and a gleam in their eye."

"Opening Lecture of The Lady Wexley, House of Langley, Angin Nation" collected in her <u>Writings and Drawings of the Utter East</u>, 823A.

The next morning, Rev, Yarrow and Dan started repairing the town walls. They stripped to the waist in the sun as Rev mixed mortar under Yarrow's tutelage and Dan made bricks. Rev wanted to be interviewing folks about the murder, but he must balance his tasks, and took seriously the Ruskiya warning about the Chisen goblen army. His shoulder ached from the tattoo, otherwise he enjoyed this uncomplicated work.

Dan expressed amazement at Yarrow's skill at mixing and spreading mortar. "I thought you worked cattle for years, Yarrow. When did you learn to be a mason? You're not that old."

Yarrow smiled. "I remember the first trees in this valley, youngster." His voice creaked with such age that crows rose, cawing, from a pine. "Why, I helped build these walls the first time they went up."

Rev laughed aloud.

"You don't believe me?" Yarrow said, in an injured tone.

"Not particularly, my friend."

"Well, I suppose I could be younger than all that." Yarrow completed another course of stones.

118

Then, "Look there," Dan whispered.

A pair of golden creatures darted back and forth above the wall. Rev at first thought they were insects, but each was as large as his hand, and resembled a winged reptile. One spit a tiny stream of fire at the other.

"Dragonets." Yarrow identified them. "Ain't seen any of those in a while, speaking of time passing."

The two creatures wove through an elaborate fire fight.

"I thought dragonets were extinct," Rev said. "Weren't they supposedly companions to dragons? Some song once said dragons would come back when the Empire was restored."

He worried about the Disk of Dragons, but sensed no trace of it. Everyone else wanted the thing, while he just wanted to be rid of its haunting influence.

"Dragons," Yarrow shuddered theatrically. "Dangerous fellows, you'd think, not the sort you generally invite to supper."

"I suppose you've met dozens," Dan teased.

"Sure. Remember how old I am?" Yarrow stretched expansively. "I like to say when Lord Vos was hanging stars in the sky, He gave me a couple to hold until He was ready for them. Weren't much for size, but whooey they were hot. Burned me right here."

He showed Rev his palms, each with a circular scar.

Rev shook his head, smiling, and handed up the next batch of mortar. He liked Yarrow, but didn't altogether trust him. Or maybe he just did not understand the man.

Yarrow seemed carefree, but had a deadly detachment. In teaching swordsmanship, he patiently made each move easy to learn, but Rev never came close to penetrating his defenses. Rev would have been making a name as a swordsman if he had such skill, but fame did not seem to concern Yarrow.

In their lessons, Yarrow had no time for formality, or dueling conventions. Or building a reputation.

"You're trying to stay alive," he would say. "Use everything you got to hand in your surroundings. If there's a chair, kick it in your foe's way. If there's a stick, use it as a shield or a bludgeon. If you're down, grab dirt and throw it in your enemy's face. Blinding your opponent for a moment can be enough. Nearly anything can be used as a weapon, and at some point, has been. Survive. That's the only rule of fighting I follow. Like the way you had to fight in the slums, only with a blade not a fist."

That was the way he taught Rev, fighting rough and dirty, taking any slight advantage. It gave Rev the beginnings of confidence.

#

After noon, Rev rode out into the ruins. Yesterday Dan found an abandoned house built of planks. The house was in decent shape, and Rev intended to snake the planks back to town to rebuild the town gates. Yarrow promised to head out later to help.

The work kept Rev busy until, on his third trip into the ruins, he came upon a girl by the side of the path through the brush. She was orcen, her gingham dress torn and dirty. He recognized Lot Sun's daughter, though he did not remember her name. She wore a white sash.

"Sir Rev, I need your help," she said, as he reined in his horse. "My father, he's..."

She burst into tears.

"What is it, miss?"

"I'll show you." She plunged between two walls too close to ride between. Doubtful, he looked at the passage. Aspen saplings and cedar grew thick there, making an even tighter fit. How had Lot Sun got himself in there? Rev dismounted and followed.

Near an aspen tree, the girl turned.

"Sir Rev? I'm awfully glad you came." She swayed.

Was she ill? It was not that sort of a sway, however.

His suspicions grew. "Your father?"

"He's over that way." She did not seem concerned anymore. She smiled at him.

He backed off, wishing he had not left his sword on his horse.

Her brow furrowed. "Now," she cried.

Men rushed out from concealment, but he was not where they expected. He turned, only to confront Khat Trun and Lum Tar, holding spears.

The thugs flung their weapons. Rev dodged, but Khat Trun's spear ricocheted off his shoulder. Pain lanced across his muscles. He plunged to his right. A thug chopped wildly at him with his spear. Rev knocked it aside, then fled.

The thugs gave chase as he ran for the forest. Branches scratched him. He felt lightheaded already from the loss of blood. He turned for town, but several thugs angled to cut him off, forcing him deeper into the woods.

"Rev," Yarrow called from up ahead. "This way."

Rev glimpsed his friend between a pine and a large rock, and raced that way. Passing into the shadows, he had a disorienting sensation. Ahead, he saw a gold-tinged path in the woods.

Pounding down this path, he somehow saw two worlds at once, the bright, real world of day and another world behind the first, sheltering and mysterious.

A faintly glowing path branched to that Other Side. He took it, and in a few strides he burst forth upon the banks of a creek. He nearly tumbled into the water, but stopped himself.

Panting, dizzy, he heard no pursuit. Anyway, the river was on the other side of town. Had he run that far? Where was Yarrow? He slipped between two thickets, hoping his pursuers would miss him. His shoulder throbbed, bleeding.

Small animals stirred in the brush. With a sinking sensation, he remembered this disoriented feeling when leaving the monastery. He'd been in that strange not-place. Was he there again?

Maybe he should not be so fretful. He *had* escaped.

He turned to find the source of the golden path. Behind him a golden disk floated in the air, the image of a dragon on it. The Disk of Dragons. It hovered over the golden path. He turned his back, not wanting to think about how that Disk might be controlling his choices.

He plugged his shoulder wound with moss. Khat Trun's spear had not flown true or Rev would have been stuck like a pig. He felt lightheaded and thirsty, and lowered himself to drink.

Beneath the surface, the stream hid a world where creatures scuttled and fish hovered, making him feel like a huge intruder peering into an unfathomable life.

The stream splashed his face. He jerked up, having nearly passed out and fallen into the water. He needed shelter. With his last strength, he burrowed under a bush and fell into a swoon.

#

Rev awoke face down, his shoulder throbbing. The forest was quiet in the evening. The unearthly beauty of this spot struck him. What was here, *belonged*. Only he himself was out of place. He crawled to the creek, drank, then struggled to his feet. He thought of the Disk of Dragons, and a stubborn rebelliousness took him. He was hurting too much to put up with this foolishness. He turned to the path, saw the Disk. He focused his will to take control of the Disk with shi.

A crashing sound arose across the creek interrupted his efforts. Something huge was approaching. He hesitated, then released shi and hurried away.

The crashing noise followed. He cursed and increased his speed, stumbling on the uneven ground. The woods thinned to a clearing around a small hill topped by a rectangular stone, which was half as tall as he was. He climbed up the hill and put his back to the stone. He drew his belt knife, his head spinning. Maybe trying to control the Disk had not been such a good idea.

A huge, shambling bear-creature emerged from the shadows, with fur of gold-and-brown stripes and a long, thin head. Its dimensions were wrong for a bear, the shoulders too blocky, the teeth too long. The bear was three times his size. He reached for shi to push away the creature.

The bear swelled up. A surge of shi knocked Rev back against the stone like a leaf hitting a wall. The bear roared and Rev's nerve broke. He fled, the bear in pursuit.

At the bottom of the hill, he leaped up at a pine tree, catching a branch and drawing himself upwards. Below him, the bear raked his leg with its claws. Pain seared his leg.

He pulled himself higher as its fangs clashed, missing his foot. The bear slammed against the tree, then grabbed a branch, but it snapped off. The bear coughed angrily and struck the tree to dislodge him. Rev hung on as the tree swayed.

Finally the bear quit, and sat back on its haunches. The stench of incense, a side effect of shi, was overwhelming. Rev brandished his knife, and the monster roared.

Its eyes narrowed, as though in thought. He did not like that.

"I'm sorry, Disk," he whispered. "I didn't mean it."

Disk of Dragons

Maybe talking to the Disk of Dragons was foolish, but he was desperate. "I believe in you, Disk. I believe. Really I do."

The golden bear waited, like an executioner watching a condemned man. Still, for the moment Rev seemed safe. Exhaustion swept him. He looped his arms through the branches and slept.

#

He woke in a half light, throat dry, arms numb, shoulder pounding with pain. The bear was gone. Had the Disk of Dragons forgiven him? He heard birds and decided it was safe. He climbed down stiffly. He thought about returning to the stream to drink, but since the bear tracks went in that direction, decided against it. The shoulder wound had scabbed, but blood still trickled from the claw marks.

Was the bear the product of his own imagination, brought into existence in this spot? A disturbing thought, but it implied he had some ability to create his reality here.

He fixed his thoughts on hearing a cardinal whistle. Nothing.

Maybe he did it wrong. Before, he had not been trying as hard. He tried to relax, staying open to sensing a cardinal. Still nothing.

Did he have to appeal to the Disk, or worse, submit himself to its power? What would happen to him? At last, he imagined himself open to the Disk, sensing it with shi, accepting its will as his own.

"Cheer. Cheer." A cardinal's call.

He ignored the uneasy sense that he was becoming a puppet of the Disk of Dragons. When he imagined a glowing path ahead, the path appeared.

But his fear kept imagining the bear behind him.

He heard a woof. He took the path and ran. Two worlds appeared around him, the shadowy Other Side and the brighter, more mundane world behind it.

He could hear the bear lumbering closer.

The glowing path divided. He took the brighter path home. Something flickered at the corner of his eye. The shadows changed direction.

He tumbled onto the forest floor, his head spinning. The bear was gone, left behind.

Lifting his head, he recognized the picnic spot in the woods where Bhat Sun had been killed. This was the mundane world. His leg was bleeding.

Why hadn't the wound scabbed? Had the bear's claws been poisoned? He was growing weaker.

He needed the healers, needed Gabryal. He rose and stumbled off towards town.

#

Gabryal headed out for her garden seeking dandelion and ginger for an infusion in the hot afternoon. To her surprise, someone lay unmoving in the street, his leg bloody.

It was Rev. Her heart skipped an anxious beat.

"Ma'tha," she called. "Ma'tha! Rev's wounded. He's been clawed."

As she located his pulse she realized how fast her own heart was beating. His pulse was fast, weak and erratic, and his skin felt hot. Ma'tha arrived with a jar of vinegar, which Gabryal poured on the wound. Claw wounds often had bits of meat in them and infected easily, but vinegar helped prevent that. Rev shuddered but did not waken, even at such a shock.

"Something's wrong," Gabryal said. "The wound isn't scabbed over. He'll bleed to death."

"Magic is keeping it open. Help me lift him, Gabryal."

#

On a warm Sennaday morning, the eighteenth of Goblenmoon, a gentle breeze was blowing through an open window of the hospital recovery room, carrying the scent of blooming hyacinths, the sort of day Gabryal thanked the Goddess Luwana she was alive to enjoy. Gabryal sat on a chair alongside Rev's bed. Yarrow and Dan stood at the foot of the bed. Yarrow carried a dashing hat, brim curled up on the sides, and wore a black shirt and trousers.

Something about him made Gabryal uneasy. He was so still, so detached.

Dan on the other hand was friendly as a lark's whistle. She considered Dan the best argument that Rev was a good man. Good people had good friends, in her experience.

Rev finally awoke. His eyes flickered when he saw Yarrow.

"Heard you call... tried to follow. Got lost." His voice was a croak.

124

"You escaped, that's the important thing. I drew the thugs off on a false trail." Yarrow gave a sharp-toothed smile. "I'm afraid a few fell in the river."

He shook his head. "Friend, you got to get better at avoiding creatures with claws."

"I'm practicing best I can." Rev tried to smile. "Maybe... give some pointers?"

"Sure, here's a tip. When its fangs are as big as your face, run away."

Gabryal chuckled.

Rev's hand grasped at the white sheets. "Yarrow, the thugs got my horse."

"No, I gathered her in, she's at the stable, fattening on grain. Your sword is there by your hand. One of the refugees brought a new scabbard to pay for some favor you did them."

Rev leaned back, looking relieved. Yarrow glanced at Gabryal, who became aware of how close she was sitting to Rev. She blushed.

"Maybe you two should go, my friends. He's pretty tired."

"No, let them stay, Gabryal. Tell... what's been happening."

Dan sat down on a wicker stool. Yarrow remained on his feet.

"We've been having trouble with the thugs," Dan said. "They attacked a caravan two days ago, robbed a freelance miner yesterday. They're thinking to draw you out, looks like."

"Signed on for the job," Rev murmured. "Do what I need to do."

"Absolutely, but not alone. You got help, hunt-brother."

"Don't let them choose the ground," Yarrow said. "Scout around for a place where you have the advantage when you face them."

"Any evidence of magic on these raids?" Rev's voice was stronger. Improbably, the conversation seemed to be doing him good.

"Still hunting Bhat's murderer?" Yarrow asked. "No, they've not been using magic."

"Maybe they don't have any," Dan said.

"They'd use it if they did," Rev said. "But I... Khat Trun is still suspect. If he got hold of someone else's spell..." His voice trailed off.

"You need more rest," Yarrow said, as Dan rose, "so we'll be off. We're working on your plan to fix up the town wall. The southern gate is almost working, and we cleaned away a lot of rubble. Found fellows to help, with the merchants kicking in wages. I'll show you when you're up and around."

He waved goodbye, and Dan and he left, gabbing cheerily.

"You have good friends," Gabryal said.

"Dan's been with me my whole life."

"Yarrow is a fine man, too."

"Wouldn't want to cross him. Some part of him... hard as granite."

"Then it's a good kind of granite." She took his hand, and they sat quietly together.

#

It was nearly night. Rev woke as Gabryal entered the room. He looked better, the color returning to his face. "Thank you for caring for me. Afraid I've been in a bad way."

He made a little gesture. "When I was hurt, thought of you first."

"You're welcome," Gabryal said, pleased. "What attacked you? It took Laia's strongest magic to heal those claw marks. There was magic in the wounds."

"Don't know. A bear?" Rev started to explain about some strange place he had gone, though after mumbling about a golden light and no sun, he fell silent.

No sun? Disturbed, Gabryal wondered if he had Crossed Over.

No mortal being could travel to the Other Side. But vampyren could.

The Other Side was a duplicate of this world in spirit, just on this side of the Veil of Vos, and the abode of many magical creatures.

Mechanically, she changed his bandages. If Rev were a vampyren, why tell her he had Crossed Over? Rev was resting now, his eyes closed.

He acted so trusting, but that only spurred her panic. She couldn't give him everything he seemed to need. A thousand crazy fears rushed through her. She couldn't trust her own thinking around him. She couldn't be falling for any other man after Zhac, it was too soon.

She fled the room, found Ma'tha arranging bandages, and confided her fears.

"You think he's a vampyren, Gabryal?" Ma'tha stacked the bandages on a shelf.

"Ma'tha, who else can go to the Other Side? No vampyren is slow enough to be caught by a bear, but there were only three claw marks. That wound came from no bear."

"Unless the bear lost a claw. Anyway, even if a vampyren were weakened, they'd never go to a mortal healer. He isn't a vampyren, even if he did Cross Over."

Ma'tha led her back to the room where Rev lay. His eyes opened.

"Do you know where you've been, Bounder?" Ma'tha asked brightly.

Gabryal frantically signaled her to be quiet, but Ma'tha went on. "We think you went to the Other Side."

"The spirit world?" Rev roused. "...stories as a kid about spirits on the Other Side of darkness... Cross Over as ghosts. That place? Crazy."

"It is crazy. No one can go over bodily to the Other Side, you know."

"With one exception, Bounder," Gabryal said coolly. "Vampyren."

"Think I'm a vampyren, Gabryal?" He grinned, then winced at the pain. "Ain't they near indestructible? And powerful? Kitten could knock me over."

"What of Crossing Over to the Other Side?" Gabryal asked.

"Don't dragon folk also cross the Other Side?"

"You don't look much like a dragon to me," Gabryal said, with some heat.

"What gave it away? Lack of scales? My skinny wings?" Feebly, he flapped an arm. He did not seem to take her concern seriously. Infuriating.

"Bothers me," he went on, "that bear creature overpowered... with shi, but I thought shi strength... related to purity of intent. I'm not *that* bad a man, or I couldn't even use shi. So I'm wrong. So who *can* use shi? Not just good folks."

She glanced at his shoulder. To her astonishment, the spear wound was nearly healed. Vampyren healed quickly. "You're healing too fast. You *are* a vampyren."

Someone chuckled: Laia, entering the room. "Certainly he's healing. I spent half last night working on him, Gabryal. You're so lost in suspicion you aren't thinking. Rev, a vampyren? No, no. I would know this." Laia patted her arm affectionately.

Gabryal blushed. Last year, Gabryal had come upon the trollen woman sitting on a stump outside the Chapter House of their Order, looking homeless. Gabryal asked if she needed help, and offered food, before discovering Laia was a senior member of the Order of the Grey Women. The trollen had been touched by the kind gesture, saying Gabryal reminded her of her own daughter, lost years ago.

Recently, Laia had mentioned that Gabryal and Rev were going to know each other a long time. That was unsettling.

Laia departed after checking on Rev. Gabryal sat watching Rev fall asleep, remembering what he said about thinking of her first. No man ever said anything like that to her. Even Zhac, wonderful as he was, always considered his beloved Defenders and their king first, though honestly (she firmly put down the tiny feeling of old resentment) she had loved that about her husband, such strength of purpose. And Zhac had returned her love. Her eyes misted. It bothered her that she used to remember exactly how Zhac's voice sounded, but often now couldn't hear him in her head at all.

How much does mourning ease due to the simple gift of forgetfulness? Some details remain sharp forever: how his smile crooked to one side, the strength of his hands; but most memories blur as new experiences overlay them. Oh, something may remind us on occasion, a scent or a thought, and the memories re-bloom, but how many memories are never brought back? Yes, the old is put aside to participate in the new, but only when enough time has passed. Until then we guard our losses jealously.

So while Gabryal enjoyed Rev's interest, it also put her out of sorts, as though she were expected to do something. She felt guilty over the stirrings she did have, the selfish part that enjoyed how Rev was so intent on her. Some deep, animal part of herself enjoyed Rev's attention, that was the plain truth. She liked this sprawling, rebellious youth, always trying to be a better man than he was.

She was still in love with her husband, but she liked Rev. Maybe too much.

She found herself whispering her secrets to his gently snoring self, telling him how she cried herself to sleep each night, how she despised this armor of hate, rage, pain and emptiness that kept her from sharing with others, from laughter, from the carefree life she yearned to have. But she still loved Zhac. Two years was not enough time to put her man behind her. Not yet.

At last she fell silent. Rev slept on.

She felt relief at that, but with a tiny, wild regret. She brushed his cheek with her lips, and departed.

#

Through the dusk dimness the band of karken roved the countryside, scouting. Their leader reminded them to avoid the hairless ones. Orders. But he was remembering how good the hairless ones tasted. Others around him licked their chops as well.

After moving through a thick woods, the karken came across an isolated farm. An orcen man worked out in the fields, far from any weapon. A fat woman was hanging clothes. Soft, young ones ran about. The wind brought their smell, the raw meat, succulent.

One of the juveniles charged. Then the whole band rushed out, orders forgotten.

The woman screamed, and the children tried to flee. The karken chased them down.

P M F Johnson

Chapter Thirteen

"Seeing the future is no simple thing. Only certain possibilities are discernible, the greatest threats or opportunities appearing most easily. Not every seer can predict equally far, since selfishness blinds us, and no trollen but a mature woman sees the future at all. The current Oracle of Gy Pe, most selfless among us, may see six days into the future. She is supported by the Seven, who may predict five days ahead. The further one sees, the better one heals. As women age, some see further and heal more, gaining wisdom and trust in the Goddess, but most remain limited. Humbling for most of us, growing older, but evidently no wiser."

"Far-fetched Claims of a Trollen Woman," from Legends of Other Races, an Oral History, *edited by Proctor Linse, published under the auspices of the Council of Historians in the city of Remula, the nation of Ilmari, Year 919A.*

The first morning Rev could move around, despite every bone aching, he saddled up Grace, and reluctantly rode over to Lot Sun's ranch. He was sweating freely under a merciless sun by the time he presented himself at the door.

Elladay being the day of rest, and Lot Sun being home, the rancher found Rev a cool drink, then sat with him. Lot Sun wore a fine brown lamb's wool vest, but unbuttoned. His cotton shirt was not tucked in, and his reptilian head shifted restlessly, like a snake hunting.

"How can I help you, Bounder?"

"Sir, I don't know how to break this news."

Lot Sun's daughter entered the room, wearing a red silk dress bound by her white sash, and moving with a dignified bearing. Rev rose and bowed. He told the tale of the ambush, leaving out her name.

Lot Sun was suspicious. "Who was the girl who spoke to you, Bounder?"

"He lies, Papa. Absolutely false," the rancher's daughter cried before Rev could speak.

Lot Sun stiffened. "A serious issue. Who were the thugs?"

When Rev mentioned Khat Trun, the old man smacked down his tail. "You said he was gone." Lot Sun did not look at his daughter.

She drew herself up. "Khat Trun is stronger than you'll ever be. You're as blind as this stranger to what's coming. I spit on you both." She fled.

Lot Sun stared out into nothing. "That ain't done. A child oughtn't do that before a guest. And she didn't address you respectful."

Rev felt acutely embarrassed.

"Is this what you came for, sir?" Lot Sun's tongue flicked over his lips.

"Actually, I had another question, concerning my investigation. Your brother, Bhat, was friendly with the lady, Gabryal?"

"Never talked to her that I was aware of," Lot Sun said in a distant voice.

Rev felt surprised. Had Gabryal lied about what she was doing at the murder site? It twisted his heart that someone he felt such affection for could put him off with a casual fib. "Bounder, I'm afraid you've inadvertently caused my family some loss of face," Lot Sun said. The rancher took his cane in hand, prepared to rise.

"I'm sorry, sir." Rev stood. "I thought you should be warned."

Lot Sun waved it off, but his manner was icy. In accusing his daughter, Rev lost him as an ally, no matter how obvious her guilt.

We speak of living rationally, but is it always wise to do so? We support our families, which perhaps is wiser than rational logic, for love buoys us; and a daughter needs her father's love all her life, with its redemption.

Still, the rancher did not ask for Grace back. For him, to withdraw the horse would be to admit losing face, so Rev would be allowed to keep Grace so long as he kept his job.

Returning to the stable, Rev was glad. The mare was so intelligent and affectionate.

As for himself, he would work to the best of his ability; he had changed since Shendasan, when his whole purpose was to get away with as much as possible.

Only as Rev reflected on what happened did it occur to him that somehow he must have availed himself of the power of the Disk. The Disk's involvement in his life, inexplicable and unexpected, was not just a burden and restraint, but actually conveyed some benefits. The thought cheered him, though his very cheerfulness made him suspicious. Was that the Disk's doing as well? Were any of his thoughts his own?

Well, he would act as though he were in complete control of himself. What else could he do?

#

First thing the next morning, Lunsday, Rev sat down to write a thank-you note to the Ruskiya. The scabbard he loaned to Dunortha as a splint for her knee had been damaged, so she had sent another as a gift, bearing an elaborate design stained into the leather with a complexity that his eyes had difficulty following. It raised the hackles on his neck. The scabbard was a breathtaking work of art, and his sword fit as though the sheath were made for the sword, a far better gift than he deserved. More choked up than he should be, he found a youth who for a copper would run the note out to the Ruskiya and read it aloud to them in the traditional fashion.

#

That afternoon, as the sun slanted over the ruins outside town, an acolyte appeared at the door to the temple near which Rev waited patiently in the shade of a crabapple.

"The High Priestess will see you," the boy intoned. The White-Sashers shunned honorifics. It actually made them more disturbing, rather than less so.

Rev followed the acolyte down a dark hallway and into an atrium where a fountain burbled in a garden and flagstones lay in straight lines, giving an effect of rigor and everything in its place. He intended to question all the local magic users. A bird sang in an apple tree above an ornate wooden chair in which sat the High Priestess Uulong, who was severe-looking, and thin for an orcen. Her head was almost entirely white, indicating a dignified age; orcen could live up to 120 years. She wore a blue robe with gold embroidery, with a white sash.

"What may I answer for you?" she asked in a high, thin voice.

"Priestess, I'm trying to meet with the members of the community to understand them and begin discussions I hope will prove fruitful." He was

132

embarrassed at how stilted his words came out, but how did one politely say, *I think you may be a murderer?*

The priestess snorted. "An admirable goal, but I have little time. You wish to understand me? Simple enough. I seek to bring people to the Goddess. You wish good relations with me? Yield the respect and deference befitting my station."

"Why did you come to this valley?"

"The Goddess sent me. I obey Her words."

Rev bowed, stymied. He wanted to approach this carefully, not ruin things with clumsy questions. "This is a beautiful room."

"I enjoy this atrium. An indulgence which I permit myself."

He smelled the heady scent of flowers, and noticed a stand of eastern lilies. Were lilies the smell of priestly magic, like ozone marked elemental magic?

"You have not attended any of our services," she said. "They occur on Lunsday evenings. You will find our Goddess a loving Mistress."

"I appreciate the invitation." Rev hesitated. "You knew the dead man, Bhat Sun?"

"Only most casually. He did not attend our services often."

"There seems to be tension between your congregation and that of the priest Qur Sil."

The priestess narrowed her eyes. "Do you have a specific complaint about my people?"

"No. But I am wondering if that tension could have played a role in Bhat's murder."

"My people never overstep themselves. I suspect none of them of murder."

"Where were you the morning of the murder?"

To his surprise, she did not seem to take offense. "I was here leading services. Do you wish me to call in my assistants to give witness?"

"That won't be necessary," he said hastily.

"I also aver that every acolyte of my temple was here."

"I appreciate that," Rev said, embarrassed, but grateful for her cooperation. His eyes fell on a small brass knickknack on a table, a small toy doorway nestled among plants in containers. He felt the urge to palm it, then a burst of shame. Some demon inside him seemed constantly pushing him to steal.

"I do have a point to clean with you," she said. "You harbor refugees on land that is not yours. Harboring thieves and villains is no way to endear yourself to the Goddess."

"They refugees are under my protection. You got a specific complaint about their actions?" He turned her question around.

"I want them gone." She turned her face away.

Was she a bigot? Who thought of a priest having irrational hatreds? She closed her eyes in disdain. His fingers moved, and the brass knickknack was cool against his skin, inside his waistband. Excitement swept through him like a great wind.

"Perhaps you should talk with them." He hoped she attributed the tension in his voice to their disagreement. "I find them a good people, they might listen to your wisdom."

"Such creatures obey no law of our race, I do not intend to speak with any of them."

"Priestess, I'm confused. Dunortha, their leader, said you already have been among them, preaching for the Goddess."

"Enough insolence from you." Her eyes sparkled with anger. "Go."

He bowed, fascinated at having caught her in an inconsistency. Had he gotten under that cool? More to the point, was she the killer? She hid something. Why else would she care if he knew she was proselytizing? Wasn't that what priests *did*? His neck prickled as he departed, but he exited from the Temple unimpeded, so they didn't know he took the doorway. Yet.

The priestess Uulong had an alibi, though he cynically wondered if her acolytes would simply swear to anything she said. He felt clumsy questioning people, but how else could he go about it?

He tried not to think of the consequences when his theft was discovered. Why worry about the lies of others when he was himself a thief, his whole life a lie?

#

Rev sat on a wicker stool in the waiting room of the hospital while Gabryal attended one more patient. He intended to ask her opinion about the small brass doorway, which felt warmer than it should, and disquieting

134

to carry, as though something watched him, aware he held the doorway, waiting for some mistake. The watching feeling was similar to that he experienced in Shendasan, but subtly different. That one raised the fear of eyes hidden in the shadows, this one the shame of a young boy under the glaring eye of a ruling mistress.

Afternoon sun slanted in the windows. He was happy at the chance to see Gabryal, but nervous. Would she guess he had stolen the brass doorway? He rose and paced. The doorway was a weight in his pouch. He vowed to get rid of it as soon as possible, maybe drop it in the dust near Uulong's temple.

Laia swept into the room like a teacher catching a truant student. "Let's see what you're carrying, Bounder."

"Healer?" He had said nothing to anyone about the doorway, but the trollen waited, her eyes narrowing dangerously – if she could read the future, how could she not know the recent past? His face heated. Feeling ridiculous, he drew forth the brass doorway. She studied it, moving her fingers as though to feel any emanations.

Gabryal entered the room and he felt doom descending. Laia would confirm that he was a thief. He would have to leave town, leave even Dan behind. He deserved no more.

What is the purpose of acting self-destructively, except to give us the excitement of shame? There is no reversing such actions. Try as Rev might, he would never change any choice of the past.

"What is that, Lady?" Gabryal asked.

"A small magical gateway, my friend, with an evil feel. For communing with creatures on the Outside, I believe. Where did you find it, Rev?"

Shocked, he wondered if she just sensed the power of the doorway, rather than sensing exactly what he had done. Clinging to that hope, he instantly lied again. "In the ruins near the temple of the priestess Uulong."

"So the doorway likely belongs to her or her people," Gabryal said. "Something they're guarding, maybe. Are you intending to return it, Rev?" Her glance seemed sharp.

"Of course." He hoped he was not blushing. How could he escape all these lies? Even lies arguably good, like this one where he was trying to

135

find a killer, made him feel terrible. Maybe there were no good lies. He shied from that thought.

Terrible thing for a thief to have, the desire for honor. On the other hand, honor might protect you from feeling like this. If you don't lie or steal, you don't feel bad. He wondered why no one ever put it so simply to him before.

Anyway, he wasn't the only liar. The more he investigated, the more tangled webs he found: the evil doorway (did that make the priestess evil?), Lot Sun's daughter mixed up with the thugs, Gabryal lying to conceal her secrets.

No, thinking he lied because they did was crazy. But was it so wrong if he lied, too? At least he was lying to advance the murder investigation.

Laia stared at him coolly, and his emotions sank. He was sure she knew, and waited for him to confess. Why not confess, right now? It would be a relief.

At that moment, someone started shouting outside.

"We've been attacked."

Torn between shock and relief, Rev ran to the door, and saw a man outside in a wide-brimmed hat. The stranger stood before a group of citizens. "A farm on the South Road was attacked, and a whole family killed."

Rev raced off to shut the town's south gate, then sent people to close the other gates. As he went, uneasy murmurs ran through the crowds. To avoid panic, Rev detailed Yarrow to arrange a militia to defend the walls, and Os Gar the wagon wright to lead a patrol through the streets.

He sent runners to warn the mine owner Ash Wal, the refugees, the conjuror Skarii, the priestess Uulong, and others outside the town walls.

Last, Rev assembled a posse to go to the farm, including Dan, a mine supervisor named Yil Ben, the White-Sasher Kek Nin, a young Ruskiya refugee, a few goblen and himself, while Dan wangled horses from Dril Plu, the stable owner. Gabryal insisted on joining them.

"It's dangerous, Gabryal," Rev protested.

"That's why I'm coming along, Bounder. To protect you."

Astonished, Rev yielded. "Come along then, but arm yourself."

They headed on horseback out the west gate. Gabryal carried only a short sword and a long staff, and rode the piebald gelding belonging to the Grey Women.

Rev worried, but she was an adult, and the other posse members seemed glad to have her along. He remembered her saying she knew some magic. True, he was glad she was close by, but he wanted to keep her safely away from danger.

Not for him to control.

He led the posse to the shacks in the ravine and to Lot Sun's ranch, warning people, then led the posse south into the darkness, the stranger, a packer with a mule train, guiding them.

One posse member was Los Fun, whom Rev thought of as the town drunk. Rev was surprised the man joined them.

"I fought in the Murkung wars, sir," Los Fun explained briefly.

"We served together, Bounder," Dril Plu spoke up.

That explained why Dril Plu overlooked his friend's drinking and treated him as an equal. A brotherhood of warriors who had saved each other's lives would override other social conventions, even among the stiff-necked Afen. Los Fun rode a horse belonging to the stable owner, and sat his saddle well. Rev felt reassured to have veteran fighters along.

The packer described what he found. Several of the posse recognized the description of the farm as the Dor Falk place, and began discussing the family in low tones: hard-working orcen who grew flax and wheat, a quiet family with a passel of children.

Shortly before dawn, the posse reached the farm. Mist over the fields lent a lonesome, haunted feeling. The gnawed bodies of the dead, the bloody clothes strewn, and the tracks indicated this had been no bandit attack. Rev drew his father's sword, somehow feeling his father guiding his hand, an eerie, comforting thought.

"The karken do this," said the lanky young Ruskiya orcen who had come along with them. He carried his spear like another limb. "We do not see them this far south before."

The comment drew a dark look from other posse members, and Rev could guess their thought, *Not until you folks drew them.*

Rev remembered the Ruskiya's name from the building bee: Hunorn Papendurshin. Hunorn was one of those rough youths who learned to fight

137

as soon as he learned to walk. No one spoke against him, which might
have been because of the necklace of claws around his neck, claws from a
very large panther, or because of the scars on his left arm, evidently from
that same panther, or the vast number of daggers he carried. Anyway, he
was polite and well spoken.

"What are karken, cousin?" Dan asked. All Ruskiya claimed each other
as cousins.

"Cruel beasts, like apes," Hunorn replied. "Travel in packs. Almost
human-size, I beg your pardon, Rev. Too intelligent for beasts, not as
smart as the mortal races. Their masters, the Murkung, give them evil
intelligence."

The Murkung were legendary for cruelty.

"Does this mean the Murkung are coming this way, Hunter?" Yil Ben
shifted uneasily.

"Perhaps, Miner. We are trail in our retreat by the karken, but why for
so many leagues? We think they are under the direction of someone."

"This happens from allowing liberties and loose morals," sneered the
White-Sasher Kek Nin. "We're being punished by the Goddess. People
must return to the old ways."

"Ha," said Yil Ben, "not if it means being in your White Sash cult, Kek
Nin."

"We are no cult. We seek the truth."

"Tell us about the karken, Hunorn," Rev asked, interrupting.

"Sa. They are as strong as orcen and fast as goblen, the young have red
coats, the older ones silver."

"I've seen ape tracks," Rev admitted to Gabryal. "I'm sorry I didn't
mention them."

"You didn't know what they were."

Rev looked around at the scattered bodies. "We need to lay these
people to rest. Does anyone know who their relatives might be?"

Several farms lay in the area, along various creeks, so Rev sent trios of
fighters, one led by Yil Ben, the other by Dan, to warn them. The rest of
the posse dug graves with spades from the barn.

Rev considered, as he worked. If karken were allied with the Murkung,
that implied the Murkung might be hunting the Disk. "But why would the
Murkung order an attack on a remote ranch?" he muttered aloud.

Hunorn answered. "This attack is not Murkung orders, Rev, this the karken do to feed."

Rev felt sickened.

By midday the posse had dug sufficient graves. Saddest was finding two children in a corner. The boy had protected his infant sister with his own body, but both died. Rev's fury rose. These beasts would be dealt with, and their masters pay vengeance price. But how?

Rev listed a few questions aloud. "First, where did they go?"

"Their tracks lead north, Bounder," said Hunorn.

"Second, why attack here?"

"Farmers would be easy pickings, sir," Los Fun said. "They weren't in defensive alignment, the man caught out in the fields, helpless."

"How can we stop this from happening again?"

No one had an answer for that.

Hunorn and Kek Nin went down to the creek to look for blackstones.

Rev paused near Gabryal. "I'm thinking that the murders of Bhat and these people are related."

"You don't see this as an attack by wild animals?"

"I think these karken were brought to Zhopahr, and whoever guided them is responsible. The karken, the mages and the thugs, even that vampyren have all come hunting the Disk of Dragons. If I had solved Bhat Sun's murder, maybe this latest tragedy would not have happened."

"You can't blame yourself, you did the best you could."

Rev was grateful for her loyalty, but shook his head. "It's my job to keep the peace."

During the morning, others farming families appeared, until some forty-five people arrived, using ashes from the fireplace to mark their foreheads in mourning. Rev urged them to return to town for safety, but after they talked together, their spokesman, a gangly older orcen named Pep Hin, declined for them all.

"Already planted the corn, sir, have to protect the seed or the animals get it. Can't abandon the crops or there'll be nothing to show for our efforts. We'd be ruined."

"You can start again, friends," Rev argued, but the farmers would not agree.

"We'll stay armed and pair up in our homes," said Pep. The other farmers nodded. The youngest children buried their heads in their mother's skirts.

Rev was not one for forcing people, but how could a small posse protect people all over the area?

Pep said a few words over the graves, then blackstones were passed to gather wishes. After the graves were filled in, the farmers' families headed out.

Rev called the posse together. "Friends, I think we should follow the karken's tracks to where they're hiding."

The posse members grimly agreed. Rev and Hunorn began to work out the trail. At least a score of the creatures had departed eastward through scrub forest towards the bluffs. The posse followed, only to find their quarry turned north at a stream, heading toward Zhopahr.

At a point where the ground climbed from the flats into some low hills, Rev caught a flicker of movement on their left.

"Ambush," he shouted and grabbed for his sword.

The karken charged from behind a screen of trees. Gabryal spoke a few words, and a bright dart shot from her staff and exploded into a ball of fire, consuming a knot of the apes. Ozone scorched the air as the horses shied and whinnied.

The lead ape leaped at Rev. Rev's training came into play without forethought. He lunged, driving his sword into its heart. The lead ape fell and the others fled, leaving behind their dead.

A half-a-dozen karken lay killed by Gabryal's magical fire. The stink of burnt fur and flesh rose. The posse stood gape-mouthed. She looked fierce, ready for another engagement.

"Impressive, Mage," Hunorn said. Coldly, she nodded her thanks.

Rev let out a low whistle. He had no idea she commanded such power.

"War magic," Dan Zee said, awed.

Gabryal tended the two casualties. Los Fun, the town drunk, had been badly bitten on the shoulder, though he killed the karken. A fell light smoldered in his eye. And Dril Plu broke his leg when a karken pulled him from his saddle. He lost his weapon in the fall, but Hunorn skewered the karken.

The stable owner thanked Hunorn profusely, and the refugee acknowledged the thanks. Fighting was nothing new to the Ruskiya.

Gabryal bound Dril Plu's leg with a splint and applied a bandage to Los Fun's wound, adding a magical cantrip to aid the healing.

Dan was the only other posse member who had killed an ape. "They were fast," he said.

"I'm glad we won." Rev was shaking in reaction. "Thank the Goddess, Yarrow is teaching me sword work or I might be dead."

His father's sword had leapt into his hand unnaturally fast, and the rich brown design on the scabbard glowed hypnotically, while a faint, spicy floral scent dissipated. Humbled, he realized the Ruskiya had given him a great gift: ensorcelment imbued the scabbard.

The posse continued, alternately walking and trotting their horses, holding spears ready. The karken forded the river disturbingly close to town, crossed the west road, then headed north into the ruins.

There a rear guard of the apes tried to surprise them, but Gabryal blasted them with a second, smaller fireball, and the karken scattered, leaving behind two more dead. At each elemental spell cast, Gabryal seemed more confident, but also more alien, as though the magic were somehow replacing her spirit with that of a pitiless, deadly foe.

The posse involuntarily drew back from her, until Dan broke the tension with a shaky laugh. "Whew. You are one dangerous woman."

The comment seemed to return her to herself, a little. "Why, thank you, Dan." She curtsied.

In the ruins, the posse discovered a hastily abandoned camp on a rise between several half-fallen walls, where it was possible to watch the road.

"They've been hiding here for some time." Rev eyed the piles of bones.

Dan nodded. "Why were they watching the traffic toward Khav?"

The question made them all uneasy.

"I think we should search for other such camps," Rev said. "Flip over all their hole cards if we can." The others concurred.

"Look at this, Rev." Hunorn pointed to a man's tracks. A spot where the man's tail trailed on the ground proved he was an orcen, while the footprint showed a notch missing out of the heel. A shiver ran up Rev's spine.

It was the same track as the one found at the site of Bhat Sun's murder.

Chapter Fourteen

"The extent of the danger to the Heart of Light became clear, and a watch was set on the Hall of the Empire, until a dragon approached the Empress, offering a way to close the Hall, using a magical seal. From that day forward, without the Disk of Dragons the Hall could not be opened; but soon the Emperors were misusing the powers of the Disk, forgetting its purpose."

"Beginning the End," from <u>The Chronicles of Sinnesemota</u>.

As the sun descended, the posse followed the karken north, but the apes traveled faster than horses, and the posse had not prepared for a long journey. At the northern rim of the valley they abandoned the chase.

"That boot track proves someone at Bhat's murder is working with the karken," Rev said to Dan as they walked their horses back to town. "It links the killings. This ain't a pile of coincidences."

In Zhopahr, the posse broke up. Several members acted shaken by the killings, the miner Yil Ben even wondering if it were time to find safety in the city of Khav.

Gabryal leaned close to Rev to say goodbye, and he felt a frisson, then a certain emptiness, as she rode away. Would they ever be more than friends? He wanted to step up his courtship, despite everything else happening.

For now, Dan and he took care of their horses, then turned them out in the stable's corral.

As Rev started for the keep, Los Fun approached. "Bounder? I, I was thinking the town needed a night watchman, and hoped you'd give me a chance." He stood humbly, no reek of alcohol on him, his shoulder bandaged where Gabryal had tended it.

"That's a position of tremendous responsibility, Los Fun."

The orcen nodded. "Yes, sir."

"How can I know you won't get drunk on the job, exposing us to an assault?"

Los Fun flinched. "I give my word I won't ever drink again." His mouth set in a determined line.

Rev felt a stir of hope. "I can only afford to pay ten coppers a week."

"I'll take it, Bounder. Can I start tonight?"

"Yes," Rev said, amazed at the turnaround in the orcen and hoping the man could stay sober. But he had never known an orcen to go back on his word when delivered so plainly, and since Rev had been given a second chance himself, he would not deny one to another.

As it turned out, Rev's trust was well placed; with such a purpose to his life, Los Fun excelled as a watchman, and never drank again.

A short time later, Rev entered Ema Vil's Sleeping Kitten Tea House. The tea house was large, two dozen tables. One wall was open to the evening air, and small fires burned in grates here and there, combating the cool of the evening. The staff bustled among the tables, waiting on the customers. The Tea House even boasted a wooden floor.

The priest Qur Sil invited Rev to sit, and Rev accepted with gratitude, soon enjoying a stew and tea.

"Qur Sil, I'm wondering if there's anyone you can vouch for, the morning that Bhat was killed," Rev asked, as he ate. "Folks you were with."

The priest's eyes narrowed. "Lot Sun and I were discussing matters of the temple, as I believe he told you, Bounder."

"He did, yes." Rev felt no embarrassment at being caught in a subterfuge, checking stories was his job. "The priestess Uulong moved here not long ago. What do you think of her?"

"All priests are in the business of bringing comfort into people's lives. People find solace knowing the Goddess Luwana loves and cares for us. Have you been attending her services?"

"Not yet."

The priest smiled, mockingly. "Are we to see you at my service, then?"

"Ain't my job to take sides. Any ideas who killed Bhat Sun?"

Qur Sil tapped his tail in a gentle rhythm. "Those I know best are my own congregation, and I cannot imagine any of them doing such a thing."

"Any got a pet leopard?"

"What?" The priest seemed momentarily taken aback.

"There's a leopard roaming the area, I'm wondering if he belongs to anyone."

Qur Sil's mocking smile widened. "I know of no one with a pet leopard. Frankly, I've never heard of such a thing."

"Nor me, which has me wondering if maybe if it's a trick of some magic user. Who uses magic in town?"

"I don't make an inventory of people's flaws, Bounder."

"Magic use is a flaw?"

The cleric adopted a teacher's tone. "Righteous Power flows only from the Goddess, all else is the deceit of the Chaos Gods."

Rev learned nothing more of use, for despite the priest's courteous language, he had a slick, religious answer for everything.

That night, as Rev, Dan and Yarrow patrolled before turning the guard over to Los Fun, Rev filled in Yarrow on events. Maybe it was the after-effects of witnessing such brutal action, but his words tumbled out, as Dan's torch cast a flickering light along the street.

"Why are the karken around?" Rev asked. "Hunorn says they attack like that to feed, but the boot track hints they're in league with Bhat's killer."

Yarrow nodded, and drank from a skin of ale.

"There's so many cards here in play. Who's the killer? What are the motives of the White-Sashers? Is everyone here to find the Disk, even Gabryal and the healers? Seems doubtful that absolutely everyone is."

"Keep tugging at strings, eventually the ball of yarn falls apart," Yarrow said.

"Great saying, friend." Dan took the skin from Yarrow, and drank. "Haven't the slightest idea what you mean by it, though."

Yarrow chuckled. Ahead, a shadowy figure stood at a lighted door, then went in and closed the door, leaving the street dark. The weavers lived down this way.

Rev sighed. "I don't understand how the world works. I want to trust in Vos and Luwana. Without the Gods, what good are our lives? But if Luwana is good, how can evil creatures use shi? Shi is supposed to be the life energy of Luwana spilled across the world when She died. It's all wrong that an evil creature could use shi, yet that bear-monster did."

"Can we say the bear was actually evil?" Yarrow innocently looked up at the stars. "May've just been trying to eat you. Not a personal thing."

"Some might even consider that a good deed, looked at objectively," Dan said.

Rev mock-punched his shoulder.

"Anyway, maybe there's only strength and power," Dan said, "no Goddess and no reason to be good. After all, even the stories agree that Luwana died."

"Don't give me that," Rev said. "You light candles to Luwana every night, nobody in the valley's more regular about it."

"Well, I was brought up right," Dan answered, slapping his tail for emphasis. "Anyway, I'm still here, proof enough the Goddess has taken care of me."

They found the northern gate closed and barred. Rev felt proud the town gates were repaired and the walls being rebuilt; Yarrow and Dan were doing most of the work, but a dozen townsfolk also pitched in.

At the western gate, Yarrow, Dan and Rev climbed the stairs to the parapets. The pale ruins glowed beneath the moon. Beyond them lay the mysterious, dark forest.

Dan set the torch into a crack in the wall.

"I remember stories about shi when I was a child," Rev said, taking the ale skin, "how truly good monks had this tremendous shi power. I don't get it. The Elder Fu told some of those stories, and he's a lot of things but he ain't no liar."

"The Elder Fu Vehma?" Yarrow said. "From Shendao monastery?"

Rev felt his face heat. "You know the Elder Fu?"

"Old friend." Yarrow got a distant look in his eye. "A very old friend."

He shook himself, like a cat preparing to go hunting. "Monks learnt shi from the dragon folk, who taught the monk Shendao in thanks for returning the Heart Jewel. So the stories tell, anyway." He tossed a copper into the air, caught it. "He taught his followers, and so on, right down to you."

"I could believe that," Rev said, handing the skin back to Yarrow, "but I've never known anyone who saw a dragon. They probably all died out."

"I always wanted to meet a dragon," Dan said.

"You got the strangest ambitions." Yarrow winked.

Silence wrapped the midnight land. A lone torch burned over at the hospital, and Rev morosely considered it. His latest shi exercise involved sensing the movement of energy at a distance, but little stirred tonight. He practiced every day, but shi was a lifetime study, fraught with failure, as when he probed the brass doorway but gained no sense of its purpose, even when trying to imagine the Disk helping him. A shi master would have done better. On the bright side, the Disk hadn't fried him for this latest attempt, though when he felt his emotions draining away, he quit immediately.

Rev showed the doorway to Yarrow, but his deputy had no idea what it was.

"Evil, Laia told you?" he said. "Those trollen are canny. It tells us something about the priestess Uulong, it truly does."

"I asked the town priest about Uulong, but he wouldn't say a thing."

"Maybe she ain't truly a priestess." Dan was nearly drowsing.

"Or maybe the goddess she worships ain't Luwana," Yarrow said, cryptically.

A golden light streaked past the corner of Rev's eye. He turned, but saw nothing more. Or did he? Puzzled, he furrowed his brows. Almost... another light flashed. Like a momentary halo, two lights circled Dan Zee's head, then whisked off and vanished.

"What was that?" Rev asked, amazed. "I thought I saw... you had falling stars around your head, Dan."

Suddenly Rev was wide awake, the hairs on the back of his neck rising. Was the Disk punishing him again for using it?

"Falling stars?" Dan chuckled. "Glad they didn't drop on me."

"Circling," Rev said, knowing it sounded foolish. "They, wait, I thought..."

Rev tried to bring forth the image of what he had seen. "Dragons. Little ones."

"I didn't see anything," Dan protested.

Rev *had* seen something hovering around Dan's head, but whatever it was did not return. Was it those dragonets? Nothing further happened, thankfully.

Yarrow started to tell stories. He had traveled the whole continent of Hazhe and told lurid tales of the wild Abar of the tents, fighting the Hebiru

...

over the sacred city of Pacesacre far to the west, and of the regimented Nipa, a nation of goblen who lived in holes on an island east of the Chisen empire. The goblen mage Xul Bil Be was from there. Yarrow's tales were mostly amusing, of people suffering for superior airs or scrappy heroes succeeding against powerful enemies, but each revealed a sympathy for the common person and a sorrow for the losses of life. Yarrow never played the hero in these tales, only an interested observer, occasionally the butt of a rough joke. He was a humble man, thankful, and he laughed often.

Their torch guttered and went dark. A few streets away, Los Fun's lantern bobbed along.

"Well," Yarrow finished the ale-skin, "time to turn in."

For the second time, Rev's eye was caught by a gleam in the darkness. "Over there. Do you see *that* light?" he hissed. This time, what he saw did not vanish – out beyond the ruins a line of faint, flickering lights wended through the woods, a ghostly procession, silent and solemn.

They gazed in wonder and unease.

The lights were a different color than the Disk, but there was still a feeling, like the Disk was getting involved in his life again. Should he pretend not to notice? Disregarding the Disk hadn't worked out well.

"We better find out what that's about," he said.

They descended the stairs, retrieved their bows, then found Los Fun patrolling the streets. The orcen watchman agreed to close the town gate behind them. It closed with a quiet thud, and they headed northwest, pursuing the lights. Yarrow guided them through the ruins and into the darkness under the trees without a stumble. Overtaking the lights, they found them to be torches carried by miners brandishing spears and pickaxes.

Rev, Dan and Yarrow snuck along behind. Ash Wal, owner of the silver mine, marched at the head of roughly forty men. With his scarred face and thick neck, he looked like a bruiser, but he wore a dark silk shirt and boots, with a kerchief around his neck and his hat at a jaunty slant, as though to be the very picture of a hero leading troops to battle. All for show. Rev did not much care for Ash Wal.

He felt an uncanny sense of watchfulness, in the darkness beneath the trees. Was that Watcher in the shadows here? He hoped not. The feeling only lasted a moment.

The miners entered a meadow, at the far side of which loomed two buttes marking the western edge of Bhat Sun's ranch. Between the buttes lay the wooden fortification of the Ruskiya refugees, completed since Rev last visited. Torches lit the walls, and along the palisade, Ruskiya guards watched. The column of miners hesitated.

The voice of Dunortha rang out. "Who are you in the depths of night come like thieves? Declare yourselves."

"Witch," called Ash Wal in his deep voice, "take your people and leave this valley. Go peacefully, or my men will burn your fort to the ground."

Rev was stunned. This he had not anticipated. He shouted, furiously. "You think no one knows you in the dark, Ash Wal? These refugees are my guests, do you forget?"

Yarrow rumbled. "Be aware, fellows, Rev ain't alone."

The miners stirred. In torchlight themselves, they could not see how many people hid in the darkness.

"Rev, these are Ruskiya, not Afen," Ash Wal argued. He rubbed at the scar on his face. "Common rabble. No one has a kick against your mercy, but this ain't no place for these folks. They'll bring the Murkung down on us. Murkung hate the Ruskiya."

"It doesn't matter if they do," Rev said coldly, "I've offered these refugees guest right, and I won't be dishonored."

"Our town ain't gonna be dishonored," declared Yarrow. The certainty in his bass voice was a fierce thing. Armies could break against that will.

A new voice broke in. "How many can you fight, Ash Wal?" It was Gabryal.

Rev was astonished, but glad she was here.

Branches rustled off to the right, as though fighters were forming a battle line. That would be Dan Zee, fooling the miners into thinking more people hid in the bushes.

The miners muttered uneasily, finding themselves between the armed Ruskiya and who knew how many townsfolk. None wanted to fight their neighbors, and all had heard of Gabryal's display of prowess with magical fire.

"I want the refugees out of here," Ash Wal shouted, his voice embarrassed and defensive.

"Then let's talk about it in a town meeting," Rev said, hunting for a peaceful solution. Ash Wal seized Rev's way out. "Tomorrow. We get our say. I'll hold you to that, Bounder."

The miners cheered. Holding his head up, Ash Wal led his men away, while Rev and Yarrow eased aside to let them pass, staying out of sight.

"Wise move, Rev," Gabryal said, after they were gone.

"Thank you for being here, Gabryal. I thought they might fight anyway, though Ash Wal doesn't have any White-Sashers among his miners, egging them on."

"Rev," called Dunortha, "again you trouble yourself for strangers. Your word is strong. We are in debt to you."

A rumble of agreement came from the men on the wall.

"I offered you guest rights, Lady," Rev said, his voice thick. "I ain't going back on my word." He could feel the presence of the Ruskiya in their camp, and he knew they felt him out here. It was good to have such allies.

"We are in the debt of you all, this we acknowledge. Tomorrow mid-morning, we ask you five to join us here."

"I'll be here, Lady," Rev said, fiercely.

"And I, Lady," said Yarrow, Dan and Gabryal all together.

"And I, Dunortha." Laia's voice rang out, surprising Rev while explaining Dunortha's count. The Ruskiya scouts were good. Rev smiled.

As Yarrow, Dan and Rev started for town, Gabryal and Laia emerged from the woods.

"Ma'tha stayed behind with an ill child." Gabryal explained. He saw by the shine in her eyes that the attraction between them was real. They walked side by side back to town, brushing arms, the heat growing between them.

"I'm glad you're here, Healers, but how did you know to come?" Dan asked.

Rev wondered if the Disk were directing them all. But why would it?

"Los Fun is a friend of mine from many years ago," Laia said. "He told us the direction you were headed, friends, and we deduced the rest."

#

The next morning, after Lot Sun had given Rev the week's pay and Dan went to buy breakfast, a knock sounded at the door.

To Rev's surprise he found Ash Wal outside the keep, head down, tail sweeping the dust.

"I was thinking maybe, Bounder, we don't got to, don't need that town meeting." The mine owner spoke in a stilted way, as though reciting words from memory. "I mean, since the whole town agreed to guest the refugees, probably I was out of line."

"We can let it pass, Ash Wal," Rev agreed, though he was puzzled.

"You understand, I didn't mean for it to come to a fight, I thought they'd just leave. They're nomads. They don't belong here, even they got to know that."

"The blood would have been on you," Rev said, disgusted.

"I dishonored my name." Ash Wal rubbed the scar on his face, acting uncomfortable, as though he had been told to say these words. "I'm gonna make it up to those I harmed." Ash Wal would not look Rev in the eye. "I'm sorry, Bounder. Wanted you to know that."

The mine owner walked away, leaving Rev to wonder if Ash Wal were just someone who led with actions rather than thought.

Rev had no idea how rash the mine owner would soon turn out to be.

Chapter Fifteen

"Delphin, the elven queen who first discovered magic, strove to counter Helgast's creation of the vampyren. She infused mud with the pure blood of Luwana to fashion a new race, breathed into their mouths to add her own spirit, then heated her new creatures with fire until they had life, creating humans. Perhaps this was blasphemy, for her efforts failed. The human folk were not wholly good; she worked in fear and so brought forth beings ideally fashioned for war. The other elven were loath to involve themselves with these new people. True, humans were creative and daring, but to the elven this just made them worse."
<u>*The Histories of Teren: The Age of Legend.*</u>

As Ash Wal departed up the street to the east, Yarrow and Dan came down the street from the north. "Biscuits and mountainberries for breakfast," Dan said, raising a basket he carried. Laia and Gabryal approached from the south, Gabryal leading their gelding.

"There's enough for all, Healers," Dan said cheerfully.

Gabryal wore her long green dress, over which she added a cream-colored shawl. Rev had never seen her so beautiful. Laia wore her grey cape, with a yellow blouse and dark green skirt, a pleasing combination with her dark eyes. Her antennae stretched out in anticipation above her triangular face. Even Dan sported a new buckskin vest, but Yarrow was the surprise of the morning in a red linen shirt and matching tri-cornered hat, with dark brown pants and boots of ornately tooled leather, showing off his golden hair and skin. Rev realized in mild surprise that Yarrow could be a bit of a dandy.

"It's Vosday, so we got paid, friends," Rev said to Yarrow and Dan. He handed out their coins, styling himself after Lot Sun's matter-of-fact manner, proud that Gabryal could see him as a man of means.

The day was cool, the heart of springtime, with a fitful wind. Along the forest path to the refugees' fort, trillium and lily-of-the-valley sent up shoots where the sun filtered through. Yarrow laughed at everything, delighted with the world, and flirted with Laia outrageously. She loved every minute of it. He seemed to sense a sadness inside Laia and worked to lift her spirits, and though neither took the flirting seriously, somehow, they seemed to understand each other on a deep level.

Yarrow and Laia easily kept up with the horses. Rev was more comfortable these days riding on Grace, and Gabryal as always looked born a-horseback, but Dan rode his horse grimly, since despite his recent purchase of the dun, Dan was not particularly happy atop a horse; he never knew where to drape his tail.

Gabryal and Rev rode side by side, and it felt good to be together, pointing out little discoveries, the rich, humid scents, a stone shaped like a fat dwarven, a jay's cry. At the fort, the Ruskiya guards let in the companions. The encampment was militarily clean. Everyone gathered in the central quadrangle as Dunortha approached, flanked by a middle-aged woman and by their war leader Kormenthon. Dunortha wore a leather dress, her necklace of claws, and knives in ornate scabbards on each hip, while her companions dressed in similar fashion, but did not wear necklaces. Eagle feathers adorned Kormenthon's hair. Before the Ruskiya clan, each companion was gifted. Yarrow, Dan and the women received silver scarabs, the men from Kormenthon, the women from Dunortha's own hand. Then Dunortha directed Kormenthon to give a necklace of gold to Rev she personally had crafted.

"The necklace protects you against the magic of our enemies, Rev," she explained. "Wear it and war magic does not touch you. So the Ruskiya pay their debt."

Rev had never been given such a grand present. "Thank you, Lady," he whispered, embarrassed they should see his tears. No one cried in the slums. To cover up, he explained how Ash Wal that morning had withdrawn his wish for a town meeting.

Dunortha was pleased. "You are strong, Rev. People respect you."

Girls in doeskin dresses brought chairs, so the honored guests might sit on each side of Dunortha. They enjoyed a feast while the young warrior Hunorn played mournful tunes on a stringed instrument. "Baile," he named the instrument, when Rev asked. The ceremony was strangely subdued, but as the music played Rev felt a kinship with the Ruskiya.

Somehow, he belonged here. He felt loyalty to these people and accepted by them; his emotions welled, as he sat with pride among his friends.

#

After the feast, Rev rode off alone to interview the goblen conjuror, Skarii. Atop the ridge that held her home, he reined in to look about. Eastwards, the Great Spice Road wended ribbon-like to the white peaks of the Hiyin mountains, Pillars of the World, to the south stretched a dozen farms in patchwork squares, scrubland beyond them, while westward lay the sharp hills and lush valleys of the Afen nation. He loved the vastness. Closer to hand, several paces away stood an unpainted shack, surrounded by a garden in which a goblen woman weeded.

She wore a purple dress, loose to allow for her four legs, and had silver wrist bangles, but she had not a single partner in view, much less the usual pod of six. Tall for a goblen, she was grey rather than brown. The stable master had explained the conjuror Skarii was cranky and could be deadly, Rev therefore approached with some trepidation as she straightened.

"T, t. That path isn't going anywhere." Her harsh, hissing voice was menacingly low in pitch. She did not speak with Afen honorifics. "You best be heading back the way you came."

"It brings me here, ma'am, and if you're the woman named Skarii, this is where I meant to come." Purple, yellow and white flowers poked their cheery heads out of an earthenware pot nearby. "Are those pansies?" he asked.

"Three different kinds, t, t, t." Her mandibles clicked warnings, but her voice softened. "You want your flowers easy-growing in a climate like this, it's harsh up here on the ridge. I am growing them for greens during the winter. Get some even under the snow."

"Wintergreen is good for that, too," said Rev, "but not such pretty flowers. I like gardens. Worked in one once."

"Tt, tt, you're looking for Skarii, you found her. What do you want?"

"I'm Rev, the new Boundskeeper. I'm trying to get to know people."

"I know who you are, now you are knowing who I am. Satisfied?"

"To know who people are, not just their names. For instance, why has a goblen woman settled among the orcen?"

She folded her arms. "T, t, t. I'm not seeing how that's your business."

153

"It might seem intrusive, but I figure understanding people will help me do my job. Don't goblen generally use two names? You must have a second one."

"You're not good at asking questions, are you?"

"I haven't been on this job very long." He felt awkward, but Skarii made no welcoming gesture. Grace shifted, stamped a foot and snorted, asking why he had not dismounted yet.

"Shows. T. I came here because I was wanting a change."

Rev did not trust her to tell the truth. She was a Chisen goblen and though the Chisen had their own notion of honor. They called it duty, but it amounted to the same thing. It did not apply to non-goblen, or even to goblen from the Nipa or Vien nations. An orcen of whatever nation would not lie, a Chisen would lie the moment it became convenient.

"The Chisen goblen mostly live in communities. You don't care for that?" he asked.

She contemplated him for so long he felt uncomfortable. He dismounted and led Grace to a tiny pond. The gusting wind nodded the flowers.

"I'm here for the magic. T, t, ttt." She clicked in a mirthful pattern, but sharply enough to deny any real humor. "Someone has been shipping raw magic from this town."

Everyone seemed to be in on some huge secret he was not. "What's raw magic?"

"Tt, you are an innocent, aren't you?" Skarii made no move to offer him a seat. He suspected she did this to gain an advantage. Grace having drunk her fill, he tied her to a sapling, away from the garden, but within reach of shade and good grass.

"T, t? You're from the Shendao monks, aren't you?"

"How did you learn that?"

"T. My imps told me. If you know the monks, you know what shi magic is."

"Shi ain't magic," he protested. "It's manipulated energy. Life energy. The energy of the world."

"That *is* magic, young man." She rattled her mandibles. "Come have a cup of tea. T, t, ttt, you're no threat to me."

Grateful at the invitation but nettled at such a casual dismissal, he followed her into the one-room shack. He sat at the rough wooden table while she revived the fire, put on water and brought out bread, dedicating two pairs of eyes to her work and one pair to him.

"Your shi is only one type of magic, Bounder. There are several more. T, t, take mine." A second pair of her eyes swiveled to him. "I conjure imps from the Other Side to do my bidding. T, useful fellows, usually invisible. Two of them behind you right now."

He repressed an urge to look around, but he did catch the faint odor of sweat that marked conjurations. She clicked with amusement at his stir of uneasiness.

"T, t, ttt, magicians of other schools use raw magic to increase their power. T. It is energy contained and concentrated in the earth. But raw magic is not useful for your monks, since they don't use it with shi."

Rev pulled out the glowing stone from his belt pouch. "I found this dropped in the woods. Is this raw magic?"

"Yes. T," she clicked thoughtfully. "Other schools of magic may or may not use raw magic. Take healing, which Ma'tha and Laia do so well and your girlfriend so poorly, it's a different sort of spell casting, not using raw magic."

Rev was lost between defending Gabryal's skills, denying she was his girlfriend, and asking what sort of magic healing was.

"You enjoy putting me off balance," he said.

"T, t, ttt. Just stating facts. I'm the person weighing everything before she makes a decision. Cautious, call me. Your Gabryal, she knows two types of magic, healing and elemental. T, t, ttt. Healing's a form of oracular magic, where the healer is seeing inside the body. No human is good at that, Gabryal's wasting her time. Ttt. Better to do like Ma'tha Mahn. Ma'tha uses a variation of conjuring, by asking trollen spirits to help her heal. Facts. Base your life on facts, you won't be going far wrong."

Skarii put the pot on the table, along with a plateful of cookies. He took one, and found it surprisingly sweet, tasting of molasses.

"T, t, elemental magic, which some folks are calling war magic, relies most on raw magic of all the disciplines, so maybe your friend Gabryal secretly came to this valley to find that raw magic, t?"

She finished a cookie with gusto, took another.

Gabryal knew about raw magic? He wondered if he believed Skarii. Somehow, he did, but that would mean Gabryal had dissembled. Honest Gabryal.

He grinned. He would have to ask her about that. Contrarily, he was liking Gabryal more as he discovered her flaws.

"Ain't spells dangerous even for the caster?"

"T, t? Who's been telling you that?"

"Personal observation. People get distracted. Distant. Cold, when they cast spells."

"I hadn't noticed. Goblen are not known for their warm, fuzzy personalities. T, t, ttt."

Rev laughed at her dry tone. "I suppose not. You've heard I'm interested in finding Bhat's killer?" He sipped his tea.

"T, you're the law, and the law is always trying to figure out who committed some crime. Me, I could care less, unless I did it, t, t, ttt." Her mandibles rattled cruelly.

"Who's been shipping the raw magic?"

"That I don't know, they stopped before I came here." She hissed in annoyance.

"Raw magic must be valuable," Rev said.

"People kill for it. I'm thinking there's a mine of raw magic around here."

She split the last cookie with him, and the gesture was not lost on Rev.

Rev felt pleased at finally getting somewhere. "Maybe that's what is drawing all the strangers. I've not been able to understand why there are so many new people in the valley."

"T. In addition to that Disk of Dragons people have been hunting, digging holes everywhere like sloppy dogs. Ttt. The Disk would be worth a hundred raw magic mines, since anyone who has the Disk can be calling a dragon. But what do you do with a dragon after you've called it?" She rinsed off the empty plate, put it back in a cupboard. "Or with the Disk, for that matter? How are you keeping anything that powerful from controlling you? T, t? No, leave me away from the Disk."

Skarii was cranky, but strangely, he trusted her to tell the truth; she was too no-nonsense to be devious, though she certainly seemed capable of holding back information, and she had one danger of the Disk straight. Uneasily, he remembered his own troubles with the Disk.

She clattered breezily. "T, t, are you suspecting anyone in particular of this murder?"

"Anyone who can use magic, especially elemental or conjurative. That would include Gabryal as well as that mage Xul Bil Be."

"Why, that would be including me as well." She clicked in mock horror.

Rev found himself enjoying this small, tough woman. "You ain't any more of a suspect than any other magic wielder."

"But I might be?" All her eyes focused on him, and he wondered if she were about to cast a spell. Instead, she clattered amusement.

"T, t, ttt, I like you, Bounder, nothing wishy-washy about you. And you sent that man to warn me against the karken, no one else ever did anything like that for me. Tt. I appreciate it, not that I need any such warning. Keep investigating, I won't hinder you. Might even clean out some of that riff-raff before you get killed. T, but stay out of my way, I do warn you that."

"I'll bother you as little as I can. But where were you the morning of the murder?"

"When was that?"

"The twenty-fourth of Dwarvenmoon."

"T. I was up here in my cottage all week, never left, no one visited." She looked amused. "No alibi, Bounder. T. I'll be giving you another thing to think on: before Bhat died, a ne'er-do-well vanished. Fellow named Zan Zan, an orcen. Thief, ttt, or at least no better than he had to be. Curious he'd be vanishing, too. No magic to him, as far as I know."

Rev stood. "I'll look into it. Thank you, Skarii."

She hissed. "T, t, be careful, human, it's deadly out there."

#

Rev rode through the streets of Zhopahr. He could check much of what Skarii said. He did suspect her of holding back information; why did she live so far from everyone else, for instance? With his mind in a turmoil, he felt an incredible urge to steal, and went to the marketplace, looking over the goods displayed on the tables: wool, clothing, hardware for the caravans. Much was small and easily pocketed. He was aware of the heavy weight of the brass doorway in his belt pouch, and felt guilty all over again.

Why did he want to steal, did he need any of these things? He reined in Grace. He never stopped before to ask why he stole. He had not had this strong a hunger to pilfer for weeks, so why now?

Asking the question led straight to its answer. He was scared of Skarii. She was a deadly woman and he did not understand her.

But why steal just because he felt some way? He did not want to be run by his emotions.

He felt someone's eyes on him. Yendre Pindo, the goblen rope maker. Was the White-Sasher looking for a weakness? The man's table was off by itself, since merchants on either side had shifted away, possibly because the priestess banned her people from dickering, which annoyed other merchants, dickering being like breathing to the Afen. Forgoing the joy of bargaining for set prices, where was the fun of that? Where was the sociability?

Rev himself enjoyed the faintly exotic flavor of the dickering, filled with friendly bantering, less businesslike than at the market in Shendasan. As the influence of the White-Sashers increased, other merchants took to dickering more furtively.

Tensions were growing, and Rev saw little to stop it. He clucked to Grace and rode on, the desire to steal having faded. He felt pleased with himself, though he could not have explained why.

#

Late in the afternoon, Gabryal collapsed onto a hospital bench, exhausted. She spent her time interviewing people, poking into alleyways, hunting through the ruins, searching for anything that might lead to the vampyren.

Laia entered the sitting room. "Dinner is ready, Gabryal."

Gabryal laughed. "Thank you, Laia." One practical use of an oracle companion, Laia always knew when everyone would be ready for dinner. It was unsettling, really.

She wanted to ask Laia more about the troublous idea of Rev and she being together, but the slump of Laia's antennae made her put aside her own concerns. "Are you not feeling well?"

Disk of Dragons

The trollen turned away, but Gabryal saw tears in her friend's eyes. The earthy stench of divinatory magic was thick.

"What is it?" Gabryal rose. "Something in the future?"

Laia bowed her head. "Nothing we can change. Some things are hard to understand, my friend. Sometimes you want to shake whoever made this world so difficult."

Gabryal gave Laia a hug. Over the last few days, her friend had been distracted and strangely sad, moving equipment around, failing to eat, staring out the doorway and whispering to herself. This must be around the anniversary of her daughter's death. Gabryal tried to recall if her friend had been so out-of-sorts last year at this time.

\#

As Rev and Dan finished mortaring the last row of stones, it was nearly nightfall. Yarrow was on patrol.

"Every day I work on this wall," Dan said, putting a last brick in place, "I grow more in awe of Yarrow's skills. I mean, he could even teach *you* about masonry. Now there's patience."

"Hey, hey," Rev objected. "I'm good at what I do."

"I can't even argue that, which is exactly my point. He's nearly single-handedly rebuilt the town walls, *and* the gates, *and* knocked down the nearby ruins that might lend protection to attackers. He could brick me up in a contest, he's that much better. You hired a genius in that man. All those goblen he got to help us with the wall? He's doing more work than all of them put together. He even has a few orcen volunteering."

This was the last section of the wall to be restored. The repaired areas still needed to be built up to the level of the battlements, but Rev felt more secure already.

As they put their tools into a sack, Rev spotted someone creeping over the wall.

Dan noticed as well. "Leaving town after the gates are closed?"

Rev and Dan snuck along the parapets to where the orcen was lowering himself down on a rope. Why had the man not simply walked out the gate before nightfall?

As the man reached the bottom of the wall, Rev recognized him. "Ash Wal, what are you doing?"

The mine owner ignored him, and walked away in a wooden, stumbling manner.

"Is he drunk?" Dan asked in an amused tone.

"Or ensorcelled." Rev did not know where that last thought came from. He grabbed the rope to follow, but something hissed past with an ugly sound, too fast to see.

An arrow, shot from outside the wall.

Dan and Rev flung themselves behind a merlon. Astonished, they peered through an embrasure, but saw no one. Rev's heart raced. "Another assassin."

"Or Ash Wal. Suddenly I'm very interested in where he is going," Dan said.

Easing along the wall, they studied the landscape, but did not spot the ambusher. Since neither had brought their bow, they dared not go over the wall after Ash Wal.

At last, frustrated, they made their way back to the safety of their keep.

"Ash Wal didn't shoot the arrow," Rev said, once inside. "I was watching him."

"Does that brawler Lum Tar owns a bow?"

"The thug I fought? That would make some sense. The way I see it, we're making the killer nervous with our investigation. We must be making progress, Dan, even if we don't know how."

"Exactly what is this progress, hunt-brother?"

"That is still a question, ain't it? You know, we could put you out there as bait next time, and watch to see who puts an arrow in you, that might work."

"Only if you give me hazard pay and take over the cooking."

"I've eaten my own cooking," Rev said mournfully, "I couldn't stomach that."

#

Near midnight, Ash Wal waited in the correct clearing in the woods, nervously rubbing his scar. Stars blazed. His skin felt clammy. Soon he heard the slow, controlled breathing behind him, and smelt the rot of mortal decay.

His heart pounded, and not entirely out of fear. To have such deadly strength, to be part of such an organization! Ash Wal was an aide to a great power, and the thought enthralled him.

"What did you find, servant?" the vampyren's voice came out muffled. Disguised.

Ash Wal explained the results of his spying.

"This happened last night? You saw it taking off in flight? So the presence I have sensed IS a dragon. That confirms how to proceed, well done."

Ash Wal felt an explosion of pleasure, only the second time he had been so rewarded. The pleasure went on and on, raging excitement and power and heady joy, increasing in intensity until it was painful, until he was screaming and tears sprang from his eyes. The sensation ceased, and Ash Wal collapsed, trembling, gratified by its power, by the offer, unspoken but assumed, that Ash Wal would someday control such power. The corpse of a rat landed on the turf beside him, used up by ritual magic. A red aura around it flickered and vanished.

"Master, what are we seeking?" Ash Wal kept his head down.

"That Boundskeeper has been asking you questions," the vampyren's voice turned icy. "You have curiosity now where you had none."

Ash Wal was consumed in a searing pain that lasted only a moment, but left him writhing in terror, excitement, and a yearning he dared not examine.

Then, to his surprise the vampyren chose to explain. "We seek the Disk of Dragons, which has sundry abilities to increase the power of our lord, the Cabalmaster. The Disk also serves as the key to open a certain Gate. Were the minions of Thana to find the Disk, the Goddess of Death could open that Gate and enter this world. We vampyren want no such god ruling us."

It paused. "You made amends to the Bounder?"

"I did, Master." Ash Wal clumsily regained his feet.

"Do not call such attention to yourself again, I need no tool watched by every sloven in town, the refugees are no threat to me. Now, show me where you last saw this dragon."

#

Later that night, deep in the woods, the vampyren stood behind Ash Wal, who was on his knees, chanting the simple, repetitive phrase it had taught him. The vampyren added a contrapuntal chant, building power that glowed in a scarlet haze around two orcen corpses sprawled at Ash Wal's feet, the remains of a couple newly arrived in town, whom none would miss for some time. The lives of a married couple could be leveraged off each other, making a spell far more potent. Why mortals made themselves vulnerable through love and marriage, the vampyren could not understand.

To perform ceremonial magic was to taste the life energy used, a heady feeling the vampyren rarely experienced, but tonight ceremonial magic was required to fight a dragon. No other magic was as potent. This spell required the vampyren's presence, no triggering the spell from a safe distance, and the cooperation of Ash Wal. This was his first ritual spell, and the depths of spiritual hunger and fear that affected unshielded casters of such magic would surely damage his mind. A necessary sacrifice.

Dragons hunted vampyren, so it was destroy or be destroyed, but since the vampyren was attacking from ambush, the odds were in its favor. No Child of Shadow voluntarily took on a dragon, but duty required it to remain in the valley, despite the vampyren's nearly insane fear of death; the Cabalmaster, Lord of the Vampyren, was not to be disobeyed. The Watcher was here, with its attendant sense of expectancy. The vampyren felt sure this spell was what the Watcher wanted from him.

Since the spell would be traceable at completion, any who followed back the spell would be led here, and a dragon would come quickly indeed. Of course, the vampyren intended the spell to succeed, after which the dragon would not matter, and the ritual magic would create a channel allowing the vampyren to capture its life's energy.

This spell would liquefy earth and stone, sinking the dragon and trapping it forever as the stone re-solidified, an ideal use for a ceremonial spell, as ritual magic was a magic of destruction and re-ordering. Of course, great magic often went awry, but the vampyren had protections, and if the local mortals died, well, more would breed.

The night was at its oldest, when other races slept most deeply. Careless fools. Run by petty emotions and passions, they deserved to die.

The vampyren's hand flicked, and a wave of force lashed out through the earth into the ruins that ringed the town, melting walls and buildings as it went. Countless red lights flared everywhere, the souls of beings rising where they died, the lights flickering as though whipped by a firestorm raging through the ether. The physical devastation headed straight at the dragon in its den in the ruins. The stench of decay exploded.

The vampyren miscalculated. The dragon *was* aware of the vampyren, and cast a counter-spell using shi, reflecting the original spell right back at the vampyren.

Only survival skills honed through eons saved the vampyren: it had already prepared a counterstroke. The original spell, reflecting back, struck the counterstroke, and the power of both deflected sideways.

Straight at the sleeping town of Zhopahr.

Chapter Sixteen

"When these faithful souls approach, dear Goddess Luwana, we ask that You not close Your Heart, but take them to Your Peace, and may Your Light that shines through shadows lead them home. May Your boundless Light lead us home to You."
"Chant for the Dead," from <u>The Book of Vos</u>, Chapter 6, Verse 12.

Gabryal jerked out of her sleep, confused. "What...?"

Ma'tha slumbered on, in her own bed. Laia was lying down, whispering the intonations of a prayer. The three women slept in the curtained-off area at the back of their small house. Nothing was wrong, Gabryal thought, relieved, only a dream.

Her eyes took in the bowls of water magic on the table, where the water was sloshing and glaring red: the vampyren had cast a spell of ceremonial magic. A huge one.

Rumbling started.

"Earthquake!" Rev shouted in the distance.

The world went mad. Gabryal screamed as the floor liquefied beneath her bed. She was thrown against the wall, only to have it collapse. The bed sailed through, with her perched precariously on top. Dust billowed, and her bed disintegrated. A chasm yawned beneath her. She grabbed a beam of lumber sliding along, and was yanked away from the hole.

The beam slammed into an obstruction, flinging her into the air.

She landed on the stone steps of the town wall. The wall swayed, then settled. Terrified, she looked out in the dawn and saw the profound chaos after someone lost control of magic.

A band of *darkness* crossed the sky. The air crackled, the ground boiled like a tide around jagged rocks, and buildings shuffled like feeble old people from spot to spot, until one after another they collapsed. A deep, grinding roar blocked out thought.

Disk of Dragons

A tragedy large enough takes on a spirit those inside apprehend directly, as though we can look out and see the Gods marching above, eyes cold and bright, raining destruction and plucking up souls. The world is revealed as directed, callous and cruel.

A scarlet butterfly hovered above a swaying flower, unable to land in the chaos. Gabryal prayed for it to find a safe perch.

The earthquake ended. Silence reigned under a grey sky, then screams arose. People trapped in the rubble. The sense of the uncanny evaporated. Concern for Gabryal's comrades flooded her. She raced up the street.

Rev was at the ruins of her home, digging with his bare hands. "Gabryal!"

"I'm here."

He spun and gathered her in his arms, but she broke away. "Ma'tha and Laia must still be trapped in the house."

Rev threw himself back to work, flinging aside lumber, rocks and trash. Digging beside him, Gabryal was amazed at his power. Seemingly unaware he was doing so, he used magic to help lever out each piece of rubble. They cleared away a collapsed wall. One, then two people crawled out: Laia and Ma'tha, dazed, frightened, covered in grime.

"Four patients were in the hospital," Gabryal told Rev.

Rev turned to the rubble-buried hospital, as she treated her companions for their injuries.

Cries and moans filled the air where half-a-dozen buildings had collapsed. Dan Zee pulled a woman from under a fallen wall. People stumbled about in shock.

The miner Ash Wal stood in the ruined street, mumbling.

The hospital's roof had partially caved in. Gabryal prayed their patients survived. Laia had a deep cut on her leg and Ma'tha received a blow to the head. After treating their injuries, Gabryal helped Rev, who was like a man possessed, a circle of shi-calm surrounding him. An hour's glass passed and he did not slow in his work.

An orcen couple joined their efforts to tunnel into the wreckage. They found one person, then a second, both unconscious. As Gabryal bound their bloody wounds, Rev carefully uncovered the body of a young woman. She was gone, nothing he could do. Tears coursed his cheeks.

Finally, Rev found the body of the last patient. The small boy had been recovering from a pierced belly; now he was dead, his body broken. The couple working alongside them were the boy's parents. The mother gave a heartrending cry and flung herself down beside her child.

Rev stood respectfully for a moment, then joined Yarrow and Dan, digging at another building.

"Follow him, friend," Laia said to Gabryal.

Surprised, Gabryal saw the trollen was sitting up, grimacing at the wound to her right leg, antennae stiff with determination.

"These I can tend." Laia waved at their patients.

"I thought you could read the future, Laia. Why couldn't you avoid this?"

"Some things cannot be avoided without worse consequences."

Not understanding, Gabryal hurried after Rev. She was astounded at how much rubble Yarrow and Dan had cleared, half a building. In short order, Rev and Gabryal helped find two more people. Rev's Ruskiya friends came in and set to work, as did the conjuror Skarii.

#

Three days later, numb with shock and grief, they called off the search for survivors. The last few victims they merely reburied with blackstones. As best Rev could tell with shi, no one still lived under the rubble. Sixteen people had died, forty were wounded but likely to survive, two had simply disappeared.

In the next few days, Rev used shi to find places where the homeless could safely rebuild and Yarrow, Dan and he pulled down several unsafe buildings.

Even a half-dozen thugs came to help, dirty, tough men who risked their lives to save people whom in other circumstances they might have robbed. Khat Trun was not among them.

Afterwards, Rev offered these men the peace of the town if they gave up their outlaw ways. All but one accepted. The life of an outlaw was harsh and the money slight. Something in their past had set them on the wrong trail, now with a chance to change and the gratitude of the community for support, they leapt at the chance for a legitimate life.

The one who declined said he could not live here after the horrors he had seen digging up the bodies. He made his goodbyes on a drizzly

Sennaday, then set off on the south trail, declaring he wanted to learn for himself whether it ended at the sea.

#

One cool afternoon, after the healers finished with their patients, Gabryal called a meeting with Ma'tha and Laia in an exam room that had survived. Her alarm spell had warned of ceremonial magic cast just before the earthquake, which implied a vampyren killed all these people. That vampyren must face justice.

More and more Gabryal found herself making decisions. Laia withdrew into herself, perhaps reminded by the tragedy of her own lost daughter.

Ma'tha managed her healing, but something had broken inside her, and she came fretfully to Gabryal for even simple decisions. Only when Gabryal solicited opinions on how to shore up a wall or reconstruct beds did Ma'tha act more like her old self. Her interest in men became all-consuming.

Gabryal, on the other hand, felt more decisive. Though she had not the healing talent of Laia or Ma'tha, she could do much even without magic. "We need to warn the Chapter House, friends, someone must let the Abbess in Khav know a vampyren is here."

Each Chapter of the Grey Order had a House run by an Abbess. The closest Chapter House stood in Khav, two weeks journey westward.

"I will go, my friends," Laia said.

"You're the best healer, Lady," Ma'tha objected. "Anyway, it's dangerous. I can go."

The trollen woman shook her head. "I have *foreseen* this. It is my journey to take."

After a moment, Gabryal said, "So be it. You're strong enough to take care of yourself on the road, Lady, probably better than either of us could."

The trollen bowed her antennae in acknowledgment. "A fight comes, like a wall of thunderclouds approaching. Take care of yourselves, and remember my affection for you."

Then she nearly whispered, "When the time comes, Gabryal, have Rev bring me home to my people." The loamy scent of a foretelling mingled with an icy sense of despair.

167

"Don't worry," Gabryal said, confused but determined to fight that despair. "The Abbess will send you back, we'll see you in a month." She hesitated. "Won't we?"

"To *see* the future, we choose the Goddess' Will, not our own," Laia said, sadly.

#

The next morning, under a gloomy sky, the town held a sorrowful ceremony in their small cemetery, commending the victims to the Goddess Luwana. Gusts of cold rain fell. It was the 19th of Trollenmoon, but felt like a day much earlier in the season.

Rev and Dan stood off to one side, Rev trembling with fury as the town priest delivered the eulogy. Rev had discovered the trail of destruction that expanded in a cone into the ruins, a path that veered straight for the town, proof of a magical basis to that earthquake. Someone had attacked their town and deliberately murdered people.

"Everything I've tried has failed," Rev murmured to Dan. "All these people are dead that I was charged with protecting. If I'd done my job better, they could have been saved."

Dan kept his voice low as well. "That's too harsh. You did everything you could to help."

But as the mourners departed after the memorial, the White-Sasher Kek Nin strode over. "Rev, I blame you. My wife died and you're at fault. You caused this."

Gabryal and Ma'tha were just approaching.

"You think Rev caused the earthquake, orcen?" Gabryal asked in disbelief.

"The displeasure of the Goddess is on him. He must come to Temple, make homage and ask forgiveness." The White-Sasher marched away.

"What was that about, Rev?" Gabryal asked.

"I have no idea, Gabryal." But Rev remembered the stolen brass doorway. His face heated. Everything he ever did wrong came back to humiliate him.

Gabryal studied him. "Evidently the White-Sashers are mad at you for something. Be careful, they're not ones to take lightly."

Rev and Dan walked the two women back to the hospital.

"Where's Laia?" Rev asked. "Taking care of patients?"

Gabryal shook her head. "She's preparing to leave this afternoon."

"To ask for more healers?" Rev shook his head. "So much damage done. Who could wield the power for such a massive spell?"

Gabryal hesitated. "Rev, the spell that caused the earthquake was ceremonial magic."

"Ceremonial? Like from a vampyren? Why?"

"For something the vampyren wanted badly, or feared greatly. That spell was aimed into the ruins, but reflected back at its sender, before it deflected into town."

"So there was a fight?" It would explain the path of destruction.

"A thwarted attack, I would say. The town may have only been hit by chance."

Slowly, he nodded. "So who did the vampyren attack?"

"Someone strong enough to turn aside such a deadly spell."

"The vampyren is still responsible for all those deaths," Rev said. "It cast that spell to hurt someone. I'm off to ask Xul Bil Be some questions. That spell started near his tower."

They came to the hospital door, but this was not the time to be courting, and Gabryal went inside without a kiss. Rev longed for more normal times.

#

Rev smacked on the door of the tall tower in which the goblen mage Xul Bil Be lived. The rain stopped, but a foggy mist remained, cloaking the disquieting sculptures, birds and fountains and strange creatures all around. No sculpture was finished. He remembered none from his previous visit, and had the uneasy sense that each was forming with infinitesimal slowness from the landscape itself – here stood a bird that had been a log, there a fountain lifted where he was sure a small pond once lay – as though the land itself took on form and intent, becoming alive, giving shape to an ancient, powerful hate. The area was silent, oppressive. No birds whistled. Rev felt as though eyes spied on him, but that only made him more angry.

The door opened to reveal the golden-skinned goblen conjuror, resembling a hulking cockroach. "Yes?" Xul Bil Be sneered. No honorific, no politeness.

"Why are you here in the valley?" Rev demanded.

169

"Tt." Xul Bil Be clicked his mandibles in surprise at Rev's vehemence. "For research."

"On what?"

The mage's mandibles clattered contemptuously. "You wouldn't understand."

"I got a town full of people mourning their dead children. They deserve answers. I won't let you put me off again. Once more, why are you in the valley?"

Xul Bil Be turned to leave, but Rev put his shoulder against the oaken door, keeping it from closing. "I'm not through with you."

The mage's eyes took on a flat, insane quality. Rev didn't care. They matched stares.

"There's been raw magic shipped from this valley," Rev said. "But raw magic ain't used in conjurations. A conjuror, that's all you are, right? Not a practitioner of some other sort of magic that uses raw magic?"

"T, t, t. If you wish to live, you had best leave."

"The earthquake was caused by magic, ceremonial magic from a vampyren."

The man's features flickered. Fear? No, pride. Pride at the power of the spell.

"You," Rev said, disbelievingly. "You cast the spell. You killed those people."

Xul Bil Be smiled in contempt. "Mortal, you are a fool to admit you know that."

Rev grabbed for Xul Bil Be's throat.

Xul Bil Be knocked away Rev's hands with amazing speed. The mage spat out two words. A name? Something landed heavily on Rev's shoulder, and a sharp pain stung his neck. He stumbled under an engulfing weakness. Crushed by the weight of a conjured imp, Rev fell to his knees, his emotions confused as it sucked at his life energy, draining him.

He slapped at the imp, but his hand passed through it. The imp was insubstantial.

He slammed himself into the base of the mage's tower, but that did not dislodge it.

Xul Bil Be watched hungrily, until a disembodied mouth appeared and whispered something. The mage reluctantly nodded. "I am most unfortunately called away. I would have enjoyed the taste of your mortal soul, human."

The vampyren entered the tower and closed the door.

Weakening rapidly, Rev visualized shi as a hammer and struck at the imp. The draining paused, but resumed. Desperate, he stumbled away down the slope, hoping the beast would quit if he fled. He yearned to lie down, to rest.

He needed to think. It was his only chance.

Could he use the Disk somehow? He looked for a path to the Other Side, and found the faint glowing line. He must trust the magic of the Disk. He strove for the calmness that shi demanded, and started down the path. He entered that dim, second world, where no tower stood.

The imp still clung to his neck.

Maintaining his centeredness against the fear, he struck at the imp with shi. The weight lessened. He attacked from a different angle to push it away, then used shi to form a vortex which sucked at the beast. As it countered that, he reversed the flow of energy.

The creature flipped off his shoulder.

He flung wave after wave of shi at the creature to keep it away as he scrambled down the path. The moment he reached the mundane world, he abandoned his view of the Other Side. The golden path vanished. The imp did not follow – he had escaped.

He collapsed to the ground. Was this how Lord Bhat had died, his life sucked out? Rev's hand grasped the necklace Dunortha gave him. It was supposed to protect against magic, but against war magic, not conjurations. The necklace was evidently of limited use.

At last, he rose and headed for the healers.

#

When it is given to the wisest prophets to know the hour of their own deaths, they may choose the manner in which it arrives and so affect the world. Great good can come from such a sorrowful choice, though so often more is risked than a single life, we are glad such a gift is rare.

Along the Great Spice Road, strange funguses and strangling vines covered the trees in the gloom of evening, and oppression and fear hung about a foggy hollow into which the road dipped. Laia along walked steadily as movements stirred the undergrowth, as though demons from the hells tracked her. She ignored the rustles, and the sense of watchfulness. The scent of loam was strong, burying the stench of decay.

Out of nowhere, the vampyren Xul Bil Be appeared beside the road, a black skeleton with flames for flesh, shadowy wings, claws and fangs poised, a magnificent use of ceremonial magic calculated to make its victim hesitate, terrified, for one fatal instant.

Laia had already paused. She had an air of calm acceptance, which gave her power against the terror of ceremonial magic.

"Trollen," Xul Bil Be said, annoyed she had spoiled its dramatic entrance, "my imp warned me some magic wielder fled to Khav for help, but I did not expect you." Its eyes narrowed. "You knew I would find you here. Why have you come anyway?"

"Child of Shadow, you have weakened yourself uselessly." She looked pleased, *seeing* this truth. "Your power is nearly depleted, and you will never gain it back."

"Quiet, mortal," Xul Bil Be hissed. "I have strength enough to kill you." But Xul Bil Be felt wary. Her words were disturbing because some were true; the earthquake spell had drained the vampyren, but the dragon still lived. Not that this would avail the trollen, but why had she come here? Trollen were the hardest mortals to kill, since they could foresee enough to avoid their own deaths; nevertheless here she stood, defiantly.

"Are you a trollen that cannot see the future?" Xul Bil Be speculated.

She waited, her eyes bright with determination. "I am of the Seven."

The vampyren hesitated. One of the Seven of Gy Pe? How could one of the Seven be here? The vampyren grew furious. This was a trick.

Xul Bil Be would not let her pass, for cruelty was in the vampyren's nature. It showed its fangs, knowing she must perceive what was to come, and who could know their own future without despair? Oracular magic was most disheartening for its wielder. Though trollen rarely chose death, mortals were foolish, and if she were of the Seven, her death would replenish its power, by giving it her life energy. The vampyren ignored its own rising panic, knowing it must act coolly.

Xul Bil Be cast an elemental spell of flames at her, but like a huge mantis she lashed straight through the flames at the vampyren. As Xul Bil Be leapt back, a stone turned under its feet. It stumbled.

Her teeth went for its throat, but as Xul Bil Be twisted away she bit deep into its arm instead. Panicked, the vampyren drove its own fangs into the back of her neck, and gave a tremendous shake. Her neck snapped. The trollen collapsed to the ground, lifeless.

Standing over her corpse, Xul Bil Be trembled at how close it came to dying. The vampyren felt an agonizing pain in its arm; the magic of healing could also bind two beings together. She bound herself to the vampyren through her bite. Had that been the point of her attack? Why bind herself to one of the Shadow Folk when the act cost her life?

Xul Bil Be breathed deeply, reassuring itself the trollen no longer mattered. She was dead.

Annoyingly, her attack foiled its intent to replenish its strength with her life force. She had outwitted it. In fact, the vampyren was worried by how vulnerable it was. It had gambled, thinking its spell would kill the dragon. Although the vampyren expended much strength, the death of a dragon would return power tenfold, but the dragon remained alive. Centuries had passed since Xul Bil Be had last been so bereft of power. Worse, the vampyren could not withdraw to rebuild power, since the Cabalmaster demanded that Xul Bil Be keep hunting the Disk.

Xul Bil Be cringed. The Lord Kukulque was not a forgiving master. The vampyren would rather die at the hands of mortals than face the Cabalmaster after shirking its duty.

Now that despicable mortal Rev had driven Xul Bil Be from its lair, the vampyren worried about its peril. And the pain in its arm was not lessening, meaning the wound from the trollen was not healing correctly. Disgusted, Xul Bil Be kicked the corpse and departed.

#

On a pallet in the hospital recovery room, Rev lay regaining his strength, aided by some foul-tasting tea Ma'tha kept forcing on him. He felt like a small boy taking his medicine, which tasted like black tar melted into a liquid, but each mouthful brought back more energy, so he drained off the latest cup. Then, just as he sat up despite the protests of Ma'tha and Gabryal, a small light incandesced in the other room.

"The bowls have lighted," Gabryal said in a tense voice. "A spell was cast. Out west."

An amulet around Ma'tha's neck flashed.

"Oh, dear Goddess. Laia's been attacked."

The women raced for the door. Rev struggled to his feet. Outside, the women went for their horses. Fighting weakness, Rev ran for his own horse, determined not to be left behind. He would not let Laia down. He reached the stable, saddled his horse on the double, and rode out to the street as the women cantered their horses past.

They took to the road at a gallop. Rev gritted his teeth against the pain and held onto the pommel with both hands, thankful that Grace kept her pace smooth.

Eventually they had to slow or risk injuring their horses, but they pushed on as quickly as they could.

Gabryal explained as they rode. "I added a spell using water magic, linking Ma'tha's amulet to the one Laia wears, so each warns of danger to the other."

Rev grimaced. "What sort of attack was it, Gabryal?"

"Ceremonial magic."

"The vampyren, then. And you have magic specifically set to tell you that." The wind blew past as the horses' hooves thudded. "You're hunting that vampyren, ain't you?"

She made no answer.

"The vampyren is Xul Bil Be," he went on. "When I told him the earthquake was started by ceremonial magic, he admitted the spell was his and attacked me."

She looked at him in amazement. "You were lucky to survive." She shook her head. "It doesn't even make sense. But you always have been full of secrets and tricks. One must have helped you this time."

#

Late that night, they came to a hollow in the hills, where the setting moon cast a pale, noble light upon a slender figure lying in the road.

"Laia!"

Gabryal jumped off her horse and dropped to her knees beside her friend.

Ma'tha dismounted and lit a torch, which showed Laia in the dust, the snarl on her face looking strangely triumphant.

Gabryal looked up, tears streaming down her face. "Dead. I failed her."

She drew a silver amulet, half melted, from around the dead woman's neck. It was the scarab Laia received from Dunortha. "The magic protected her from elemental magic, but that wasn't enough."

"A powerful vampyren, my friends," Ma'tha said, "to use conjurations and elemental magic, not just ceremonial spells."

Rev remained on his horse, bow ready. The hollow made him uneasy. He had a sense of despair, and the stench of decay was strong; the traces of a magic battle.

"Are all the Grey Women vampyren hunters?" he asked.

"We swore an oath not to discuss our mission," Gabryal said.

"One last question, then. Does ceremonial magic use raw magic?"

She looked at him, bleakly. "Yes."

"So maybe that's why the vampyren is here. At least we know what Xul Bil Be looks like."

Gabryal shook her head. "No, the vampyren mimic the features of the mortal races. This vampyren can look like anyone. It will just take on a different face now."

They built a fire and camped beside the road, then blackened their faces with dirt and ashes in mourning, tore their clothes and held vigil for the dead, while Gabryal fought back her tears to sing the old, slow dirges. Afterwards, Rev held her as she cried, and Ma'tha sat head down, her shoulders shaking.

Great loss is too hard to take in all at once. The body must absorb it, little by little. Grief is a loss the body feels first, a physical blow.

"Laia was so strong," Gabryal whispered. "She never talked much. She was shy, but truly loyal. She took good care of me, making sure I ate, that I dressed warmly enough. She paid such attention to everyone around her."

Ma'tha nodded. "You wouldn't think it, but she loved little practical jokes, frogs on your pillow, those sorts of things. Gentle though, nothing hurtful ever."

"I thought she could see things coming," Gabryal said. "Why couldn't she avoid this?"

The hollow in the hills was an alien place, and they huddled near the protection of their fire as mortals have for endless years, facing the overwhelming dark. Ma'tha seemed overcome by this last deed, and said little the rest of the night.

At dawn they raised a pyre, and with cleansing flames released her spirit to its journey, the practice of the trollen race. Then they recited verses from The Book of Vos.

Finished, Rev cast around for tracks, but found none departing the area.

"Vampyren can Cross Over, remember," Gabryal said.

Rev nodded reluctantly. Now was not the time to follow it to the Other Side, when it might expect them to give chase.

Once the flames cooled, Gabryal gathered the ashes to be returned to Laia's family. They raised a marker in her memory, then departed for Zhopahr.

So no warning reached the Chapter House of the Grey Women in Khav, and the plots of the vampyren were left to increase, unimpeded. Would the Chapter House have survived, otherwise? Perhaps, but the vampyren were ever a devious race.

Chapter Seventeen

"Of Artifacts there be Nine:
the Disk of Dragons opens the Hall of the Empire;
the Trollen Rose gives understanding for alliance;
the Vampyren Labyrinth allows passage to the heart's desire;
the Gnomen Eagle answers an honest question;
the Wolfen Cup heals the earthly wound;
the Elven Lance guides the victory in battle;
the Dwarven Scales returns the needed wealth;
the Orcen Staff reveals liar and the lie;
the Heart of Light brings in the God Outside."
"Closing Passage," from <u>The Chronicles of Sinnesemota</u>.

The next morning the town held a ceremony honoring Laia, including a stirring eulogy by the night watchman Los Fun, who related that Laia once saved his life. The day was bright, the wind kicked up dust enough to make the eyes water.

What could be said after such a loss? Too soon, the wind alone would know her name, still, she was loved and would be missed. Sweet Laia.

After the service, Ma'tha passed a blackstone to gather the wishes of the townsfolk, then departed to bury it where Laia had died. Yarrow tagged along, after a quiet request from Rev that he keep an eye on her. Not that Rev believed even Yarrow could do much against a vampyren, but from now on people should travel in groups whenever possible.

Gabryal and Dan accompanied Rev to the vampyren's tower, since Rev wanted to examine it, despite his lingering weakness from the imp. Reaching the tower, they found the door ajar. All was silent in the strange landscape; no water ran in the eerie fountain, only a slimy pool remained. The place felt abandoned.

He led the others inside, where they found the main room empty, aside from a few broken cages and debris on the stone floor. The layout was similar to the Bounder's keep, with a first floor comprised entirely of the main room, and stairs against the circular wall leading to the upper floor.

"Looks like no one has been here for centuries." Dan gazed at a dusty altar beside an ancient fireplace.

"Oh, a vampyren lived here," Gabryal said grimly. "The landscape outside is twisted. The earth itself rebels at the evil of their magic."

Drawing his sword, Rev led the way up the staircase. The upper floor consisted of a single circular room, where the dust was thick, seemingly undisturbed. Taking his father's sword in hand was oddly comforting, as though his father were somehow looking down, protecting him.

"I intend to bring this vampyren to justice," Gabryal said.

"Please don't go after Xul Bil Be hotheaded," Rev said. "Vampyren have been hunted a lot over the years, and they're still around. Best be cautious."

Gabryal gave him a tender glance. "Thank you for your concern."

Frisson sparkled between them. It had been too long since they had taken time for each other. So much had happened, and they both shared a hunger, a yearning for relief, for affirming that they were young and alive, with reason for hope.

Dan interrupted. "Gabryal, do you have magic that can track Xul Bil Be?"

Gabryal turned from Rev. "I can try."

She took small bowls from her slingbag, and filled each with water from Rev's canteen. But the seeking spell refused to work properly. The water did glow, proving the vampyren had been here, but each bowl glowed equally, showing no direction to seek it, despite her trying until the air grew redolent of ozone.

At last she gave up. "Vampyren have been foiling spells for a long time."

Her face was washed free of emotion, so that she seemed withdrawn and numb, noticeable after the electricity between them so recently. A dangerous disassociation occurred after wielding magic, Rev concluded.

"If we're done in the tower," Gabryal said, "I'm going to search the area, see if I can learn where the monster went."

"You can't go into the woods alone after a vampyren," Rev objected.

"This is what I do, Rev. Someone has to face them, bring them to justice for their acts."

"I'll go with you."

She nodded, but acted ambivalent about having his company. So, after Dan went back to guard the town and the two headed into the woods, Rev kept quiet, giving her time. Women were tricky, that was sure.

As the day passed, he admired her sense of purpose, and at one point, she commented on his skill in the woods, which kindled a glow of pleasure in him. She seemed to find as much comfort in their friendship as he did, but they had no success in tracking down the vampyren.

At nightfall they gave up.

#

The next day Rev headed out eastward, on a different mission, following directions from Yarrow. His neck and shoulder ached, lingering effects of that battle with the imp. By mid-morning, he found a spot in the woods to hobble Grace in a meadow close by a fast-running stream with plenty of forage.

Upstream and on the far side of the stream lay a camp matching Yarrow's description of the hideout of the thugs. The camp was a mess, neither cabin had a door, the latrine was not far from the stream, and debris lay everywhere, but the thugs were not slack about everything – two lookouts perched on bluffs near the road.

Rev approached, careful not to break any branches underfoot, intending to confirm an assault could succeed coming down off the ridge behind the camp. The thugs had been causing trouble long enough. Rev studied the ground for any tracks having a notch out of the heel, but the thugs had not wandered into the woods since the last rain. He heard shouts and hoped they might be quarreling, but they were simply noisy. The stream burbled past, hidden in the bracken.

He studied his route and decided the brush near the water was too thick, he must retreat up the ridge or cross the stream over a nearby fallen tree. On the far bank, the soil appeared disturbed by tracks. Was there any way across this stream other than the tree trunk? He felt uneasy, but attributed that to the nearness of the enemy.

He crawled onto the tree trunk out over the water, sneaking closer. Halfway across the stream, he felt a surge of power as the air itself hardened into a snare.

Magic.

He threw himself off the trunk, head-first into the water. The trap tightened around his leg, but the current yanked him downstream, and he slipped free.

An invisible bell rang, the sound reverberating through the woods. The magical scent of burnt roses flared, and shouts arose.

He tumbled down the stream like a rag doll, grabbing for shi to help traverse this chute, but too desperate to calm himself. He smacked against a rock that nearly knocked the breath out of him. He seized the rock, but the deluge shoved against him, loosening his hold.

Again he sought tranquility, falling into the discipline he practiced daily. His grip failed and he slid away downstream, but the pause gave him a chance to sense shi. He drew in the power to guide his way down the chute of water, avoiding rocks. He even turned to travel feet first.

The shi heightened his exhilaration, until he was bursting with joy and a sense of invulnerability. A delusion. Too late, he noticed the stream dropped over a waterfall. Over he went, plunging into a shockingly cold pool, where the powerful current sucked him under.

The current rushed through a narrow crack in the rocks, pinning him against the crack. He desperately levered himself upward, trying to reach the surface, but the current slammed him back. His head banged the stone. Darkness surged.

His lungs labored. Fighting panic, he tried to draw himself away with shi, but the water focused too much energy through the crack. He sought for any shi not following the power raging through the crack. There. A small line of energy angled off.

He aligned himself with this thin line of power, and kicked his legs and arms with all his might.

He popped straight upward, launching half out of the water with the force of the energy.

He lunged at a shelf of rock and caught it, clinging by his fingers, gasping in huge breaths as the churning pool sucked at his waist and legs.

With his last strength, he pulled himself from the pool onto the shelf of rock.

Stunned, he lay panting. Darkness pulsed at the edge of his vision.

At last, he rolled over on his back. Well, that was one way to learn to work shi. He smiled wanly; but he was still stuck down a hole, feeling wobbly, with the enemy coming. The pool lay in a stone cauldron formed by falling water over countless years, its sheer walls rising to twice his own height. Water poured out through the crack at one end of the pool, but he was not skilled enough to redirect the water's energy to lift himself out of the hole.

The thugs would be looking for him. The walls of the cauldron overhung the pool, so if he wedged himself back against the stones he would be hard to see. Maybe he could use shi as a cloak to hide himself further.

A log lying on the shelf gave him an idea. He dropped one end into the water, then shoved. Sure enough, the log sank and caught at the spot the water drained through the cleft in the rocks below the surface, a dark mass difficult to see in the current.

He heard men approaching and sat. Be just another part of the landscape, he told himself, ignoring his throbbing shoulder. Be calm.

"Goddess of Death, he must've slipped off that log like a turtle, slicker'n mud down a hole." Khat Trun's mocking voice rose above the others. "Or that spell would've caught him."

The thugs gathered at the edge of the cauldron, almost directly above Rev.

Be part of the landscape.

"Boss, you think he might survive the stream?"

"Don't want to say too soon."

"Remember Olk Stuy, Boss?" came Lum Tar's surly voice.

"He was drunk," said Khat Trun. "Don't count. Found him in this pool, though."

"Hey. Something IS in the water," said Lum Tar. "You think he's trapped down there?"

"Why, I believe he is." Khat Trun roared. "Fool got his foot stuck."

The thugs whooped. A few edged around the cauldron, looking into the water.

P M F Johnson

Be part of the landscape.

"Shall we fetch him out?"

"Nah. Let him rot." A burst of laughter.

"Ale jar to go around when we get back to camp," Khat Trun shouted.

That got their attention. They cheered, and headed back for camp. Their voices faded into the distance.

With an effort, Rev brought himself back from his state of serenity. It was difficult, perhaps because he was so tired, as though all his emotions had washed away. Was shi sucking his self away? Was the use of magic a huge, subtle trap?

Fear jolted him, helping him to recover. Anyway, he had learned the thugs had magic, and their spell had the same stench of the magic that killed Bhat Sun.

Khat Trun had just become the primary suspect in the murder.

Rev focused on escaping the cauldron. A quarter of the way around the pool, there was a place in the wall with enough handholds that he thought he could do it. Problem was, to reach the first handhold, a crack in the rocks, he would have to jump out over the water, and reach backwards at the same time to catch hold. If he missed his grip, he would fall in and be sucked under. Then he saw a way to improve his odds At his feet was a chunk of stone. He picked it up.

Wet and shivering, he edged over to stand directly beneath the crack, hesitated, then crouched and leapt. Reaching as high as he could, he thrust the stone into the crevice. It jammed, creating a handhold. He held on to it, dangling, then levered himself up.

A moment later, he was out on the forest floor, heart pounding, free of the trap. He had succeeded so far, but must still hurry, someone might sneak back to rob the drowned man. He clambered to his feet. His knuckles stung where the skin had rubbed off, but he was alive. He made his way to his horse, finding Grace hidden deep in the brush. Relieved, he called in a low voice and she came eagerly. He gave her a wet carrot from his belt pouch.

He rode off, exhausted and bruised. Thinking of the distance to town, and seeing how low the sun had fallen, he decided to camp in a sheltered ravine.

It was a decision he would regret the rest of his life.

182

#

As Rev rode into town early the next morning, he was met at the eastern gate by Ma'tha.

"Rev, the thugs attacked the town last night. Khat Trun killed a little Ruskiya girl. Stabbed her with his sword."

Stunned, Rev stared at her. "Whose girl, Ma'tha?"

"Senyanna's daughter, Vantra." Her expression was pinched with guilt. "She lost too much blood, I'm not Laia, I couldn't save her. She was only nine. She'd made a friend and was staying in town. Khat Trun laughed as he struck her down."

Senyanna was a young widow who had lost her husband to the karken. Now her only daughter was gone as well.

Rev had failed the refugees. Despite his big words, he had not been here to protect their girl. "Where did Khat Trun go?"

"Yarrow and Dan and half-a-dozen other men drove the thugs off. They fled east."

Back towards their camp, then. Rev wheeled Grace around. Drawing his father's sword, he urged his horse into a gallop.

"No, Rev," Ma'tha called out. "I don't want to be responsible for losing you, too. Don't go," she wailed, "oh, what will I tell Gabryal?"

#

The sentries saw him. Even high upon their bluffs, they quailed at his fury. They loosed arrows, but their aim was not steady, and he rushed past as they bleated on their horns.

The warning roused the other thugs, and seeing only one man, they laughed. A dozen thugs lounged about a fire, and two raised bows, but he had taken up the power of shi and their arrows flew wide.

What is the fury of a righteous man? Those who commit evil always have some niggling uncertainty, an unquenchable fear they are in the wrong and must someday pay, but the righteous man has no such doubts, and slices through his foes like a sword splits twine. The heart of shi is directing the will with certainty.

Such power Rev bore. And the Disk of Dragons responded. Even without wielding the Disk directly, he had become attuned to it, and the Disk's aura flooded him like an icy wind pushing from behind. His focus was so pure, no scent of incense trailed him – his power was in complete balance.

Lum Tar, the orcen thug Rev once fought, who had sworn Rev's death, charged, swinging his sword. Rev parried, lunged and skewered the man.

With the same move, Rev came off his horse, landing on his feet. Shi guided him, the dance of blades took him. He dodged left, putting the two closest thugs one behind the other. Utterly calm, Rev slapped aside his first foe's blade and drove his sword into the man's chest. As the body fell he went over it at the second man, who, not expecting an attack from that angle, was an instant slow in raising his blade. Rev thrust into the man's heart.

Watching a wielder of shi at a distance one sees nothing to explain what happens. It is unnerving, as the shi master moves, while opponents waver and hesitate, unable to act against him. The logic of shi is clear, who masters his will masters the battlefield.

Three foes down, Rev turned to the others. The cold look in his eyes, even more than the lightning speed of his attack, struck doubt into his foes. They surged forward, a dozen strong, but their own numbers restricted them, few were able to strike cleanly, and the power of the Disk weighed against them. Rev danced before them, striking hard. Shi helped him ignore the blows that strayed off mark, and parry the accurate swings. His blade sliced this throat, entered that eye, cut another's artery, attacking over and over, proving they were mortal, they could be hurt, they would die.

His blade itself cowed them. Forged eons ago, it gleamed unnaturally in the sun, and swung so smoothly it almost guided his blows. Made for the hand of a shi master, the blade resonated weirdly with the power of the Disk, the soul of his ancestors in his hand. The arrogance of the thugs collapsed as Rev downed them left and right.

Seeing their most powerful fighters fall, the rest broke and ran.

With the image of that girl in his mind's eye, an innocent child cut down just for their amusement, Rev was merciless. Two more men died by his blade as the rest scattered. Three fell into the stream and were swept away. One last thug turned and fought, a brutal-faced orcen and a great swordsman in his day, judging from his stance, but the tide of the fight was against him, and perhaps doubt tightened his muscles. After a series

184

of thrusts and counters, he was a shade slow on one parry. He died on Rev's sword, a sneer on his lips.

The last thugs fled into the trees, dragging themselves across rocks, crying in terror. Even the sentries had fled. Rev stood panting, in the center of the camp, alone.

Khat Trun had not been there. Feverishly, Rev searched the camp, but the leader of the thugs had fled after he killed the child. The coward. The evil, murderous coward. Rev would find the man. There would be death to pay.

P M F Johnson

Chapter Eighteen

"Oh, we have the joy of a sailor's lot,
But it's not a lot have we.
Live our lives all wet
Not a coin to bet
Or to pay for a bit of she."
Drinking Song of the Samu Gnomen in a Tavern in Shinpayamuru, as recorded by the roving ethnographers of Ilmari before they organized into the Historians of Remula. Year unknown.

Late that afternoon, when Gabryal learned that Rev had attacked the camp of the thugs single-handed, she confronted him in the marketplace, with what seemed the entire town watching. "What in Luwana's world did you think you were doing, Rev? You think you're immortal? One man against twenty? Don't *ever* do that again. You didn't even let me know, and you could have been killed."

"I had it to do, Gabryal," he said, embarrassed.

"Why didn't you ask me for help? What do you think I'm your friend for?"

"I wasn't thinking things through very well," he admitted.

"I'll say you weren't. I thought my heart would stop when I heard. You are the luckiest man I ever met, Rev Caern." She hugged him hard, confusing him at the change. "I care about you, Rev," she whispered. "I don't have many friends, too few to lose one."

"One thing I learned," he said. "I found the tracks of that notched heel in their camp. One of the thugs was involved in Bhat's murder."

#

Rev did not know how he could face the Ruskiya after he had failed them. But that evening Dunortha herself came to the keep to tell him the mother of the lost girl appreciated he had done what he could. "It is a brave deed to face so many, Rev. A good deed."

186

"Tell her I am so sorry for her loss, Lady," he said, sadly.

#

Rev, Dan and Gabryal had dinner that night at the Local Teahouse, chatting about little things. Gabryal and Rev thought alike in many ways: determined to improve their world, cynical about the current state of affairs, loving a laugh. Rev gave her a bunch of wildflowers, over which she exclaimed happily, then took a deep whiff. She swayed towards him and his mind filled with kisses, but Dan's presence restrained them. In a way, coming close to each other, backing off, then returning even closer like this was fun, heating them both up like crazy. In a way, it was driving him mad. Her eyes just laughed at him.

Dan had made a discovery. "Turns out people have been going to Madame Coo for love potions, curses and such."

"You don't think it's foolishness?" Gabryal asked. "Do love charms ever really work?"

"Jho Iun said people think she's quite effective. The word is, people seem afraid of her, maybe there's more to her magic than you'd think."

"Could she be supplying Khat Trun with magic, then?" Rev asked.

"Khat Trun and Lot Sun's daughter just broke up," Gabryal said. "Ma'tha heard they fought over Madame Coo."

#

Gabryal and Rev spent days in the woods, hunting for Khat Trun and Xul Bil Be, while Yarrow and Dan protected the town. For Rev it was an unsettling blend, being with her and hunting the killers. They had to concentrate on what they were doing, so he could not spend every moment courting her, but he could not ignore the fire he felt. By the sparkle in her eyes she felt it too, but she maintained a certain formality, giving him no opportunity to steal a kiss. He might have given up, but they worked together so easily, making meals, setting up and striking camp, it was as though they had known each other all their lives. That was encouraging.

The first night she even put her hand on his bicep, in passing. When he followed after her, she only giggled, slipped into her tent and pulled the flaps closed, sticking out her head and shaking it. "Not now. Not yet."

"When?" he asked, his voice thick.

"I don't know," she whispered, a tinge of sadness in her voice.

187

To distract himself, the next night he asked her to teach him the rudiments of elemental magic, but shortly into the lesson, the energy exploded in his face, singeing his eyebrows. The edgy stench of lightning burned the air. He swore never to touch war magic again, despite Gabryal's amused assurances that the misfire proved he had talent.

Likewise, in trying to learn shi, she quickly gave up. "Too much is sitting silently with nothing happening. It's not a very manly... that is, it's not a strong magic, is it?"

Rev was embarrassed. "What do you mean? Shi is powerful."

"Rev, war magic is straightforward." A blaze of her flame struck a dead weed. "Shi is all avoiding trouble, stepping out of the way, not being there. What's powerful about that?"

Rev stomped out the weed before the forest caught fire. Her use of the flame seed fascinated him. He had discerned its pattern of energy. "Shoot one of those little seeds at me. I want to try something."

"What? You'll get hurt."

"You're the one saying I'm not manly."

"You're manly, Rev. Gods." She shivered. "I was only teasing you."

They stared at each other with raw need, but as he took a step forward, she looked away. Her face showed the act of will that small move required. But no was still no.

What was wrong with her? He narrowed his eyes. "If I'm such a man, then shoot a fire seed. A little one. Anyway, you're a healer, if I'm a failure at my magic, you can repair me."

Her eyes met his. So much was being said, having nothing to do with words.

"I don't wish to."

It only made him feel colder, more hurt. She would not even let him prove himself.

"Now who's the coward?" he said. The words filled the air between them, creating a separation, making them both miserable. This was insane.

Something released inside. Suddenly he felt calm, enfolded in shi.

"I test a method of protecting us. Do it." Shi was in his voice. Everything else stopped mattering. There was only the calmness.

"Fine. Ready?"

Her trigger phrase was short – the seed shot right at his face. He was so in tune with shi he sensed the magic forcing its way through more delicate energies, like a hammer swung through raindrops. But the hammer could be manipulated. Push there and...

...the fire seed whooshed past his ear, missing him.

"So maybe shi is manly enough." Rev turned to make sure the latest seed hadn't started any fire. He was feeling distanced from his emotions, maybe not such a bad thing at the moment.

When he turned back, annoyance was on her face. "No. That's what I'm talking about, shi is all tricks and shifts. I'm a straightforward woman, I don't like shi."

He burst into laughter. In an instant she was laughing with him, and they were friends again.

But their laughter trailed away into silence. Friends or not, here they were alone together, the perfect time to flirt, instead they somehow erected an invisible wall. He felt helpless to change their relationship. He wanted so much to take her in his arms and kiss her like flames, but not tonight. Maybe not ever.

So he thought about something else. Dan said only about twenty thugs joined the raid that killed the girl, which meant Rev's vengeance probably had not struck those responsible, assuming the guilty thugs fled with their leader. The thugs in camp might have had nothing to do with the killing of the girl.

Rev told himself all the ruffians posed an ongoing threat, Lum Tar had even tried to kill him, but he felt ashamed. What if some had been there by coincidence? He understood now why the Afen demanded proof before punishment, and why Yarrow mentioned a judge. True, the townsfolk were delighted Rev killed so many thugs, but that did not make him feel any better.

Rev shook his head. "One thing I don't understand. These Afen have proved courageous enough, so why didn't they help Los Fun when the thugs were whipping him?"

Gabryal seemed relieved to have something else to talk about. "Being the town drunk dropped Los Fun to the same caste as the thugs. No one cares what outcasts do to each other."

"These castes the Afen believe in seem wrong to me."

"The caste system does a lot of good. Nobles and higher status people like Lot Sun have obligations, like giving money to any struggling to improve themselves."

"Except outcasts."

"Most outcasts choose to be so, thieves and thugs and drunks. Anyone who is sober and trying to improve themselves, lords are bound to give them money."

"I don't like castes. I won't allow them in Sinnesemota."

She laughed. "As if you could stop people doing what they want."

#

The next day, they admitted they were not going to find the vampyren nor the remaining thugs. Inside the town gate that evening, Gabryal paused uncertainly, brushing her toe across the dust. "Rev?"

He turned to her.

"You're..." She ducked her head uncertainly. "You're very tall. Such wide shoulders."

Their eyes met. He moved forward and kissed her, the most natural thing in the world.

She spun and fled for the hospital. He watched her, confused. Had he done something wrong? He thought she wanted him to kiss her. Defeated, bleak, confused and hopeful, Rev cared for Grace at the stable, then walked over to the Jaunt's End.

Mindful of Afen social rituals, the orcen woman who ran the restaurant, Ha'a Iun, curtsied, then guided him to a corner table. She wore her white sash with pride. "Bounder, thank you for your patronage. We have goat and white yams tonight, with vegetables picked this morning."

Rev nodded thanks and eased his aching body into a chair. In the dark room, lit by candles at the tables, he became aware of a man staring with a disquieting interest. An orcen with half his tail cut off. Rev recognized him with surprise – Eg Bror, an orcen guardsman from his hometown. The last Rev had seen him, he was rapidly losing a fight to the goblen invaders in a Shendasan alley. What was he doing here in Zhopahr? He was alone and smelled of drink.

The nondescript assassin had mentioned Eg Bror just before he died, which made Rev doubly wary. This orcen was associated with the Watcher, somehow.

"I remember you." Eg Bror's voice held an edge of triumph and cruelty.

Rev shook his head. "I don't think we've ever been introduced, orcen."

Jho Iun shuffled into the room, his face down, his hands perpetually dry-washing each other. "Bounder, how are you doing?" His voice squeaked eagerly and his tail waggled.

Rev's heart sank. He had forgotten the greasy barrel-maker was Ha'a Iun's husband. Worse, Jho Iun now wore a white sash to match his wife's. "Greetings, Cooper."

"Have you found the thugs?"

"They may have left the valley."

Jho Iun barely waited for the reply. "Tell me, how many did you kill in your attack?"

Rev looked at him with distaste. "I couldn't say."

The fat cooper bounced in place. "A lot, I bet. Wish I'd been there. When are you joining our Temple? Half the people in town have. The High Priestess protects us."

"I don't know how welcome I would be."

"The Goddess takes all," Jho Iun said, his voice rising. "Remember the words of our priestess, you mustn't mock the sacred, nor shun the serious, Bounder."

"Husband, leave the Bounder alone." Bearing a plate of steaming bread, Ha'a entered the room. "He needs to eat."

Rev rose to thank her.

"You're Boundskeeper here?" said Eg Bror. "You've come a long ways."

"You know our Boundskeeper, stranger?" Jho Iun spun to Eg Bror.

"Jho Iun, I need your help in the kitchen," said Ha'a. "You may chat later."

Jho Iun reluctantly followed his wife from the room.

Rev wished fervently he had not entered this restaurant, despite his policy of spreading around his custom. Jho Iun had a morbid streak, and now the man would weasel what he could from Eg Bror about Rev's past. And how would the Watcher use that?

"We should talk," Eg Bror said.

Rev did not trust the man. "Did you lose your job in Shendasan? Why are you in town?"

Eg Bror hesitated, as though he did have a secret, then hissed. "Make you a deal. Trade your sword for my silence. Save your position here, maybe even your life."

"No deal for my sword. Ever." Rev walked out.

Rev's heart was beating double fast. He hurried away, but Eg Bror did not follow. Was the orcen sent by the Watcher? Going after the sword implied as much. Did he mean he would not let the Watcher know where Rev was? But if Rev gave up the sword, the Watcher would not care about him, so did Eg Bror mean something else? Or did the Watcher want not just the sword, but *him*?

Was Eg Bror not involved with the Watcher at all? But then why would the assassin have mentioned him? It was hard to believe Eg Bror could be bribed, if he working for the Watcher, but much easier to believe he would pretend to be bought off, and then betray Rev anyway.

Rev's head swirled with desperation, wanting to avoid having folks here know Rev's past in Shendasan. Rev felt a twist in his stomach; revealing his history of stealing could cost his job. Worse, what would Gabryal think of him?

#

Ma'tha had been feeling brittle recently, not herself, all jangly and uneasy. With no patients needing help, she prowled the half-repaired hospital, her tail whipping. First the hospital lost, then Laia. It was too much. She did not do well when she got to feeling this way, but she knew the answer. She was a single woman, good-looking, in a town full of eligible men; so after putting on her best blue dress, draping a strand of smoky obsidians around her neck and adding a blue parasol, she found a fine table in Playa Usp's Local Tea House where she drank tea and awaited developments.

The Local Tea House was not near the busy streets, catering more to townsfolk. She had had enough of rambling men, she wanted a steady fellow. The heavy drinkers went to the taverns, and the worst sort went to Madame Coo's, so here she sat in a tea house as Vosday wended its way into evening.

A gentle breeze wafted through the door, but when Playa and a client engaged in some friendly dickering over the cost of tea and a meal, a

White-Sasher in the corner loudly accused Playa of deliberately setting her first price too high, of lying, in fact.

An unpleasant moment, of which too many were happening these days. Had the White-Sashers taken leave of their senses? Both Playa and her client knew what price they would settle on – the client took tea here every day, how could that possibly be lying? Fortunately, the White-Sasher finally departed and peace returned.

A handsome orcen appeared at the door, his tail thick and majestic. By his rough clothes and, there was no polite way to put it, grime, he was a miner. Miners were strong though, and he did brush the dust off his clothes and stamp his boots clean outside.

He informed Playa that he sought supper.

"Oh, do sit with me, Miner," Ma'tha called, "I could use some conversation."

"Yes'm," he said, ducking his head and approaching with a shy smile.

Playa brought out the pot, whisk and strainer, and went through the ritual of preparing tea at the table, during which it was impolite to speak, since the man was supposed to enjoy this ritual, but Ma'tha felt impatient, though she did admire Playa's elegant manner of whisking the tea. At last Playa withdrew.

Ma'tha took a sip. "You have business in town?"

"Business, ma'am? Oh, you mean the mining? I don't own the mine, I just work there." He looked befuddled and a bit nervous, as though he had sat down with a leopard who was making polite inquiries after his health. Such a delightful shyness.

"Your name, friend?"

"I'm Ori."

"Ori? So nice to meet you. You may call me Ma'tha. Mining must be such hard work." She smiled, and switched her tail. "Is that true?"

#

Two days later, a short-stepping orcen gentleman emerged from the clothier's shop in the northwest quarter. He wore a fine wool jacket, a linen shirt, and blended wool and linen pants, all too tight. The shirt was striped purple and white, the jacket a checkered chartreuse, the pants an eye-catching shade of saffron. His boots, incongruously, were the large black work boots of a miner, otherwise he bore no resemblance to the man

193

named Ori. His tail was greased, his face scrubbed raw, and his eyes revealed a desperate, trapped quality.

From the shop emerged two goblen men and an orcen woman.

"Papas, you've done a divine job," Ma'tha enthused. "I love the color of those pants."

Papas Sekulto bowed. "T, t, an expensive dye derived from crocuses in the mountains, Madame."

"You have the finest tailor in the kingdom, I swear it must be true."

He clicked happily. "My partner Drinhe. Oh, I think you are right," he answered in a confidential tone. "He is such a dear and happy little worker. Aren't you, Drinhe?"

"I still wonder if he mightn't look better in mauve, friends." Drinhe Sekult-te used four eyes to review his creation, keeping his last pair on his Papas. "It would work so well with that lovely grey skin tone, and draw attention away from those droopy eyelids."

"Absolutely, tailor," Ma'tha burbled, "but you've done so well with this outfit, it's impossible to find fault. You are working with a miner here, allowances must be made. Anyway, we must leave something for the next outfit."

A slight moan emerged from the gentleman being discussed. None of them paid the slightest attention. He remained motionless, eyes staring like a deer whacked upside the head by a log. Even when she reached into his pouch for money, only the faintest trembling of his tail indicated what he might think. His jaw was clamped firmly shut, as though he had bitterly learned the cost of opening it.

Ma'tha waved a cheery goodbye to the clothiers. "Ta ta. It's off to the cobbler with us."

She steered her man down the curving street. "I haven't had this much fun in ages. I'm so glad you asked me out, aren't you, dearest?"

She did not notice the involuntary jerk of his muscles.

"I'm thinking we should have a nice house on the slope east of town," she cooed. "The hill will protect us from the morning light, so I'll have you all to myself longer before we have to leave our bed." She squeezed his arm. Sweat dripped down his forehead.

She spun him to face her, and stared intently into his eyes. "Darling, I can't help but notice how *quiet* you are. Is something the matter?"

He gave the narrowest shake of his head, terror writ plain on his face.

She looked about, her expression a puzzled grimace. "I have the sense that something is missing, a feeling I don't have, that I should have. Something with us, with the two of us. Do you know what I mean?"

Almost he made the mistake of answering her. Only the faintest narrowing of her eyes as he opened his mouth safely strangled the words in his throat. "Ah... ah... aahh I am, that is, I don't... that is, nothing's... ma'am..."

The utterly cold look on her face remained fixed until the last whimper faded. Then it was replaced with a look of satisfaction. "There. I'm sure I'm mistaken. Now here we are at the hospital, be an angel and wait while I look over my patients. Then we can go to replace those horrid boots. Evening's coming soon." She hauled his face down to kiss him before entering the hospital, humming to herself a tune about spiders and the flies who love them.

She had let him out of her sight for the first time since they met. Astounded, the miner gazed about wildly. Spotting the open South Gate, instantly he was in full gallop through it, and out into the wilderness, leaving behind all his worldly possessions.

The miner was never seen on the continent of Hazhe again.

Years later, a sailor off the west coast of Meriges, half the world away, said to his companion, "Hain't you one of them orcen from the Afen kingdom? I been there."

That sailor was accidentally swept overboard in a high sea that night. No one else ever connected the miner to any lands where his terror might still walk the earth in search of him.

#

Rev paused outside the hospital's door in the evening, his mouth dry, his palms wet. He intended to tell Gabryal of his interest in her. She confused him. Maybe part of his dream of leaving town last night was from fear of what might happen with her, maybe part from resentment that she would not commit. He felt miserable in this uncertainty, so he would tell her, and then see.

"Rev, you're standing in the street for a purpose?" Gabryal appeared at the door in a long green gown that showed off her blonde hair and hazel eyes. She was gorgeous.

He flushed. "I was coming over to ask you to tea, Gabryal. Is this a poor time?"

"I think this would be a very good time."

At the Local Tea House, Playa set them up in a quiet corner. Rev hoped to make his intentions clear, but despite how comfortable he felt with her, he remained nervous, so he talked first about something else. "You use raw magic in your spells? Like that glowing stone at the scene of Bhat's murder?"

"Yes."

"So why did you fib about the raw magic when I first found it?" The words were out before he could recall them. His job was to learn about the murder, but how had he reached the point where duty took precedence over a pretty girl? Evidently some stubborn, inner him was getting integrity. Blame it on the Disk. He rubbed at the table top with his thumb. "You said you didn't know what raw magic was, that day."

She blushed. "I suspected you could be the killer, so I wasn't about to tell you anything."

She had not objected to his directness. "Gabryal," his words spilled out, "I find you very interesting. I'd like to get to know you better. Have a chance... the opportunity to court you."

He kept his head down, unbelievably unsure.

Her hand covered his own. He looked up to find sympathy in her eyes.

"Thank you. There is no greater compliment a man can pay a woman. And I like you, Rev. But..." Her voice trailed off.

He felt the lash of disappointment. He'd expected it. Would she have anything to do with him now that he made a complete fool of himself? Her hand was warm, soft.

"You know, Rev," she looked down, "since we found Laia, I've wanted to see my family again. It's like I've lost a near-mother in Laia, and it makes me want to see my own mother. I miss her. Maybe afterwards I can think about, about us.

"Anyway, first I have my duty." Her voice hardened. "I will *not* let this vampyren get away." She hesitated, as though surprised at herself. Her gaze softened. "Can you be patient with me? I don't deserve it, I know. I'm all spiky edges, tough where I should be soft."

She leaned toward him. As though inviting him to speak. Or to kiss her.

Such a moment for a young man has so many possibilities, so much hope for the future bound up into one glorious instant of anticipation. He may afterwards relive such a moment throughout his entire life with pleasure, remembering how the mystery played out, how well she responded, how the joy began.

Or maybe not.

"WHERE IS HE?" A woman's voice roared, drowning forever what he was about to say.

Gabryal and Rev both jumped. In strode Ma'tha, hand on her dagger's hilt.

Gabryal rose in confusion. "Who are you seeking, Ma'tha?"

"Don't tell me I've lost *another* boyfriend," Ma'tha shouted. "I won't have it. He is *not* getting away. Do you hear me, people?" She glowered around the tea room. Playa was conveniently in the back room. The other patrons pointedly pretended to talk, avoiding the humiliation Ma'tha heaped on herself.

"He's the third one *this year*. Where do they get to? One minute they're here, the next..." Ma'tha plunked herself down at the table and burst into tears.

An hour's glass passed before Ma'tha calmed down sufficiently for them to start back to the hospital. The moment with Gabryal was irretrievably lost, but Rev still wanted to be with her.

Ma'tha, crying floods of tears, left them at the door. "Good night, you two. Be thankful you have each other. I'll just have to go... be alone." She hurried inside, dabbing at her eyes.

Gabryal hesitated. "Thank you for the tea." Her eyes met his.

He felt the heat return. "You're welcome, Gabryal. I enjoyed being with you."

She was standing close, her eyes bright, and he wondered if he dared kiss her, really kiss her this time, but he felt too shy. She said she was not ready yet, but she did have a small smile on her face, so there was reason for hope. If he did not pursue her, he would never forgive himself.

"May I make dinner for you tomorrow?" he asked, stumbling over his words.

"I'd like that, Rev."

Hope burst through his veins. "Until tomorrow, then."

P M F Johnson

Chapter Nineteen

"I have myself seen a master of shi lift five men in one hand, and not small men, but ones amazed and exclaiming at the power of the master. No man, it is said, approaches a master of shi who wishes it not. For proof, one master invited me to come against him. I was unable even to commence, such was his power. A strange weakness kept me from doing what I previously determined with all my heart to do. We are fortunate such masters exist only among the humble monks of an obscure sect in the Hiyin mountains."
<u>*Report to the Angin Minister of Trade*</u>*, made by a roving diplomat in Xan Her, year 624A.*

The following morning, Rev set out to prepare a fine dinner. Knowing nearly nothing about cooking, he was in a panic until he ran across Ma'tha at the marketplace. She wore a sassy pink dress, which belied her sad expression.

"You're here to meet someone, Healer?" he asked.

"My man bought flowers from this very merchant, Bounder."

Sure enough, the proprietor of the flower stand, a huge, burly man, cowered from Ma'tha, his eyes wide with terror. They had indeed met.

"I'm sure he'll return," Ma'tha said mournfully. "When he does, we'll be united again."

"I got a problem," Rev blurted out. "I promised Gabryal I'd cook dinner tonight. I want it to be nice, but I don't know the first thing about cooking. Can you help me?"

Ma'tha turned. "You want help on a meal?"

"Not if it's too much trouble."

"A fine meal isn't any trouble." Her eyes began to gleam in interest. "Gabryal likes fish, not anything too heavy. A meal such as this shouldn't be too heavy anyway." She grabbed Rev's arm and walked him along the street. "Where are you to eat this meal?"

"I was thinking I could pay one of the tea houses to sit at their table."

"Oh no, *no*." Ma'tha waved her hands in horror. "At your home, Rev. You want her to know she's special."

"I don't have any way to serve a nice meal," he said meekly. "And what about Dan?"

"You will have a way. When we're done, you most certainly will." She strode along, tail high, lost love forgotten. "And Dan is our friend. We can handle Dan. Just you follow me."

#

Rev felt a bit dazed. The most dangerous storm could never have been so effectively devastating. The main room of the keep had undergone an amazing transformation, colored rocks carefully arranged made a fascinating sculpture, a thick, soft rug covered the floor, a green woven cloth rested on the table. He did not know the place anymore. And oh, demon's flames, the food Ma'tha was cooking.

Telling him he was cooking, of course, but she was the one with the ladle in her hand. He never smelled anything so succulent. His task was to act as errand boy. Ma'tha even met Dan upon his return. Dan cautiously drew away, until Ma'tha murmured something in his ear, after which he grinned, impishly waggled a finger at Rev and rushed off on some task.

Rev, alarmed at that little exchange, vowed to ask Dan what that was about, later.

Everything was almost ready. Rev hurried to find the flower seller, since he was to have "wildflowers on the table, and no saving coppers, mind you," but at the marketplace, a sneering orcen in a greasy coat and white sash confronted him.

"Bounder, I hear you set yourself up as a man of virtue and goodness here." It was Eg Bror, the last person he wanted to see.

Rev brushed past. "Talk to you later, Eg Bror."

Eg Bror shouted after him. "We'd better, or I'll be talking to everyone else around here. Understand?"

Merchants and shoppers turned. Rev hunched his shoulders and hurried on, hoping the situation with Eg Bror would somehow resolve itself.

#

That evening, Gabryal gazed around Rev's keep, delight on her face. Even the stone walls gleamed. A fire crackled in the fireplace and the window revealed a sky darkening to a gorgeous midnight blue. "Everything looks so beautiful, Rev."

"Thank you, Gabryal," Rev said, wondering if she realized Ma'tha's role in putting the evening together. "It's a comfortable place, I've discovered."

Gabryal had said it was too soon to court, but he did not want her deciding it was time, then finding someone else. Even if he was risking their friendship, he had to try. He liked Gabryal so much; imagine if they could find love together. His heart beat like crazy.

She had paused, and he realized he was supposed to take her cape.

"Let me," he said, and she smiled at him. She wore a cream-colored dress, cinched at the waist, and tiny white flowers decorated her hair.

"You look so pretty," he said, his yearning for her rising into a sharp pang.

She curtsied her thanks. He found a hook for her carry-bag. He felt like an imposter pretending to be suave. On the other hand, it was fun. "Something to drink?"

"I would enjoy that."

He hurried to a chest situated on one side of the room. He opened the chest without knowing what Ma'tha had stashed inside. It contained two buckets of cool water, in each of which rested a bottle. He gazed at them with consternation.

"I seem only to have wine," he said, then flushed at how that sounded.

"Wine would be delightful," Gabryal said, her low voice sending a thrill through him. She was enjoying this little play as well. Their eyes burned into each other.

He was first to look away, fearing to chase her off. He poured them both a glass of a pale wine, then his uncertainties about the meal spiked. What had Ma'tha said about timing? He decided to sit with Gabryal a few moments before he served dinner.

Gabryal smiled and they raised their glasses.

"To your beautiful hazel eyes," he said.

"Now you're flattering. Thank you, I love it." Her grin was so impish they both laughed.

They made comfortable small talk, amazed by their luck in finding each other, by this chance to be together.

The whistling sound of steam arose from a pot near the fire, and its lid rattled.

"My dinner." Rev jumped up in a panic. Gabryal followed him. He yanked the pot off the coals, spotted a towel and used it to lift the lid, discovering his brussels sprouts were small mounds of mush. Sadly, he gazed at them. "I so wanted this to be nice."

"I'm sure they'll taste fine," Gabryal said in a comforting tone. "What do you have cooking there?" She pointed at a portable two-handled oven.

The oven stood in the coals. He lifted the lid to discover a fat trout inside, cooked until the flesh was separating in chunks. "Oh, oh, oh," he said in despair. "I don't know what to do."

Gabryal gazed at him in astonishment.

"Well," he said ruefully, "it's not as though I've ever been a cook."

She laughed. "Look at this wonderful meal. What did you do, conjure it?"

He hesitated. "Ma'tha helped."

"Helped?" Her voice was brightly innocent. "Ma'tha?"

"All right, she kicked me out of the kitchen. I've never seen any of this food before."

Gabryal put her hand on his chest and laughed so hard tears came. He put his arms around her, she raised her face, and then they were kissing.

The meal was forgotten and their reluctance fell away. All the time they waited, courted, flirted, and hungered for each other finally exploded, and they moaned as need overcame them. Then it was all kissing, touching, exploring.

They were reaching an intimacy so far beyond their first kiss, that when a red light flashed he did not notice and she did not care to.

The light flashed again, bright, insistent, interrupting.

She swore, bitterly, and shoved at his chest, pushing him off.

"What?" he asked, confused. The light flashed yet a third time, inside the room.

She was already pulling herself back together. "Vampyren. That's a warning of ritual magic being cast, by Xul Bil Be."

She rushed over to her carry bag.

He felt a flush of cold. "Burn Xul Bil Be. Can't it wait?"

She lifted out a flashing amulet. "I don't know this magic well. I received this amulet from the Grey Women in Khav. The intensity indicates the spell was cast in the valley, but probably not inside the town. It's a killing magic, though. Someone just died in sacrifice."

"We better see about Ma'tha," Rev said, instantly worried.

Gabryal paused for a moment to rest her hand on his chest, her gaze amused, and something more primitive. "I'm glad you had a rug on that floor."

He growled, and she giggled. They hurried off.

Ma'tha met them at her door, her face strained. "Another seeking spell, friends, much more powerful this time. Xul Bil Be surely killed someone."

The main room of the Grey Women's home was surprisingly spare, with little more than a table, a few comfortable chairs, a pantry and fireplace. Of course, Ma'tha had decorated with fresh flower arrangements along the walls, frilly curtains over the windows, and a matching curtain that blocked off the back room.

Ma'tha rubbed her arms with her fingers. "The vampyren is still after the Disk of Dragons."

"The vampyren moves wherever it wants, whenever it wants," Rev said. "I don't think it fears us at all."

"It fears us, Rev," Ma'tha said. "Remember, vampyren take the long view, they prefer to outlive you rather than fight you. There's always tomorrow for a vampyren. For this one to come out of hiding means it wants something badly enough to risk itself. That's a strong argument for the Disk being in the valley."

"If this Disk of Dragons is so valuable, why not ignore us and flat-out look for the Disk?"

"Think of it from the vampyren's point of view." Ma'tha's tail thumped nervously. "If some mortal does find the Disk, it can always ambush that person and take the Disk away. What's the hurry?"

"We have a reason to hurry," Rev said, "we got to find the vampyren. It will kill again."

"There's one more thing we haven't tried," Gabryal said. "Maybe it's time. There may be reason for the vampyren to fear us yet."

Something in the determined shine in her eyes made Rev uneasy.

Gabryal drew aside the curtain to the private living area, and went to a laboratory set up on a wide desk. Alembics stood by beakers, lined up near two small stoves, powders and liquids in jars stood along the back of the desk. She took a wand from a drawer, then sorted through her jars of powder until finding two she wanted. From a metal bowl she took a glowing stone, raw magic. In a drawer, she found a pouch of black silk, from which she removed a half-blackened bit of metal. "The amulet Laia had on when she died."

Ma'tha gasped. "Gabryal?"

She had evidently fathomed what Gabryal intended.

"We have to ask her," Gabryal argued. "She knows how important this is."

"It's wrong." Ma'tha's voice was nearly a squeal.

"Not if she agrees, it isn't."

"But she will. That's not fair, you know her. It's wrong even to ask."

Rev had no idea what they were arguing about, but Gabryal looked stubborn and Ma'tha dissatisfied.

"It's dangerous," Ma'tha said. "I don't want to lose you, too."

"Don't worry, I know how the spell works. Anyway, Laia dedicated her whole life to this, wouldn't she expect to be asked? I would. We have to do something, how many more people will we let die?"

Ask Laia? Laia was dead. What did Gabryal mean?

Ma'tha squinted in sudden suspicion. "Gabryal, it isn't even elemental magic. How can you cast this spell?"

"I can't. You're the one who knows conjurations. But I have notes on how to cast the spell. Will you help me?"

Ma'tha's hands froze in mid-movement. She looked wildly from Gabryal to Rev. "I can't... Do you know how dangerous calling a spirit can be?"

Gabryal waited.

"You're asking me to cast a spell from *notes*?" Ma'tha stared at Gabryal, then down at the bowl. At last she closed her eyes, took a deep breath, and let it out. "You're right, we have to try, how else can we fight a vampyren?"

Gabryal turned to Rev. "Do you still have that small brass doorway?"

Rev blinked. "You heard what Laia said. It's evil."

"It's a connection to the Outside, that alone makes it evil. What we're doing, well, we're going to give her a choice, Rev. We're not forcing anyone to do anything."

He pulled the doorway from his belt pouch.

They returned to the front room, Ma'tha drawing the curtain closed, then moved the chairs and table aside and rolled up the rug, leaving an empty space. Ma'tha motioned Rev to a corner chair. Gabryal put a sheaf of papers on the table as Ma'tha drew a circle of powder in the middle of the dirt floor. The powder glinted. Metal? She placed the brass doorway inside the circle. Her face had already gone emotionless.

"Close your eyes when we light the fire," Ma'tha told him, "we're not going to be very smooth about this, I'm afraid." She looked more unsettled by the thought of doing something inelegant than accidentally conjuring some beast that might devour them all.

She studied the notes, then began to chant in a soft voice. The language had many guttural sounds and sudden stops. Gabryal joined Ma'tha, their voices blending.

A strange lethargy stole over him, but he strove to pay attention. Gabryal was gesturing with a burning wand. The room was cold, the front door open. The candles blew out in a growing breeze. The hairs on his neck prickled; the wind whipped in a circle. Ma'tha had a flame cupped in her hand. As she applied the flame to the metal powder, he shut his eyes. A brilliant light seared through his closed eyelids. The chanting broke off.

After a moment, he opened his eyes. The room was dark. The wind stopped.

He had the terrible sense that a presence was in the room, but different from the Watchfulness. This presence felt closer, more driven by passion, an anger very different from the cold dispassion of the Watchfulness. Rev felt completely unprotected. Something crashed, a distant, unearthly sound. The presence had stepped outside the circle of protection!

In a quiet tone, Ma'tha asked a question. The presence hovered, as though it stood in another place and looked down at them in this room. Again, Ma'tha asked. The candles flared and Gabryal recommenced her chant. The raw magic pulsed a deep orange, highlighting her face, then darkness gathered as Ma'tha asked a third time.

The presence grew closer, more like a part of this world. It crouched down until it fit into the room, a shadow in the darkness, a well of recklessness and despair.

The shadow sprang away, out the door.

The chanting stopped. Rev woke gasping, as though a bucket of water had been thrown in his face. Ma'tha and Gabryal clung to each other, wide-eyed. They had released something terrifying and enraged into the world.

By the Hands of Vos he hoped they knew what they were doing.

Chapter Twenty

"The dragon folk may have fashioned the first mortals, following some purpose of the Great Mother. Perhaps Luwana looks for a reuniting of all peoples with Herself, repairing the world. The prophets speak of this, as does the holy <u>Book of Vos</u>, but we common folk know little of such secrets. Whether a Goddess may die and yet live to guide us remains a mystery, though many believe it to be so."
<u>*The Histories of Teren: The Age of Legend.*</u>

Later that night, Dan and Rev followed the street that circled inside the town wall. Fortunately, the wall stood on bedrock and needed few repairs after the earthquake. The wind was fitful and cool, the stars shone steadily.

Rev concluded, "...so the presence Ma'tha brought into the world was the spirit of Laia."

"Ma'tha did that with conjuration magic? I thought you had to protect yourself from a spirit when you call it."

"Not if the spirit isn't hostile. Most are. They don't want to come back. Even friends or family can be deadly, so Ma'tha took a big chance asking if Laia would become a Ghost Hound."

Rev felt an unease, as though the Disk itself were restless. He remembered that sense of struggle long ago between light and darkness over the city hall of Shendasan. This had the same feel of mighty forces grappling.

"What's a Ghost Hound?"

"Laia's ghost somehow put into an ethereal hound. A Ghost Hound is driven by rage, or vengeance, hunting down the being that killed it. So evidently this Hound has power against the vampyren."

"The dead ain't meant to stay in this world." Dan slapped down his tail. "Trouble's coming from this."

"I can see why Ma'tha was reluctant. You could feel the wrongness."

"Magic's got consequences," Dan said, "your friend the Elder Fu told us. You think Ma'tha has condemned Laia to an eternal existence as a ghost?"

"I don't know. Any one of them would pay such a price to kill a vampyren. Those Grey Women are tough, Dan."

"You're getting involved with one."

Rev nodded. "I told Gabryal if I'm supposed to tell her when I do something dangerous, she has to tell me as well. She became so cold and distant. Magic does that. Chasing down that vampyren will make the town safer, so I'm inclined not to object to their spell, but what am I going to do about Gabryal? Her and me?"

Dan sighed expressively, and looked away without answering.

Rev did not know how to interpret his friend's response. He was at that delicious, unsettling, unhappy moment when a young man is deeply interested in a woman but unsure if she is equally interested, that early time when he does not yet feel comfortable, does not understand the signals, but wants to press ahead, a young bull ready to jump out of his pasture for the pretty heifer in the next paddock, and flames take the fences.

Dan and he checked Zhopahr's west gate to be sure it was barred, then stopped at the stable so Rev could feed Grace an apple.

A shadow moved in the corner. "Good to see you tonight, Bounder. You as well, Dan." The same soft voice as Dril Plu, the stable master who died in the earthquake, but a little higher pitch: his son Ton Plu-shin. No, Rev thought sadly, his name was just Ton Plu, now that his father had died, another loss to the town. Even Laia was dead. Who else might die?

They exchanged a few words as Rev fed the apple to Grace. Rev was proud of Dan. His friend had changed, people treated him with respect. Dan had never been a swaggerer, but he walked with confidence now, and exhibited a deep concern for others. Having responsibility caused him to bloom, as though he were born for this life.

Back at the keep, they sat to eat the burned leftovers of Rev's abandoned meal.

Rev could barely eat. "Dan, how did I fall for such a complex woman?"

Dan pointed a fork at him. "She's a woman, they're ALL complex. Question is, do you like her?"

"I love her intelligence, her quick laugh, her graceful as a dragonfly way of walking."

"Graceful as a dragonfly? You ARE besotted. You'll be making up bad poetry next."

"She's always improving herself, something I'm determined to do myself." Rev grinned. "And she's tolerant of Ma'tha's quirks and foibles."

"It does bode well, you being a man of quirks and foibles yourself." Then Dan looked serious. "I'm concerned, though. You two are so different."

"Opposites can like each other." Rev felt defensive.

"It's not that. I think you're a lot more serious about your relationship than she is. I don't want you to get hurt."

"She's still in mourning for her husband, I understand that. We're going slow."

"No, Rev. She's going slow. Or was trying to, before tonight. That's what worries me. One heated grapple isn't likely to change her long-term view, she's not as much of a kid as you. Anyway," he hesitated, "you're seeing a lot of each other, I don't hardly see you anymore."

"You're jealous," Rev said, amazed. He bused his dishes from the table to wash them.

"It's not that. Or maybe I am, but it's more than that. You're off with her all the time, not protecting the town. That bothers me."

"I *am* protecting the town, by trying to catch that thug Khat Trun and the vampyren. What I'm doing is dangerous, Dan, I'm not shirking anything."

"I know that, but do the townsfolk? People are talking about you and Gabryal. If they can't see what you're doing, they'll think you're doing nothing."

Dan took up a towel to dry the dishes.

"Let them think what they like," Rev declared.

They worked in uncomfortable silence.

"I do want you to be happy." Dan hesitated. "You think you and Gabryal will happen?"

Rev handed Dan the last dish. "She fascinates me. Maybe I am being a fool over her. I can see what you mean, she's being hesitant, but who wants to never be a fool in love? You were with Ma'tha."

"I'd hardly call that love." Dan turned dark grey with embarrassment. "Anyway, you go ahead with Gabryal. If you don't start a fire, nothing gets cooked." He changed the subject. "What ever happened to that map of yours?"

"I've been working on it." Rev pulled it from a drawer, placed it on top of the table. "I've marked the murder site, and where everyone was. It helps keep track of the people still not accounted for, Xul Bil Be, Skarii, Madame Coo and the thugs being the main ones. Skarii lives alone, so her being on the list is not surprising, but I don't really suspect her."

Dan studied the map. "It shows the White-Sashers were all in their temple at the time of the murder."

"Which gives every one of them an alibi. Uulong told me they were there."

"Rev, that was a Vosday morning. Who goes to service on Vosday? People go to services on Lunsday, Luwana's day. And on the 24th of Dwarvenmoon? That's not GreeningDay, or any other holiday I can think of, so what were they doing?"

Rev hesitated. "I don't know. I never went to services like you, so that didn't occur to me, but no one else recalls seeing the White-Sashers that morning, so I'm pretty sure they were in the temple together, whatever they were praying for. Does it really matter?"

#

The next morning, after opening the gates, Rev headed toward the hospital. He never made it. As he crossed the market, he was intercepted by a familiar, annoying figure.

"Well, Bounder, you willing to talk with me now?" Eg Bror sneered. The man swayed, already drunk, his voice loud enough to turn heads.

Rev felt a stab of concern that this man would threaten his position, then anger took him. "We don't got anything to say to each other, orcen."

"You won't pay for my silence?"

"To a man who tortured children when he caught them? No."

Eg Bror shouted aloud. "You weren't any more humble when fleeing arrest for theft, were you? Do you people know this man was a thief in Shendasan?"

209

"That's a lie," Rev shot back. "I was never in Shendasan." Instantly, he realized his mistake, many people knew he was from Shendasan, including Gabryal. His face heated.

"You deny it?" Eg Bror pounced.

"No, no. I am from Shendasan, that part is true, but I never met you before in my life."

"So you admit you stole?"

Rev felt the heat of his own confusion. He didn't know what to say. He wanted desperately to lie, to flee, to slug this man.

A man who lies to cover up his actions will give partial answers at different times to various innocent questions, and unwittingly build up a web of contradicting assertions. People may not notice at first, but something disturbs them, maybe they are even concerned, and press the man to see how they can help. This makes it harder for the liar, as they notice that his answers don't make sense, and their questions grow more pointed, their suspicions grow, they bring up his previous answers and ask for an explanation.

He can either admit his lies and begin to be honest, or strain to make all his previous comments tie together sensibly, at least those he can remember in the desperate moment. He continues in his foolishness, denying what is obvious – he cannot remember everything he said, he cannot make the contradictions match up, he cannot talk his way out of it anymore.

Rev was brought to this moment by an enemy, and the choice paralyzed him. Sometimes no choice is a choice in itself.

"Your silence proclaims the truth," Eg Bror declared, "you're a common thief. Hear that, people? The man you expect to protect you is a sneak thief. He even stole that sword. It's mine."

The White-Sashers nearby whooped and hollered, screaming jibes at Rev. "Give him his sword back."

"Did you steal, human?" asked the orcen merchant Bov Whin, who had been examining a table of fruit nearby. Tall and thin, with dark lines under his eyes, he was always scowling at something. He was not a White-Sasher, but looked at Rev with suspicion.

Dan was making his way through the crowd toward Rev.

Disk of Dragons

Rev felt so ashamed he wanted to fade into nothingness. True heroes never had to face this sort of thing. He didn't want to lie anymore, but he had not yet been driven to the point of telling the whole truth.

"When I was hungry," he admitted, but deep down, he knew even that was a further tangling of the deceitful web, and his voice quavered unconvincingly. "But the sword is mine."

Eg Bror pranced in circles, his stub tail waggling. "Rev's a lying, petty thief."

Every eye accused him. His heart pounded loudly in his own ears.

Reprieve came from an unexpected quarter. But not a good one.

A young man galloped his horse into the market place. "Goblen soldiers. North of town, headed this way. We're gonna be attacked."

An attacking army? The crowd surged in fear. Women screamed and merchants grabbed their wares. People jostled each other and scuffles broke out. The mine owner Ash Wal bellowed, drunk and swaying, his fine clothes smeared with dirt and the feather in his cap broken. Someone had to take charge.

A man bumped a little girl and she fell. Rev picked her up and put her in the arms of her mother, then started giving orders. "Dan, go alert Yarrow and the town garrison. Bov, send your sons to tell the guards to close the gates."

The moment of accusation was forgotten. Eg Bror slipped away. But the moment would have damaging consequences.

"People," Rev raised his voice. "Those who own weapons get them and report to the town wall for defense. Mothers, have your children fill buckets of water for putting out fires. Fana," this to Bov's wife, "have those unable to fight report to Ma'tha to assist at the hospital if needed. Everyone, calm down. We'll find out what they want and deal with them fairly." He kept his voice steady, and the people did settle down and obey him. A miracle. His mind was running rapidly. How many soldiers? Were they in battle formation?

He needed more information. The blacksmith was close, so Rev sent him to saddle Grace. After he departed, Rev directed people to stations on the town wall, put Yarrow in charge of the immediate defense, then ordered older boys to ride out to the nearby farms, ranches and mines, making sure to mention Skarii Hesketh, since they might need a conjuror.

211

Rev rode out the north gate to gain more information. The road climbed through the ruins, then crossed a plateau to a vast downslope. Rev reined in.

Far down the road, a score or so of soldiers were visible, so distant that only traveling in formation gave away their military background. Closer, a single figure on foot ran toward him. Rev thought he could see a saffron robe. A monk from Shendao?

The soldiers were catching up to the monk, so Rev urged Grace into a gallop down the road. The small figure in saffron started to sprint for him. The soldiers waved their spears.

Having the advantage of the slope, Rev reached the fugitive well ahead of the soldiers. To his astonishment and delight, the monk was his old friend, the Elder Fu Vehma.

"Jump on." Rev pulled his friend up behind him, started Grace back up the hill. He resisted the urge to gallop her. The quickest way to kill a horse was to run it uphill. The soldiers were less than a thousand paces away, but Rev kept Grace at a deliberate speed. If he went too slowly they would catch him. He wanted to run in a blind panic. Instead he slipped off Grace, and led her at a walk.

He could hear the faint shouts of the soldiers behind, voicing curses and imprecations in the Chisen tongue. The soldiers kept closing the distance, but still Rev kept Grace at a walk, until the soldiers closed half the distance between them. The Chisen were starting to labor.

The crest of the hill was some distance ahead when a spent arrow fell to his left, proving the soldiers were within bow shot. The Elder Fu clutched at the saddle, exhausted.

Rev started to run. Beside him, Grace broke into a smooth trot. Another arrow fell off to the right, a third ricocheted off a rock.

Rev cleared his mind of fear, trying to sense the arrows. One struck the road nearby, surprising him. Fear lurched, but he created a wave of shi overhead, flowing from right to left. The faint scent incense hinted the magic was at work. Another arrow struck, off to the left. Deflected? Rev took steady breaths.

Another arrow struck, farther behind. He glanced back. The soldiers had halted, heads down and splay-footed, exhausted. His gamble to keep his pace steady had paid off. Rev had saved the Elder Fu.

But these soldiers were only the vanguard. Far behind them rose the dust of a large mass of troops. An entire goblen army approached.

Chapter Twenty One

"Love unifies, hate separates. This is the only test to know the Will of a Loving God."
"Meditations," from <u>The Book of Vos</u>, *Chapter 2, Verse 1.*

Rev and the Elder Fu rode double under the stone archway of the town gate. Dust drifted in the air. People were screaming on every side, but the noise was so profound that nothing could be understood, the entire world had become unintelligible; violence threatened on all sides. It's Elladay, Rev thought, a day dedicated to peace. How could war come on Elladay? In the plaza, he reined in and the Elder Fu hopped down.

"Is it true, Bounder?" The terrified voice of Jho Iun broke through the noise. "Is an army out there?"

"Who are they, Bounder?" someone called.

The Elder Fu answered. "Over a thousand fighters of the Chisen Empire approach, marching from the city of Shendasan. They have massacred two towns that surrendered to them."

From Shendasan? Had this army been sent by the Watcher? Rev could not possibly be so important, there must be another motivation. Hunting the Disk of Dragons, perhaps, or even simple conquest. Picking him off at the same time would be only a side issue.

No more time for that. The growing hysteria of the townsfolk spurred Rev to step up onto a knee-high stone. "Citizens, we got a good wall and a couple hundred fighters to man it. Will you fight to protect your families?"

"Yes," the shout resounded.

"Will you have me lead the defense of the town?"

"Yes." The cries were not as loud. Rev wondered whether Eg Bror had been spreading his poisonous rumors, but nothing could be done about it.

Rev called for captains to lead the town's defenses. Ash Wal announced loudly he would defend the eastern wall with his miners. The Ruskiya had come into Zhopahr and their war leader, Kormenthon, agreed to marshal the defense of the western wall. Dunortha would lend him magical aid. Yarrow volunteered to captain the north, where the bulk of the assault might be expected. Lot Sun claimed the right to head the townsfolk protecting the south.

The captains of the town's defenses departed. Others clamored for Rev's attention, but he held up his hands. "One moment, friends. Elder Fu, can you use shi to protect our northwest corner?"

The elder bowed. "I will be able to do something, Rev."

"Thank you, old friend. I've missed you over these last months." They clasped forearms, then headed together to the Elder Fu's position on the northwest wall.

"It seems like a tremendous coincidence to have you show up here."

The elder bowed, as a smile lit his round face. "A great coincidence, yes, if I did not know where you were. I did say that I would hear of you, young one."

Rev laughed. "I'm glad to have you, though for your sake I wish you hadn't come just in time to be trapped with us. Any idea what sort of magic they wield?"

"Chisen armies generally include a pod of conjurors."

Rev felt a stab of concern. "How can we fight such a force, if they have six conjurors? We have a couple hundred fighters at most." He felt a surge of anticipation, as though the Disk prepared for battle. Was he to be just another weapon it flung into the fray?

The Elder Fu spread his hands. "The town walls give us an edge, and we will plan for magic against groups of defenders. Much can be anticipated."

Finding a short stick, the monk sketched in the dust three typical tactics of assault used by the goblen and how to defend each. Rev wrote out the information for the captains and handed them off to runners, before heading over to the north gate. The walkway atop the wall was wide enough for three people to walk abreast, and the stone parapets were chest high, with merlons rising like stone teeth at regular intervals, giving more protection to the defenders.

Rev was amazed at the work Yarrow and his helpers completed. Only a few merlons were missing. Men were spaced at the embrasures, but Yarrow also had men on the street pounding wooden planks together into constructs. Rev joined Yarrow, where the walkway arched over the town gate.

"I don't understand." Rev pointed at the men. "What are they doing?"

"I have them in reserve. Meanwhile, they're constructing wooden screens as protection against missiles. We'll put the screens wherever we haven't finished the merlons. When the attack comes, I'll throw my reserves in where the fighting is heaviest."

At the west gate, the Ruskiyan war chief, Kormenthon, had made similar dispositions, also holding a small reserve. The war chief stood on the steps between the west gate and the Bounder's keep. His wall was missing some merlons, but all his parapets were chest height. "I am glad you are in charge, Bounder. Only you, we trust and follow."

Rev told him about Yarrow's idea for screens, and the Ruskiya leader immediately put his own fighters to work on the project.

Heartened, Rev moved on to the south wall. Here the wall was in worse shape, with the parapets incomplete in a couple of places and few merlons giving protection above that. Lot Sun had all his fighters on the wall. The rancher paced the walkway. But when Rev explained how he preferred the troops situated, with a reserve held back, the rancher looked away.

"Has the Bounder experience of war?" His voice was cold.

"I'm commander, sir."

"My question is not answered." He impatiently tapped his cane on the stones.

"I don't," Rev admitted, embarrassed, "but those who *are* experienced are arranging their fighters in that manner."

"I have fought. I'll arrange my own troops."

Rev was taken aback. "Are you saying you won't obey my orders?"

Lot Sun gazed into the distance. "I'm not just passin' through, shunnin' the serious. I got more at stake here than any human."

Flummoxed, Rev said, "They'll kill me just as dead as you if we're taken. Anyway, what has that to do with how we arrange our defenses?"

"I'll see to the defense of this wall." Lot Sun walked away.

None of Lot Sun's men would look at Rev. And to hear Lot Sun quote the White-Sashers' 'shunning the serious' phrase disturbed him.

"The other commanders are building screens to place where the wall ain't complete," Rev said loudly, so Lot Sun's men could hear. "You can get wood to do the same from the ruined buildings in town."

Rev headed down the stairs, seething inside.

On the east wall, Ash Wal stood proudly at the head of the stairway beside the gate. The wall was in better shape, but Ash Wal had also appointed no reserves, and showed the same attitude as Lot Sun. "We have no truck with thieves here."

The mine owner would not look at him.

Shame cut through Rev. "Explain to me, Miner, how that matters. Is all this political bickering, who will and won't do what, going to keep us alive?"

"We'll do our part." Ash Wal waved his tail in a dismissive gesture.

"You won't even know what your part is, if you don't work with the rest of us."

"I'll have nothing to do with a petty thief." The mine owner leaned on the parapets, hunching his shoulders.

"And the Ruskiya will have nothing to do with you. If you don't want me as leader, find a better answer."

Ash Wal gave a cold smile. "Folks will have their answer soon enough."

There it was. Half his fighting force would not obey him.

As Rev headed back to the north wall, he felt a rush of the old urge to steal, but that was just covering up his fear and shame. He was terrified at the rebellion, and at having responsibility for the lives of everyone in town. His past thieving had come back to haunt him at the worst time possible, driving a wedge through the town that could get them all killed. He had to solve this rebellion, fast.

He could not resign, since the refugees, a quarter of their fighting force, said they would not obey any townsfolk other than him, but he had an idea.

He found Yarrow on the north wall and explained his dilemma.

"Divided armies fail," Yarrow said, looking out over the wall.

"I have a solution. It's me they don't care for. If they think you're operating independently, they're likely to listen to you, so anything we want done, you send the idea to them as though it were your own. That'll keep them informed, anyway, and the lines of communication open."

Yarrow's eyes narrowed. "Not ideal. We could replace them as leaders."

His voice was so matter-of-fact that Rev knew the acts of replacement if done by Yarrow would be swift and permanent.

"No, no," Rev said. "We don't have to go that far." The full burden of being a leader during war crashed down on him. "Not yet, anyway."

The thought made him almost ill.

"As you will," Yarrow said, as though discussing the butchering of chickens.

Shaken, Rev hurried away. He needed a moment to come to grips with the fact that, if the fractiousness of Lot Sun and Ash Wal endangered the entire town, the lives of hundreds, he would choose Yarrow's solution.

Rev was growing up in this moment, and he did not much like it.

The rest of the day, Rev held the west gate open for local refugees, keeping a watch to warn if any Chisen came too close. Folks poured into the town. Leaving the gate open was risky, but Rev wanted to give as many people a chance for safety as he could. Only at last light did Rev order the gates closed.

The next dawn arrived with the weather sweltering, an oppressive heat that hinted at blood and sorrows; it was the second of Wolfenmoon, the second day of summer.

The Chisen army filed into the valley, their dark carapaces glittering in the sun. They set up skirmish lines, and behind them, camps. By noon, Zhopahr was besieged.

Chapter Twenty Two

"Farmers! Craftspeople! Are you adventurous? Looking for a chance to improve your lot in life, maybe make a fortune? Your opportunity is here.

"A few brave souls will be chosen to form a new Empire in the East. These lands have never known a plow, and any seed planted springs up overnight in such rich soil, and the climate is so mild that your health will improve in miraculous fashion. Have you always wished you lived in ancient Sinnesemota? It's not too late. A NEW paradise is forming. Only ten gold coins to buy a share in this new Empire. Officers are taking deposits at the Rectory of Simmon. Don't Miss Your Chance!"

Handbill from Remula at the Time of the Great Eastern Migrations, @203A. Countless pilgrims joined these east-bound wagon trains, only to discover the reality of treeless plains, thin soils, and natives hostile to their invasion. Provenance of preservation spell on this handbill unknown. Collection of the Museum of Thehar.

Rev cradled a small incense burner as he cowered in a doorway. The afternoon was sweltering, with the sun in a cloudless sky. The sweat of shame dripped down his forehead. The town had been besieged, and here he was, filching things. Walking down an alley, he had noticed the burner on a table inside an open door.

How could he be a leader, protecting people, and yet be stealing from them every time he got upset? It would be laughable, if he did not feel so bad. He had to return the incense burner.

The army needed leadership, his thoughts argued, *he had no time to return it.*

Well, he should have thought of that when he stole it.

He would be found out if he tried to return it.

He should have thought of that when he stole it.

219

P M F Johnson

Rev returned to the house, where, not even looking around, he entered and replaced the incense burner where he found it. To his relief, no one was there.

Still, his obsessive stealing would destroy any chance he had in this town, even if they did turn away the army. Worse, his reputation as a thief would probably ruin Dan Zee's prospects as well. How could Rev learn to stop? He seemed to have no control over himself.

He headed to the north gate. From atop the wall Yarrow called down. "They haven't sent out a herald, Rev, they're thinking to let us fret a mite, first."

The golden-haired man had the intent look of a hawk contemplating prey.

Rev climbed up beside him. The invading army had bivouacked around the town, tents laid out in hexagonal patterns throughout the ruins. Half-a-dozen tents were larger than the rest, and white rather than brown; around these centered considerable activity, while the sole red tent commanded a wide clearing, where goblen with gold braid clustered – the army leaders. Six other bright blue tents to one side caught Rev's attention.

"Conjurors," explained Yarrow.

Sweat dampened Rev's clothes. How could the town withstand six mages, let alone a thousand veteran soldiers? Then his natural optimism reasserted itself. The town walls sat on bedrock, no one would tunnel under them. The townsfolk could win this fight.

Finally six goblen, with four legs each, spidered toward the front gate, holding the golden flag of parley, so Rev sent for Dan and the town captains. At a proper speaking distance, the goblen heralds drew up. They wore shoulder braids and scarlet velvet clothes. Three wore pants, three wore skirts, each one sneering more haughtily than the last.

Rev stepped up to the battlements. "Who are you that threaten our home?"

He felt the Disk stir, a flicker of power inside.

The six heralds hissed angrily. One stepped forward. "Tt, tt. We are Speakers for the Unity who centers the Order of the Empire of the Chisen, represented here by his Eminence, Norwe Hesketh, for whom we speak. T, t. Who are you broken-pods to be denying the imperatives of Order?"

220

Rev felt stunned. Norwe Hesketh, here? The man had ordered the death of Rev's father. Rev wanted to strangle the man. Dan put his hand on Rev's shoulder and the ferocity passed.

"We are the people of Zhopahr, defending ourselves against invaders bringing hate and violence," Rev answered, finally.

"T,t,t. You have an insolent tongue."

"You invade with an army of a thousand killers to attack a peaceful people who never did you harm, and you don't like OUR words? Go, or you'll leave hundreds of your dead on this ground and still never conquer us. Go."

The town defenders roared approval.

The heralds stood stone-like until the cheers and jeers died away. "T,t. By tomorrow, you must be leading out twelve sixties of the cattle called *neve* to feed our troops until proper arrangements are made for governing this valley. As proof of your honorable intent, we are requiring you send out thirty-six women, and not crones you do not fear to lose. Ttt. Last, you must yield the Disk of Dragons. We will return to hear your answer tomorrow."

Lot Sun brandished his elegant sword. "You can have neither my cattle nor my daughter, goblen. Get you gone before I kill you where you stand."

The lead herald quailed. "You threaten a herald pod?"

He fled, galloping away, and his pod followed as the townsfolk shouted defiance.

Lot Sun barked a laugh without mirth. "That solves that. Those're impossible terms."

Ash Wal spoke. "Do we have this Disk of Dragons, sir?"

"Those were insane mumblings, Miner," Lot Sun answered, "dreams and foolishness a thousand years gone. I'm as interested in finding a deal as anyone, but the cattle are running free in the canyons yonder, the women we won't give over to their cruelty, and the Disk don't exist. If you can't find any grounds for negotiating, you can't make a deal. We got to fight."

As afternoon faded, Rev sought to take counsel with his leaders, but both Ash Wal and Lot Sun refused to meet with him. Annoyed, Rev joined the others in a tea house.

All agreed they could not accede to the insane demands.

"They wish our death," Dunortha stated.

Qual Hich waved his hands. His red mayor's hat sat crookedly on his head. "We cannot be sure, Lady, but they make unfortunate demands, truly. People will not stand for it."

"My friends," Rev said, "our count of fighters is around two hundred, against twelve hundred Chisen, but with the rubble cleared away, they have no hiding places within an arrow's flight of the wall. We can hold out. Dan, how are stocks at the hospital?"

"Not enough for a major battle, but they'll do the best they can. Ma'tha is holding up despite her recent sorrow."

"That man fled days ago," Rev said.

"That was another fellow, Rev." Gabryal held up her hand. "This one was new."

Everyone chuckled. The healer's man-hunger was well known.

"Elder Fu, what can you tell us about this army?" Rev asked. "Who do we face?"

"They are goblen, Rev, a people who desire order above all, and only agree to action after consulting each other. They operate in pods of six, though one member called the First is dominant, and one pod is dominant over five other pods, and so on up to the dominant pod over the Empire, led by one they call the Unity. The Chisen fear chaos. We may be able to take advantage of that, since a change in leadership is very disorderly. Disable one of their leaders, and the rest may retreat to choose a new leader."

The Elder paused. "Rumor says a vampyren leads the Chisen Empire, masquerading as their Unity."

Dismay followed this, though Rev was not surprised. He looked at Gabryal. Was the vampyren that led the Chisen in collaboration with Xul Bil Be? Were they both working at the behest of the Watcher? News that a vampyren already hid among them could not be kept from a war council, so Rev outlined his suspicions.

"I believe the vampyren was disguising itself as Xul Bil Be. The mage vanished after the earthquake."

"Could the vampyren here have asked the Chisen vampyren for help?" asked Dan.

"Almost certainly, my friend," answered the Elder Fu. "Aside from a few renegades, all vampyren cooperate, seeking the return of the Shadow Years."

"The vampyren are after this Disk of Dragons, Bounder?" asked Qual Hich. The mayor kept one hand on his red hat, nervously holding it on.

"Evidently, sir."

"Does this Disk have power?" Dunortha idled at the table with the tip of her dagger.

"The legends say it controls dragons, Lady," Gabryal said.

"So we put our hands on this Disk and a pair of dragons, and we win this fight," said Dunortha, flipping her dagger and catching it by the hilt.

Yarrow chuckled.

Rev also grinned. "If we knew how to use it. But we don't have the Disk to hand over." He reminded himself even if the Disk were really influencing him at a distance, he had no idea where it actually was in the physical world.

"Anyway, it is no honor to accept such terms," said Dunortha. "We must fight."

#

Rev walked with the Elder Fu back to his post through the darkening evening. Nervous or not, Rev needed some help. What is more difficult than to admit something truly shameful, an activity we secretly wish to continue? But Rev could not go on living this way.

"Elder, I got a difficulty." He explained about his trouble with stealing, how he had worked not to steal, and his failure on that very day. The old monk listened sympathetically.

Rev felt relief as he concluded. "What can I do, Elder?"

"Thoughts are powerful, Rev, they lead us into all sorts of foolishness. When I have troubles, I pay close attention to my own thoughts. If I concentrate on something foolish or hurtful, I end up doing something foolish or hurtful. Perhaps learning to focus your thoughts will work for you."

"My thoughts are always chattering away about some nonsense or other."

"No one said this is simple," the Elder said. "It's related to shi. To work the magic, I must control my thinking. Just so with any time I try to change myself."

"I've had success with shi. Some. I've been working on it."

"Good for you. Celebrate your progress, it is hard won. For me, I also pay attention to my emotions. Am I afraid? Why? Is anger driving my thoughts?"

"I can't imagine you angry."

The Elder laughed. "If I were a perfect being, I wouldn't be on this earth. No, I have trouble with my thoughts. But I have success when I feel whatever I feel, without trying to shunt it aside, or solve it.

"Feeling badly never hurt me. It's in acting to avoid feeling badly that I hurt myself and others. When I allow myself to feel badly, soon such feelings vanish and with them any urge to act the fool."

Rev felt as though those words went straight into his center. A profound change shivered through him.

So much of his stealing happened when he did not want to face some painful situation, but stealing made him feel worse and never solved the problem. And how many times was the pain due to the consequences of his own stealing? As though he wanted to hurt himself.

But he remembered the rushing joy of stealing, the triumph, the superiority. Could he reject such feelings forever? He wanted to. At least, most of him did.

As Rev and the Elder Fu reached another corner, half-a-dozen orcen in white sashes confronted them, led by the goblen rope maker Yendre Pindo.

Torches on the town walls cast eerie, shifting shadows.

"T, t. Bounder, the disasters we've had are due to you," said Yendre. "You've been high-handed since you entered this town. You must make amends to High Priestess Uulong. T, t, t. Come now."

Surprised, Rev stopped. "I have to see to the defenses of the town. I got no time for the priestess today, Yendre."

The orcen crowded around.

"You've stolen from her," the goblen insisted. "Only she may hold the item you have. Return it to her. T, t, t. We are all cursed until you do."

Panicked, Rev remembered the brass doorway. She needed it for defending the town? It was evil.

He almost said as much right there, but it did not matter, he was wrong in taking the doorway. "Give it to her."

He took the doorway from his belt pouch.

Yendre jerked back his hand, and the doorway dropped to the ground. "Tt. I can't touch that, I'm not worthy."

"I got no time for this," Rev said, shame making him rough. He pushed past the goblen, with the Elder Fu following him.

They went on in silence. He felt the heat of his humiliation before the Elder. He looked up to the dark sky. "Did you ever have trouble with stealing?"

"I have had trouble with many things in my life, young friend. I have lived a long time."

They reached the stairs at the base of the wall.

"You did the right thing, in returning the door, Rev," the Elder said in a comforting tone. "You try to do better, that is most important. You do better if you work at it, but improvement comes slowly. Be patient."

Rev bowed as the monk moved away. Rev felt a little less shame, being accepted by the Elder Fu even with his horrible flaw. He always thought if people knew his deepest secrets they would hate him. Maybe that was not entirely true.

He promised himself he would follow his own thoughts, catch the urge to steal when it crept in. At the moment, fortunately, he had no such urge. Maybe just admitting the urge removed it forever. He felt a tiny spark of hope.

#

In the night shade beneath the trees, the vampyren Xul Bil Be met with a messenger from the Chisen army. The messenger quailed, seeing fires burning where the vampyren's eyes should have been, bones gleaming beneath a tattered cloak.

The messenger could not keep his mandibles from clattering in fear. "Tt, tt, tt. What, what can you be telling us of those who resist us? Tt, tt, tt."

"The townsfolk have elemental, conjurative, and priestly magic. Some have fought in battle, many have not. Agents inside the town will help us. Expect this."

The goblen soldier bowed. "What of the disposition of the valley, after? Tt, tt, tt."

The vampyren felt contempt for those who would consider such trivial matters. "If your army conquers this valley, we grant it to your leader as a reward. You are dismissed."

The goblen fled.

Despite the flaws of the mortals, Xul Bil Be was pleased its compatriot had sent the army to help hunt for the Disk of Dragons. Success seemed inevitable. Doubtless this army was here at the behest of the Watcher. The strange presence would continue to apply pressure here until its goals, whatever they were, had been met.

But as the vampyren was departing the meeting place, a surge of overwhelming sadness and despair rushed in.

An ambush.

The vampyren dove into the brush, casting a protection spell to ward off physical assault. An embarrassing mistake. The attacker was not mortal, but a female Ghost Hound, two spans in length, black in color, radiating an unearthly cold along with the paralyzing emotions. Her icy fangs lunged for the vampyren.

Xul Bil Be dug a pinch of corpse powder from a pouch and flung it. The powder dissolved into a sparkling mist. The Hound hesitated just long enough before plunging through that powder to give Xul Bil Be time to speak the trigger phrase of a prepared spell.

Instantly, the vampyren traveled to the Other Side.

Unfortunately, the Ghost Hound clamped her jaws on the vampyren's shoulder and was dragged along, but here on the Other Side Xul Bil Be could touch the beast. The vampyren grabbed the Hound's jaws. The Hound let go and slashed the vampyren's arm.

Xul Bil Be screamed in pain. The Hound went for the throat, but the vampyren knocked her aside.

Desperate, Xul Bil Be threw up a wall of energy, but before it was completed the Hound slashed the vampyren's hamstring.

Xul Bil Be felt an explosion of pain, but the wall of magic was raised.

226

The Hound tried leaping around the shimmering magic, but the wall blocked her.

Behind its bulwark, the vampyren breathed in huge gulps of air, pulse racing as its body frantically repaired the damage. Over eons the vampyren learned that even massive pain could be ignored. Grimly, it prepared its next spell. The only source of power was its own life, but the Hound was too dangerous to let go free.

The vampyren released the wall, which vanished. As the Hound leapt forward, Xul Bil Be flung a pale silvery net of energy, capturing and entangling the Hound.

The vampyren's own life energy fled out in a rush.

#

The vampyren awakened on the ground of the Other Side, under a pale sky. Pain scorched its legs and shoulder. Vampyren mended unless they were killed outright, but the healing would be slow, since it had little power left.

Xul Bil Be felt uneasy. So many things had gone wrong. Maybe Xul Bil Be should simply leave. But how could Xul Bil Be report to the Cabalmaster that it had allowed mere mortals to take the Disk? Pride stiffened its resolve, and the memory of thousands of successes. It avoided thinking about the punishments the Lord Kukulque meted out for failure.

The Hound remained bound in the silvery net, but the despair and sadness emanating from her affected the vampyren, who angrily shook off the feelings.

It studied the Hound, deciding how to fashion a more permanent binding. The best power available was the Hound's own life essence. The Hound could serve as trigger for her own destruction.

The vampyren smiled thinly, concocted a fitting spell to enact its vengeance, cast it on her, then departed.

#

The Ghost Hound huddled, buried under the spell. She felt bereft. All through her mortal life she had known the future, but that ability was gone, and her memories were fading.

She must kill this vampyren quickly. Mists dimmed her sight and she was slipping away. She possessed one advantage, an attachment to the vampyren through which she could affect the net spell binding her.

227

Bindings that could be manipulated could be loosed. One memory flamed in her: this vampyren had devoured her daughter's soul. Only the vampyren's death would release her daughter, along with any other taken souls, to begin their final journey to peace.

The Hound gnawed steadily at the bindings of the trap.

Chapter Twenty Three

"Where goes the soul upon death? None knows, but spells have been crafted that bring souls back for short periods. The Ghost Hound is one such dire magic. A person who possesses a powerful intent, but dies before that intention is fulfilled, may be brought back as a Hound to complete the task. The magic opens a channel through the Veil to the Outside, beyond even the Other Side, but the cost is high for any foolish enough to cast such a spell, though that cost may not be perceived immediately."

"Mortality," from *The Grimoire of Deth Henan, Archmage of Pacesacre, 103A.*

Just after dawn, Norwe Hesketh stood among his five pod mates. As governing pod of the Western Hiyin province of the Chisen Empire, they rated most luxurious accommodations: rugs of silk and wool, furniture of cherry wood. The tent smelled faintly of mildew, however.

That Norwe stood while his pod mates remained seated on their soft ottomans showed his unusual dominance. Though he did not notice, the space they kept between him and themselves revealed their dislike for him, not that he would have cared. He had been third to join the forming pod during melding season nine years ago, and so by rights should never have been selected as provincial governor over his two senior pod mates. Only slick dealings with likeminded outsiders won him the position, leaving resentments among the pod.

Norwe was different from his mates. He was a rare grey goblen among the dark brown Chisen, and nervous, always tapping his claws or clacking his mandibles. And he had a cruel side that made his pod mates uneasy. Norwe continued his rant, started when he received a letter during breakfast.

"Ttt. My sister is here," he said, not so much to his pod mates as at them. "Her letter taunts me. She plotted with my very parents against me."

"Tt, is that why we came to this desolate place?" said Likye, using his claws to preen his mandibles in an insolent fashion. Likye was most vain, wearing only dramatic red silk shirts and black pants. "Obtaining vengeance on a broken-pod relative of yours?"

The pod tensed, since all knew orders to march on this town came down from the Unity. Truly, their own pod was near breaking. Norwe twitched, but otherwise did not acknowledge the insult, perhaps not knowing how to respond.

Instead, he turned to the door. "Var," he roared for his aide.

"Yes sir." The feral human slunk in and dropped to one knee. Underfed, looking more like prey than ally, the human's gaze skittered from the uneaten portions on the breakfast trays to the round bed pods favored so goblen could sleep tail to tail, protecting each other's backs; the beds were unused – the pod did not think with one mind anymore, the evidence was plain.

Of them all, only Sensii noticed Var's roving gaze. She narrowed her eyes. Trust the slinky human Var to use that information to his advantage. Sensii was the quietest of the pod, plotting patiently to take advantage of any openings. Despite being second in seniority, she always wore dark colors, the less easily to be noticed, the more easily to observe.

"Yes, Lord?" Var repeated hesitantly.

Norwe stared at him in suspicion. "T, t, t. Human, you look too much like the man who has been speaking for the rebels on the town walls. T. Like an enemy."

"Humans do look alike," Var said in a most subservient tone.

Sensii found him gratingly false, but she could stand her arrogant pod mate no longer. "T, tt. Third mate, are you planning on killing yet another of our aides?"

Norwe jerked in surprise. "Tttt. No, my pod mate, this human will be living."

The man Var seemed relieved.

Norwe continued. "Var, I am wanting you to take a message to the general. Tt, tt. We suspect a traitor is harbored in the town. She is Chisen, but of no pod. Grey-hued. T, t, t. Is that surprising you, human?" His voice rose to a near roar. "Let him give the order that she is to be cut down wherever she is found. Are you understanding, Var?"

230

"Yes sir. The grey-skinned goblen woman in town is a traitor, to be killed where found. The order must be communicated to all the troops."

"Ttt. She is broken-pod, Var, you forgot that part of the message. Now be going."

The human Var bowed and departed. Sensii looked after the aide, thoughtfully. He was a clever one, this human. Var had lasted as an aide to Norwe four times longer than any other. The governor even seemed to like Var, at least more than he liked his pod mates. Var, one of the conquered citizens of Shendasan, had risen far in the few years since the conquest of that city, displaying initiative and cunning. How could she use him?

"It's too bad you won't be witnessing the death of this broken-pod," she said to Norwe.

"Why shouldn't I?" Norwe wheeled on her.

"Tt, tt. The soldiers will kill her long before you get there." She kept her expression neutral, having sown the seed. Oh, she knew the story of his broken-pod sister, another one of his monstrous secrets. Let him worry.

"T, t. We shall be speaking to the rebels again in two hour-glasses of time," Norwe said, as though he were pod master, rather than merely third in rank inside the pod. "See that you are prepared. I would not be humiliated." He left the tent.

Likye clattered contempt the moment Norwe left. "Ttt. A bit high-handed, we are growing, wouldn't you say?"

Sensii sympathized with Likye. "T, tt. He does seem to think we are here solely for his benefit, rather than all for each other."

"I wonder how he would like life as a broken-pod." Likye examined himself in a mirror.

"Likye?" Sensii was scandalized. "Tt. That would be endangering all of us."

"Not if we can find another to join our pod. We would be the same as blended, then." Likye was fourth in rank inside their pod and his lowly status irritated him. If their pod re-formed with a new member, he might rise in rank. Better food, more mating.

"You have someone in mind?" Sensii asked, intrigued.

Gornwe spoke for the first time. Their most senior pod mate used a detached, disdainful tone. "T, t. Blended pods never have as much stature as an original."

Likye turned on him. "You are enjoying the fruits of our social position so greatly?"

Gornwe clicked in amusement. Their First was fatter than them all, his carapace glistening with oils, and so slow it was not surprising that Norwe had outmaneuvered him. "Being mates of a governor does have its perquisites." Gornwe liked to taunt the other males in the pod. Norwe mostly ignored him, but Likye always rose to the bait.

"Tttt. We should all be governor, sharing power," Likye said, his voice screeching in an unseemly fashion. "What IS a pod if not a team?"

As the tent heated, Sensii began cooling herself with a small wicker fan.

Murmii languidly raised her arm. "I for one do not wish the botheration of such work. Norwe is enjoying it, let him." Murmii was beautiful, lazy, absolute last in rank, and perversely enjoyed the position of least responsibility. Sensii wished politics had not required her to be one of their pod mates, but: "Allies make when pod is formed, so safe the children may be born."

"He is bringing us all down," Likye said. "He's digging for disaster, he never thinks of our pod, of us. You've seen him." He went back to studying his reflection in the mirror.

"What you are proposing is just never done," Gornwe said, waving his claw in disdain.

"Tttt. It is and has been," Likye said. "It just happens quietly. Order in public, always; I believe that as much as you do, but there must be change for advancement. If we stop appearing with Norwe in public, others will notice. No chaos, no disorder, only a subtle sign. Letting him make first entrance into this dreary town alone, for instance. He'll be champing to go after that broken-pod, so he won't be paying any attention. He'll probably even go in before the defenses are fully broken, the fool. Solve our whole problem for us. Anyway, if we find another pod for Norwe to join before we publicly break our own pod."

"Letting the new pod have the glory, and us have the safety, is that it?" Sensii asked. It came out cattier than she planned.

Likye drew himself up, formally. "Tt, tt. I am wishing to have children."

It was as though lightning crackled through the room. All hissed in tandem.

"Are you being serious?" Gornwe asked, for once breathless with surprise.

"Norwe will never stop long enough for us to nest," Likye said stubbornly. "And it is an excuse to break the pod even the Unity would accept."

"T. Be not saying excuse." Jorii spoke for the first time. Sometimes she went whole days without speaking, but now her mandibles clattered with excitement. "Be saying reason."

"Then you are with me?" Likye asked.

"T. I am." Jorii said.

"Tttt. Children are too much work," Murmii said, annoyance in her voice.

"Gornwe?" Likye asked.

"I will not be the one choosing to break my pod," Gornwe said. "There are two of you, you need three."

As one, the pod turned to Sensii, and she felt the heat of their attention, the choice hers to make. "Tt, tt. T," she clicked. "Yes, I am voting to break our pod. I will no more live in fear of my own pod mate. Let Norwe have power and rank, I will be choosing a family, a nest, the love of a true pod, of those who care for each other, as it was meant to be."

A slight breeze lifted the flap of the tent.

"Since you three have decided to leave the pod," Gornwe said slowly, "I will be joining you." Just like that, he dropped to fourth in status, after being First. "But I say we still appear with Norwe this morning. Think this through before we are making our move public."

"I am joining you as well." Murmii hissed delicately. "Who would wish to be alone with Norwe?"

"Let Norwe have his power?" Likye repeated softly, examining himself in the mirror. "Tttt. Oh, no, my mates. No, we will be doing better than that, now that I am First."

#

Two hours after sunrise, heralds from the army approached again. Rev was on the north wall, Yarrow and Dan at his side. The lead herald was a thin-faced goblen, grey rather than the usual cockroach brown, wearing golden robes and a circlet of feathers, carrying a silver scepter. Rev recognized the governor, Norwe Hesketh.

Five other goblen followed him. They must be his pod mates, all splendidly attired, but none dressed anything like each other. Did that lack of conformity mean something?

The governor spoke. "Ttt. Have you decided about our demands?"

"We'll have no dealings with bandits brandishing weapons at our door," Rev said.

Norwe's mandibles clicked in contempt. "Be considering this." He waved imperiously. From the Chisen camp soldiers emerged, carrying people like sacks, two peasant boys and a Ruskiya youth. The boys did not struggle.

"T, t. A few brats we caught. You are knowing them?"

A soldier yanked one boy's head up by the hair, giving a brief glimpse of a frightened face. On the town wall, a man screamed in grief as he recognized his son.

"T, t, ttt," Norwe laughed. "So you foreigners care about your children. T, t. Until you open your gates, we will be killing, slowly and at intervals, each of these vermin."

Rev's hope froze. Even the other heralds looked shocked.

"How many children have you seized, Chisen?" cried the stable master Ton Plu.

"T, t, t. You must guess. T, t, ttt. You will be having opportunity to make an accurate tally, you will be hearing them all." From the tents a fourth young boy screamed in agony.

"T, t, ttt," Norwe clicked in cruel amusement. "You will know whether we are having any left, they will only fall silent when all are gone. T, t. I will be returning at noon for your decision." Smirking, he departed. The townsfolk were stunned.

Spurred by this, the leaders of the town gathered in their headquarters. Prominent townsfolk joined them. All heard the faint screams of a boy being tortured in the Chisen camp.

Rev hunched his shoulders, not wanting to feel this terrible helplessness. He remembered what the Elder Fu said:

It's in acting to avoid feeling badly that I hurt myself and others.

234

The faces of his companions reflected a loathing and rage equal to his own.

"We have to make this decision as a community," Rev declared. "I believe they'll kill us if we open the gates, people."

"Council members," said Ash Wal in a cold tone, "I won't take the advice of a thief."

"Nor me, Council," said Lot Sun, to Rev's chagrin. The rancher would not look at Rev, and he wore a white sash. So Lot Sun had gone over to Uulong's Temple. Rev rued confronting him about the actions of his daughter; another cost come home to roost.

"Are you cowards, not to face the truth, townsfolk?" asked Dunortha. "See you not the cruelty in them? I back our leader, Rev Caern."

Her war leader, Kormenthon, nodded.

"I got to agree with Dunortha, friends," said Yarrow. "I see no reason to trust them killers, the Chisen'd slaughter us, first chance. It's hard, hearing that," he gestured in the direction of the ongoing cries, "but it shows what monsters we're fighting."

"I won't be led by a ruffian, Yarrow," Lot Sun said, "I got my honor to consider. I won't allow a thief to speak for me." He pointed his cane at Rev.

Ma'tha shook her head. "My heart grieves for those children, but we shouldn't all die out of spite, sir. We must work together."

"We have to save those children," said Gabryal, "but not by sacrificing all in division and recrimination, my friends. There must be another way."

"Do any oppose the choice to fight?" Dunortha looked around. No one raised an opposition. "So, rancher, that much is decided. At noon, go and tell them our decision."

Lot Sun glared at her, but she returned his gaze coolly until he rose and departed.

As the council broke up, Rev walked out. He felt an emptiness inside. His stealing had caused a division in their ranks. He wanted to blame it on weird Afen notions of culture and class, but none of this would be a problem without his own stupid actions. He had to change. Why hadn't he already? He felt a helpless shame.

They had faced so much loss: Bhat's death, the slaughter of the farm family, the depredations of the thugs, the earthquake. Now an army threatened; the stakes were going up and up. Surely these deaths were all tied to the Disk. The notched track found at the scene of the murder, along with the one at the den of the karken and the one at the camp of the thugs suggested someone thought Bhat Sun knew about the Disk and killed him to obtain that knowledge. And that person had kept on killing.

The thugs, the vampyren, the karken, maybe even the refugees, all were here for the Disk. Until it was found, no peace would come to the valley.

#

Rev could see the Chisen army checking their blades and fastening on their armor. It was the third of Wolfenmoon, summer already. In the morning heat, the Chisen armor would be sweltering. They deserved to sweat.

Dan had set the armorer, cooper and blacksmiths to making shields. The shields were small and crude, but better than nothing.

An obscuring mist arose over the enemy. From it, purple tendrils floated towards the town. Alarmed, Rev watched them approach, but far down the wall, the Elder Fu *gestured*. Three tendrils snapped, whipping back dangerously at their creators. The Elder Fu gestured again, and more tendrils snapped, one lashing back against the conjuror who raised it. The man collapsed. The mist faded shortly thereafter, and the Chisen did not try that spell again.

Still, looking upon the enemy, what Rev saw chilled him. Think of being surrounded by twelve hundred people who wish you dead. You are no more than an ant to be crushed beneath the heel, nothing to raise you above utter insignificance. The mind refuses to dwell on this, lest you go mad. You must laugh. Or lose yourself in duty, or drink, or hate. Rev looked out at the glittering ranks of the enemy in a cold way. This is the mind of war. He felt the glowing Disk inside him, hardening his soul.

At midday, Norwe returned under the flag of parley, his pod behind him. He called out contemptuously. "T, t, t. I am not seeing the gate open."

"We reject your terms, sir," Lot Sun cried. "Free our children and bother us no more."

Norwe clicked in amusement. "T, t, ttt. You are choosing your own fate."

He galloped back to camp. Two screams arose from the tents, high piercing sounds that bubbled as they faded. Several townsfolk burst into tears. Rev felt sorrow and fury, with an edge of fear. Here was the fate the Watchfulness intended for all the mortal races.

The Chisen army raised their shields and attacked.

Chapter Twenty Four

"Luwana, the Goddess of Love, yearned for union with the One God, Who is both Elho and Elha, male and female, the ultimate Unity, but since Luwana could not directly overcome division among the Gods, She chose to die to accomplish the unity of all beings. By this act Luwana showed even death cannot divide us, for we are united in spirit. The day will come when all unite, if we strive for that. Even the Gods of Chaos and Order will join."
The Histories of Teren: The Age of Legend.

Under a brilliant sun, the Chisen goblen battle line rushed forward in pods of six. Arrows flew from defenders on the wall, but most struck only shields or missed their targets.

"Patience, friends," Rev shouted, on the north wall. "Pick your target. Aim."

Down the wall, Dan coolly worked his bow, leading the archers. Behind the attackers, energies flared like cones of flame as the Chisen magic users cast their spells. Rev tried to empty his mind to find shi, but in his excitement it was impossible.

A huge, insubstantial creature rose behind the enemy lines, a demon of purple smoke as tall as the town wall. It had no head nor arms, only two massive legs; cruel flames ignited here and there inside its body. The Chisen soldiers drew aside in fear as the creature strode up to the north gate and smashed into the timbers, destroying itself.

The gate burst into flame. Defenders on the wall screamed as sheets of fire struck them, and two men collapsed, engulfed. Rev felt the shock of their deaths.

Suddenly, his fears were gone and his training took over. The Elder Fu taught him to visualize shi as water of different colors, and he felt the shi like water currents everywhere. Through the energy against his skin, he sensed what was happening, as though his body extended where he wished, and his will could direct the currents.

Energy gathered over the Chisen conjurors like a purple orb, and the new orb *felt* like the previous demon of smoke. Rev worked the shi above the attacking army, preparing a counter magic, primitive but the best he could do. He suppressed the energy rising from the goblen army, like a coiling spring. As the new smoke demon crossed the area, he released his coil of shi. The energy shot up, driving the monster high into the sky. It exploded far above. Wisps of smoke floated away, with a faint scent of sweat.

Rev sought the Disk, but did not sense it.

A bead of fire shot toward the Chisen mages: Gabryal's war magic. The enemy mages had lined up a throng of pale imps, and though Gabryal's magic struck one imp, exploding in an oily black cloud and the stench of ozone, the smoke dissipated to reveal the imp and the enemy mages behind it unhurt.

The Chisen soldiers lifted ladders against the wall. Rev ran down along the parapet, shouting encouragement. "Fight. Find aim. Fight!"

Pods of goblen foot soldiers climbed up, and the defenders engaged them with spears. Dan stood with the archers, loosing arrow after arrow. Two tiny dragonets circled Dan's head like a spinning golden halo, diving, rising, spitting fire at the foe.

"Knock down the ladders," Rev ordered, leveraging aside one with his sword. The ladder fell as defenders jumped off. To his right, on the wall beyond the north gate, the priestess Uulong screamed for destruction, atop a merlon in full view of the enemy. No arrow struck her. She waved a small brass object that caught the sun. The doorway.

"The woman's crazy," Dan declared.

To the left, Yarrow stood atop the wall, swinging his massive sword with the gargantuan cry of a man battling the very gods. As though a mist had lifted, Rev could see the true heart of the man in his inhuman delight in battle. None withstood him, few tried.

Two enemy conjurors worked frantically, but Yarrow took on their greatest demons with a mighty laugh, and the power of his presence kept the otherworldly beings at bay.

For a moment, Rev felt the sense of something high above them all, looking down, directing the battle.

Immediately, the power of the Disk was there, luring Rev:

I can protect you against the Watcher.

An arrow exploded against the wall, stinging him with shards. Ignoring the Disk, he knocked down the next ladder. Other defenders pushed off ladders, slowing the assault.

"Bad magic coming, Rev," Dan called.

A whirlwind streamed into the air above the Chisen conjurors, a demon spinning into a tornado. The whirlwind headed for their wall. Rev's heart skipped a beat, but he threw a directed line of shi against the tornado. His will struck it, but the blowback knocked him off his feet.

The demon's power was too great, but stubbornly, he clambered up again.

The tornado sucked up attackers as it approached – the mages directing the demon showed no concern for their own troops. The goblen army fled to either side.

Desperate, Rev submitted to the power of the Disk, hoping to use it against the tornado. The power seized him. He waited for guidance, but sensed only a distant satisfaction. The Disk was not volunteering any help, now that it had him. He'd been decoyed.

Or had he? At least the sense of watchfulness was gone.

The tornado struck the wall. Defenders, ladders and spears flew everywhere. Rev frantically tried imagining the golden glow of the Disk driving against the tornado, but the whirlwind hung in place, and the wall began to crumble. One stone flew at Rev. He ducked it.

Unexpectedly, the tornado changed. Wobbling in a widening gyre, it suddenly looped crazily back toward the attacking mages, struck the throng of conjured imps protecting them and blew several creatures apart, destroying itself in the process.

Had the Disk done this? Then Rev realized the Elder Fu had taken a hand, turning the tornado back on the Chisen. The Elder Fu had saved the wall.

The goblen army regrouped. Once again the Chisen army pressed forward, and arrows flew up so heavily the defenders had to seek shelter behind the stone merlons.

Rev worked shi to dissipate the fire raging at the town gate, but the energy was difficult to handle, the flows whipping back and forth. The chaos of the fire baffled him, but he drew some of its energy skyward, a simple enough task for his limited skills.

The fires died down. He drew away energy until only flickers remained, then lassoed the last flames to send darts at the nearest soldiers. The attackers screeched and jumped back. The gate was blackened, but held. Beyond it, Uulong raged on, using a terror that emanated from the doorway to drive back the Chisen.

Dust hid most of the wall, so Rev could not see Dan. He hoped his friend was all right. The Chisen conjurors were summoning smaller beings, which meant their largest spells had been cast, he hoped. Better yet, the imps were going berserk: the Elder Fu was still fighting.

An arrow slashed past Rev's face and he ducked. His ear stung. He raised his hand to his ear and it came away bloody. He had dropped his shield while weaving the flows of shi. Chagrined, he hefted his shield again before he looked out.

Unexpectedly, he caught a pungent whiff of roses. Before he could trace it, a goblen vaulted the wall and lunged at him. Rev deflected its spear with his shield. A defender beside Rev swung a sword and the goblen fell, headless.

The battle raged. Three times more the goblen troops gained the walls, three times Rev helped throw them back. The Chisen conjurors sent magical beings clambering up the walls, but the Elder Fu and Gabryal foiled these assaults. Once, Gabryal shot a bolt of fire through the remaining imps and wounded a goblen conjuror.

At last, horns rang above the fray, and the attack broke off. The goblen troops retreated, bearing their dead and wounded. The sun was nearly down. The gate smoldered. The defense had held, but bodies lay strewn along the wall. The town had paid heavily.

Where was Dan? Rev searched along the wall, as the shadow of fear suddenly clutched his heart. Darkness slowly covered the field, but Rev did not his friend.

#

That evening, in the tea house, Rev took counsel with the town's leaders. They sat at a table in the heat, without a breath of breeze, as the

241

groans of the wounded rose in the distance. Dan did not join them. In shock, Rev still hoped Dan would turn up alive.

The others waited, but Rev did not know what to say. Where the wall had been weak the casualties were heaviest. He had not done enough to build up the wall, not insisted people work on it more. The icy weight of the magic he had worked today created a wall between him and his emotions, but he supposed he must be feeling guilt and anger.

While eating beef stew, the commanders reported assaults had been thrown back on every side. The fewest casualties came on the south wall, where the ravine hampered the attackers, the most casualties occurred on the north, where three of the six enemy mages concentrated.

Skarii's imps proved equal to facing an enemy conjuror, but she slumped at the table, exhausted. Dunortha also succeeded in countering the enemy's spells, though Rev had no idea what magic she wielded.

"But not alone," she said. "The Elder Fu helps this day, or it goes ill for us."

Gabryal ate silently in one corner. Rev was grateful beyond words that she survived. Slowly, his emotions trickled back in. The tavern owner Pura Rew, her tail drooping, reported twenty-five town members killed, another thirty-seven wounded.

Concerned about the damage to the northern gate, Rev directed Yarrow to have his men pile stones and timbers against it to prevent a breach. Kormenthon decided to have the Ruskiya do the same on the western gate, and when Yarrow asked, Lot Sun shrugged. "I could do so, Yarrow."

But Ash Wal refused to block the east gate. "Why seal ourselves in? We need some chance of escape if the fight turns against us." His voice was strangely tense.

The High Priestess Uulong hissed at him. "Betrayer. Servant of the shadows, you think I do not see who you truly are? You will beg for mercy as the Goddess gives you to the flames."

Enraged, Ash Wal rushed at her. White-Sashers surged in to protect their mistress and three miners raised their spears.

Rev leaped between them. "Stop."

Using shi to strengthen his muscles, he held the two combatants at arm's length. "Stop this. We're playing our hands for our enemies. Don't you understand?"

The priestess glared. "In not thwarting evil, Bounder, you assist it. You, too, will feel the wrath of the Goddess." She swept away, her followers trailing her.

"The Bounder may consider himself thanked," Ash Wal said, sarcastically.

"Get out of here," Rev told him, disgusted.

The man swaggered off. What sort of leader was Rev, not to have his troops obey him? This had to do with the poisonous words Eg Bror had spread, but Rev could only change his future choices, the past was over and done. *Feeling badly never hurt me.* He remembered the Elder Fu's words. They were not much help.

The meeting over, the others departed. All but Gabryal.

Rev and Gabryal stared at each other. Whether spurred by the danger of battle, or some deeper need, they left the teahouse together and found an abandoned building.

A dim light from torches atop the town walls shone through the door. Their first, frantic kiss was endless, their hunger all-consuming. His hands roved her curves, enflaming them both. Her own hands became insistent in turn, then it was all giving and receiving and heat in the shadows.

#

In silence, he gently traced his finger along her cheek, across the sweet lobe of her ear, down her neck. She rested her hand on his shoulder. So that was love. He had learned this much before he died, what it was like to love a beautiful woman.

Duty called them away, but their parting kiss was tender.

"You are a dear man, Rev," she whispered. Then she was gone.

#

Rev never slept that night, shoring up the town's defenses. Nor did he ever find Dan Zee. When White-Sashers attacked goblen laborers, calling them traitors, Rev broke that up, knocking down one man with the flat of his sword. The followers of the priestess used the incident to whip up fury, and ever more people seemed to regard Rev with hatred. Several times he was spit at.

The sun came up majestically. Watching the sky take on a golden glow, Rev felt light-headed, half mystical, as though some secret of the universe were about to be revealed. But out beyond the town walls, the enemy army waited, and he feared what that secret might be.

Chapter Twenty Five

"Is not death necessary for life? All life rests on the sacrifice of others. The deer sacrifices herself to the wolf, the earthworm to the hungry fox. We submit, and as the Goddess requires, we give our lives. In this way our people remain strong in faith, and She cares for us."
Blasphemy of a Follower of the Goddess Thana upon the Scaffold During the Murkung Wars, 602A.

Rev waited on the town wall alongside Yarrow, but morning passed and the army remained in place.

"They might be thinking siege." Yarrow scratched a dog's ears, as calm as though he had not fought at all. It made Yarrow seem inhuman, but Rev felt glad the blond lion of a man was on his side. He wondered if Dan had fallen off the town wall, and lay among the bodies there. The grief was too great. He could not think about it anymore.

The besieging army fanned into the ruins. Laborers hauled stones to lay into courses, building a stone wall against the defenders' arrows. The wall snaked forward, protecting the workers as they toiled. The master of the project directed the workers from half a hundred paces beyond range of Rev's bow. Yarrow made a nasty face, found his own massive bow, and when the man turned away, loosed an arrow. It vanished into the sky. A long moment passed, then the arrow transfixed the man. He collapsed.

Yarrow nodded. Confusion reigned on the project the rest of the morning.

Considerable action roiled around a tent the enemy set up for their wounded and in the area they buried their dead. Still, despite the cost of the assault, the Chisen heavily outnumbered the town's defenders.

"We got cattle and grain enough for a month or more," Rev said.

Yarrow shook his head. "They'll poison the river to ruin our well. The well ain't deep, and the ground here is mostly rocky, not much sand to filter the water."

Dismayed, Rev hurried off to find Pura Rew in the central plaza. He told her to have people gather water into basins, tubs, whatever could hold water.

Her tail waggled. "Jho Iun could make more barrels, sir."

"Good. Have him do that, Pura."

Then, from afar, Rev spotted Dan on the street, a bandage on his head. He was alive!

Rev ran the whole way there, laughing in disbelief. "Dan, hunt-brother. Are you all right?"

"I'm dead as a door jamb," Dan answered weakly. "Looks worse than it is, actually."

His shaky smile brought tears to Rev's eyes.

Rev danced in a circle of joy. "I told myself you had to be alive. I couldn't go to the hospital, I was afraid you wouldn't be there. I looked everywhere else, so I just couldn't. Forgive me, Dan."

Rev cried freely, seeing his friend whom he feared gone forever. "You get right back in the hospital and let the healers take care of you, I don't want you risking yourself."

"We're all risking ourselves now," Dan answered somberly. "Anyway, Ma'tha thought it would be fine if I got out for a few moments. Not long, though."

"Let me find you a place to sit."

Rev spent a quarter of an hour's glass in the shade of the plaza willow with Dan before returning to the cares of the town.

Yarrow was right. The next morning, when they tested the well water on a chicken, it went into convulsions. Rev felt a sinking feeling. Their water source was ruined.

"Another way you've betrayed us, human," one of Uulong's guards said with contempt.

Rev went to find the Elder Fu, atop the wall.

"Can we use shi to make the water pure?"

The Elder Fu shook his head. "Shi is energy flowing. We can make the energy respond to our will, but poison is simply an element in the water. I have not the skill to remove it."

Rev found Skarii on the opposite wall.

She shrugged. "T. Conjured beings have no ability to remove poison from water, human. I'm sorry."

Gabryal was moving chairs out of the hospital. "Making more room for pallets inside," she explained.

But she could not do what he asked, either. "I don't know any elemental spells that do what you propose."

An extra tenderness was between them, but her voice reflected her exhaustion.

Ma'tha, at the hospital door, pursed her lips. "What you ask isn't healing, it's a purification, Rev. My spirits can't help either, I'm afraid."

Rev's frustration grew. With all the magic available, none could do this key thing. The Watcher was outthinking him. At that thought, he had a rush of warmth, and the image of the Disk was suddenly before his eyes – blocking him from feeling the Watcher. If he could not sense it, it could not sense him. That was the help the Disk was offering. Everything else he must do on his own. But even without feeling the Watcher, he knew it was out there, an evil, taunting presence, working to destroy his town, simply because it could. He wondered what its next move would be.

#

When he returned to the central plaza in the afternoon shadows, the leaders of the town had gathered, including the mayor Qual Hich in his red hat, Ash Wal, Lot Sun and the burly blacksmith Man Usp. Yarrow stood there, as did Dunortha and Kormenthon.

Lot Sun used his cane to wave Rev over. "We had a meeting, Bounder. People ain't happy with the direction of the fight. We decided a change in leadership is needed."

Rev had been relieved of command.

Ash Wal nodded, with a satisfied expression. Yarrow stood stone-like, Man Usp and the mayor wore unreadable expressions.

"Who will lead the refugees?" Rev asked.

"For the duration of the battle, Bounder," said the mayor Qual Hich, holding his hat atop his head, "we've agreed to follow Kormenthon's orders."

Kormenthon's face was compassionate but his words were stern. "Bounder, we unite as a battle force when we do this. You understand?"

If the townsfolk did not wish to follow him, he would cause no dissension, too many lives were at stake. "Kormenthon, I yield command to you. What do you want of me?"

"We speak of your skills later. We are first deal with the threat to our water supply. Gabryal holds skill with the magic of fire, sa?"

"She does," he said, numb.

"This is good. We have water, fire, we distill water for drink. Kill cattle, salt some, smoke some. Cattle we eat first, save our grain against a longer siege. We schedule our watch, half a day on, half a day off, that no one grows too tired. All understand?"

The gathered leaders nodded.

"I review the lines of leadership. We make a method to our defense." This last he said to Ash Wal, who nodded, sullenly.

"Go to your tasks. Rev, I speak with you now."

Once the others were gone, he spoke quietly. "Rev, an army fights on food. As the army comes, I send youths to drive off the *neve*. The Chisen are have little food. This makes them vulnerable. I ask you slip over the wall tonight, disturb their camp, destroy their supplies. Hunorn sees you have forest skills when you are hunt for the karken together. You can do this."

What he asked made sense. Cynically, Rev also understood that if he failed he would die, removing a point of dissonance among the townsfolk. "I'll do as you ask."

#

Rev found Dan on a wicker chair outside the hospital.

"You alone against an army?" Dan said incredulously. "You'll be killed."

"We got to do something."

"I'm coming along." Dan struggled to his feet.

"No, you're not." Rev gently forced his friend back into the chair. He was disturbed at how easy it was to do. "You ain't in any shape."

"You're my heart-brother, Rev, I don't have anyone but you. We've done everything together. You can't do this alone. Don't leave me."

"I'll be back." Emotions welled inside him. "You ain't strong enough, heart-brother."

"Then take someone else. Yarrow or Gabryal. Someone strong."

"I'm thinking on doing this alone. Why kill someone else?"

"At least tell them what you're doing," Dan pleaded. "Do that for me."

"I will tell them," Rev promised. "And I'll be back. On my honor as a slicker."

"Oh, that's a comfort," Dan said.

They both grinned.

#

Rev found Yarrow by the north gate, telling Gabryal of Rev's demotion. Her face reflected her sympathy.

Rev waved it off. "Something new has come up. I agreed to sneak out to burn the Chisen supplies."

Gabryal's eyes widened. "The Chisen will be on watch. You can't do it alone, I'm going with you."

"As am I," Yarrow rumbled.

"Gabryal, the town needs your magic for fires to distill drinking water, and the Chisen could attack again, any time."

"You need my magic, too. If they don't have sense enough to keep you as leader, I'm not worrying about them too much. People don't need magic to start fires. Flint, steel and tinder works fine."

He turned to Yarrow. "You know too much about tactics to be taken away from the northern wall. You got a duty to your men."

"Qual Hich can take my place, the mayor fought in a siege once before. Rev, I didn't hire on to the town, I hired on to you. Town'll take care of itself. Anyway, Zhopahr can't stand a long siege and the army'll send for reinforcements, so we got to move quick."

Rev felt a tiny stab of hope, but shook his head. "Here's the issue, I got a plan for getting outside, but I'm not sure I can bring anyone else."

"How's that?" Yarrow asked, a glint in his eye. Amusement?

When Rev explained about the golden path, Yarrow nodded. "Passage to the Other Side. If you open the way, anyone who's touching you can follow."

"You're sure of this?" Rev asked, surprised.

"So the stories say." Yarrow shrugged.

After full dark, the three gathered in dark clothes and charcoaled faces near the east gate. The moon would not rise until near dawn. Rev felt

249

thankful for Yarrow and Gabryal's support. He took Gabryal's hand and she took Yarrow's to form a physical link between them.

Each time he Crossed Over, the vertigo lingered longer, but he gritted his teeth and took the golden path. Sure enough, by holding his hands, his companions stayed with him. On the Other Side, he led the others east to get beyond any guard posting on the mundane side.

All through this, he was feeling the presence of the Disk, a warmth in this limbs, an image of the golden Disk whenever he closed his eyes, hiding his movements from the Watcher. Something told him if the Disk were not hiding him, this little jaunt would be found out quick, and end brutally.

At last he halted. "We'll need to be silent when we return to the mundane world."

Yarrow drew a long dagger from a belt sheath. "Ready."

Rev shivered.

"I expect their supply wagons will be near the golden tents," Rev said. "Gabryal, can you set the wagons afire?"

"Yes." The certainty in her voice gave him confidence.

"Then let's play out this hand." Rev sought the golden path back to the mundane world. The light changed, and the familiar stars appeared. They were out of town, far enough away from the Chisen army that Rev heard only the usual noises of the night. They looped around to the northwest, well outside where pickets might be stationed, then finally turned inward.

In a couple hundred paces, using shi, Rev sensed a sentinel. Heart pounding, he pointed.

Yarrow slipped off. That was a job for one alone. Rev sensed the deep shi flows of the army. His vertigo eased, maybe because he was not moving.

A huge form loomed. Yarrow. The big man wiped fluid from his blade, his eyes cold. They continued. Rev grew aware of more soldiers. A pod slept nearby. Rev held up a hand, but Yarrow had already slipped ahead. How could such a big man move so quietly?

Twice more they encountered pods of sleepers, and though Rev wanted to lead the team around, Yarrow went after the sleepers each time. The big man was calculating and deadly. Rev shuddered. But they needed such an ally that night.

They reached the supply train, but no supplies remained on the wagons, so Rev led the hunters onward. They saw a pile of boxes ahead. The supplies. A sentry sat at a fire, arrow nocked. Yarrow's dagger blossomed in his chest. The goblen slumped, his bow clattering.

Rev tapped Gabryal's shoulder. She raised her staff.

"Yalkatanthe is, hai quanthe resdolor..."

Of course she had to speak her spell aloud. Ozone filled the air.

"Yrech!" someone shouted in the goblen language. Rev felt a lurch of fear.

The boxes exploded in flames. Soldiers shouted. One rushed up, crying out. Rev stepped from the shadows and lopped the man's head off.

Yarrow cut another soldier down.

"Rev, to the Other Side," Yarrow called.

Their only chance. Rev sought the golden path, and despite his fear found it. He raced onto the shining line, and in a few paces found the second, dim path heading to the Other Side. The noise of battle vanished. Instantly he became so dizzy he fell sprawling. Yarrow halted beside him, but no one was beside Yarrow.

Gabryal had been left behind.

Chapter Twenty Six

"In that land was ruination. The rivers were stopped with bodies, livestock lay bleeding in the ditches, the buildings were thrown down, the people taken into slavery. A wind blew across the empty fields."
"The Fall of Pacesacre," from The Last Days of Sinnesemota, *by Kol Dar, 23A.*

In the dim light of the Other Side, Rev realized Gabryal must still be in the camp of the enemy. Using his sword, he frantically levered himself to his feet, but as he started back, Yarrow intercepted him. Running into his arm was like hitting a tree trunk.

"Easy, friend," Yarrow said. "They'll be lying in wait."

"She'll be dead." Rev struggled to free himself. The effort increased his dizziness. The idea of Gabryal at the mercy of the Watcher was almost more than he could bear.

"If so, she already is. If she ain't, they'll have caught her and taken her for questioning. We'll need to free her."

Rev paused, panting. "They torture those they catch."

"So we move quick. I've watched them bring their prisoners to the golden tent. It's this direction." Yarrow led off through the trees as though he had been on the Other Side a thousand times. He was the coolest man under pressure Rev had ever known. With him leading, the vertigo eased.

After a hundred paces, Yarrow paused. "We Cross Over to the mundane, cut our way into the tent, grab her if she's there, and Cross Over to the Other Side. Can you do it?"

Rev lifted his own sword. "Let's go."

He released his will to the Disk, found the golden path and stepped forward.

The lighting changed. Firelight revealed a night campsite. Ahead rose the wall of a tent, just as Yarrow said.

Rev slashed the canvas and charged in.

Five goblen soldiers inside the tent faced Gabryal, who fought the grip of a sixth. Her head was bloody. Their spears were out. Rev plunged his sword into the kidney of the nearest soldier.

A second goblen turned, eyes widening. "*Yrech.*"

Rev thrust his blade into the man's throat, as Yarrow stabbed another.

Two goblen leaped out the door, yelling. "T, t, t. *Kanse il resen.*"

The goblen grappling with Gabryal turned, but Gabryal drove her fist against his head, staggering him. Rev's sword finished him off.

Gabryal grabbed her staff and they fled through the rent in the canvas. Outside, Rev found the golden path, keeping one hand firmly on Gabryal. As they Crossed Over, the world behind them exploded in flames.

On the Other Side, exhausted by their near disaster, they sank onto a fallen log.

The starlight was dim, the east lightening. The forest looked primordially beautiful.

Rev kept replaying the scenes in his head, the blood, the screams, the terror on Gabryal's face. She rested in the crook of his arm. He checked the wound above her right ear, found it bloody but not deep. He kissed her hair.

"We're out, now," Yarrow said. "We can escape the whole fight. Shall we? The town seems doomed, most folks would say."

Rev looked at his friend in astonishment. "Abandon the townsfolk?"

Only then he noticed that Yarrow carried two orcen boys, evidently rescued from the tent, both covered with lacerations and dazed. One was Gil Plu-shin, the stable master's son, the other a Ruskiya boy.

"They rejected your leadership, Rev, and half would cheer if you died. Are you truly going back? The White-Sashers are your enemies, they mean you ill."

"Not everyone in town wears the white sash."

"Not even most, but would you really take Gabryal back into that? Or these boys?"

Rev felt a wrench. He could keep Gabryal from danger.

"I can't leave Ma'tha," Gabryal said.

"Ain't you returning with us?" Rev asked Yarrow.

"You're going back in?" Yarrow asked, a strange glint in his eye.

To Rev, it was not even a question. How much he had changed. "I owe the Elder Fu, and I gave the refugees my word to protect them. Anyway, Dan Zee is there."

Yarrow nodded. "I'll stick with you, but we best hurry, the army won't wait after learning their supplies are ruined, they'll launch an attack right away."

Rev noticed a dark stain on Gabryal's arm. "Let me see that."

Blood. Her arm had been sliced from elbow to wrist.

"We got to get you to Ma'tha." Rev took off his shirt and fashioned a makeshift bandage, fighting his vertigo.

"Do you have anything to drink?" Gabryal asked.

No one had brought a canteen. Rev had been twelve ways a fool. He assisted her as they moved off through the twilight, while Yarrow led the two children.

#

They emerged onto a street in Zhopahr near the east gate at dawn.

"Next attack will come any moment." Yarrow departed for the north wall.

As Rev assisted Gabryal and the boys to the hospital, a tremendous roar arose. "Yarrow was right," Rev said. "Here comes the battle." The greatest push yet by the Watcher to destroy their town.

Rev was still dizzy. Men screamed and magic whooshed as they reached the hospital.

"Ma'tha," Rev shouted. "Gabryal is wounded. Ma'tha!"

Ma'tha rushed out and guided Gabryal to a bench. "Let's see, Gabryal."

Dan Zee stepped out, with a bow and quiver. He was bandaged, but upright. "You sure can put a scare into a slicker. You survive?"

"With Yarrow and Gabryal's help."

"See, that's good. I thought bringing friends would help." Dan strung his bow. "Go on. I'll be along as soon as I can."

Rev clapped his friend gently on the back, gave Gabryal a kiss, and left them all to Ma'tha. He could see from the hospital door the fighting had not reached the south gate, so he headed east, weaving from dizziness.

He rounded a corner to find Ash Wal at the east gate, lifting the crossbar.

An instant of confusion reigns when we are confronted with something that goes against common sense. At that moment death hovers closely.

Rev took a fatal moment to recognize that Ash Wal was letting in the goblen. Betraying the town. The Watcher had reached inside their walls and turned one of their own against them.

"Ash Wal, stop," Rev roared.

The gate swung open. The enemy poured in. Half-a-dozen spears caught Ash Wal, lifted his body like a rag doll and flung him aside.

Only two defenders were in a position close to what was happening: the clothier Papas Sekulto and his partner Drinhe. The two townsmen charged out into the street before the attacking soldiers, and braced themselves. Chisen spears crashed against their shields, seeking their hearts. They dug in harder, stemming the tide of the enemy for a few desperate moments.

"People," Rev cried, "the gate is open. The enemy is inside. To the east gate!"

Alone, Papas and Drinhe blocked the way. One spear after another struck them, but they refused to fall. Finally, their shields shattered.

The Chisen soldiers overwhelmed the two defenders, and the army swirled in, but Papas and Drinhe had bought time for townsfolk to rush down off the wall, and for Rev to gather shi.

The Chisen whooped and flung their spears. Rev used shi to divert them. A thin line of defenders crashed into the attackers, halting their advance briefly, then slowly giving away as more Chisen warriors poured in, the full weight of the Watcher behind them. The fate of the town hung in the balance.

Remembering a trick the Elder Fu once showed him, Rev slapped his hands on the ground, channeling shi. The soil rippled, and Rev directed the ripple at the charging goblen, knocking them off their feet. How else could he use shi as a weapon? He tried cracking the ripple of shi like a whip. It worked. The shi snapped two goblen into the air, clicking and screaming. One hit the town wall hard, another struck a building. Both crumpled.

A dozen more defenders joined the fight, their spears red with blood.

"Close the gate, people." Rev drew his sword and charged. Other defenders joined Rev, while the Chisen raised spears and cried out in their tongue.

Half split from the fight and raced off into the city streets.

Again, Rev had the strange feeling his sword guided him. He parried a spear and lunged, scoring a wound on his opponent's wrist. He danced back as two other attackers struck.

The power of the Disk flooded him. He felt a connection between the Disk and sword. He remembered moonlight highlighting the sword high atop the City Hall, that power contending against the Watcher. Here again, the Disk set itself against the vampyren, and their great, secret power. So he fought, and his blade glowed with a golden light.

Was the Watcher hovering there before him? Suddenly, in the midst of the battle, Rev felt as though he confronted a vast Shadow, with eyes of darkness that sucked at his soul. Hate and emptiness faced him, an unfathomable abyss drawing him forward to his doom.

But his sword was in his hand, and it had faced this enemy before. Power blazed from the blade, light throwing back the darkness. He stepped forward, and the Watcher fell back, not caring to confront its power directly.

Another time would come.

With that, the Shadow passed.

Rev found himself near the open city gate. He slammed the gate shut and dropped the bar. Cut off from reinforcements, the last of the Chisen inside fell to the blades of the defenders.

The townsfolk had prevailed here, but only eight defenders still stood. Rev felt a cold lack of emotion, as the power of the Disk roared through him.

His own people stepped back, dismayed by the look on his face.

"Are they all gone?" His voice sounded alien even to himself.

"Some Chisen went to open the south gate, sir."

"We go there." Rev ran for the south gate, his power sweeping the others along. Halfway down the first street, he found a pod of Chisen facing a squad of townsmen.

Rev attacked, throwing the Chisen into turmoil. The other townsfolk scattered the goblen, leaving two dead.

Rev stared at his father's blade, amazed he survived a fight against skilled soldiers. The magic blazed, and he felt like a pawn. The Disk had taken him. So be it.

"To the south gate," Rev shouted, rallying the townsfolk.

They gave a harsh cheer.

He charged down the street and around a corner, with the townsfolk following him. The enemy soldiers had indeed opened the south gate. Lot Sun and his men fought the enemy hand-to-hand. Near the hospital, Dan plied his bow, Gabryal beside him, her arm in a bandage. Her staff flared, but the resulting fireball was weak, striking only two Chisen. She was wounded and tired.

A trio of Chisen conjurors entered the gate, preceded by six ghost-like demons. Behind them marched six more pods of soldiers, and behind them, triumphantly waving a jewel-encrusted sword, the governor Norwe Hesketh himself, champion of the Watcher and locus of its power today.

Sure that nothing purely physical could affect the demons, Rev sheathed his sword, raised a shi whip and struck at Norwe. A demon blocked his strike, and the enemy conjurors shouted contempt. Rev swung at the demon.

By luck, his whip hit a vulnerable spot, breaking the magic that bound the demon to the mage's will. The creature vanished in an oily puff of spoke.

Gabryal launched a fireball. One demon staggered, but survived. Dan's arrows bounced off the demons. Rev alone could stand against them. The demons broke off stones from nearby buildings. Rev used shi to redirect the hail of stones, sending them crashing into the buildings. The demons simply snapped off more stones and timbers.

One demon advanced. Rev tried his ripple magic against it, to no effect.

Then, with a suddenness like jumping into a cold lake, the power of the Disk deserted him. His shi wavered, but he could not flee. The defenders must hold.

A building collapsed with a roar. Dust billowed, then cleared to reveal a conjured demon nearly upon him. Rev dropped to the ground as a stone flew over his head.

He cracked his shi whip around the demon's legs and yanked it off its feet. The demon floated sideways, into the aim of its comrades. Two stones bounced off it.

Rev snapped his whip, hoping to break the bindings that held the demons. He drove the nearest demon back with the fury of his attack.

Two other demons stepped to one side to better strike at Rev. Inadvertently, the goblen conjurors and Norwe were left unprotected.

Wheels had turned against wheels, pawns moved against pawns, sacrifice, pain and loss, all for this one moment, with the Watcher lined up against champions of hope, the battle in the balance, and an opening the Disk itself perhaps had prepared, setting up the players for one last fling of the dice.

A tiny imp shot past both attackers and defenders, splitting the gap between the demons, trailing fire. It struck the champion of the Watcher, Norwe Hesketh.

Flames enveloped him with a whoosh. The goblen leader screamed. He dropped to the ground, engulfed by flames and an oily smoke that died away to reveal his charred body.

The leader of the Chisen goblen was dead.

With that, the strength of the Watcher was broken, the flaws of its tools revealed. Just as the Elder Fu had predicted, when the Chisen leader fell the fight went out of the their whole army. Their conjurors backed away, calling for their demons to protect them.

They fled through the gate, and the Chisen soldiers broke and raced after them. The deepest instincts of the goblen, their very nature, overwhelmed any subtle prodding by the Watcher.

The goblen rank and file was left with this thought: no one wished to be last to die. Let their former governor have the honor. He had wanted this town so badly, let him stay in it.

They did not even rescue his body on their way out.

Just like that, they were gone. Dust roiled as Rev slammed the town gate shut. Dan and he dropped the crossbar in place together.

"The Chisen are retreating, Bounder," a man called down from the wall.

Bodies lay scattered everywhere. Someone approached through the haze. Rev drew his sword, but it was only Skarii.

She walked up to the corpse of Norwe Hesketh. She must have conjured the fire imp that killed Norwe. She spit in the dead man's face.

"My brother. My full name is Skarii Hesketh. Ttt. He killed our parents. Killed my pod mates, in his ambition. I fled, vowing his death. He was always wanting to conquer. Told me he was wanting to rule even the

Afen, even the Pers. Sooner or later, that meant coming west through this town. T, t, t. You never hate anyone like you hate your relatives."

"What of the Chisen still in the city, Skarii?" Rev asked.

"Who knows? Ttt. They're probably all dead."

That was it. Silence slowly descended on the city.

"I'm going back to the hospital," Gabryal said, at last.

"Me, too," Dan said. "To sleep for a week."

Gabryal kissed Rev, then she and Dan departed.

Rev stared down at Norwe Hesketh, the man who ordered his father's death. He felt no satisfaction. The Disk had left a gaping void inside him.

He left Skarii alone with her brother's body. In the next block he entered the doorway of an empty home. A zinnia bloomed in a vase on the table. He crammed the flower into his pouch and walked out.

Somehow, after that he could focus on the town again. Skarii was correct, all goblen soldiers inside the walls were dead. A pod tried to open the northern gate, but Yarrow leapt down from the wall onto two soldiers, killing them, as his sword lopped off the head of a third.

The others fled, but he cut them down within a few steps, then prowled the town, ensuring no other Chisen lived.

Rev climbed the wall. The Chisen army was breaking camp. Their leader killed, they were leaving.

Back at the east gate, Rev found Ash Wal's corpse. Killed by the invaders he let in. He made his betrayal, gambled and lost. If he had won, all the townsfolk would be dead. The Watcher had reached him, and twisted his thinking. What had he been promised? A few coins? Some place at a royal table?

Rev's skin prickled. The Watcher would stop at nothing. Rev could almost feel sorry for Ash Wal, knowing how it worked: look how powerfully the Disk controlled him, without his even physically wielding it yet.

Yet? He shivered.

The Disk was alien, its demands strange and heartless, its rules not his rules. The thought frightened him. But it opposed the Watcher, and guided him and his allies into a situation where their own bravery, and willingness, could carry the day.

Under a pile of goblen, Rev found the bodies of Papas Sekulto and his partner Drinhe Sekult-te. The two had fallen among the enemy, shields shattered and spears broken, but facing the gate, their wounds in front, partners to the last.

Rev arranged their limbs with reverence, placed their weapons at their sides, and stood in silence for a moment.

Near the gate lay a familiar looking body, an orcen with a cut-off tail: Eg Bror, who tried to blackmail Rev. Another agent of the Watcher. Was he dead as well?

Rev turned to search among the bodies on the far side of the gate. He felt the ghost of shame. What if the man were alive? But since the same question pertained to the bodies he was checking, he continued. The state of the maimed corpses should have made him sick, but he felt nothing, checking every defender and invader mechanically.

All dead. At last he walked over to Eg Bror. Dead. He never would get Rev's sword.

Rev rubbed the petals of the stolen zinnia in his pouch. Would just stealing little things satisfy his craving? And just once in a while. Things of no value, so he didn't hurt anyone?

The seductiveness of that thought scared him. Where would it stop?

He vowed to tell Gabryal about his stealing. Maybe if he did not keep his actions a secret he would be shamed into stopping. He didn't want to feel this terrible, anymore.

First, he had work to do. As long as the Disk physically remained hidden, the town's troubles would continue. The Chisen had far greater armies, they would be back to hunt it again.

If someone else discovered the Disk of Dragons, would Rev be released from its power?

Maybe, but what if the vampyren were the one who found it?

#

From the forest, Xul Bil Be watched the retreat of the Imperial Army of the Chisen. Typical mortals failing in their one purpose, to rid the valley of the interfering locals so the vampyren could hunt the Disk – not that any could have anticipated the tricks of the townsfolk, especially that human Rev foiling the double-cross by Ash Wal.

The Boundskeeper deserved a slow death.

But over the years, Xul Bil Be had learned how powerful the Watcher truly was. Another army would be summoned in due time. Meanwhile, this army unearthed one priceless jot of information, worth the whole battle, information perhaps the whole battle had been arranged to reveal. One of the townsfolk could physically Cross Over.

The prophecies from that vile Book of Vos declared such a mortal would appear when the Disk of Dragons appeared, and the battle for Sinnesemota began. The Watcher was subtle enough to have arranged this whole escapade to bring this one man out into the open.

Furthermore, Xul Bil Be recognized the soldiers' description of the man appearing out of nowhere and vanishing, the key to bringing forth the Disk of Dragons: that Boundskeeper, Rev.

#

Through the next day youths trailed the goblen army, and reported it headed east, returning to the Chisen Empire. People laughed at finding themselves alive when death had been so close, then burst into tears at the losses suffered. The priestess Uulong claimed her Goddess had protected the town. Her followers rejoiced.

That evening, Rev, Dan, Gabryal, Yarrow, the Elder Fu and Ma'tha rested in the wicker chairs outside the hospital. Of the forty-two people brought into the hospital, only five died, a tribute to Ma'tha's skills and doggedness.

Two remained in some danger, but all had been tended and were resting.

Rev and Gabryal sat together. Rev drank his tea. The evening was warm. Occasionally, someone reached for the fruit on the table. The Elder Fu, in a cross-legged position, amused them by floating upward a few times, then settling back into his stool; he didn't seem to notice.

"The children Yarrow found in the Chisen tent were the last Norwe was holding." Gabryal shook her head. "They killed four other children. And the goblen army might return once they choose a new governor. What's to stop them?"

"Well, they did lose," Dan answered.

Rev stared at the brightening stars. "I got a feeling we're witnessing the beginning of a great war, a long struggle. And not one between good and evil, but between two monstrous evils, with innocent people caught in the middle."

"Lot of things suggest that," Yarrow rumbled. "The vampyren and goblen stirring at the behest of the Cabalmaster, the karken and Murkung on the move for the Hand of Thana. Two great evils, indeed. But don't discount the power of those who want justice and peace. We'll be fighting as well, Rev."

Rev nodded.

He wondered where his brother was. He hoped Var survived. The two brothers fought often, growing up, but Var was the only member of Rev's family who might be alive. Rev remembered his older brother giving him a loaf of brown bread once; no food ever tasted better.

"Where's the vampyren, I want to know," Gabryal said.

"And the killer's still uncaught," Yarrow said.

"Like to know where the Disk is," Dan said. "That's why the Chisen sent an army here. If we get the Disk out of here, there'd be no reason for that army to come back."

Rev had the sense of ghosts rising from the battlefield, mourning.

#

The next day, the priestess Uulong stood in a forest clearing at the entrance to the raw magic mine, a tricky entrance to find in an otherwise unimpressive low limestone cliff. The humid air made the day seem heavy, awaiting some dread event. The feeling annoyed her. She preferred clean winter, with its cold that drove out the riffraff. She was actually sweating. Intolerable.

She had repeatedly searched this mine, despite the dangers posed by the emanations of raw magic. Returning once more seemed useless. Yet spies in the Chisen army insisted they had orders to search for this mine, which implied the vampyren believed the Disk of Dragons was concealed here.

Uulong's guard stood behind her, spear ready, trembling. He should be nervous, they were all failing in their duty to the Goddess Thana, the Goddess of Submission, whom the fearful and unbelievers called the Goddess of Death.

Uulong prepared her question once again. The preparatory prayer was slow and complicated, and her frustration rose. Prayers were tricky, the Goddess demanded a person formulate their prayer precisely. But she navigated the language flawlessly, until the rote portion of her prayer ended, and the power was hers.

"If the Disk of Dragons rests here, Oh Goddess," she prayed, "please give us indication."

Like a stroke of lightning going out, the power vanished as its purpose was accomplished.

Nothing happened. All wasted.

Uulong slapped down her tail. She had made no mistake.

With an effort, she mastered her emotions. She must accept the will of the Goddess, a greater wisdom than her own. She could only conclude the Disk of Dragons did not rest in this cave.

She turned away. "Guard, return to the temple. Tell them to prepare a full sacrifice. I go into town."

#

But her guard did not reached the temple. As he reached the edge of the woods, an invisible fist seized him by his throat. He struggled to scream, but could not.

In a cold voice, his captor ordered the conjured being to ease its grip so the man could gasp out answers.

The guardsman was only too quick to comply, spilling everything he knew as his eyes bulged and his legs kicked annoyingly.

Xul Bil Be contemplated what it learned. The priestess Uulong knew the location of the raw magic mine. And this man promised to lead the vampyren there, in exchange for his life. A trap? Uulong best hope not. Xul Bil Be indicated for the man to show the way.

The mortal pointed northeast, this small hope twisting his face. Most distasteful. The man led the way to a clearing near a limestone cliff, which held the mine's entrance.

Even from several dozen paces away, the vampyren could feel the pulse of raw magic. No wonder the vampyren's spells failed to discover the Disk. So much raw magic would mask it. The Disk of Dragons must be here.

The vampyren found the orcen guard only too eager to discuss Uulong's actions. Coward. Evidently she did not realize the Disk must be here. Good. The guard knew little else, so Xul Bil Be took advantage of the fact that the mine would mask any use of ceremonial magic, wrapped one hand around the man's throat, and sucked out his life's energy.

Finished, Xul Bil Be cast the body aside. Pleased with the infusion of strength, the vampyren approached the mine. This place made Xul Bil Be uneasy. No magic could give warning if enemies approached while it was inside the mine.

Nevertheless, the vampyren slipped inside.

The raw magic glowing in the walls provided light. The vampyren traveled until reaching a dividing of the corridor. The right-hand way ended at a narrow shaft that rose to the surface and provided air. Judging from the one-pronged pick on the ground, this place had not been mined since that sort of pick had been favored, at the end of the Empire of Sinnesemota.

The vampyren showed its fangs at those ancient enemies, then tried the second corridor. This one slowly descended, and the glow of the walls faded; no mining tunnel, but some secret exit out of the ancient city. The vampyren sensed no trace of the Disk ahead. The vampyren stopped, sure the Disk of Dragons was not this way.

Xul Bil Be retraced its steps. The power of this place felt extremely discomforting. Mortals could not abide here without incurring some harsh illness. The vampyren reviewed the facts. The mine predated the tunnel; the passage from the city reinforced suspicions the Disk was hidden here, since someone expended great effort to build the secret passage. But the vampyren found no place where the Disk could rest, no other corridor, no little niche.

So where was the Disk? The priestess had not found it, even using her best magic.

Could the Disk be hidden on the Other Side? That must be it. This place was obscured by the emanations of raw magic, which would hold true on the Other Side as well, and only the rarest of mortals could Cross Over bodily, so the Disk would not be found by accident.

And because the Disk was not actually hidden in the mine, but in an analogous spot on the Other Side, the magic of the priestess failed, since she had not known exactly how to phrase her prayers. An excellent hiding place, but now that Xul Bil Be knew the trick, it would Cross Over and—

The wall the vampyren struck, invisible and undetectable, threw it back painfully.

A magical shield prevented the vampyren from reaching the Disk. Annoyed, Xul Bil Be moved out into the forest a few hundred steps, Crossed Over, and approached the mine again. Once more it hit the invisible barrier. Infuriating.

Methodically, the vampyren tried misdirection, decoys, and magical assaults, but found no way to pass that barrier. Until a small creature on the Other Side passed the barrier effortlessly on its own little business.

So the barrier did not apply to every being. The vampyren grabbed another of the beasts, a sort of magical chipmunk. But when compelled to go find the Disk, the chipmunk was suddenly prevented from passing across the barrier.

What sort of monstrous spell was this? The spell must work specifically against the influence of any vampyren. Furious, the vampyren sucked out the chipmunk's life force, an old habit to which the vampyren succumbed whenever it needed to think.

The vampyren had to hurry. Others hunted the Disk, after all.

Abruptly, the vampyren laughed, seeing the solution. Let someone else find the Disk and return past that barrier. That must have been the intent of the Watcher all along. The execrable Boundskeeper possessed the skill to Cross Over, let him do so.

Once he found the Disk, the vampyren could seize it, while getting a bit of much-needed revenge. For Xul Bil Be was coming to hate Rev.

Yes, Rev should be easy to lure here through his soft, foolish heart.

And the vampyren knew just the bait to catch the man.

Chapter Twenty Seven

old oak
atop the hill
lightning at nightfall
Poems of the Waterfall, by Chi Basso, 327A.

As Rev passed the east gate, he met Uulong entering the town.

"Rev, you are hereby relieved of your position as Boundskeeper," she declared. "My followers will see to the safety of the town from now on."

"Only Lot Sun and the Town Council can end my employment, Priestess."

"That will be arranged." Uulong's eyes took on a shiny light. "A thief who helped the vampyren and the Chisen, we cannot have as Bounder."

Hearing her loud voice, people appeared at doors. White-Sashers gathered to her, but other people hurried over as well. The mayor Qual Hich marched down the street, his dusty red hat quivering determinedly.

"Priestess, with Chisen soldiers all around, the Bounder snuck into their camp to save us. He fought the thugs alone, fought the karken, even protected the refugees. We owe our lives to the Bounder." The mayor's voice gained power. "Don't you harass our Bounder."

To Rev's astonishment, many of the townsfolk gathered behind the mayor. As rumor of a challenge to Rev passed through town, mothers rushed up with babes in their arms, and men strode forward, tools of trade in hand. Dan Zee appeared and Yarrow with him.

Even the cooper Jho Iun showed up. "The Bounder saved my nephew Gil's life, Priestess," Jho Iun declared, his shoulders hunched. He dropped his white sash in the dirt. "I support our Bounder."

The opposition made the priestess more stubborn. "Rev is a thief, Cooper. He must be outcast."

"He's been giving away his money to the old and the sick," the mayor shot back. "Quiet as he could, not to impress anyone. He's made our town

266

safe. What he did in some distant past somewhere else is never-mind to me. He's our Bounder."

Both mayor and priestess glared. The mob of White-Sashers behind the High Priestess swelled, but other people lined up behind Rev, until his supporters, orcen, goblen, and human, far outnumbered the White-Sashers.

"Bounder," they chanted. "Bounder. Rev's our Bounder."

Uulong sneered at the mayor. "I curse your business, merchant. May you have naught but sorrow before you."

Qual Hich laughed at her, waving his red hat defiantly, showing off its stains and rents. "As though my marketplace might do bang-away business with the town in ruins."

His wife put her arm through his.

Uulong stomped off. Not nearly so many followed her as before the battle.

People cheered and pounded Rev's back. A tavern owner brought out a keg of spirits, and the town held an impromptu celebration. Their Bounder was a hero and they let him know it. Dan led the toasts.

Rev wished his stealing was as far in the past as the mayor believed, but surely this support would help keep him from ever stealing again. However, in the midst of the victory party, no one was watching anything. Left alone, Rev began roving the town, and literally had to run out of a store to prevent himself from filching something. He was horrified. He should throw himself into the river to prevent himself from hurting anyone anymore.

In desperation he sought the Elder Fu.

The monk had taken up residence in an abandoned building. The walls, once plastered, peeled here and there to reveal large limestone bricks, giving the place a relaxed, imperfect beauty. The Elder Fu occupied one room, similar to his cell at the monastery. The room's only decoration was a blooming delphinium.

Rev told the Elder Fu everything, since he was not getting better by keeping his lies a secret. He trusted the old monk with every evil and nasty thought, every lie, every theft, and admitted the cost to everyone of what he had done.

"I don't want to live this way. I can't even tell which thoughts in my own head are true, anymore. Can you help me?" His voice went very small. "Will you?"

"Rev, Aspirants agree to help each other. It's in giving such help Sinnesemota will come again. Not as a place of perfection, but where people strive to do better, and help each other. When we help each other, we enjoy a moment of serenity, happiness. That's the true Sinnesemota. What motivates us, me as much as you, is pure greed. A greed to be at peace for a moment. That's Luwana's paradox: it's in helping others we help ourselves."

"I don't want to be a thief anymore."

"Admitting that is the first step to change," the Elder Fu said. "You have reason for hope. It will take a great deal of work, of serious intent, but you can be different. Rely on your own hunger for happiness."

#

Gabryal was sitting in the hospital that night, exhausted, rousing to bring water or change bandages, collapsing again. In this strange mental state, a voice in the back of her mind whispered, asking where Laia had gone. Was her friend safe?

Curiosity tugged at Gabryal until she arose as though in a dream, departing her body and heading into the dimness, seeking the ghost of Laia. Muttered words guided her in some weird way, though she did not understand them. Part of her accepted this travel as her spirit floated down an alley, through the town gate, and out into the shadows under the stars. Another part of her, knowing this was no usual dream, grew fearful.

In a clearing in the woods near a limestone bluff, she found Laia trussed like an insect in a web, bound with the glowing traces of a spell. Laia seemed unaware of Gabryal. Gabryal felt a welling sadness and recklessness – the corona of emotions surrounding a Ghost Hound.

Laia was working at her bonds. She had nearly loosened a strand of magic attached to a brown mass of muddy energy. But a separate, pale line returned from the dirty mass to her, the channel for a return stroke.

It was a trap. If Laia finished undoing that strand, the magic would be set off.

268

What would result? Gabryal feared the vampyren knew only too well. She tried to catch Laia's attention, but her friend remained unaware. Gabryal was not physically present here.

Her gut knew this was real. The twilight sky and the haunting beauty of the place hinted this was the Other Side. Rev could reach this place.

She hesitated, embarrassed. She did not want to ask, to be beholden to Rev. On the other hand, she could count on him. Gabryal turned back, without giving thought to what had lured her here.

#

Rev and the Elder Fu sat playing cards. A new closeness existed between them. Rev knelt on the visitor's mat, tea cup at his elbow, as the Elder Fu dealt out the cards. Coppers rested on the mat at the monk's knee. An annoyingly smaller pile remained on Rev's side of the playing stone.

"What I'm hoping is that the murderer was killed in the war. We lost a number of people. And maybe the army came across Khat Trun and wiped him out."

"That would be a most convenient war," the Elder Fu responded, raking in the pot. "Nor do you account for the vampyren, unless you think Xul Bil Be also murdered Bhat Sun."

"I ain't sure who killed Bhat, but no, I don't think any vampyren would get caught by a stray arrow. Luwana is the Goddess of Life, not Impossible Luck. Elder, do you know why I'm getting this dizziness, Crossing Over?"

"You must be mindful of shi when you walk the Paths, young one. Otherwise, the vertigo will grow so immense you will be unable to walk." The elder happily won another small pot. The Elder Fu certainly must be an honest man, but he held great hands with uncanny consistency.

The cards rustled as Rev dealt them across the playing stone. "I'm dizzy right now. How long will this last?"

The Elder Fu made a sympathetic clucking noise. "If you continue to Cross Over heedlessly, the dizziness could become permanent."

He discarded two cards. Rev dropped one.

"I have to hold shi the entire time I Crossed Over?" Rev's latest card filled out his hand nicely. Pleased, he increased his bet.

The monk matched his bet. "You must focus on your center at all times. Shi is the art of balance. Balance is not something you put on and take off

269

like a coat. Crossing Over rouses the effects quickly, but any use of shi will cause such dizziness if you ignore the energy flows."

"I have to hold the magic always, even when not using it?"

"It's a deal of work, young one." The Elder, even while pulling in the latest coins, somehow seemed humble. He tapped the deck for luck and dealt another hand. "Being mindful is also what you must do to overcome your hunger to steal. The same skill."

"That's not fair." Rev chuckled. "But I remember saying something like that before. Didn't make no difference then, bet it won't now."

The Elder Fu, a cherub-like look on his round face, barely looked at his cards in the candlelight. Rev knew every trick. The old monk couldn't be cheating, so how come every hand went his way?

Rev dropped his latest cards in disgust. He wondered if he should mention how the Disk seemed to rule his life, but feared he would sound too crazy even for the Elder Fu. "How can I maintain my shi center all the time?"

"Find shi now."

Rev reached for shi. "How much energy do I wield?"

"You need not wield it, you must simply be mindful of it."

"Mindful of it? You mean just stay aware of it? You do that?"

"At all times." The Elder was dealing again, with a satisfied grin.

Rev winced. The elder loved playing cards and Rev wanted to humor the man, but this grew expensive.

"If Crossing Over is using shi, why would it make me feel dizzy?" Rev found himself holding a nearly excellent hand, but somehow knew it would not be good enough. He discarded one card.

"You are not sensing the flows. Like riding a tiny boat in a huge sea with eyes shut – not knowing what will happen next, you are constantly taken unawares, and grow dizzy."

The Elder tossed another coin. It clinked into the growing pot.

"That's why the vertigo was less strong when I used shi on purpose?" Rev stared mournfully at the Wise Man. The card did not fit his hand.

"Because you were aware of the flows, yes."

"So, what's the back deal? How do I get better at this?"

"Practice," the Elder Fu said. With a saintly smile, he pulled in the last of Rev's coins. "You grow better with practice."

#

Working to remain aware of the calmness of shi, Rev found Gabryal at his door later that night. Nervousness and hope burned through him, until her tone sobered him.

"Rev, remember the Lady Laia came back as a Ghost Hound? The vampyren has trapped her on the Other Side. Will you help me free her?"

"Absolutely."

She led him off through town. He was so pleased to be going with her as the stars were appearing that he ignored the uneasy feeling of being watched.

Outside of town, Rev took Gabryal's hand and they Crossed Over. It was brighter on the Other Side, although evening-dim. A few birds whistled. The feeling of being watched increased, but who could have followed from the mundane world? Was this the Watcher, somehow? Keeping a sense of shi, sure enough, he did not grow dizzy.

Near a low bluff Gabryal paused, her brow furrowed. "I don't know where... oh, flames of the hells, there she is."

A huge hound lay in a clearing. Laia? Rev felt a rush of despair – the Ghost Hound, affecting him.

"Laia, stop working on that knot," Gabryal called. "It's a trap."

The Hound raised her head to them, then thumped her tail in acknowledgment. The aura of recklessness increased as they came closer.

"Stay back, Rev, there's an invisible trap around her. I saw it in my dream."

"I sense it."

He spotted a dark opening in the limestone bluff. A cave? He felt disquieted, as though something powerful hid there, foreboding but tempting.

"We have to unravel the trap." Gabryal made a face. "But I can't see the trap and you don't know any elemental magic to disarm it."

"So we'll work together. I'll describe the spell, and you figure it out."

The magic flowed in complex patterns around the Ghost Hound, colors that mingled red to maroon to purple to blue to green. The Hound lay quiet.

Rev put aside the powerful urge to search the cave. First things first. He began to describe the spell, weave after weave.

271

Gabryal nodded. "It's as though ideas of ceremonial magic have been implemented in elemental magic. Tricky."

At another sense of being watched, Rev reached out with shi.

Something slipped off into the trees. The vampyren? He gripped the hilt of his sword, but the shadow passed beyond his sight. He had not felt the intensity of the Watcher, but it was a disturbing feeling all the same.

During the next break Gabryal was more hopeful. "I'm starting to understand. Ceremonial magic operates off the energy of living beings. That thread connected to Laia has to be the trigger. It runs between her and the main energies of the spell. The trap would suck Laia's soul out in its release, using her own life against her."

"Better not release it."

At last, Gabryal exclaimed. "That's it. That thin strand, it has to be that one."

She took a deep breath. "Take that strand in your hands. Carefully. Snap it."

The spell collapsed, releasing Laia.

Gabryal shouted in relief as the Hound leaped up and scampered about.

Rev smiled shakily.

Gabryal knelt before the Ghost Hound. "I am so sorry for calling you back. We'll free you from the conjuration that binds you, it wasn't right to ask that of you."

But at that, the Hound growled. She still wanted vengeance.

Gabryal buried her face in the Hound's coat. "Thank you. I'll try to be worthy of you."

Rev took Gabryal's hand, and curled his other hand into the Ghost Hound's fur. They followed him back to the mundane world. The Ghost Hound immediately bounded away into the brush, back on the hunt.

#

Rev and Gabryal rested on the wicker chairs outside the hospital the next morning. Rev felt nervous. "We have to talk, Gabryal."

He wanted to tell her about the stealing, but avoiding the moment, first he went back to one clue he never chased down. "You remember that scent of burnt roses around Bhat's body? Does war magic create that?"

"No, Rev. Only the after-lightning smell. And healing gives a green, growing smell, like first spring. The Lady Laia's oracular magic was close, an earthy, loamy smell. But I remember, as a little girl, seeing a magician doing a spell at the Pers court, and noticing the smell of roses."

"What was the magic?"

"I don't remember. The magician brought forth magical birds that whistled. Is this what you asked to talk to me about?"

"No."

She had the right to know, if she were to become involved with him. He bowed his head and told her his story, all the stealing, all the lies.

"I want to be completely honest," he concluded, "I can't bear the lies any longer. This is who I've been, but I hope not who I'll be ever again. I ain't going to do it anymore."

It was as though a door slammed shut. Her face went distant, hard. "Do you expect me to cheer because you're an honest thief? I'm sorry, Rev, but I have to absorb this. Please, go."

He nodded, feeling lost and ridiculous. Had his stupid thieving cost him even this? She said nothing as he left.

#

Gabryal felt a heavy sadness, that a good man bore such a shadow.

Rev was a liar.

Who is not suspicious of such a person, and rightly so? If we accept the apologies of liars protecting their weakness, why, they immediately hurt us once again, then proffer the exact same twisted words, the familiar, deep and heartfelt apologies.

And yet, and yet, how do we feel for such people? Angry? Hurt? Betrayed?

They do suffer, caught on their own rack. They may give love as best they can, they may be generous, sacrifice themselves for others. Contradictions tangle in each of us. Can we feel, at least, compassion for people caught in such lies and weakness, fearing that without grace in our lives – a grace not of our own doing – we might be in their position, lost, suffering, inflicting pain on ourselves and all who care for us?

And hope is possible. People do change. Not always, perhaps not often, and rarely to the extent we might wish, but sometimes to an extent greater than anyone could imagine.

No one sees the future, except the wise women of Gy Pe, a little.

273

Gabryal let out a long, slow breath. Did she want to call him back? She still missed her husband, but sometimes most of a day would go by where she did not think of him. Living through grief was like slowly wading toward a distant shore.

She liked Rev. He accepted her, he did not demand any charade, did not demand she give up her dreams. But could she trust him? No. He had stolen only a day ago. Sorrow welled in her.

She had the unsettling feeling that she kept reaching out to Rev, awkwardly, not knowing what she wanted, exactly. Laia had said he would be in her life a long time, but never said he would be the love of her life.

Gabryal missed Laia. She felt the sharp grief of separation.

\#

Xul Bil Be stalked through the woods along a tall ridge. That featherheaded human could not find the Disk under his very nose. Nor did the woman discover it, even lured to the very spot where the Disk was hidden.

Were they numb to its power? But Rev had sensed the vampyren itself. Rev was simply stupid. The vampyren should have destroyed both of them.

No, it still had a use for Rev.

What most disturbed the vampyren was an ongoing psychic tug from the Hound. The Hound might nose through its deceptions and find it again. That last fight had been too close.

Nor had it expected the humans to solve the trap.

Maybe if the vampyren lured Rev to the mine, then showed him an open passageway to the Other Side, he would get the hint. But how to lure Rev without giving away its presence to the Hound? The lure would have to be someone Rev would value dearly, but not anyone connected to the Hound.

Chapter Twenty Eight

"The cave glowed with its own light, a sickly orange that cast horrific shadows on the faces of the miserable men who had made it thus far. These few were maddened, for raw magic enflames the lust for power more even than does gold. First one, then another assailed his companions, until all were fighting to be the sole possessor of the Mines of Galacia. Blood mingled with the strange magic in that place, until all there lay still. They killed each other. Yet in the pulsating glow, shadows still moved in a weird dance as the ghosts of those wretches, trapped by the magic, fought on with no surcease. May Luwana have mercy upon their souls."
<u>*True Tales of Most Evil Magic*</u>, *by The Lady Wexley, 825A.*

Lonesome afternoon light slanted across the town. Rev paced the streets, sure he had lost Gabryal, but he could not indulge himself – he hunted information about magic and murder.

He found the Elder Fu meditating in his tiny home. The delphinium had been replaced by a single red rose. Rev explained about the killing of Bhat Sun and the clues, including the mysterious leopard.

His mentor added wood to a fire to heat tea. "A leopard that acts human? That is strange. Perhaps it is someone under a spell."

"A spell? Could the vampyren use shi to change someone into a leopard?"

"If a vampyren learned shi it could become powerful indeed, but shi cannot change one being into another, young one, that would be a different type of magic, either the ceremonial magic of the vampyren, the illusory magic of the gnomen, or the power of a God focused through clerical magic."

"Why would the vampyren alter someone into a leopard instead of killing the person?"

"Out of cruelty," the Elder Fu said. "The person is trapped as an animal as long as the spell lasts, which may be as long as the vampyren lives – and vampyren do not die unless killed – a punishment of endless sorrow and frustration."

"The leopard may have witnessed the murder," Rev speculated. "If we changed it back, the person could tell us who killed Bhat."

#

The woman named Lada stared at Rev suspiciously, as though already aware of why he had come to her door.

"Lada," he said, embarrassed, "I was the one who took your chicken."

He held out three coppers, for the chicken he stole and then lost. She stared at him coldly.

"This replaces the one you lost," he went on, determined to continue admitting the truth, admit his weakness. "I'm sorry I stole from you."

She took the coins, not letting his hand brush hers. "I wondered about you, Rev. People said you were a thief, and I said, no, he's honest and open, but I wondered. Now, here it's true. You hurt my trust in people, you did that."

"I am sorry."

"But I thank you for warning me, so I can take care of myself. Keep you away."

When she said no more, he walked away, saddened at the pain he caused, but relieved he had been honest with her.

He tried to explain to Dan at lunch. "Lada knows who I am, so I can't steal around her, she'll be watching me. I'm safer, because I can't deceive myself into thinking I could deceive her."

"She's not your personal Bounder," Dan said. "You have to set your own bounds and live by them. It's not anyone else's duty."

That sounded right. Rev had tried to make amends, and it turned out a painful mess. Still, he owed people that – even now he felt the urge, an instant away from stealing again. Only around the Ruskiya did he feel safe, without the urge to steal, and that was only due to the magic of the tattoo. Must he join the Ruskiya, live out the rest of his life among them?

#

Later that afternoon, Rev slipped out the town's eastern gate, hoping to solve a puzzle: Uulong entered the town through the east gate the other

276

day, although the north gate led to her Temple, and traveling without a guard. He could not pick out her tracks from other travelers after this much time.

Buzzards circled the woods to the northeast.

He headed there. A circle of vultures flapped off. Sure enough, a corpse lay sprawled across a bush, a man in the white sash of Uulong's acolytes. Had she killed someone? Rev felt revulsion and dismay.

He took a moment to compose himself before approaching the body. Was this to be his job – being first to find the dead bodies, and deal with the more gruesome side of life?

Bruises marked the dead man's throat: strangled. Uulong's tracks were nowhere to be seen, though other tracks covered the area. Tracks of a biped, barefoot. The vampyren?

Only by sheer willpower did he keep from fleeing in fear. After a time, he continued. He recognized the clothes of the dead man as Ruskiya, so this was a refugee. How had the man come to join the ranks of Uulong's followers?

No tracks left the area. Had the vampyren Crossed Over in departing? Rev felt a deep relief that the vampyren was gone.

#

That evening, Rev entered the refugee's clan hall and told the Ruskiya of the murder. Sorrowful murmurs swept the gathering. When he described the clothes and tattoos of the dead man, one family burst into sobs, recognizing their kin.

"Grievous news," said Dunortha.

A man exclaimed. "Why remain in this evil valley among people who hate us, when we can seek no vengeance?"

"I'll search for the killer." Rev's words sounded hollow even to him.

The refugees were silent as he mounted Grace and rode away.

Despite the late hour, Rev headed to Skarii's hut, finding the goblen conjuror bundling clothes into a carrying pack by lantern light. The door was open, but he pounded politely on the doorjamb.

"You're leaving? What are you going to do? Where will you go?"

"Tt, you're still investigating?"

"No, I'm concerned for you."

Her tone softened. "Tt, thank you, human, few enough have ever said that."

She made a curious, lost gesture. "I don't know where I'll be going. There are not many places safe, and I cannot be returning to my home among the Chisen. Perhaps west."

"If I find the killer, there will be the ranch as reward," Rev said. "You could stay on until you chose a direction."

"T, t, ttt, you're courting a goblen?" She clicked in amusement.

He blushed. "I didn't mean, that is, you're very pretty, any goblen would be lucky..."

"T, t, t, enough. Leave me the scraps of my dignity."

"I like you, Skarii. I'd miss you, that's what I meant."

"Tt, I'm gruff and cross."

"Your best qualities," he answered breezily.

"T, t, ttt, at least my most ineradicable. These days are hard. The Murkung and karken are spreading, vampyren have taken over my nation, t, t, and everywhere I am seeing war. I'll search for a place such evil hasn't reached. I have no better purpose."

"What if we find the Disk of Dragons?" Rev asked. "Couldn't we use it to bring back the old days, the Empire of Sinnesemota?" His heart stirred.

She paused, considering, and he was caught by the marvel – never would a mage in the fullness of her power have listened to him as a scrap boy on the streets of Shendasan.

"Tt, surely you aren't thinking such a search would be easy," she said dubiously.

"Isn't the Empire of Peace worth fighting to restore? Where harmony and justice ruled? The Disk could give us the Hall, which could give us the aid of Vos. We don't have to live forever in war, with only the promise of war for our children. It's a dream I have."

"Farfetched."

"But what do you have better to do?"

She went to pour tea, clicked her formal agreement. "Tt, tt. T. Yes, it's a dream I could be following."

Rev threw his arms around her. "Thank you."

Startled, she stood still, then put her arms around him tentatively. "But humans are not my type," she warned him.

278

Disk of Dragons

He swung her into a dance around the floor of her shack. The lantern flame whipped, and she screeched and laughed. He had to lean down to dance with her, and soon they were laughing so hard they had to sit down.

Skarii caught her breath. "T, t, t, one thing is true – evil is growing. If we take the Disk of Dragons, t, t, t, people will be seeking to take it from us, wishing the power for themselves. We are weak and they are very strong."

"Maybe the Disk does call the dragon folk. That would help."

"Tttt, calls, but not controls. You best be friends with any dragon called."

"Is that why it's called the Disk of Dragons?"

"T, The Dragon Queen made it, and a dragon gave it to the Empress of Sinnesemota as a gift, that's why."

"A dragon?" Rev had a sudden memory from an old story. "Do you remember the name of the dragon who gave it to the Empress?"

"Ttt, it doesn't matter, surely."

Rev let the thought go. "I have a question. If a mortal were transformed into a leopard, could you change him back?"

Skarii turned all of her eyes to him. "You mean that leopard wandering around? I've been herding it away with conjurations, I never thought it might be a mortal. Tttt, no, I don't have the skill to change it back."

"Would Xul Bil Be have been able to transform it? As a vampyren."

"Tt, Xul Bil Be is a vampyren? They have many strange skills, using the life energy of people. T. Yes. A vampyren could twist someone into the form of a leopard."

"How about Uulong? Could she do it?"

Skarii hissed. "T, t. Different priests have different powers. What can a God do, what will a God do... Gods won't grant power to just anyone. They want evidence of piety. The more pious a person, the more power. Be careful of her, Rev. Many priests of Thana keep a sacrifice to their Goddess prepared, ready to give them quick access to great power. A mortal, held on an altar in the heart of their temples. Likely Uulong has such an unfortunate held somewhere, so do not underestimate her. Thana would grant her much after such a sacrifice.

"But dislike of Uulong is growing. People wait for a chance to turn on her. Gods don't like their priests unpopular. Ttt. Uulong must be careful,

279

her Goddess may be considering her replaceable. T, t, ttt." Skarii clicked in amusement. "Don't underestimate how Uulong miscalculated, telling the Afen they can't dicker. On such trivialities nations hang.

"T, anyway, it might be amusing to try for the Disk. T tt t, you are bringing out the adventuress in me, human. Once I wondered at the possibilities, rather than at the losses. Maybe I return to that way of looking at things. You have my gratitude. What if I were to look back someday and see naught but years lost in bitterness? Tt, better to be a fool with a dream, even bound to fail."

"Do you think Uulong is here to find the Disk?"

"Tt, the Disk adds power to any magic cast. She would be wanting it for that and its power to open the Hall. To gain the Heart of Light residing there and use it to bring Thana, the Goddess of Death, into our world. T, t, t, there's the reason to keep the Disk out of her hands."

"Do the priests of Thana use a spell like what killed Bhat Sun?"

"T, t? How did he die?"

Rev explained about the bloodless corpse.

"T. Yes. A common torture by the priests of Thana, using a spell that sucks the blood out of a man. Ttt."

"The spell wouldn't leave wounds?"

"Blood just sprays out of the victim's skin. Ttt, ugly spell."

"Rev, I have taken an interest in your hunt, and my imps report that hussy in town, Madame Coo, is Murkung orcen, and Khat Trun's sister. T, t, t. She has been casting spells of priestly magic. Small spells, but with the stench of death. Thana's magic."

"So she might be the killer, working with Khat Trun." His gaze wandered over Skarii's things. Why was he thinking about stealing? Because he was frustrated, tired and lonely.

He missed Gabryal. He wanted her to be part of his dream of Sinnesemota.

"T. Rev, something to think on – you're an annoyance."

"Why, thank you."

Her mandibles clicked in amusement. "T, t, ttt. You've been sticking your nose into everyone's business since you entered town."

"Don't hold back, tell me the tough stuff first." He grinned.

She held up a hand. "T, t, t. Vampyren are well known for eliminating annoyances. Since you're alive, it must be waiting on something."

A sobering thought. "What would that be?"

"T, Vampyren only do things in their own interest. Do you have something it wants?"

"I don't own much more than this shirt and an old sword. It might be after the sword, though. Family heirloom."

"How about something you know? Or something you can do, no one else can?"

Rev felt a flare of interest. He could Cross Over. Was the Disk hidden on the Other Side?

He was so busy with his thoughts he rode the whole way home before realizing his desire to steal had vanished.

Chapter Twenty Nine

"The trollen may be meek and mild
but nothing deadly, nothing wild
will ever hurt a trollen child,
'cause they can see tomorrow.
Their women know just what to do
to heal whatever's wrong with you,
but when they want they kill you too,
'cause they can see tomorrow."
<u>Children's street rhyme</u>, *from the Foreign Quarters of Ekhander,*
Capital of Gy Pe.

The circle tightened like a noose around the vampyren at its center, hidden near the mine of raw magic. Many centuries had passed since it felt such fear; the horror of its proud life being extinguished was almost too much to bear.

The vampyren's fears were well-founded, for it could not hide the spark of its very being. The Ghost Hound Laia coursed on its scent through the woods. Nor was the Lady Laia alone – another person waited near the mine, shadowing the vampyren, desperate for freedom and vengeance.

#

Rev and Dan stood atop the wall of Zhopahr. Morning haze obscured the valley. "It's like time stopped long ago," Dan said, "leaving mysteries undisturbed."

"You're getting to be a mystic. Careful, or you'll be taking up with the Oracle in Gy Pe."

"I've gone from homeless vagabond to deputy Bounder, respected of the community, why not Chief Dreamer for an empire?" Dan chuckled. He waved at the ruins in the valley. "What would this city have looked like during Sinnesemota?"

"More to the point, was that mound to the northeast the temple of the priests who protected the Disk of Dragons? Find the Disk, and we'll lure the killers into the open."

"Paint a big target on our backs, you mean."

"Don't look," Rev told him, "but the bull's-eye is already there."

"I'm getting used to it. I never saw myself enforcing the law, but it feels right. As though we each have a purpose in life, and this is mine."

Rev patted his friend's shoulder. "My big dream is elsewhere. I'll reestablish Sinnesemota or break myself trying." He hesitated, fearing they had somehow begun to talk of parting. He stumbled over the next words. "But I'll recommend you for my position when I leave, if you want."

"Honorable, and I thank you," Dan said with a wry smile, "but I'm going with you. We're for Sinnesemota together, hunt-brother." He glanced away, embarrassed to show emotion. "If we ever accomplish our dream," he went on in a rough voice, "I could see myself being a Boundskeeper someday, that's all I'm saying."

Rev was swept by a sense of the impermanence of life. Where would they live when this was over? Someplace where if he stole... he shook off the thought with a shudder. "You know, I was saving money to buy you an apprenticeship."

"You did what?" Dan asked, his tail stiff with surprise.

"Figured it would cost maybe fifty silvers," Rev said, embarrassed. "I always thought you needed a job with honor. Anyway, I have most of the needed silver here." He removed a pouch looped around his belt and handed it to Dan. "I was hoping you'd take it, maybe use it against that day when you do retire."

"I don't believe..." Dan's voice ran out. His tail quivered. "You were always the best friend a man could have." He drew forth a similar pouch. "I was saving to buy you an apprenticeship after you got tired of stealing."

"You demon," Rev cried. They fell to pummeling each other about the shoulders with gales of laughter. Rev snatched back his own pouch before Dan could open it. "No doubt you've saved twice as much as I. So you keep yours and I'll keep mine, and we'll buy each other a great meal, a cask of ale and celebrate that we neither of us left the other fellow behind in some dull life as needle sharpener or scribe."

"And we'll reestablish Sinnesemota, even if the rest of the world thinks we're crazy."

"Agreed." Rev threw his arm around his friend and laughed, as crows cawed over the fields and a pair of dragonets flew in joyful loops above, unseen.

Footsteps came rushing through the ruins. Rev spun, fist on his sword hilt, but it was Gabryal coming around a tumbled wall. His heart leapt. "Gabryal, it's good—"

She interrupted. "The Lady Laia found the vampyren in the woods. Come quickly."

Startled, Rev and Dan started after her. Rev said, "But what if we confront it?"

"We kill it," she said.

#

Ginsa Rew-va waggled her tail in annoyance. Her friends did not want to go any farther into the gloomy woods, they were scaredy-snakes, not companions fit for an orcen princess.

Today she was a princess. Yesterday she had been the pirate captain of a magic boat sailing the High Seas. Her friends loved to have her lead their games, since she was so inventive. She had plenty of time, since her Momma, the famous Pura Rew, had taken over so much responsibility for the town during the war. Momma did not watch her as closely, which was just fine by Ginsa. Now, something exciting drew Ginsa deeper into the woods, a stirring and muttering in her mind. In her imagination, she followed the tracks of the cruel foe that had stolen her... whatever. Brother? That was good. Stolen her brother. She always wanted a little brother to save. She waved her reed spear. She loved the woods, the mystery of the place. She helped her mother with the bucket brigade during the battle, and considered herself the bravest girl in Zhopahr. Her tail waved proudly.

"Ginsa, wait up," called her companions, their voices taut with fear.

Ginsa paused. "I'm here, you two." Maybe it wasn't fair to make them follow her, after all, the woods *were* creepy. Maybe she would wait, just to protect them.

She noticed a shadowy spot in the cliff face nearby. "Look, a cave."

Ben Hich-shin examined the place dubiously. "There could be bears in there."

"Then there would be tracks, silly." Ginsa crept forward.

"There *are* tracks, Ginsa," cried Do'ra.

At that moment, Ginsa discovered a limit to her own bravery.

A scary person in a dark cloak emerged from the cave. It wore the clothes of that magician Xul Bil Be, but he was a goblen, and this thing had no skin, no flesh, only bones that glowed a horrible white. Fear rolled out from it, and she found herself terrified, unable to flee.

Flames burned in its empty eye sockets. The stench of things rotted for a thousand years overwhelmed her, and she gagged. "Let me be. Help. Mommy! MOMMY!"

The monster raised its skeletal hands. The finger bones wove a spell as the monster intoned in some twisted language that tortured the air.

"Mungul raspakar, theth kherutar, mokhu..."

Too late, she recognized it as the same voice that whispered in her mind.

Her skin heated, and her eyes felt like fireballs.

\#

Despite the vampyren's caution, its own evil left it vulnerable, a target of vengeance. As it concentrated on ensorcelling the children, a sleek form raced out of the woods behind it.

The vampyren's spell failed as the snow leopard struck. The flaming skeletal image vanished, replaced by a pale, ugly creature, the true aspect of the vampyren.

The children were released.

Instantly, Ben tugged at Ginsa's shoulder. "Run away, Ginsa."

For the only time in Ginsa's whole life, she did.

\#

Furious, Xul Bil Be threw off the leopard. The vampyren looked from the fleeing children to the leopard. "You will die in their place."

The vampyren started a spell to freeze the cat's blood.

If the leopard had been the only trouble Xul Bil Be faced, the vampyren would have overcome the large cat. But at that moment, a streak of fire from the woods struck the vampyren.

Xul Bil Be shrieked, stumbling away. Gabryal had arrived.

Xul Bil Be shrugged off the elemental magic, but its own spell was ruined once again, and its defenses weakened. It could not take too many blows like that.

The leopard threw itself back on the vampyren, but knocked the vampyren aside, causing Gabryal's next fire spell to miss.

Xul Bil Be struck the leopard, spinning the cat through the air to hit a tree. It crumpled.

The vampyren faced the woman emerging from the woods.

"For my Zhac." Gabryal launched another spell, but the vampyren waved a hand, and her flames spun off harmlessly.

Xul Bil Be sneered. "Do you think I have never faced war magic? I shall taste your soul, woman." The vampyren cast a ceremonial spell to drain her soul.

A sparkling cloud of billowing energy, the color of rotted wood, flowed toward her, sucking life, leaving the vegetation brown and withered as it passed.

Gabryal raised her staff to counter the spell, but of course no elemental magic could—

The sparkling cloud halted. To the vampyren's dismay, it reversed course, moving back at the vampyren. Stopping such a cloud was a trick of shi. Rev was here.

Then some fool started shooting arrows from the woods.

#

The vampyren was trickier than anticipated, and avoided Dan's arrows even while struggling to control the sparkling cloud.

Gabryal flung another fireball, but the vampyren waved its hand and redirected the fireball at Rev, as he emerged from the woods.

Gabryal screamed. "No. Rev!"

The flames exploded. But the gold necklace Dunortha gave Rev saved him. The necklace shattered, but the flames did not affect him.

Rev had not stopped concentrating, and the sparkling cloud encompassed the vampyren, forcing it to counter its own spell.

As it did, Gabryal flung her last fireball. Fire exploded and the vampyren screamed. It collapsed, writhing. Gabryal drew her belt knife and charged, sobbing the name of her husband.

Even now, despite Gabryal's fire, Rev's shi, and the arrows Dan loosed, they were not strong enough to overcome the vampyren. Yet they kept the vampyren distracted, so it did not sense the true danger.

Out of the woods, faster than any living thing, shot the Ghost Hound. For this foreseen moment, Laia had lain down her life: her chance at the monster that devoured her child.

As Xul Bil Be struggled to rise, the Ghost Hound's teeth clamped around its neck.

An immeasurable agony of fear took the vampyren. Its pride crumbled, its bowels turned to jelly. Vainly it struggled.

Laia ripped out the vampyren's soul. The putrid, dirty yellow thing flickered, faded, vanished in the sunlight.

The vampyren sank to the ground. Its body dissolved, and its bones crumbled into dust. Laia's child, Gabryal's husband, those who died in the earthquake, and the dead from a hundred centuries of murder, souls bound to the vampyren, all were released.

The souls flew free, with an impression of music like the song of angels.

Gabryal felt a burst of joy, as a great darkness departed the world.

Then she looked upon Laia. Such sorrow etched the face of the Ghost Hound that Gabryal's breath caught. This was an ending for her friend, an ending Gabryal helped create.

As Ma'tha arrived at the head of a column of townsfolk, the Ghost Hound looked up with an expression so distant and lost that Ma'tha fell to her knees, tears streaming down her face.

Gabryal wanted to cry out: No.

But, duty done, the cost must be paid.

The Ghost Hound turned, responding to a call beyond their ken. She loped away, vanishing into nothingness, going to the places only the heart may know for sure.

For the rest of her life Gabryal would remember, with an overwhelming guilt.

#

A transformation overcame the leopard. Its trunk and head shortened, its legs lengthened and its fur melted away, until a skinny orcen lay in the clearing. Rev took off his shirt to cover the man's nakedness.

287

The townsfolk gazed in astonishment. Pura Rew put her arms around Ginsa, the tails of mother and daughter shuddering.

The transformed orcen leveraged himself to his hands and knees.

"Orcen, are you the man known as Zan Zan?" Rev asked.

As the orcen raised his head, a woman from the crowd threw her arms around him.

"Zan, I was so worried. I thought you left town."

The woman was Zan Zan's former wife, a laundress.

"Did the vampyren change you into a cat?" Rev asked.

Zan Zan nodded. The crowd murmured, not altogether encouragingly. Zan Zan's thievery had plagued the town for months. His ex-wife shifted away from him.

"The vampyren is dead, the killer caught," Uulong proclaimed. "Praise the Goddess."

"Not so easily as that." Rev felt the weight of duty. "Priestess Uulong, during the battle with the Chisen, I smelled burnt roses, the same smell at the murder site of Bhat Sun. The smell of magic being cast. But the only magicians near me were the Elder Fu..."

"...who was not here when Bhat was killed..." Dan interrupted.

"...Gabryal..."

"...in town at the time of the murder..."

"...and you, Priestess." Rev turned. "Zan Zan, you witnessed the murder of Bhat Sun. Please inform these folks who committed the murder."

At Rev's unyielding gaze, the goblen spoke. "The priestess Uulong, sir."

In astonishment, everyone considered how cruel the priestess had been, how her followers bullied folks. It is never wise to lord it over others, then become vulnerable to them.

"Murderer," shouted a hundred throats.

Pandemonium broke loose. Lot Sun and his men raised their weapons, roaring. Uulong fled into the mine. Her bodyguards formed a skirmish line, but the townsfolk cut them down. Rev leaped past them and chased after the priestess.

The tunnel walls glowed a strange orange hue. His emotions roiled under the pressure of the raw magic like a sea in a midnight storm: rage, then fear, then hopelessness, until he felt scattered, a bird lost in a tempest.

The tunnel split in two. The left hand passage had a recent wash of energy, so Rev headed that way. Uulong had outpaced them. Enough to stop and prepare a nasty surprise?

Using shi, he searched ahead for concentrations of energy that might indicate traps. The path descended and veins of raw magic grew more scarce, until most of the light came from behind. At last, in the deep shadows, the passageway ended in a door.

To Rev's dismay, shi indicated someone waited. He stopped, but his approach had alerted the ambusher, who yanked open the door.

An orcen, his head painted red and black. Khat Trun grinned evilly, and raised his sword.

P M F Johnson

Chapter Thirty

"Are there dragons yet alive, somewhere in the vasty world?
Folks will say it must be so, for they're immortal, as you've heard.
Luwana's Angels, they are called, but some are evil, some are good,
while some don't care for you at all. They're wrought of gems from
mountain hurled,
in stone-hard scales they go abroad. On wing and singing each to each
They visit in the midnight sky, where none can spy, where none can
seek
But other dragons. High above you they converse, and what one sees
Is quickly known to all. By daylight, some in mortal guise will teach,
Or watch, or hunt, or seek for treasure, what may give a dragon
pleasure.
Golden eyes and golden skin, deadly, mystic, wise old kin."
<u>Song of an Unknown Minor Bard</u>. *Often attributed to the dragon Ya*
Rao, who delivered the Disk of Dragons to humanity.

Khat Trun's sword came down. Rev parried desperately. Khat Trun, more skilled, knocked aside Rev's blade, lunged...

...and a Ruskiya knife struck him in the eye. The thug collapsed.

"So he dies for my grandniece Vantra," growled Dunortha, drawing another knife. "Kick his body out of the way."

Behind her came Dan, Gabryal and half-a-dozen townsfolk. They entered a room of stone, at the far side of which rose a staircase. Rev raced up it into a shadowy room. An altar stood encircled by four black candles and the scent of burnt roses hung in the air.

The presence of Thana, the Goddess of Death, hung there, unseen, but thickening the air until they nearly choked with the foulness of rotting bodies, death and decay.

The priestess Uulong herself stood at the altar, and raised a dagger over a young boy lying there. The boy was held down by three acolytes, who

290

bent the boy backwards, exposing his chest. A terrible glow surrounded her, as the fury of the Goddess possessed her. All were trapped in its web.

She drove the knife down.

Only Rev was quick enough to react, empowered by his sword.

He dove, knocking Uulong aside. Her blade flashed, as though it too were furious, slicing a bloody groove along the boy's chest but missing his heart.

Rev had thwarted the spell the priestess was attempting to cast.

The priestess hissed like a serpent, and struck at Rev. Rev blocked the unexpected blow, but the dagger snaked around his sword like a living thing.

He grabbed her wrist, but the knife bucked, lunging for his life's blood. It inched closer, a Goddess demanding sacrifice.

In that instant, he had a vision. The hand of the priestess appeared desiccated, with knifelike fingernails, stained with dried blood. An evil power emanated from it like a blue aura. He saw not the mortal hand of Uulong, but the Hand of Thana acting through her, the remote High Priestess of Death, who carried out the will of the Goddess from a hidden tabernacle far from here, surrounded by spells of malediction and hate.

The dagger demanded a death.

With a wrench, Rev deflected the dagger to the only other heart within reach. The knife plunged into the chest of the priestess Uulong.

With that act, the Hand of Thana became aware of him. Here was an enemy thwarting her power, denying her Goddess.

The vision faded.

Before him, the priestess Uulong screamed, a thin sound that faded away, as though drawn into a far distance.

She muttered an incomprehensible phrase, and crumpled.

But the Hand of Thana knew of Rev now, and through her, the Goddess of Death Herself. He had made an implacable enemy.

The eerie sensation of *knowing* ended.

He stood alone, confused. Ruskiya warriors seized the acolytes.

"Did you stop Uulong's curse?" Yarrow asked in a peculiar, commanding tone.

"I don't know." Rev felt compelled to answer. "I don't feel cursed."

Yarrow's tawny eyes narrowed, and Rev felt forced to explain further. "The dagger seemed alive, and demanded blood. So it killed her. She mumbled something as she died."

"Then the curse succeeded."

Yarrow shook his head as though in regret.

The compulsion on Rev abruptly ended. He felt a cold shock. Astonishment, or simply release?

"She's dead," Dan argued, "so what does it matter? Rev ain't hurt, is he?"

"Uulong's curse called the Goddess of Death."

"What does that mean?" Rev asked, with a sinking feeling.

The Elder Fu answered. "Best practice your shi, young one. You will have a steady stream of unwelcome visitors, whose goal is your painful death."

Rev shook off this pronouncement. He had more tasks, and such a danger seemed remote.

They made their way back through the tunnel, to where the townsfolk awaited. Lot Sun's men held Zan Zan in the noonday sun, where Ma'tha was healing him.

Rev asked, "Why did the vampyren change you into a leopard, Zan Zan?"

The unfriendly eyes of the townsfolk turned to the goblen.

He lowered his head. "Tried to steal from him, sir. Thought a magic user would have useful things."

"Why were you near Uulong when she killed Bhat Sun?"

"I was hoping she'd change me back to normal, but Khat Trun chased me away."

"Why did she torture Bhat?"

"She was asking about the Disk of Dragons. He kept saying all he knew about was the mine, and showed her the raw magic he got. Blood spraying everywhere. It was horrible. She kept at it until he fell silent. I don't think he had any idea where the Disk was."

Rev blew out his breath. There were the answers.

But what to do with Zan Zan? The thief was a trouble to their town.

Disk of Dragons

"Zan Zan, because you helped those children we'll show mercy, but four roads lead from this town. Take one and go." Rev turned on Madame Coo. "You as well. Go."

The crowd parted as the two departed. The laundress who had been Zan Zan's wife made no move to join him. Rev felt a pang. Such was the lot of thieves, chased away, unwanted.

"Rev, I examine the boots of Khat Trun," said Hunorn. "His are the prints we find in the camp of the karken, and at the site of Bhat's murder."

"That makes sense. Karken are servants of Thana. Uulong must have sent Khat Trun to give them orders."

"So Uulong murdered my brother," Lot Sun said. "She tortured him to death to find the Disk."

Rev nodded. "Bhat must have been mining the raw magic, sir. She learned where the mine was, found the tunnel ended at that building and chose that building as her Temple to make it easier to explore."

"She moved into her Temple the day after the murder, as I recall," said Gabryal.

"But there's no evidence of the Disk in the mine." Yarrow's tone was deceptively casual. Rev's friend had an amused glint in his eye.

"There ain't, Yarrow, it's true, but I know where it is, I bet. I can even point at the guardian of the Disk."

Yarrow's smile widened.

"I remembered the story," Rev went on, "where a dragon herald brought the Disk as a gift from the Dragon Queen to the mortal folk. Skarii reminded me. The herald's name was Ya Rao. But dragons are immortal, ain't they?"

Rev made a sign he remembered from the Elder Fu. His left hand formed a curve as though holding a ball, but with the thumb widespread and a gap between the middle fingers, mimicking three talons. The sign of the dragon. Yarrow laughed and returned the sign.

"Or should I say guardians?" Rev asked, turning to the Elder Fu. "There do seem to be two here."

"Rev, what are you talking about?" Gabryal asked.

"Dragons, my dear. I'm talking about dragons."

Yarrow and the Elder Fu Vehma bowed, their golden skin glittering.

293

Gabryal looked from one to the other. "I don't understand. You're dragons? You don't look like dragons. Where are your wings?"

She took Rev's hand. He felt happy that she looked to him for protection.

"They're in disguise as mortals," Rev explained. "I never heard about the golden skin, though."

"Are you saying the Disk of Dragons is here?" Gabryal asked. "Why couldn't any spells find it?"

"I imagine the searching spells couldn't penetrate the masking power of the raw magic in the mine. Anyway, the Disk is hidden on the Other Side, so most people couldn't bring it forth."

Gabryal understood. "But you can."

"You trained me to Cross Over, didn't you?" Rev asked the Elder Fu.

"Your friend Yarrow helped." The monk smiled.

"Is it time to bring forth the Disk?" Rev asked.

Yarrow shook his head. "We do not interfere in the choices of mortals. Whether to bring forth the Disk is for mortals to decide."

"Faugh," said the Elder Fu, "you are too cautious, Ya Rao. You ask for advice, young one, I give some. Shadows arise, and the Watcher has returned, the ancient weapon of the vampyren Cabalmaster. It would be good if Vos could speak with His people once again, but the Jewel through which the God speaks resides in the Hall of the Empire, which cannot be opened without the Disk."

Rev hesitated. "But there's a cost to this as well, ain't there?"

The Elder Fu bowed. "Your wisdom grows. The Disk and the Shield, these are all the same in the mystical world. If you take up the Disk, you become the Shield for your people."

"Why is the Disk first?"

The old monk's mustache quivered in amusement. "Your suspicion grows alongside your wisdom. The Disk demands honesty. We cannot be true servants of the Goddess without honesty, first of all."

"And if we don't get the Artifacts, the vampyren will."

"Or the White-Sashers, those who follow Thana. We must bring the Artifacts to the Hall to participate in the ceremony to reach the Heart of Light. Bring the Goddess of love into our own hearts, and so prevent the enemy from bringing forth their own Gods, the Gods of fear. Remember, the same process will work for evil, if our goodness fails."

Rev felt the weight of this moment. "And so the great war commences. But I'll take up my part. I got to, if our world is to have peace."

Gabryal whispered. "Come back safely."

She kissed him lightly on the cheek.

He relaxed, taking in shi. It was Lunsday, Luwana's day, the 9th of Wolfenmoon. He entered the mine, and saw the path to the Other Side, but instead of one golden line becoming two, here one divided into three, and the third line blazed. The Path of Peace. He walked forward into a place that multiplied his serenity like a bell might echo off the hills in harmony with itself.

Three steps ahead lay the Disk of Dragons, no larger than his splayed hand, resting on a golden table. It gleamed innocently. His old uneasiness returned. Even now, he could not be sure how much his actions had been influenced by it.

He sighed. Not that it mattered. He lifted the Disk and bowed in reverence to the Goddess Luwana, whose life blood formed this Path of Peace. For the rest of his life, he yearned to walk further on that Path of Peace. But not yet. Not yet.

Bearing the Disk of Dragons, Rev Caern emerged from the cave, blinking against the sun as the people of Zhopahr cheered.

But the Elder Fu leaned close to Yarrow and murmured. "So the Prophecy of the Disk comes true. Now the Dark Battle begins."

THE END

295

P M F Johnson

About the author: I am a lifelong fantasy reader, trying my hand at writing an epic tale. I live with my wife, the author Sandra Rector, in Minnesota. You may learn more about the world of Sinnesemota at my web site, PMFJohnson.com

If you enjoyed this novel, please try *Trollen Rose*, next in the Saga of Sinnesemota series.

P M F Johnson
Twitter: @PMFJohnson1
Facebook: https://Facebook.com/PMFJohnson1

Made in United States
Troutdale, OR
12/12/2024

26190377R00183